THE IRISH FAIRY TALE

THE IRISH FAIRY TALE

A Narrative Tradition from the
Middle Ages to Yeats and Stephens

VITO CARRASSI
Translated by Kevin Wren

JOHN CABOT UNIVERSITY PRESS
Distributed by
University of Delaware Press

Published by John Cabot University Press
www.johncabot.edu

Distributed by University of Delaware Press
in partnership with The Rowman & Littlefield Publishing Group, Inc.
4501 Forbes Boulevard, Suite 200, Lanham, Maryland 20706
www.rowmanlittlefield.com

10 Thornbury Road, Plymouth PL6 7PP, United Kingdom

Originally published as *Il fairy tale nella tradizione narrativa irlandese. Un itinerario storico e culturale* (Bari: Mario Adda Editore, 2008).

British Library Cataloguing in Publication Information Available

Library of Congress Cataloging-in-Publication Data
Carrassi, Vito.
 [Fairy tale nella tradizione narrativa irlandese. English]
 The Irish fairy tale : a narrative tradition from the Middle Ages to Yeats and Stephens / Vito Carrassi ; translated by Kevin Wren.
  p. cm.
 Includes bibliographical references and index.
 ISBN 978-1-61149-380-1 (pbk. : alk. paper) — ISBN 978-1-61149-379-5 (electronic)
 1. Fairy tales—Ireland—History and criticism. 2. Folklore—Ireland. I. Wren, Kevin, 1959– II. Title.
 PN3437.C3713 2012
 398.209415—dc23   2011049829

∞™ The paper used in this publication meets the minimum requirements of American National Standard for Information Sciences—Permanence of Paper for Printed Library Materials, ANSI/NISO Z39.48-1992.

Printed in the United States of America

For Giovanni Battista Bronzini

CONTENTS

Acknowledgments

I WOULD LIKE TO THANK most of all Professor Vera Di Natale, who followed closely the various phases of the preparation, elaboration, and drafting of the text; I am grateful to her for her attentive and competent reading, which was the source of constant and profitable confrontation and for her precious and most generous advice and suggestions. My appreciation goes to Kevin Wren, not only for the quality of his translation (contributed to in no small part by the scrupulous revision of his wife Elena), but also for the reflection prompted by our interlinguistic dialogue and for his help in deciding on the title of the English edition. I'm obliged to Professor Allan Christensen for the immediate attention and gratifying appreciation that he gave to my work, apart from the inestimable solicitude with which he followed all the phases of this project. I would last like to thank my wife, Elettra, for her affection, support, and the stimulus that she provided me, fundamental in the realization and completion of this work. My gratitude also goes to Ireland, the muse of my research on narrativity, folklore, and literature, and a field always bristling with new horizons.

Introduction

Narrativity, Between Orality and Writing

MAN HAS AN EXTREMELY EFFICIENT and almost inexhaustible means of appropriating the reality around and within himself, an instrument that allows him to model and give sense to the world that envelopes him: *storytelling*. Storytelling allows men and women to evade everyday existence and enter a world which it alone makes possible. We do not know at what moment of human History (itself the greatest tale, containing within itself all other tales) one of our forebears felt, for the first time, the need to turn an event from his own life or that of others into a tale. Nevertheless, we can intuit plausibly that the first to hear this *proto-tale* felt a new pleasure, latent within his or her intimate self, which the *proto-storyteller* brought to light, thus furnishing the first link in a chain that was to remain uninterrupted through the ages.

On that far-off day, mankind discovered a "something" that had the power to give ordered and delimited form to the patrimony of events, dreams, and fears that had accumulated progressively in his collective memory, and which could be shared with an audience of his contemporaries. He discovered in himself the ability to create an entity that could solve "the problem of how to translate *knowing* into *telling*."[1] That entity was the tale, an indispensable channel through which he could transmit both truth or mere fantasy in such a way as to involve an audience of his fellow men. The tale also allowed him to go back over an event from the past, working within himself to reinforce the memory or even to reconstruct it, a posteriori.

The tale therefore was an extremely efficacious means of stemming the passage of time, creating a virtual space in which to govern autonomously the otherwise uncontrollable flux of events. Following specific rules, this space was organized to allow the storyteller to arrange within it figures, circumstances, gestures, and actions that would mirror, on the basis of a range of theoretically unlimited modes, a reality from which—for a period of time—it was possible finally to estrange oneself in order to observe the acts, words, and even thoughts of those who for the same period of time remained ephemerally but intensely alive. As long as the storyteller prolonged his narrative performance, a parallel reality held in suspension the lives of his listeners.

His tale was not only heard, but *received* by his listeners, either with detachment or participation. Ceasing to be the exclusive property of its author or bearer, in one way or another, the tale took possession and entered into the possession of other people, thus becoming *communal patrimony*. Its destiny was no longer linked to a single creator or storyteller, but to all those who, once having heard the tale, wanted to pass it on. As they did so, they became themselves authors, performing before a new audience another tale, their own, personal version of that already heard. Better or worse, more concise or extended, more entertaining or instructive, a series of versions would gradually have displaced the original; taken together—some with more success than others—these versions would have created a first *narrative tradition*, sedimenting itself in the collective memory of a community.

Whatever the effective origin of the narrative phenomenon, the degree to which it has affirmed itself among the peoples of the Earth attests undoubtedly to its value as one of the founding elements in the evolution of humanity, revealing it as "probably the most adequate metaphor for civilization, the locus of traditions, archetypes, and the symbolic subconscious."[2] Step by step, storytelling accompanied the continual becoming of History, providing mankind with the ability of turning events into tales and thus saving them from oblivion, particularly in the period preceding the written word. By telling tales and listening to them, man kept the past alive, transmitting it from generation to generation, albeit according to a fluid alteration of form and content that depended on the succession of storytellers and on the environmental and social conditions of the time, which would prove the most powerful of modifying factors. Through storytelling, man had in fact acquired the possibility of *creating* the past (fugitive by nature), which, when deprived of the time–space support otherwise furnished by this tool, would have remained an inconsistent and amorphous accumulation of events whose existence that could not be deduced from the present. No storyteller is able to give an incontrovertible image of the past: this is humanly impossible, even for first-person witnesses of events. However, the storyteller can give a *possible* account of whatever took place at a particular time because every narration is a more or less convincing reconstruction of an event, with its beginning and end already provided, situated at sufficient distance from the storyteller so that he can *translate* a more or less real action into a virtual account composed of verbal material.

Until a means arises to definitively fix the word, it remains entirely subject to the incessant fluidity of *orality*, the original condition of storytelling. In the oral phase, a tale is never an absolute possession: in order to survive it must be perpetually *repeated*. Its fate is completely entrusted to memory and the goodwill of those storytellers who follow each other in the course of time, and to the reception it receives from those who listen to it from time to time.[3] Only active collaboration between these two components will allow the oral tale to be transmitted from generation to generation. Until it *is fixed and stabilized* in the written word, the tale maintains the fluidity of the event itself, suspended perpetually between *potentiality* and *act*.[4]

The tale, moreover, responds to the "radical need for fabulation intrinsic to the human subconscious,"[5] a phenomenon that, by its very nature, does not tolerate barriers between individuals, nor allow for social, economic, cultural, or other discrimination. Rather, this need is a typical agent of *aggregation*: around a good tale and good storyteller, there will always be people willing to stop and listen—all the more so in contexts in which no written library guarantees a repertory kept close to hand. In pregraphic culture, in which oral storytelling is the only means for preserving and transmitting a tradition received from the past, it is quite natural that a class of particularly gifted individuals should affirm themselves professional *bards*, storytellers who quickly become points of reference for the entire community and whose tales become exemplary models to which others refer in an attempt to establish the official version of this or that traditional tale. But, since one is dealing with shared universal patrimony, there is nothing to stop any member of the community—even those not belonging to the bard class—from putting into circulation his own version of a particular tale or even creating one of his own and depositing it for the first time into the traditional collection. Only time can decide which tale or version of a tale will be the most successful, since it is impossible to exercise any control over the production of tales or the birth of storytellers.

In storytelling, only the audience exerts control. No despot could successfully attempt to prohibit whoever wants to from telling a tale in his own way. To prohibit a man from telling his tale (which might be that of his own life) would be the same as prohibiting him from speaking; it deprives him of a vital need. Perhaps the despot could appeal to the need to preserve a presumed original form, through the versions of the tale generated by a class of official bards. But tracking down this "official" form would be nearly impossible after who knows how many bards—from the tale's origin to the given moment—have told the tale, with each making their own original contributions to the traditional text. Faced with this anonymous creation, in which a single and determinate author cannot be found, it is thus the *collective* aspect of the tale that emerges, in the sense that, inevitably, a tale presented to the listening public is not just the voice of whoever is telling the tale at that particular moment, but the result of an indefinable plurality of voices that have gradually annealed with each other, fusing themselves into a single entity, the expression of an entire people.

Every nation, therefore, among those factors that distinguish it from others, will develop in the course of time a traditional patrimony of tales.[6] By sharing in this patrimony, it is possible to glimpse the identity of a people, just as in the case of language, religion, uses, and customs. These factors—language, religion, etc.—form, in fact, the understructure of a narrative that, when taken together, can be defined as *traditional*, summarizing in this adjective all those characteristics previously described: oral transmission, popular diffusion, continual variation, anonymous origin, and ethnic connotation.

But a traditional tale is above all what is passed down, transmitted from one individual to another, from one generation to another, and from one epoch to another, saved from oblivion, continually suspended between mechanical repetition and creative innovation, between the desire to preserve the past as it was and to reconstruct it according to the canons of the present. One is dealing then with a tradition that, in the context of storytelling, can serve either as an ideal model to which to conform or as a source of inspiration for the creation of new models.

Its aspect as an *open system*, in my view, most clearly characterizes the narrative tradition in its oral and popular dimensions. On the one hand, the elements that make up such a system are not fixed in the sense that, in the course of time, they may change form or leave the system never to return, perhaps being supplanted by new elements. On the other hand, the system is substantially accessible to anyone and to any exigency that is oriented toward sharing its elements with what is external to it or, in the final analysis, can be absorbed within it.

Since it is an open system, the traditional tale is destined to continual evolution, to continual transitoriness. The more or less faithful transmission of its original patrimony is entrusted completely to the nature and goodwill of those who, through storytelling, allow a message deposited into collective memory to become a tale—or rather the verbal object necessary for the perpetuation of an otherwise mute tradition. A lack of storytellers poses a continual threat of extinction for any traditional tale. Some threads of the tradition will be handed down in hundreds of versions because they are particularly popular with audiences; others will barely manage to survive, thanks to the efforts of a small group of enthusiasts. Other threads will be destined to disappear for good because they come to light in a time (and in a place and society) that is unable or unwilling to take them up, thus depriving following generations of a treasure. In this case, *narrativity* will be deprived of a part, no matter how inconspicuous, of the immense reserve of "motives, plots, *topoi*, roles and functions" from which it weaves its web, "always incomplete and free to be begun again," and from which grow "continually differing *fabulae*, particular plots, and characters charged with a historical and psychological ethos, immerged inevitably in the social institutions."[7] By *narrativity*, I mean that active principle that acts upon reality and makes it possible to narrate, and also the implicit grammar that provides the structures by which, working on the basis of a real or fictitious event, it is possible to construct a tale. I am referring most of all to that quality intrinsic to the narrative tradition by which it propagates itself in time and space and by which it escapes sterilizing itself in the logic of a *closed system*, thus preserving its state of vitality and openness to the world.

However, despite the natural tendency of the tradition toward narrativity and all its representatives in flesh and blood can do, inevitably, sooner or later, in the context of solely oral transmission, something will be lost of the patrimony inherited from the past. It has already been said that, in an open system, no single element is permanent, and this is even more the case when such a system enlarges itself. For every element that is lost, another takes its place. Yet, it is also true that, in losing an element, we are deprived of a link in the long chain that connects the narrative phenomenon to its origins. This is a serious issue for the researcher trying to reconstruct the genesis and evolution of a given thread of the tradition, perhaps in an attempt to discover the traces of a historical event or to reconstruct a specific environment or context. A tool is required to arrest the dangerous fluidity of the oral tale; a system is needed to set in place a new type of tradition, one no longer permeable, a *closed system*—writing.

"By separating the knower from the known (Havelock 1963), writing makes possible increasingly articulate introspectivity, opening the psyche as never before not only to the external objective world quite distinct from itself but also to the interior self against whom the objective world is set."[8] Ong's statement provides an incisive image of the explosive revolution that occurred with the advent of writing. The written word separated and distanced from each other the two parts of a dual concept that had remained indivisible for thousands of years. The tale is extracted from the living voice of the bard, imperfect and never the same, and is transferred onto the page, from which no escape is possible. The object of narration ceases to be an integral part of the narrating subject, ceases to entrust its destiny to an unpredictable variable; instead it consigns itself to a context of unvarying predictability in which its survival is guaranteed, along with that of its forms and themes. An open system, in which there is a continual dialectical tension between subject and object, in which a constant movement filters every element through the generous channels of subjectivity, is flanked by a closed system, in which the object, once expressed, no longer has any relationship with the subject of origin and is, in fact, objectified in the stasis of the written page.

At this point, the narrative patrimony that, until that moment, had sedimented itself in a given community, finds itself at a sort of crossroads: it could continue along the same path beaten for centuries and centuries, or it could risk the new path that writing has opened up. On the one hand, the purely oral tradition continues its millennial voyage, entrusting itself to memory and the flair of the professional, maintaining intact the unrepeatable nature of the event for each narration, with each single performance of the same tale interpreted differently each time, albeit with the generous intention of preserving faithfully what was received from preceding generations. On the other, the new category, this depository of a revolutionary skill, this *writing*, begins to change the characteristics of the narrative act, imprisoning it within a text that can no longer be modified. It will repeat the same tale every time that it is read and, rather than preserving a *tradition*, it will tend to reproduce an original *work* that is immediately recognizable as unique, since it will have severed its links with the exterior, cut off its relationship with the real world, and entered into a dimension entirely its own. Regarding originality, it should also be said that oral storytelling, being linked to the memorization of a verbal sequence, and hence to the mnemonic abilities of the single storyteller, is on a formal level conditioned by a determinate *formulary* which, in facilitating the transmission of a traditional *corpus*, limits the expressive freedom of the individual storyteller, who will instead affirm his originality in "managing a particular interaction with this audience at this time."[9] The writer, liberated from the conditioning of memory, can concentrate all his energies on the formal development of the text, even when he sets about transferring onto the written page a text of oral origin.

Characteristically, oral storytelling follows and continues an ancient tradition that tends toward conservation, albeit subject to perennial, physiological evolution. On the other, written text begins a new tradition, one that tends toward innovation, particularly because it is linked to the absence of a real audience with which to interact in the course of the narration and hence of a marked interference with the intentions of the narrator, who now deals with an unalterable means of expression, no longer linked to the occasion. From the open and direct relationship with the listening public, one passes to the closed and indirect relationship between an author and a virtual public of readers. And although the author of the written text cannot sever the umbilical cord linking him to preceding tradition, far more than the storyteller, he is responsible for his work since, unlike in an oral performance, it is destined (unforeseen accidents apart) to survive him, under his name and no one else's. It is no longer part of an anonymous tradition handed down from generation to generation, in which we can consider authors "apart from the first, to the same degree the successive narrators of the tale, the representatives of tendencies and collective taste."[10]

In ancient cultures, the ability to read and write was the prerogative of the privileged few who tended, in one way or another, to create an élite within a largely illiterate society. This situation contributed inevitably to deepening the rift that separates the two distinct ambits facing each other within the art of storytelling. Unless the élite itself opposed the innovation of writing, perhaps to preserve the privilege of a class whose preeminence was built on the frequently hereditary function of official bards, oral narration survived naturally among the economically and culturally lower classes, among those people who had neither the chance nor the inclination to take up writing and thus had no alternative but to continue handing down their tales through traditional channels. In this way, the oral tradition takes on the *popular* connotation universally ascribed to it. I use the term "popular" in the strictest sense, in which it refers to the common people—the majority—rather than in a wider sense, referring to the entire community. While the oral tradition, therefore, becomes the means of expression of the people, the written tradition becomes the expression of a separate class which, both culturally and from a socioeconomic point of view, distinguishes and emancipates itself from the majority. This class lends a cultured connotation to its narrative, which now becomes *literature* in the fullest sense of the word. The word "literature" is eventually used also in the field of oral tradition, so that "popular literature" becomes opposed to "cultured literature" or, one might say, "oral literature" becomes opposed to "written literature."

These are the two components from whose sum one can determine the exact dimension and effective value of a given narrative tradition. With the passing of time, one, the written/cultured component, conquers ever more space, relegating to a more and more marginal position the oral/popular tradition. This is also due to the development of a narrative form that is able to cast off completely an inheritance that seems to limit the innovative skills intrinsic to writing. In reality, writing, in a certain sense finishes by betraying itself because it rests on the *imitation* of a model which, once established, can no longer be disputed; it is maintained to be *exemplary*, thus debasing to no minor degree the idea of the uniqueness of the written text. The oral tradition, on the other hand, conservative as it may be, is, by its very nature, open to absorbing into itself extraneous elements which, beyond the redevelopment that takes place, constitute a greater wealth by which to set into motion the process of narrativity. Given its markedly dynamic and dialectical nature, the latter little tolerates barriers between one narrative context and another, barriers that would prevent the reserves of form and content of the one being used by the other and vice versa. From this point of view, it is clear that the moment inevitably arrives in which the two fundamental components of the tradition (once one overcomes the reciprocal diffidence) meet each other on the common ground of narrativity.

In reality, the two contexts were very close at the origins of their separation. I am referring to the transcription, during the classical period, of texts pertaining to an extremely ancient oral tradition, such as, to give the most obvious example, Homer's long poems. The objective was to preserve definitively an inheritance that was too precious to be left to the mercy of the variables of occasional transmission. In these cases, writing guaranteed a model of reference, both for the community in general—which, in that immutable text, would have fixed their identity—and for the more restricted community of writers, for whom a stable and consecrated form was an immense source of inspiration. Either before or after, writing guaranteed for humanity the fruition of an extraordinary narrative patrimony consigned to it by the oral tradition. Yet it also crystallized this patrimony in conformity with the particular characteristics it had assumed in the space–time context in which it was transcribed. Thus, although the transcribed text saved certain tales from disappearance, it also arrested their evolution. Even more so, it can be said that the existence of any particular text undoubtedly contributed to the definitive eclipse or marked limitation of its oral circulation: it was far more economical to read the text than to listen to the unreliable versions offered by a bard. This obviously depended on the literacy of the given community. Until literacy became widespread, an oral tradition, parallel to the written one, prospered and hence permitted the natural evolution that the written text attempted to arrest permanently.

However, as mentioned above, the spoken and the written word cannot proceed in separate compartments. They share, in one way or another, a common patrimony, to the degree that nothing prevents their reciprocally influencing each other. This is even more so in those cases in which the bard is also a reader, or when the writer has the possibility of hearing the tale from the living voice of an authentic storyteller.[11] The transcription of texts of oral origin can be considered a kind of middle ground between two worlds that tend to oppose each other, a species of bridge that allows for the initial recognition of shared elements. Writing appropriates orality and renders it according to its rigid schemes. It may deform it, but it is nonetheless obliged to take it into consideration. And, whereas from the formal and inevitably expressive point of view it can do little to preserve it (indeed, writing's intention is to emend the characteristics typical of speech, which it considers defects), it cannot but take note—pure merit apart—of the oral tradition's by no means negligible value as a depository of "ready made plots, of codified ways of putting together basic narrative elements to produce partly new stories."[12] The oral and popular tradition, far from being the outdated residue of a past era and of eclipsed values, becomes an antidote, one that regenerates a literature that risks sterilizing itself in empty self-imitation.

The aim of my research here is to analyze the relationships that, in a determined space–time context, have been created between two opposed ambits of the narrative tradition, particularly from the viewpoint of a genre (that for the time being I call the *folktale*), which, in my opinion, provides the most obvious meeting point or point of transition between the two fundamental modes of narration. Returning to themes already discussed, the complex relationships will be analyzed, in the narrative field, between the oral and popular components and the written and cultured; between an imposing national tradition and the innovative requirements of an emerging literary form. To put it differently, here we will observe the outcome of an original interaction established between the inheritance of the past and the reality of the present.

It is a well-known fact that, under the auspices of nineteenth-century Romanticism, the need for the substantial recovery on the part of official literature of a tradition neglected, if not openly denigrated, for centuries was first declared. The proponents of the so-called "Heidelberg group" (Jacob and Wilhelm Grimm, Clemens Brentano, and Achim von Arnim) were the precursors of a greater movement that, throughout the century, dedicated itself to bringing to light and making accessible to the wider public the enormous patrimony of myths, legends, and folktales preserved through the centuries by word of mouth and kept alive by the lower classes. Whether one was dealing with "authentic relics of the ancient poetic creations of the people" or, more correctly, with "oral traditions" which, "far from being fixed and immutable forms, were subject to continuous process of innovation in the context of family communication itself,"[13] the Grimm brothers, with their collection and transcription of popular folktales, were the first to make a concrete contribution to the growing need of the literary community—and of readers—to renew their links with the oral/popular tradition. The Grimm brothers' work was certainly not a faithful reproduction of the living voice of the storytellers, but rather an artistic revisiting of material that had always been considered coarse and devoid of aesthetic worth.

However, from the point of view of our research here, this is anything but a fault. Within the ambit of a study conducted by an ethnologist and a folklorist on the traditions of a predetermined human community, the scientific approach came to the fore: a complete, literal transcription was made of the oral tale, in such a way as to allow it to form a document that would be at the service of a specific act of theorization.

The Grimm brothers, like many others, were writers approaching a tradition which, by its very nature, permitted active appropriation. Just as the traditional tales themselves were the result of centuries of evolution imposed on them by the bards, in the same way, writers boasted of the right to intervene in this tradition and transmit it in the form that they liked best. The *Kinder- und Hausmärchen* are a work of art, not an ethnological essay.

Following the Grimms' example, the rest of Europe during the nineteenth century saw a flowering of anthologies dedicated to the oral/popular tradition, whose recuperation was seen to be the duty of every nation that wanted to preserve intact its roots and most genuine expressions. On the one hand were authors who, working in a more or less scientific spirit, tried to keep as much as possible to the original form of the texts they had been gathering, with the intention of discovering in them precious proof of the various theories that, in that century, were germinating regarding the origin, diffusion, and evolution of the themes and motifs of myth, legend, and the folktale.

On the other hand, in the course of the nineteenth century, other writers, following the Grimm brothers, approached the patrimony of traditional narrative not simply with the intent of making known to a widening public the hidden beauty of the tales of an oral/popular matrix—filtered more or less through artistic awareness—but also with the explicit intent of drawing from a narrative *corpus* of almost inexhaustible proportions new fodder for a literature which, with the advent of the Romantic revolution, found itself lacking in inspiration. Recourse was again being made to a patrimony from which great authors of the past had already drawn, specifically Dante, Rabelais, Cervantes, and Shakespeare, whose greatness encompassed the supreme capacity to conjoin the higher and lower levels of literary tradition. Thus, in the nineteenth century, one was dealing with the resumption of an interrupted dialogue, according to the parameters that were gradually being formed in a century full of ferment.

We will track the evolution of the relationship between narrative writing and the oral tradition in the context that I feel is the most vivacious and interesting. Our attention will be focused on one nation that has managed to preserve the most conspicuous and significant traditional patrimony and the strictest relationship between it and its literary reworking: Ireland. From this viewpoint, it is by no means surprising that our analysis will be based on specific works by William Butler Yeats, inspiration and chief exponent of a literary current, the so-called *Irish Revival*, into which flowed a vaster cultural mobilization that lasted a century. His collections of folk and fairy tales resuscitated a rich national tradition that involved the most disparate representatives of the Irish literary scene. In these collections, one can make out the premises for works that go well beyond pure transcription and in which is set under way a profound revision of the traditional patrimony, as shall be seen in the *Irish Fairy Tales* of James Stephens. Furthermore, by examining the material lying under the title *fairy tale* by the authors cited above, it has been possible for me to undertake a narratological analysis. On the basis of the redefinition of the concept of the fairy tale, a specific terrain has been localized for the unification, beneath the same roof, of contexts and genres fundamental to the narrative tradition: *myth*, *legend*, and *folktale*. This has made it possible to dispose of a larger and more complex tool with which to cast light on the specific characteristics of Irish tradition, in particular in the attempt to isolate the gifts of *narrativity* (*explicit*, let us say) that distinguish fundamentally the Irish fairy tale and elect it to be an ideal *model* on which to build the more complex forms of narrative discourse. This will be analyzed also in a completely literary work (e.g., *Dubliners* by James Joyce), seen from the perspective of the fairy tale, so as to locate the meeting point between two apparently distinct contexts. My hope is that, by the end of this work, the reader will agree with my choice of Ireland, fruit undoubtedly of a personal preference, but dictated also by the reasonable conviction of having chosen a privileged terrain on which to analyze the narrative tradition in its entirety.

The Fairy Tale: Reformulation of a Concept

Our field of research into the narrative phenomenon is focused therefore on a specific area of Irish narrative tradition. As mentioned above, this area is that of the fairy tale, which is normally understood as just one of many narrative genres located within the horizon of a tradition that, for the time being and for convenience, we will include under the obsolete but appropriate title of *the faerie* (*fiabesco* in the original Italian of this text), a title that leads us intuitively to a context as fascinating as it is difficult to circumscribe within clear and precise confines. How should one attempt, moreover, to provide a limpid outline of a subject which, by definition, evades the most elementary criteria of verisimilitude? The field is potentially infinite, to the extent that it includes tales connected to the supernatural, to the marvelous, to the fantastic, and to the representation of a world, figures, and events that assume consistency only when narrative tradition has a faerie approach to a reality otherwise known in *natural* terms,[14] so as to reveal an image that is normally less plausible, but also more ample and profound. One is dealing with an extremely wide field of research, one that has proved resistant to coherent and synthetic classification, a field in which it is not easy to identify a category that can overcome all the terminological nuances characterizing a by no means negligible number of narrative genres. Within this group, and perhaps more visible than the rest, appears the fairy tale.[15] Despite its century-old use, widespread both in specialist study and in the popular view, the fairy tale seems to lend itself to a more complex interpretation, from which it is possible to draw a substantially new category, one capable of providing a *transversal* vision of the narrative material that has been up to now defined as belonging to the faerie. Read in such a way, the fairy tale goes beyond the narrow limits imposed by its being a genre to become a meeting point, on formal and thematic levels, of a considerable part of the narrative tradition. Amplifying (at the risk of exaggeration, I dare say) the field of reference of a term apparently so circumscribed and attempting to locate within a partial concept a general perspective means making plain a semantic potential not hitherto recognized. Our objective, obviously, is to radically rework a system consecrated by centuries of critical revision. However, no work of research may legitimately fear casting its methodological foundations into doubt, if such an approach is seen as the keystone to an innovative hypothesis of interpretation. Besides, it is impossible to separate the approach of the present work from its indivisible links with its elected field. It is necessary, therefore, to recognize the erstwhile inconceivable idea that the fairy tale is a transversal narrative category, lacking in solid connections to Irish tradition. One must also take account of the fact that only in this way would any appreciable progress have been possible using this approach to the material in question. My argument is that the Irish context, as shall be seen, is the most congenial to the verification of how a fundamental principle operates (identified in a specific conception of the fairy tale), and is capable of lending unity to a complex storytelling tradition.

The individuation of a suitable, presumably homogenous category in which to create a unitary vision formed from multifaceted phenomenon obviously involves confronting the preexisting fragmentation of the categories within this phenomenon. It is necessary, therefore, to have a sufficiently clear, practical idea of those genres, or at least the most important ones, that constitute the narrative panorama currently recognized as pertaining to the faerie. The task outlined is no easy one. One has to deal with a fully fledged corpus of terminology, given the nature and amount of threads to be found in our field of research. Beyond the absolute number of terms adopted over the course of time to indicate the various ambits of the faerie, the researcher is further inhibited by the marked variability with which any one concept is interpreted by each of the scholars who have preceded him over the same terrain. Above all, one must recognize that, in this field, far from negligible problems arise in translating a concept from one language to another. Thus, a host of obstacles present themselves as we attempt to reach a correct and complete examination of the phenomenon under scrutiny.

Perhaps it is not by chance that the narrative typical of the faerie gives rise to terminological disputes. In a context in which the most disparate forms come easily into being and evolve, possibly mixing one with the other or contaminating narrative genres pertaining to other contexts, it is difficult to come up with a secure criterion of classification. So much is this the case that, faced with an unlimited thematic and formal variability, the study of the faerie tradition has ultimately directed itself toward the extenuating circumstance provided by the degree of *credibility* that one assumes is the attribute of the single tale or narrative category. This is an extenuating circumstance that, despite its being convenient from a methodological point of view in its capacity to reduce drastically the number of fundamental genres, lends itself to generating a substantially equivocal situation.

The synthetic picture provided by Stith Thompson in his essay *The Folktale* presents an essential, yet highly structured overview of the terms employed in defining and distinguishing the different forms that together form the panorama of the narrative tradition of the faerie,[16] a synthesis that has the further merit of evincing just how hard it can be for one language to transpose a concept originally expressed in another, so much so that attempts at translation are frequently abandoned in order to maintain intact the meaning of the foreign term.

It is not surprising, therefore, that Thompson's first reference is to the concept that he considers to be most frequent in the study of the faerie, expressed by the German term *Märchen*, which he opines is inadequately translated by the English *fairy tale* and *household tale*, and by the French *conte populaire*. No mention is made of the Italian term *Fiaba*, which I believe, along with the Russian term *Skazka*, gets closest to the original meaning of *Märchen*. Without doubt, *Märchen* is best defined when describing tales like *Cinderella* or any tales that employ an unreal setting, abstract characters, and a succession of marvellous motifs and themes to which the listener need give no credence. To quote Thompson regarding the inadequacy of the term "fairy tale," it "seems to imply the presence of fairies; but the great majority of such tales have no fairies."[17] This is an interesting observation in that it questions the effective semantic relationship between the terms "fairy tale" and "fairies," an interrogative that is fundamental to our research.

Thompson likens *Märchen* to the Italian term *Novella*, citing the literary examples such as *The Thousand and One Nights* and the *Decameron*. The general structure is the same, but the *novella* differs in its realistic setting and in marvellous events that claim greater credibility. Frequently, the two genres tend to overlap in the promiscuous form of the *Novellenmärchen*.

Hero tale seems a more comprehensive term that embraces the specificity of both, insofar as the reader is dealing with a genre that can be set in the fantastic world of the *Märchen* and also in the pseudo-realistic world of the novella. However, although in each tale there is at least one hero, according to Thompson this is not enough to assign to them the definition of "hero tale," a definition that seems more appropriate for those tales dealing with the heroic gestures of heroes, such as Heracles' and Theseus' battles with superhuman adversaries. These tales concern a pre- or pseudo-historical epoch dominated by legendary figures, in which the highest ideals are reflected, those proper to the *epos*, and around which the identity of a given community is consolidated.

Thompson goes on to cite another fundamental German term, *Sage*, translated into English variously as *local tradition*, *local legend*, and *migratory legend*, and into French as *tradition populaire*. Here, one is dealing essentially with the Italian term *Leggenda*, although Thompson later assigns a different meaning to this term. With the *Sage*, we have passed to tales of extraordinary events, but located in precise places, happening to people with historical veracity, and normally based on a single narrative motif that is generally believed actually to have occurred.

English terms pertaining to local tradition include *explanatory tale* and *etiological tale*, corresponding in French to the *pourquoi story* and to the German *Natursage*. These tales are intended to explain the origin, in a marvellous way, of any aspect of the nature and population of a given place. They are frequently found within a *Märchen* or a hero tale as an ornamental motif.

Our discourse focuses therefore on a term that, more than any other, seems to lend itself to the most disparate of interpretations, but which lies necessarily at the basis of all the narratives that we are analyzing: *Myth*. From the point of view of our analysis, although this term is fundamental, for the moment it will be treated merely in the sense of a *tale*, on the basis of the classifications imposed until now. Thompson considers a myth to be a tale set in a world preceding the present order, complete with sacred beings and semi-divine heroes, in which one finds the origin of things. The form frequently comprises hero tales and etiological tales, but myths are linked to the religious beliefs of a people and are possessed of a sacredness found nowhere else. In substance, they form the substructure on which all the narrative tradition is built.[18]

The summary continues by examining *animal tales*, a highly generic term under which Thompson groups all those tales, widespread in popular tradition, centered on animals that behave like human beings, whose vices and virtues they symbolize. When the moral intention of the tale is made clear, perhaps with a crowing maxim, it proceeds to the genre of true *fable*, of which the classical example is the collection attributed to Aesop.

There is also space for brief humorous anecdotes: *jests*, *humorous tales*, and *merry tales* in English, and *Schwank* in German; in Italian, these can be translated as *Facezie*. These tales focus on the stupidity of a single character—a fool—around whom gather authentic cycles that depict the tricks played on the fool, who is frequently involved in obscene adventures.

Final mention must be made of two genres that Thompson considers to be of a purely literary matrix. The *legend*, in contrast to genres pertaining to local tradition and the explanatory tale, here refers specifically to the lives of saints, a prevalently literary genre not entirely absent from oral storytelling. The last to be discussed is the *saga*, which Thompson warns must not be confused with the *Sage*, to the extent that, in his opinion, the former refers explicitly to literary tales from the heroic age, in particular those originating from Scandinavia and Ireland.

As Thompson himself admits, and I concur, one could continue to expand the catalogue of terminology that has accumulated within the ambit of the faerie. But the picture provided seems to me enough to give a general background against which to set my proposal of improving and expanding the concept of the fairy tale. What is more, as mentioned above, these forms are extremely permeable and frequently merge or even mutate into each another. So true is this that "fairy tales become myths, or animal tales, or local legends,"[19] an observation which, however formally incorrect from the point of view of the theory I shall proceed to illustrate, nevertheless makes clear just how shifting are the lines of demarcation between one concept and another and, consequently, how plausible it is to develop a wider, all-embracing concept.

Within Thompson's inventory, it is possible to make out a fundamental contrast between two forms in particular, *Märchen* and *Sage*, which in Italian could be translated into that between *fiaba* and *leggenda*. I draw attention to this antithetical pair because, as the history of scholarship into the faerie illustrates, in the two terms in question it is possible to summarize the substance of the genres already mentioned. Above all, this is because, in the distinction between *Märchen* and *Sage*, one may perceive a clear bipartition in the narrative field that my theory is intended to dispute.

In his seminal essay, *The European Folktale*, Max Lüthi has conducted a precise analysis focused on individuating the stylistic characteristics of the *Märchen*. The specific traits to emerge are *one-dimensionality*, the *absence of perspective and density*, the *technique of episodic sequence*, the *isolation of the characters*, and the *tendency toward the universal*. These qualities distinguish the *Märchen* and, in an opposed form, the concept that Lüthi proposes as defining the *Sage*. Following in the steps of Jolles, he interprets the latter as a *simple form*, where "an event, an experience, or a deed (whether real or imaginary) is turned to speech. The subject determines the mood, and the two together, the subject and the mood, determine the form that the narrative takes." Distancing himself from Jolles, on the other hand, he sees in the *Märchen* a precise artistic elaboration, given that its form "does not derive from their content but has a life of its own."[20] The Swiss scholar's interpretation, in the wake of grimmian idea, draws a clear line between a narrative reduced to the mere recording of a given event and a narrative marked by a clear aesthetic awareness, enough to transcend the contingent event. The possibility that a *Sage* was subject to artistic revisiting is excluded, just as is the possibility of the *Märchen* recounting personal experience. No compromise exists between one form and the other.

Other such classifications give the same impression, oriented equally at dividing the field of the faerie into two distinct areas, individuated on the basis of a rigid criterion of truthfulness and of the credibility that the tale lends to the storyteller and his audience. For example, the eminent Swedish folklorist Carl W. von Sidow makes a distinction between *Memorat*, a category in which lie "first-person experience tales of *actual events*," and *Fabulat*, which include "invented narrations of *imagined occurrences*."[21] As I understand it, in the first case, the tale is born as it is from memory of a personal fact; in the second, from pure invention, as if memory and invention were entirely separate compartments, simultaneously inoperative in the mind of the storyteller. Katharine Briggs, in her authoritative *Dictionary of British Folk Tales*, chooses to divide her work into two quite distinct categories: on the one hand, "folk narratives," or "folk *fiction*, told for edification, delight or amusement," and on the other, "Folk legends," that were "once believed to be *true*."[22] On the basis of the terms adopted, this distinction seems to recognize narrative qualities only in the case of the first category, leaving the second in a sort of limbo in which, rather than a tale, one encounters simple testimony worthy of being believed.

The two examples cited reflect the general attitude of scholars, on the basis of which an irreconcilable antithesis is individuated between two utterly opposed modes of development and fruition in the case of the traditional tale pertaining to the faerie, a discourse also having roots in the context of Irish tradition. Thus, a narrative patrimony, among the largest and most varied in the world between the nineteenth and twentieth centuries, was not only kept from disappearing by the patient work of transcription, but also was divided into two well-defined categories. To use the Gaelic terminology of a collector par excellence, such as Douglas Hyde, an antithesis was introduced between *scéal* and *seanchas*, which were translated, respectively, as *story* or *folktale* and *belief*. The first is described by Hyde as "something much more intricate, complicated and *thought-out than the belief* . . . long, more or less conventional," whereas the second is "short, conversational, chiefly relating to real people, and contains no great sequence of incidents."[23] Beyond the differences linked to the length and the style of the tale, the extenuating circumstance that emerges in the case of the *scéal* is the absence of *belief*. In fact, the *scéal* complicates its form precisely because of its "aesthetic presentation," which is opposed to the "conversational" development of the *seanchas*, in which prevails "the informational value,"[24] a situation that, according to Hyde, one can verify personally by visiting anyone living in the Irish countryside: if one asks them about the existence of fairies, they will rattle off their own experiences and those of their acquaintances and will insist on being believed, since one is dealing with an everyday experience for them; if one asks them for a *scéal*, they will quote some illustrious examples from tradition, asking their interlocutor in his turn whether he knows them already, since they derive from conventional patrimony, which is more easily shared by more than one individual and does not require any direct involvement on the part of the storyteller or listener.

An objection comes spontaneously to mind: if the belief is based on the conviction that one is in touch with a tradition imbued with personal meetings with the fairies, then what would happen if neither the storyteller nor the listener believed in this at all, perhaps because they have had no such experience, direct or indirect? And furthermore, what stance would we adopt in face of the narration of "ancient stories, elaborated, told with gravity and solemnity, and not treated as inventions"?[25] A tale narrated as a personal experience could easily be considered a fable, possibly because it is deprived of concrete reference, and hence it assumes a purely aesthetic value, just as a storyteller who adds a location and a character with name and surname to a *scéal* lends to it an aspect of real experience. Admitting as an extenuating circumstance the degree of credibility attributed to a tale would therefore require, rather than a polarization around two antithetical concepts, the institution of a wide margin within the two poles, to deal with the vast range of interpretations to which the one tale can give rise.

Such a consideration seems to me sufficient to demonstrate how inefficient such an abused and excessively rigid criterion can be, and to suggest instead that a classification is required that parts from more objectively certifiable properties. The risk otherwise is to fall into terminological contradiction. Here, I refer the reader to the distinction that another Irishman, Edwin S. Hartland, in his classic work on the subject,[26] makes between fairy tales or *Märchen* and "tales about fairies" or sagas: on the one side are tales of marvellous events not intended to be believed seriously; on the other, a genre of narration, not baptized by chance as the *serious tale*, linked more or less to a historical place and characters. But above all, on both sides lies the concept of the *fairy*, called upon to individuate two contexts, which should exclude each other: if the *fairy tale* should not be taken seriously, how can a *tale about fairies* aspire to such a consideration? Hartland seems moreover to invite us to take note of the extremely extensive value of the term *fairy*, and, by consequence, of that of the *fairy tale*, a concept that will lead us eventually to the individuation of that transversal category destined to break down the barrier between genre and genre and, as seen above, generate a fair amount of misunderstanding.

In any case, the theoretical conclusions illustrated up to now, as well as the questionableness of the criteria adopted, give an accurate picture of the effective conditions to be found in our area of research, conditions that must be resolved in search of a more wide-reaching theory. Propp, to identify his field of research, has used the category *tales of magic* contained within the classic typological repertory of Aarne-Thompson, a category to which he nevertheless gives a Structuralist rereading.[27] Despite limiting his research to a determinate section of the traditional patrimony, Propp enunciates an organic set of rules of composition, which proves its validity on far wider territory. His *tale of magic*, differently from what one might think, goes well beyond the strict limits of the *Märchen*: it is enough to look at the set of types contained under this entry in *Types of the Folktale* to realize that Propp's analysis, far from isolating a single genre among the rest, has revealed itself to be a sort of *passepartout* capable of identifying the links between the *Märchen* and the *Sage* and a whole series of intermediate genres. In elaborating his theory, Propp availed of a traditional classification scheme according to plot in order to obtain a far deeper one. This rendered the traditional classification substantially superfluous, if not erroneous.

Let us consider, therefore, the careful analysis made by Mary H. Thuente of the relationship between Yeats and the Irish narrative tradition. Thuente suggests classifying the material from which the poet draws into three fundamental genres: *Myth*, which, in the manner of Thompson, includes tales set in the remote past and made up of gods and semi-divine heroes, through which the origins of the world are narrated; *Legend*, which, like the much quoted-term *Sage*, refers to tales of extraordinary events set in the "historical past"; and *Folktale*, which is reflected in the also much-quoted term *Märchen* and hence is a "strictly fictional" narrative set in an unspecified place and time and deviating from any appeal to the reality of the listener, in exact antithesis to *legend*.[28] This tripartition is intended by Thuente to mirror the point of view of Yeats himself, who recognized the existence of the same three genres, with the only difference being his use of the term *household tale* in place of *folktale*.

It must be stressed that Yeats also made use of the term *fairy tale* in a sense not synonymous with *Märchen*. He was alluding to a subgenre of the legend, as a tale referring explicitly to fairies and to "quasi-supernatural" beings "like ghosts and witches."[29] In substance, this subgenre contains all the cases of meetings with, or manifestations of the supernatural, regardless both of the setting and minor characters involved and of the specific nature of the phenomenon that forms the center of attraction. It must also be noted that, by the concept of *legend*, Yeats understood both the tradition regarding pseudo-historical, heroic characters (such as Cú Culainn or Finn) struggling with creatures and situations from *another world* (called, not insignificantly, *Fairyland*) and that regarding everyday figures, perhaps even from his own time, who had undergone experiences that defied rational explanation. In light of this, it does not seem possible to me to glimpse any real distinction between the field of reference of the fairy tale and that of the legend, all the more so if one considers the direct relationship that exists between the popular *fairies* and the *Tuatha Dé Danann*, or figures from Fairyland. Both can be considered as inherited forms originating, in a more or less direct manner, from the myths recognized as the first examples of a tradition that was organizing itself upon them. Myth, therefore, began to take form as an indispensable premise, lying at the origin and guaranteeing the subsistence of the particular concept of the *fairy tale* that I am attempting to develop here.

How should one deal, then, with the classical meaning of the term *fairy tale*, traditionally understood as a synonym of *Märchen*? We have already seen how Thompson cast this into discussion; it seemed to him that this definition implied the presence of fairies in the strictest sense, and hence a posed restriction of the wider semantic field embraced by *Märchen*. Considering that this very same concept was rendered by Yeats with the term *household tale*, and by Thuente with *folktale*, one runs the risk of a paradox—that of identifying with the term *fairy tale* a new, wider narrative category, which fails nevertheless to cover the ambit for which the term was originally coined. It seems to me that this is avoidable simply by taking into account the extended conception of the word *fairy*, which was recognized in the context of the legend: a fairy tale is not distinguished by the presence of a fairy or an elf, but by everything that defies the laws of nature.[30] And as far as I am concerned, it is rare to run into a *Märchen* in which the hero and his antagonist do without divine intervention or are themselves lacking magic powers. Therefore, the term *folktale*, too, displays the fundamental requisites to be included within the semantic field of the *fairy tale*. And the paradox is avoided.

The function of *fairy* varies notably between a legend and a folktale, according to modalities that are frequently antithetical; this will promptly be taken into consideration. But what is taking form now is a category finally equipped to embrace all that part of the narrative tradition defined provisionally as belonging to *the faerie*, but which now may be rebaptized as the *fairy tale*. In the Irish context, this narrative category finds its ideal application, since it reflects an inclination that characterizes the narrative of the country and its spirit itself: "The dimension of the supernatural, the otherworldly . . . is never absent from Irish narrative. . . . the deep and continual concern . . . with the inter-relationships between the two worlds . . . is one of the underlying continuities from primitive to modern Irish society."[31]

Faced with a vision of the world that distinguishes an entire tradition throughout its history, it seems highly opportune to me to identify a common area in which the different narrative expressions that evoke this vision can meet and recognize each other. And if the Irish ascribe to another world—called *Fairyland*—all that evades rational understanding (and without taking into account that, in the concept of *fairy faith,* are grouped the pagan beliefs handed down since time immemorial, despite the advent of a deep Christian faith), I believe that the expression *fairy tale* is the most appropriate to our ends.

Naturally, the genre is not all-inclusive. For one thing, at the level of myth, the fairy tale is an aporia, in that, as already mentioned (and treated in more detail further on), the one is necessarily preliminary to the other. Furthermore, it is by no means given that the genre *legend* or the genre *folktale* enter into the conceptual horizon of the *fairy tale*. Where the hero, Finn, struggles with an antagonist like himself, or the peasant, Donald O'Neary, runs rings around his neighbors thanks to his cunning, in the absence of a fairy manifestation we have simply a legend, whether it be heroic or historical. The same can be said of the folktale in which a king, in cahoots with his future son-in-law, punishes the pride of his daughter using a wholly human trick; the tale has only one dimension, in contrast to the multidimensionality of the fairy tale, which precisely on this plane establishes its identity and consequently its differentiation within the wider, indistinct category of the tale. However, it will be a study of the structure underlying the fairy tale that will allow us to establish with greater precision how much it distinguishes itself from the rest of narrative and how much it lends itself to an analysis that might cover a wider, even universal spectrum.

The fairy tale, as it has been defined in this introduction, passes over the classical barriers between genres, sanctioning the fundamental unity that characterizes a whole part of the narrative tradition. As long as it is entrusted to oral transmission, it undergoes continual evolution. Now, those same genres absorbed into its conceptual horizon can be read as phases which, in time, alternate in giving a specific form to a specific fairy tale. In this way, we arrive at an even more relative vision of the rigid classification governing the self-same material of the tradition, which on the surface is mutated in time and space and by the different narrative events which model it, but in its depths remains true to its origin. To form an initial idea, consider the scheme proposed by John W. Foster regarding the form adopted, in chronological order, from a traditional tale: *experience* or *event* → *first-person anecdote* → *third-person anecdote* → *local legend* → *fairy tale* or *folktale*. Along with this, the narrator also undergoes evolution: *subject* or *witness* → *informant* or *retailer* → *anecdotalist* → *storyteller*. The narration passes gradually from *personal* to *impersonal* mode. Space and time, originally specified, are slowly generalized.[32] On the basis of these considerations, it will be possible to elaborate an organic theory of the evolution of the fairy tale, a theory that is an integral part of a wider field of research, in which the specific narratological analysis is made and on which our entire discourse depends.

Notes

1. Wilhelm F. H. Nicolaisen, "Why Tell Stories?," *Fabula* 31 (1990): 50.
2. Angelo Marchese, *L'officina del racconto. Semiotica della narratività* (Milano: Mondadori, 1983), 5.
3. Cf. the concept of the *preventive censure of the community*, adopted by Petr Bogatyrëv and Roman Jakobson in "Folklore as a Special Form of Creation," *Folklore Forum* 13, 1 (1980): 1–21.
4. On this theme, the analysis made by Walter J. Ong, *Orality and Literacy: The Technologizing of the Word* (Abingdon-New York: Routledge, 1988) is especially significant. See in particular the chapter "Writing Restructures Consciousness" (77–114).
5. Cf. Marchese, *L'officina del racconto*, 6.
6. Cf. Georges D. Zimmermann, *The Irish Story Teller* (Dublin: Four Courts, 2001), 9: "People with a common stock of stories (and ways of telling them) form a community."
7. Marchese, *L'officina del racconto*, 6.
8. Ong, *Orality and Literacy*, 104.
9. Ibid., 41.

10. Giovanni B. Bronzini, *Il mito della poesia popolare* (Roma: Edizioni dell'Ateneo, 1966), 18.

11. See the detailed examination of the Irish context given in Caoimnin Ó Danachair, "Oral Tradition and the Printed Word," *Irish University Review* IX, 1 (1979): 31–41.

12. Zimmermann, *The Irish Story Teller*, 11.

13. Sebastiano Lo Nigro, "La fiaba tra scrittura e oralità," *La ricerca folklorica* 12 (1985): 8.

14. Cf. the division into three principal categories adopted by Tzvetan Todorov: "The *marvellous* involves literature which simply presents supernatural occurrences without trying to explain them. The *uncanny* Todorov defines as using what seems to be supernatural, then finally providing a natural explanation of it . . . the *fantastic*, which he defines as suspending itself between a rational and an irrational position" (quoted in Elliott B. Gose, *The World of Irish Wonder Tale* [Toronto-Dingle: University of Toronto Press, 1985], 105: my italics). Todorov makes a distinction based substantially on the degree of credibility and verifiability of the tale, a criterion that has always characterized, in the broadest sense, the analysis of *the faerie*, thus leading to an overly clear division within the same expressive field. In my proposal to redefine the concept of the fairy tale, above all, a desire to recompose an undeniable underlying unity comes to the fore.

15. Regarding the greater *visibility* of the fairy tale with respect to other sectors of popular tradition, a datum that emerges from the examination made by Carl-Herman Tillhagen of the annals of *FF Communications*, from 1910 to 1970, is very interesting, an examination aimed at purifying the space occupied, percentage-wise, by the main traditional genres. Among the twelve genres that the scholar notes, it emerges that the fairy tale occupies 49.9 percent of the distinguished journal, leaving the others far behind: Carl H. Tillhagen, "Reality and Folklore Research," *Béaloideas* 39–41 (1971–1973), 329.

16. See Stith Thompson, *The Folktale* (Berkeley-Los Angeles: University of California Press, 1977), 7–10.

17. Ibid., 8 (my italics).

18. Not only pertaining to the narrative tradition, but to the very identity of the *ethnos*: cf. Carlo Tullio-Altan, *Ethnos e civiltà* (Milano: Feltrinelli, 1995), 22–24.

19. Thompson, *The Folktale*, 10.

20. Max Lüthi, *The European Folktale: Form and Nature* (Bloomington: Indiana University Press, 1986), 3.

21. Nicolaisen, "Why Tell Stories?," 6 (my italics). In the same article, the scholar opportunely notes, in response to the thesis of von Sidow, that "in the course of more extensive and more intensive folk-narrative research, it has become quite apparent that such a clear-cut distinction is highly artificial and cannot be sustained in such a simplistic fashion."

22. Katharine M. Briggs, *A Dictionary of British Folk Tales* (London: Routledge and Kegan Paul, 1970), 1 (my italics).

23. Zimmermann, *The Irish Story Teller*, 563 (my italics).

24. Ibid., 562.

25. Ibid., 563.

26. See Edwin S. Hartland, *Popular Studies in Mythology, Romance, and Folklore* (London: Nutt, 1914).

27. Cf. Vladimir J. Propp, *Morphology of the Folktale* (Austin: University of Texas Press, 2003), 19–24.

28. Mary H. Thuente, "'Traditional Innovations': Yeats and Joyce and Irish Oral Tradition," *Mosaic: A Journal for the Comparative Study of Literature and Ideas* XII, 3 (1979): 92.

29. Ibid., 93.

30. See Noel Williams, "The Semantic of the Word 'Fairy': Making Meaning Out of Thin Air," in *The Good People: New Fairylore Essays* (New York-London: Garland Publishing, 1991), 457–75, in which the origin of the term *fairy* and its semantic evolution are analyzed. The etymological origin of the word is the Latin *fatum*, giving birth to the neuter plural *fata*, which not by chance is found in Italian. In the passage from the French *fee* to the English *fay*, or rather *fairy*, the author notes no less than four principal acceptations: "(1) enchantment, illusion; (2) fairyland, land of illusion; (3) human with special powers; (4) supernatural beings" (p. 463). In practice, from its origins, one can see in the semantic field of *fairy* (*tale*) the possibility of making it a far wider category than it has been until now.

31. Gose, *The World of Irish Wonder Tale*, 5.

32. See John W. Foster, *Fictions of the Irish Literary Revival* (Dublin: Gill and Macmillan, 1987), 216–17.

A Celtic Legacy and Christian Syncretism

1

A Methodological Introduction

REAMS HAVE BEEN WRITTEN, mostly in the last two centuries, regarding the origin and diffusion of an immense and varied, orally transmitted narrative patrimony unique to people from every corner of the world. This narrative patrimony has followed a path that, from time immemorial, has led to us, despite innumerable accidents encountered along the way. Endless discussion has considered the possibility of tracking down, particularly in Europe, a single geographical and historical area where the original narrative themes and motifs might have been born, before they spread out across the world. Research has brought to light substantial affinities between the myths, legends, and folktales (which will be our arena of discussion) of various nations very distant from each other, and profound questions have followed these discoveries. Works such as *The Types of the Folktale* by Aarne and Thompson, and the ponderous *Motif Index* by Thompson not only give us an idea of the immense size of the narrative corpus at humanity's disposal, but also provide us with the view of a patrimony that, as far as motifs and themes are concerned, is the common privilege of all of mankind. Many scholars have worked with praiseworthy self-abnegation in the romantic search for a place, a time, and a people in which to anchor our common roots and from which we are all born. For example, a highly influential current of nineteenth-century theorizing suggested that the Indian subcontinent could be considered the cradle of Indo-European *fabulation*[1] (both in the proto-historical phase, as a legacy of the migrations of Indo-European peoples from India to the West, and in the historical phase, when Indian society was so extremely civilized as to allow its narrative patrimony to spread to less developed peoples). This theory is no more than a generous and forgivable attempt to discover a common origin for a universal phe-nomenon, one which, precisely because of its obvious universality, it would be more logical to englobe in a *polygenetic* theory.

In any case, here, one is dealing with a hypothesis that, albeit sug-gestive and often well argued, can never fully demonstrate its validity, no more so than all the others that have been elaborated in this respect. One must recognize the existence of extremely precise limits for research aimed at reconstructing a past that is far more hypothetical than histori-cal. Historical truth is demonstrated with incontrovertible documents. Everything else is mere opinion—all the more so when one is faced with something that has no, as it were, *measurable* consistency. We can count the thousands of variants that exist in the world of a given tale, but we cannot enclose in a neat formula what it was that, ages ago, inspired the human mind to give birth to *storytelling*. This is particularly true in those tales pertaining to the *faerie*, whose ambit was described in the Introduc-tion to this volume. To speak the truth, one might say that, in effect, not even the variants of a single faerie motif are truly quantifiable, neither on a diachronic level (it being impossible to recover all of those lost with the passing of time), nor on a synchronic level (since it is possible that in some far-away corner of the world there exists a storyteller who has evaded the efforts of the most zealous of tale hunters). As long as it maintains its oral nature, the popular narrative tradition—and hence the themes and motifs on which it is built—does not lend itself to being in-terpreted on the basis of rigid, generalizing modules. It lends itself instead to study that considers it a product arising directly from the intimacy of all mankind. When one speaks of the *collective* value of the oral tradition, one undoubtedly does not wish to affirm that a tale comes simultaneously from all members of a community, but rather to evince the phenomenon in which a single creator cannot be tracked down, given the tale's trans-versal diffusion throughout the community. One must also emphasize the purely *human* factor, outcome apart, that distinguishes the creation of a tale or a simple faerie motif. This leads me to believe that the most appropriate research in this field lays aside the study of aspects extraneous to the narrative fact itself, and concentrates instead on the fundamental aspect of the issue—*the play of the imagination*—in which the anthropolo-gist Franz Boas believed he had discovered the universal origin of the tale.[2] If this premise is supported by an awareness that "the growth of myths and tales is extremely complex, and there have been all kinds of disintegration and accretion of foreign materials," it is fair to conclude, and still in agreement with Boas: "The original form of any particular myth may be quite impossible to discover."[3]

Considering all that has been said, it seems to me that, rather than attempting to reconstruct the genesis and origin of the entire narrative tradition, it is far more reasonable to limit the horizon of research to a determinate narrative tradition, without losing awareness that one is undertaking a partial reconstruction, conditioned, inevitably, by the material that writing has preserved in time: it is clear that oral transmission, source as it is of incessant variation, can contribute only in an indirect manner to a diachronic investigation. Furthermore, one must not undervalue the fact that the oral and written traditions have coexisted peacefully for centuries, sharing, unconsciously perhaps, a common narrative patrimony. This is true to such an extent that it is impossible to isolate a truly *traditional* ambit and one more specifically *literary*, since both have conditioned each other reciprocally, giving birth to substantially *hybrid* forms and themes that obscure the provenance of this or that single element. Our premises here are fundamental since the intention is to study the fairy tale, a narrative context in which, more than any other, a fusion takes place between traditions of differing origin. It is based on myths and beliefs pertaining to the sphere of folklore, or rather to a patrimony that groups together an entire people and which, therefore, is an integral part of the life of a certain community. But it is also true that this patrimony has been used always more widely and expertly in the sphere of literary elaboration: when Perrault tells the tale of Cinderella, he does nothing else but rework a narrative theme widespread in popular culture. Obviously, the writer approaches the tale with intentions far from those of the original. He elaborates it according to a form that mutates the theme into a classic of literature, and he addresses it to an *élite* far different from the peasants who have handed the tale down for centuries. In this way, the fairy tale demonstrates its noteworthy capacity to put into contact contexts that, from every other point of view, would have ignored each other reciprocally.

It is fair to state that, in the narrative tradition, it has never been possible to identify a real scission into two absolutely distinct sections—oral versus literary—and this is all the more so true in regard to the fairy tale. As much as it has been possible, particularly since the advent of Humanism, to develop highly elaborate forms pertaining to the ambit of the Italian *novellistica d'arte* (in particular, the collections of Basile and Straparola), and as much as writers have underlined their independence from a tradition considered outdated, inadequate, and suitable only to a humble and unprepared public, the fairy tale, and, with it, substantially the rest of narrative, has never managed to sever its primordial links with a patrimony originating in the lower levels of society and the past, even if it was precisely this idea that imposed itself from Boccaccio to the threshold of Romanticism.[4] Due to this idea, the work of recollection that lasted throughout the nineteenth century, in every part of Europe, assumed great importance, leading hosts of writers and simple scholars to focus their attention on those traditional elements that had survived among the lower classes. Examining the stages of this European phenomenon does not enter into our field of research here. In general, however, it should be said that underlying this labor of transcription was a deeply felt need to reappropriate a heritage that was capable (in that it was a universal phenomenon) of unveiling the fundamental unity of mankind, erasing artificial barriers of nation and culture. On the other hand, this same heritage was also seen as a national phenomenon, a depository of each nation's unique narrative tradition. This was even more the case with those nations subject to foreign hegemony,[5] a discourse that in Ireland, more than in most other European countries, was an important issue.

The Celtic Heritage

At the beginning of the nineteenth century, Ireland was no more than a tiny part of the immense British Empire, a dominion that had lasted for six centuries and that no insurrection had managed seriously to disrupt. However, in this highly limited and marginal context, and despite growing cultural persecution on the part of the invaders, an enormous patrimony of traditional Irish tales was conserved, unequaled in the rest of Europe. This patrimony was transmitted particularly in the cottages of the Irish countryside, where tenacious efforts were made to keep alive a glorious past and where storytelling was the only means of preserving an extremely marked sense of identity. Irish lore is all the more original in that it survived in a historically insular context; unlike the rest of Europe, the Roman legions had not occupied Ireland. In Ireland, the Celtic civilization lasted far longer than it did elsewhere, where it appeared like a meteorite and was quickly swept away by Greco-Latin civilization. Latin culture, undeniably attractive to native people, was further strengthened by the coming of Christianity; the Roman Empire eventually absorbed a multitude of weaker indigenous European cultures, thus giving the continent a highly unitary cultural physiognomy. Until the moment of the English invasion of Ireland in the twelfth century, the island nation managed to keep alive its markedly Celtic nature, and also unite it with Christianity, thus establishing a balanced, original compromise unequaled elsewhere. The surprising synthesis reached in Ireland between the new religion and ancient pagan tradition was entirely unique; in other lands, the two elements were held in decided antithesis, with Christianity favoring, if not the actual disappearance, then at least the debasement of a great part of pre-Christian tradition.[6] Considering the value of the legacy of Celtic civilization in Ireland, its preservation was undoubtedly due to the intelligence and respect with which the Irish Church approached it. This cultural patrimony was too large and too original to be ignored, all the more so because it was a resource which, if carefully managed, would serve the Church's ends. Thus, on the one hand, the Church was motivated by a recognition of the incontrovertible value of the native tradition and the need to preserve it from the risks of purely oral transmission; on the other hand, the Church wanted to appropriate this tradition in Christian terms, with a view to more successfully converting a pagan people.

The rapid spread of the Christian message in Ireland was, in my opinion, assisted by a peculiar quality of the Celtic spirit, one readily reflected by the very nature of the fairy tale. I refer to all that goes beyond mere sense-perception, to an attraction to that unreachable world lying well beyond everyday reality, to the near-devaluation of pure corporeity in the name of a striving for the absolute, the infinite; this spirit inevitably produced the visionary character and imaginative power of the entire narrative production of Celtic origin.[7] It seems in no way rash to me to glimpse in such an attitude toward the world and life itself a powerful incentive to welcome and embrace a faith that laid its accent on the spiritual dimension and guaranteed the existence of another world. Maybe, because they saw in this mental disposition terrain congenial to Christian teaching, the representatives of the Irish Church were more inclined than elsewhere to tolerate beliefs deriving from a pagan past. *Fairy faith* and the Bible could happily coexist because, in a certain sense, they reciprocally reinforced each other.[8] Moreover, without a fair dose of tolerance, it would have been impossible to preserve an entire narrative patrimony that founded its peculiarity and beauty on a belief in the fairy world itself: an extremely extensive part of the Irish tradition belonged to that transversal category in which we have defined the fairy tale.

But what exactly did St. Patrick and his successors find so precious about the island? They did not find simply a rich and varied quantity of tales, but also a society built around these tales and their storytellers. Here, they encountered a privileged ground for narrativity, in the sense that before their eyes—and above all, to their ears—they found a context that was extremely propitious for the creation, transmission, and evolution of the narrative patrimony. This patrimony formed a foundational value for every member of a community that could truly recognize and identify itself only through narration inherited from tradition. We are discussing an epoch prior to the advent of Christianity, embracing a number of centuries before and after the birth of Christ, which would be substantially obscure were it not for the tales it left behind. The difficulty of penetrating pagan Ireland is increased by a complete lack of written documents; not a single traditional tale has been transcribed. We are faced with a society in which the transmission of knowledge and the memory of the past itself were entrusted entirely to oral means and to a selected class of storytellers. Since the narrative tradition was so highly valued, it could only be entrusted to a restricted circle of professionals, selected not by right of descent but by merit. Merit was acquired and certified only after a long and rigorous training course: to aspire to achieve the rank of *fili*—the Gaelic word for officially recognized storyteller—no less than twelve years of intensive study were required.[9] This is not surprising if one considers the mass of information that a *fili* was obliged to assimilate: "the conventional number was said to be seventy times fifty, which may be a way of saying as many as there are nights in the year."[10] This passage from Zimmermann allows us to understand how, on any day of the year, it was possible to find time to listen to traditional tales—and any *fili* worthy of the name had to be ready every day to satisfy the demand for new tales. The *filid* (plural of *fili*) were the only recognized channel through which the community could learn the *senchas* (literally, "antiquity") in which were contained the norms on which society and the "categorization of the real" depended. They were also the only real element of cohesion in an island which, however small, was politically fragmented. This makes it clear that every *fili* had to be the depositary of the *coimgne*, the "complete and coordinated knowledge" of the entire narrative corpus.[11] This responsibility was compensated for by the respect and honor reserved by all the people for their *filid*, superior even to that conceded to sovereigns themselves.

Hence, for the Celts, storytelling was a very serious activity. But it was also the principal form of entertainment at every level of society. Although on the one hand storytelling made it possible to transmit traditional knowledge and the identity of the community itself, on the other it was the favorite way of passing free time, the amusement of a society that, even today, conserves an exclusive predilection for the art of the word,[12] so much so that "there is scarcely a hill, a rock, or river pool, a ruined castle or abbey which has not its own story."[13] Before a place can acquire an intrinsic value, it becomes the object of a tale, which ends by being the only value that really counts for the Irish: the *genius loci* is supplanted by the *genius fabulae*.[14] This is what I mean when I refer to a terrain suited to narrativity. In Ireland, one is dealing with an attitude to reality that traditional Irish storytelling has inherited directly from its Celtic roots, an ability to make a tale of practically every element of existence, thus rendering Irish narrative tradition as rich and varied as we know it to be today. The number of tales originating from the island is far superior to those pertaining to a common transnational patrimony.[15] Although to the *fili* was entrusted the professional and serious issue of oral transmission, a great number of non-professional storytellers also transmitted a patrimony of tales of a somewhat lower nature—perhaps noble subjects reworked in a comic or satirical key. These were wandering bards who lived off the generosity of those who, from time to time, shared the storytelling arts with them, and they were organized into a hierarchy based on the theme and modality of the tales belonging to their individual repertories.[16]

As mentioned previously, thematic richness was a dominant characteristic of the repertory of these storytellers, whether professional or amateur. In this respect, one should consider the following list drawn up by Zimmermann from the *Book of Leinster*, in which the entire patrimony of tale is classified according to the type of narrative event:

> Destruction (murdering, ravaging), Cattle-raids, Courtships (with men as active suitors), Elopements (with women often taking the initiative), Battles, Caves, Sea-voyages (*immrama*: circumnavigation involving wonders), Death-tales (the manner and circumstances in which heroes died), Communal Feasts, Sieges, Expeditions and Adventures in the Otherworld (*echtrai*), Slaughters, Irruptions (the bursting forth of lakes or rivers), Loves, Military Expeditions, Invasions (the provenance and distribution of the tribes of Ireland, Conceptions and Births, Visions and Frenzies . . .[17]

The author's ellipses suggest that one is perhaps dealing with an incomplete inventory, yet it is enough to give an idea of just how varied Irish storytelling was at its origins and of how it could adapt itself to any audience or circumstances. One should note, moreover, the perfect coexistence, or I would say, *interpenetration*, of the real and specifically supernatural dimensions that, as we understand now, were only vaguely separated in the Celtic worldview.

Analyzing *Book of Leinster's* index more closely, one becomes aware that it may definitively be read as a group of different events that, either completely or partially, can be united within one long tale—rather as an "archetypal pattern"—in which to construct the career, and hence the tale, of a hero.[18] One rarely comes across a tale that limits itself to one of the listed themes; variety is an absolutely typical aspect of Irish narration. The index, therefore, should be read as a kind of model, a reserve from which the oral storyteller could easily reconstruct those tales (or parts of tales) deposited in his memory, or from which he could elaborate new, missing elements to insert into the life tale of a traditional character. The model could be used, therefore, either in a *conservative* or *innovative* way.

It was only at the beginning of the nineteenth century that scholars introduced new, more functional criteria of classification for the legacy of Celtic storytelling. These criteria were based on the identification of four fundamental *cycles*, in which the various narrative themes are unified by their sharing the same space–time context, by the presence of given characters, and by a certain affinity of tone. The four cycles in question, ordered chronologically according to the epoch in which they are believed to be set, are:

1. *The Mythological Cycle*, which collects the patrimony of tales regarding the first invasions, focused in particular on the *Tuatha Dé Danann*, a people of decidedly superhuman character, to the extent that they were promoted to the rank of the divine; the Celtic pantheon is, for the greater part, composed of characters of this people.

2. *The Ulster Cycle*, which depicts a reality following the arrival of the *Milesians*, thought to be the ancestors of the modern-day Irish, a reality in which human heroes, nevertheless of superhuman bravery, above all the Celtic Heracles *Cú Chulainn*, face each other in interminable battles following a code of honor typical of the *epopee*. The main thread is based on the war between the champions of Ulster and those of Connacht for the possession of a magic bull.

3. *The Fenian* or *Ossianic Cycle*, which tells the tale of *Finn* and his *Fianna Fail*, or rather of a great commander and his knights, including his son *Oisin*, who fought for the Sovereign of Leinster in an epoch following the birth of Christ. In this cycle, one encounters the transition from a principally epic tone to a more fictitious one, in which a taste for magical evasion and for adventure supplants the idea of rigid heroism, as incarnated in the protagonists of the Ulster Cycle;

4. *The Historical Cycle* or *The Cycle of the Kings*, set in the Christian era, focused on the semi-historical figures of kings, the last representatives of a world in decline and the first to face the saints and clerics working for the conversion of the island to the new faith.[19]

This schematization is strictly constructed a posteriori, and the boundaries between one cycle and another should not be considered static. One should take into consideration that "characters and motifs from one cycle may turn up in another."[20] It is also possible to come across a tale that cannot be assigned with certainty to any of the four cycles: in particular, the narrative corpus relative to the first Milesian invaders comes to mind. Rolleston inserts these tales into the *Mythological Cycle*, committing an error I would think, since he himself says that, with the Milesians, one enters an epoch closer to history and beyond the mythical sphere pertaining to the first cycle.[21] These limits, however, must be accepted, above all in the absence of more adequate solutions and in view of the deductions that the scheme makes possible.

Each cycle takes in a certain phase of Irish history, which is therefore set out *sub specie fabulosa*. On the one hand, the narrative tradition is classified from a more or less historical perspective; on the other, tradition, with all its weight, influences the historical reconstruction of an entire nation. The two levels interact closely, and the farther one goes back in time, the more the boundaries separating them tend to fade, particularly when the aid of a written source of native origin is lacking. It will be difficult, therefore, to draw a dividing line between the *truth* (or at least the *verisimilitude*) of *historia*—understood in its derivation from the Greek root ιδ, or rather the knowledge that a certain event took place because one saw it and plausibly recorded it in *a document*—and the *probability* of *fabula*, a term that should be understood in its derivation from the Latin *for, faris*, or rather "what exists in that it has been created by words," in all their freedom of expression, and hence transmitted only by the tale. Both will necessarily be present in the mental horizon of the storyteller and his audience. The oral tradition originating from the Celtic past will therefore be present in the double guise of narrative corpus and of testimony (however open to dispute) of that past itself.

One will have noted moreover how, in the passage from one cycle to another, a chronological progression exists that implies a gradual growth in historical veracity. From a mythical, aboriginal context, filled with divinities and, preceding them, with "huge Phantom-like figures, which loom vaguely through the mists of tradition,"[22] one passes to a context in which the characters have become human, although they remain far from the historical concept of humanity. We can define this epoch as *legendary*, halfway between Myth and History. A further progression is encountered in the passage from the mastodontic heroes of the Ulster Cycle to the more familiar ones of the Fenian Cycle, to such an extent that "the annalists of ancient Ireland treated the story of Finn and the Fianna, in its main outlines, as sober history,"[23] although in effect one is dealing with adventures focused on encounters with supernatural beings. But, whereas in the preceding cycle they were identified as divinities, for Finn and his followers, these beings are changed into earthly fairy creatures. We enter into a more strictly historical phase in the fourth cycle, which is also the least unitary, since there are no dominant characters prevailing over the others to distinguish the entire narrative corpus: this reinforces the idea that we have entered into a context in which the heroes of Legend have been replaced by fully fledged men, whether they be kings or saints, but pertaining in any case to an absolutely recognizable historical era.

The fairy tale inserts itself naturally into the complex horizon thus outlined. As a narrative genre, it puts into contact characters and situations pertaining to qualitatively different contexts, builds a bridge between drastically distant epochs, and permits a comparison between more or less distinct conceptions of the world. This is possible because, despite the chronological succession of the epochs, the representatives of the past do not disappear but continue, in altered forms and in hidden places, to co-exist with the representatives of the present. The fairy tale forms an ideal middle ground, in which Myth, Legend, and History can flow together and interact. In chapter 4, the exact value that this concept assumes is analyzed, as it plays a concrete function in the construction of the fairy tale. Now, however, it is time to turn our attention to the filter through which the Celtic heritage discussed above actually passed.

The Christian Appropriation of Celtic Tradition

The meeting between Christianity and the Celtic world must have been in no way traumatic, since it allowed for a synthesis of great cultural value, not only for the Irish, but also from the point of view of its consequences throughout Europe. An entire apparatus of pagan beliefs, in particular that connected to the existence of fairies, rather than being totally removed in favor of the new faith was re-elaborated by the latter and made, so to speak, usable within the Christian frame of reference: the origin of the fairies, for example, was explained as deriving from a battle in heaven between rebel angels and those faithful to God. This rereading affirms itself in folklore, but should flank, rather than substitute, the idea inherited from a pagan past, according to which the fairies were, more or less, terrestrial divinities directly linked to the mythical *Tuatha Dé Danann*. In substance, the old and the new learned quickly to coexist, given that the undoubtedly power-ful force of attraction of the message spread *in primis* by St. Patrick would have been incapable (even if he wanted it to) of eradicating a traditional patrimony which, as in no other part of Europe, had sedimented itself so profoundly within the popular mentality and imagination. In the tolerant attitude of the Church should be read a fair dose of realistic pragmatism; the Church realized that it would have been pointless and damaging to undertake a full frontal assault against an enemy who did not, in any case, present an insurmountable barrier. The work of conversion could proceed with a certain rapidity precisely because one was dealing with the gradual fusion of two opposed but consonant contexts, in a reciprocal way that allowed for peaceful coexistence. The noble and warrior classes presented the greatest resistance to Christianity, in that they held themselves to be the most genuine depository of the ideals expressed by Celtic and pagan tradition. It seems plausible to me that this resistance began to vacillate when Irish monks began their work to recover and transcribe the immense narrative patrimony that was the depository of this tradition, and to secure a means by which to prevent its being swept away by the accidents con-nected to purely oral transmission. At that moment, the Irish aristocracy surely realized that they had an ally who, questionable motives aside, was pursuing an objective of undoubted relevance.[24]

One could discuss at length as to whether Christian dogma absorbed into itself pagan belief, thus rendering it inoffensive and indeed functional to its own ends, or that "the rich and widespread pre-Christian heritage indigenous to Ireland for centuries, rather than simply adopting Christian ideals, incorporated them *into existing structures.*"[25] In this light, it would mean that preexisting tradition, made strong by centuries of sedimenta-tion, worked to make Christian dogma its own, adapting it in such a way as not to disturb the existing status quo. It seems to me that the truth is to be found inevitably somewhere between the two, for the simple reason that, if one was really dealing with an absorption in one direction only, sooner or later the absorbed tradition would have finished by be-ing debased entirely in favor of the other. Thus, what effectively exists, in broad outline to the present day, is a peaceful coexistence, or rather a balanced combination: Ireland can definitely be defined as one European country in which Catholicism has its most solid roots, but one cannot ignore the traditional respect shown by the greater part of the population to their pagan heritage, as witness "the survival of a great number of . . . monuments to ancient beliefs."[26] Both elements are inextricably linked in forming Irish identity.

We are most interested in more closely examining the way in which the Church approached the transmission of a narrative tradition that it found still in full flower upon arrival in the island. It has been emphasized that to speak with some authority of a historical epoch, one must wait at least until the beginning of St. Patrick's preaching. It is believed that from Patrick himself came the first intention to preserve from oblivion a patrimony of tales that kept alive the prehistorical phase of Ireland and its people: "We are told that Saint Patrick listened with pleasure to the tales of aged survivors of the warrior Fianna and that he commended his clerics to take pen and vellum, and write down the old men's stories *lest they be forgotten*."[27] Ó Danachair is referring to conversations that the Saint is supposed to have had with representatives of the *Fenian* legend, in particular Oisin and Keelta (Caoilte), which fascinated him to such a point that he considered it his duty to preserve them perpetually in memory. In the *Acallam na Senórach* (*Conversations of the Ancients*), a Gaelic text dating to the thirteenth century, we even read of St. Patrick exclaiming after hearing a tale: "Success and benediction attend thee, Keelta! This is to me a lightening of spirit and mind. And now tell us another tale."[28] The monks who took on the task of transcribing the narrative corpus inherited from Celtic tradition thought it opportune to involve directly the Saint par excellence, as if searching for the most prestigious guarantee for their work—which began, at least according to the testimony that has come down to us, in the seventh century and went on throughout the Middle Ages, as the quoted text shows.[29]

Oral transmission did not cease; instead, it may have preserved, autonomously, traditional tales that have come down to us bypassing the filter of writing and Christianity, and hence adhering to the authentic Celtic spirit. The fact remains, however, that the greater part of the tradition doubtlessly was transmitted directly or indirectly by the texts transcribed by monks during the Middle Ages. Hence, when scrutinizing these tales, one must necessarily bear in mind the influence that may have been exerted by two originally extraneous factors. This is an influence of no little importance, one that has undoubtedly altered in many points the letter and spirit of tales pertaining to preceding epochs and characters, and not only in the chronological sense. But, how can one pretend that, after so many centuries, it would be possible to preserve integrally a tradition entrusted to oral transmission? Even if the monks had not transcribed the texts, history would have taken its course, and other agents, external or internal, would have contributed to altering a large number of traditional elements. What has come down to us is the outcome of a cultural fusion that has given an absolutely specific form to a preexisting heritage. It is this that we must approach, because it is all that has materially been conserved. Despite the freedom that one can concede to the work of transcription, it still derives from an indigenous source, which, thanks to this transcription, in one way or another will remain fixed for good, liberated from the changeability intrinsic to the oral act. I am also of the opinion that a monk, however devoted to his faith, will feel it his duty as a scribe as he sits before the performance of a talented bard, not to omit anything beautiful and worthy of conservation in what he has heard. A tale can certainly be purified of elements inappropriate to the Christian spirit, it can undoubtedly undergo damage and addition, perhaps due only to the loss of memory, but it will preserve its identity, whatever attracted those who thought it worth transcribing in the first place.

The appropriation of the indigenous tradition was certainly the most effective means that the Church could employ in its preaching, and it is incorrect to undervalue the degree of re-elaboration it could have made to the oral tales. But can we produce documentary evidence to demonstrate the kind and quantity of this re-elaboration? We have only what the oral and written tradition—the pagan heritage and the advent of Christianity—has contributed to producing and transmitting to us, a heritage that must be considered in its entirety, recognizing that it is only the visible stratum superimposed on many others that have preceded it. Besides, it is not possible in the purely Celtic tradition itself to recognize "what would be specifically 'Celtic,' what may be part of a wider Indo-European heritage, what came perhaps from more ancient strata . . . and there is little hope of our identifying an exclusively 'Celtic' way of narrating."[30]

Owing to the impossibility of reconstructing something which that no longer be directly obtained, it is better to concentrate on the narrative tradition as it has come down to us, without forgetting that orality is above all an open system to which all members of the community, including writers, have freedom of access and intervention.

Above all, one clue makes me think that the texts transcribed throughout the course of the Middle Ages reproduce faithfully the substance of the ancient Irish narrative tradition. I am referring to the insertion into these texts of the figure of St. Patrick and other minor saints, a presence explained by the desire to place the work of the copyists in a dogmatically correct context. Tales coming from the pagan past are set against a fictitious metanarrative background, in which appear and speak prominent characters from Christian history, charged with directing the content of the text in the right way. We have already read a passage in which the first evangelizer of Ireland displays all his appreciation for the tales narrated to him by Keelta, a character who nevertheless pertains to a field opposed to his own. In another passage, the Saint admits in front of his interlocutor: "Were it not for us an impairing of the devout life, an occasion of neglecting prayer, and of deserting converse with Good, we, as we talked with thee, would feel the time pass quickly, warrior!"[31] On the one hand, St. Patrick repeats the pleasure he feels on hearing the tales; on the other, he separates it from the religious life. It is as if he recognizes the division existing between the two ambits. From this, one can deduce that the copyist in question, by means of the Saint, wished to affirm his autonomy in the narrative field. Basically, the device of inventing the baptism of Keelta, introduced before he begins to narrate, is enough to furnish a key acceptable in Christian terms. It is correct to maintain that behind the work of the Irish monks lies hidden (or clearly revealed) an *allegorical* reading, a re-elaboration of the past in service to the present, similar to what happened to so many texts from classical antiquity at the hands of medieval clerics. One is dealing with an *interpretation* that distorts the original message, but not its forms and themes. In substance, it does not seem to me that the medieval copyists felt the urgent need to alter radically a consolidated narrative patrimony.

Thus, a heterogeneous body of tales of the most varied nature was given unity and organization in the medieval manuscripts, making it also possible to create the subdivisions of the cycles discussed previously. Once the transcription of these texts was complete—the *Book of Leinster*, the *Book of the Dun Cow*, the *Book of Armagh*, the *Book of Invasions*—it was possible to achieve an overview of the noblest Celtic narrative tradition. I am not using the term *noble* casually given that, in these texts, obviously, the entire tradition did not appear, but only those parts deemed worthy of transmittal. Perhaps no less deserving narrative threads were neglected, perhaps others did not have the good fortune of being heard by the copyists: in any case, all those that found a place in these collections became the tradition *par excellence*, what officially represented centuries and centuries of Irish storytelling. Writing created, in practice, a *classic literature*, the encompassing expression of a privileged class that had appropriated an oral and popular tradition as its point of reference, on a literary and sociopolitical level, particularly in its centuries-old battle with the English invaders

It is impossible to ascertain how much access the lower classes were given to this classic tradition. That with the passing of time it became a privileged source of inspiration for literature is an undeniable fact: to give just a few examples, one need only think of the medieval flowering of the so-called *Breton Cycle*, of many passages from Shakespeare's works, of the false eighteenth-century Ossianic poems of Macpherson, and even of the recent explosion of the fantasy genre. Undoubtedly, a certain influence was exercised also on those who kept up the oral tradition. Thus, one was, in fact, dealing with two contexts persisting in the same space–time. However, the affirmation of writing could not greatly interrupt the canonical mechanisms of orality, which remained alive and vital above all in the countryside, where the narrative patrimony, freed of the conventions imposed by literature, could pursue its natural evolution. Whereas, on the one hand, the narrative tradition became conventional and standardized on models considered classical, on the other, it became the depository of values proper to folklore, a context in which conservation and innovation were in perennial conflict. The fairy tale, besides being the genre charged with the task of connecting the planes of Myth and Legend pertaining to classical and pagan tradition, also became the context in which characters of popular and historical extraction could enter into contact with a reality of mythical origin that folklore, influenced by Christianity, had re-elaborated: the gods, linked to Myth, had made their entrance into History as fairies, a tradition that remained for many centuries the exclusive prerogative of popular orality. This situation existed at least until the nineteenth century, when an intellectual orientation developed that thought it necessary to fix this, too, in writing.

Notes

1. For an overview of those theories that, between the nineteenth and twentieth centuries, have attempted to explain the origin and diffusion of *folktales*, see the treatment given in Thompson, *The Folktale*, 367–90. In particular, for the *Indological* thesis of Benfey, 376–79.

2. Ibid., 389–90: "He is convinced that the origins of the narrative are due to the play of the imagination with the events of human life. But this play of the imagination in man is rather limited, so that there is every tendency to operate with an old stock of imaginative happenings rather than to invent new ones."

3. Ibid., 390.

4. Cf. Lo Nigro, *La fiaba tra scrittura e oralità*, 7–8.

5. Cf. the analysis offered in Zimmermann, *The Irish Story Teller*, 168–70.

6. See Caoimnin Ó Danachair, "Stories and Storytelling in Ireland," in *Folk Literature of the British Isles* (London-Folkestone: Scarecrow Press, 1978), 107–8: "In some parts of the world the new Christian teaching was opposed to the ancient learning. Not so in Ireland—here they *blended fruitfully*" (my italics).

7. Cf. Phillip Le Duc Marcus, *Yeats and the Beginning of the Irish Renaissance* (Ithaca-London: Cornell University Press, 1970), 22–25. A passage from an article by Yeats is particularly significant, *The Poetry of R. D. Joyce*, "Irish Fireside" (1886), 331: "Love of shadowy Hy Brasil (literally *Island of the Blessed*, synonym of an otherworldly dimension which suggests unequivocally the Christian idea of *Paradise*) is very characteristic of the Celtic race, ever desiring the things that lie beyond the actual; dreamy and fanciful things, unreal if you will, as are all the belongings of the spirit from the point of view of the body."

8. Cf. Diarmuid Ó Giolláin, "The Fairy Belief and Official Religion," in *The Good People*, 202: "There was no conflict between belief in the fairies and belief in the saints. Both belonged to the same popular religions and inhabited the same mythical universe."

9. See Zimmermann, *The Irish Story Teller*, 34.

10. Ibid.

11. Melita Cataldi, introduction to *Antiche storie e fiabe irlandesi*, ed. by Melita Cataldi (Torino: Einaudi, 1985), VII.

12. Cf. Zimmermann, *The Irish Story Teller*, 12: "The Irish are often said to have *great facility in verbal expression*, to love eloquence, and to spin tales. In actual fact, verbal agility is unevenly distributed among them and there are good and bad storytellers everywhere, but it can hardly be denied that Ireland has enjoyed a *highly verbal culture*, that conversation and storytelling have been cultivated there as a *game* or a *fine art*, and that a good deal of the narrative exchange has been perceived as 'traditional'" (my italics). If one agrees with all that Zimmermann affirms, one must recognize how a discourse on narrativity cannot do without an attentive examination of a context of major importance from this point of view such as that of the Irish, a people who, more than any other, incarnate the ability to descry in reality a constant narrative potential.

13. Ó Danachair, *Stories and Storytelling in Ireland*, 111.

14. See the brilliant analysis of the subject in Patrick Sheeran, "Genius Fabulae. The Irish Sense of Place," *Irish University Review* XVIII, 2 (1988): 191–206. In particular, 197: "The nominal sense of place means, then, not only an obsessive resort to names, but also that is sufficient to name a place in order to mark one's attachment to it." For the Irish, therefore, it is enough to *name* a place, give it, that is, a merely verbal consistency, to set up an emotional relationship with it. In this way, a world emerges that is made up of *words* rather than the concrete elements of tangible reality.

15. See Ó Danachair, *Stories and Storytelling in Ireland*, 111: "Popular and wide-spread as these international tales were in Ireland, they were still outnumbered and outclassed by the great body of stories native to Ireland."

16. See Zimmermann, *The Irish Story Teller*, 34–35, to gain a sufficiently complete picture of the "different grades among the *baird*."

17. Ibid., 35.

18. Ibid.

19. See ibid., 36.

20. Ibid., 37.

21. Cf. Thomas W. Rolleston, *Myths and Legends of the Celtic Race* (New York: Crowell, 1911), 96.

22. Ibid.

23. Ibid., 252.

24. In James Stephens' *Irish Fairy Tales*, specifically in the first and last tales, it is possible to assist at the progressive drawing together of the exponents of Christianity and the proud Celtic-pagan aristocracy, a drawing together that terminates in reciprocal acceptance due to a shared love for the narrative tradition.

25. Nora Naughton, "God and the Good People: Folk Belief in a Traditional Community," *Béaloideas* 71 (2003), 23 (my italics).

26. Ibid., 20.

27. Ó Danachair, *Stories and Storytelling in Ireland*, 108 (my italics).

28. Rolleston, *Myths and Legends of the Celtic Race*, 283.

29. See Zimmermann, *The Irish Story Teller*, 32–33.

30. Ibid., 42.

31. Rolleston, *Myths and Legends of the Celtic Race*, 283.

The Precursors of Yeats in the Recovery of the Narrative Tradition   2

SIMILARLY TO WHAT TOOK PLACE in almost all of the rest of continental Europe, in Ireland during the nineteenth century a whole series of writers—in the broadest sense of the term—undertook a task then considered laudable, that of preserving the narrative patrimony which, over time, had accumulated by means of popular storytelling. The objective was to save from the precariousness of orality a narrative tradition that reflected the deepest values of a nation, its folklore—a depository of legacy from which, until that moment, literature had kept a careful distance. It has already been seen how medieval Christian monks became protagonists of the transcription of that immense corpus of Irish tales that had been handed down for centuries, in particular by a class of professional bards to whom Celtic society had delegated the responsibility of keeping the narrative tradition intact. In the monks' manuscripts, this tradition found its first permanent expression, and was saved from the accidents of oral transmission. Obviously, the tradition had been remodeled continually by these accidents because it depended on a specific mode of transmittal: the *filid* themselves, although educated to preserve the purity of their heritage, could never prove an invincible bastion against the alterations constantly encouraged by a continually evolving environment.

Writing, on its part, avails of the faculty to remove a narrative corpus created and brought to oral fruition by the people from the influence of factors that, taken together, account for the characteristics that render each tale unique. But no matter how much literature strives to modify to its own ends the materials drawn from tradition, it will always remain the fruit of traditional knowledge, of a more or less organic apparatus of myths, beliefs, customs, and rites that distinguish a given community, whether it be national or merely local. The folklore that lies behind the composition of those texts reputed to be classics—in which all that, *a posteriori*, we consider to be the best of the Celtic tradition is gathered—is not evident, to the extent that it has been absorbed into the logic of the literary text, for which the forms and themes of narration are independent of, or at least less conditioned by, any reference to the reality that has forged them. Once literature has taken the upper hand, the tradition follows the evolution of the literary text; at its origin, however, albeit not clearly visible, lies a process of creation and elaboration proper to folklore.

The Christian clerics of the early Middle Ages made possible the recovery of an imposing narrative tradition linked to a world that, upon their arrival, was inevitably destined to disappear or be significantly altered. In the same way, nineteenth-century writers and scholars undertook the recovery of an oral tradition that also seemed destined to fade away under the unrelenting passage of time and the ascendancy of a literary culture. Patrick Kennedy, in the introduction to his collection, on the one hand, gave vent to the fear that "the memory of the tales heard in boyhood would be irrevocably lost" and, on the other, complained that the destiny of these tales depended on the memory of the emigrant Irish and second-class magazines.[1] The whole shared memory of a body of traditional tales, the only common patrimony by which an entire nation could recognize itself, was in danger of being lost for good, a patrimony not yet manipulated by writing and hence, substantially, virgin territory, still well rooted in folklore. It has already been said that a tradition genuinely free of any contact with literature is not objectively conceivable. It does not seem correct to me to assume the existence of a popular bard, and hence of a tale elaborated in an oral context, entirely uninfluenced by the circulation of written texts. However, it is equally obvious that the narrative production circulating in the Irish countryside presented itself to the intellectuals of the nineteenth century, on the one hand, as the only path by which to approach a so-to-speak primigenial, uncontaminated narrative form, and on the other, to discover an unexplored treasure that could open up new, unexpected scenarios for literature. Within this precious body of tales, there coexisted the popular re-elaboration of the classic patrimony already collected in the monastic manuscripts and the heterogeneous set of tales connected, more or less directly, to the daily life of the storyteller. In the latter context, it was possible to discern the contemporary evolution of a tradition that, although rooted in the distant past, preserved its vitality thanks precisely to the interpenetration of a system of beliefs handed down from generation to generation and a perennially new narrative act, between the collective dimension proper to a given people and the specific individuality of the storytellers spread throughout the Irish territory.

The peasant storyteller became a central figure in the Irish literary panorama, in particular from the point of view of Yeats, who ascribed to it the survival of a primitive reality that was saved "from the impurities of the modern world" because on its isolation depended "the purity of the literature preserved by the peasant," the only element capable of providing a "link to an ancient literary and imaginative tradition which could . . . rival that of Greece." The narrative tradition in its entirety enters into the field identified by Yeats, since he does not recognize the validity of a hierarchal classification which, canonically, makes a net distinction between "high poetry of bardic tradition and the simpler folk tales which spoke of fairy raths and stolen children." Both of these narrative categories constitute corresponding gates of entry for the poet to a supernatural dimension capable of compensating for his dissatisfaction with Christian spirituality, which was no longer enough to contain the poetical horizons opening to his creative genius.[2] The main theme of these nineteenth-century collections is precisely that of encounters with fairies had by one or more human protagonists, frequently identified with heroes of Celtic legend, but more often than not deprived of any precise biographical identity, and sometimes coinciding with that of the storyteller himself. In practice, almost all this tradition can be included in the conception of the fairy tale outlined in the Introduction. Thus, the fairy tale becomes the privileged point of communication between the narrative act and the element of folklore or, more precisely, it is the most important product of the interaction between the two, the most explicit manifestation of the persistence of a tradition, albeit in a framework of continual innovation.

To this tradition turned a wide array of intellectuals, among whom the dominant characteristic was a common interest in the written perpetuation of material never before deemed worthy of attention, or at least, never considered appropriate to be transferred into a literary context. In the case of many of these scholars, the boundary between the folklorist and the writer is unclear, as is the fluid barrier between scientific intentions and artistic aspiration. The resulting picture is extremely heterogeneous, because the approach to the narrative tradition is highly personal and inseparably linked to the individual judgment of those who undertook to compile the material in the first place and to final product of their work. Observing the notable diversity of orientation connected to the written appropriation of the fairy tale of popular origin—the narrative context par excellence, suspended between orality and writing, between the tradition of folklore and literary elaboration—it is possible to derive many extremely interesting ideas regarding the narrative phenomenon in its entirety. The fairy tale seems to set off a *virtuous circle* of narrativity, an inexhaustible movement in which the single element of tradition undergoes a change according to the use made of it by the writer or the oral bard himself. Into this context, Yeats' work as a collector inserts itself in an activity which, taking the form of a judicious selection of fairy tales from the written tradition that developed in the nineteenth century, identified in the *eternal return* the principle by which to found a literature capable of arising continually from its ashes. This virtuous principle of circularity becomes *vicious* when one presumes it to have reached a state of immutability, at which point the link with the original patrimony loses its profoundly dynamic nature.

The Royal Hibernian Tales

The first publication specifically dedicated to fairy tales drawn directly from the living voice of the people is the anonymous *The Royal Hibernian Tales: Being a Collection of the Most Entertaining Stories now Extant*, going back to a date before 1825, as Séamus Ó Duilearga demonstrates in a 1940 editorial note.[3] The title itself says much about the nature of this collection. It places its accent on the *nationality* of the tales, rendered more so by the use of the Latinized adjective *Hibernian* that seems to me intended, along with the reference to royalty, to suggest the great value that the compiler assigns to his work: the adjective *Most Entertaining* indicates that the anonymous collector has specifically oriented his research toward those examples of the narrative tradition most in conformity with the prime need of entertaining the public (although it should be noted that, in the introduction, reference is also made to the didactic aspect of the texts in question).[4] Finally, it seems worthwhile to note the presence of that phrase "now Extant," an expression that the compiler uses to acknowledge the partial nature of his collection, based on as much of the popular tradition as had been conserved up to his time. From this residual patrimony, he selects thirteen tales, freeing them, for the first time, from the uncertain destiny of orality and making them the first Irish classic in the genre.

In the introduction to the collection, it is argued that the work was inspired by similar collections of fairy tales from other parts of the world and by the ensuing consideration that, for Ireland, too, rich as it was in its own national tradition, the task of giving a stable and lasting form to an albeit minimal part of the immense repertory of the storytellers could no longer be delayed. We are not told if our collector effectively toured the island to hear and transcribe fairy tales directly from the living voice of the storytellers: the fact is that there is absolutely no reference to the source and circumstance of the storytelling. It is clear, therefore, that the interest is totally concentrated on the tale itself and that the teller fades into the background. What counts is to underline the *genuineness* of the stories, their value as an absolute novelty for readers accustomed to official litera-ture.[5] Both the substantial novelty of the work and the cultural climate of the time guaranteed it a wide circulation, with the volume even finding pride of place in the library of Thackeray himself.[6]

Thomas Crofton Croker and His Followers

The circulation of a work such as *The Royal Hibernian Tales* gave the An-glo-Irish upper classes the chance to come into contact with the other half of the country, the poor, Catholic classes of the countryside, particularly in the West, an area in which the ancient traditions are most tenaciously preserved, predominantly through the Irish language. Indeed, this proved a linguistic barrier—the first collectors only spoke English—that made for a decidedly partial approach to the Irish narrative patrimony, which most frequently preserved its most original tales, those having no equivalent in the rest of Europe, in the native tongue. To complete the picture, cultural and ethnic prejudices came to play, on the basis of which the first writers from the east considered the peasants of Celtic origin as an inferior class, depository indeed of a precious, unexplored reserve of fairy tales, but at the same time dominated by superstitions displaying their cultural backward-ness and irrationality.[7]

On these assumptions began the work of Thomas Crofton Croker. Croker may be considered the chief exponent of a particular intellectual orientation that, following the example of the Grimm Brothers, con-sidered it indispensable to spread among their fellow countrymen and men of letters knowledge of a storytelling tradition that could create a specific identity for the Irish with respect to other nations in which such an identity was perhaps long consolidated. Antiquarian, folklorist, and writer, Croker published in 1825 *Fairy Legends and Traditions of the South of Ireland*, the first, but also the most successful of his collections. So popular was this work that his publisher encouraged him to collect the material for another two volumes. The work received the solemn recognition of Walter Scott and of the Grimm Brothers, who translated it into German. Thanks to Croker's main collection, the narrative tradition deriving from folklore passed the confines of Ireland for the first time and was discovered in the rest of Europe.

Fairy Legends and Traditions of the South of Ireland took the form of a more or less authentic account of a journey undertaken in the southern counties, familiar to Croker in that he came originally from Cork. The aim of this itinerant adventure was not simply to gather traditional tales, but to use them to illustrate "the superstitions of the Irish Peasantry, superstitions which . . . powerfully influence their conduct and manner of thinking" and to cast light on "the very extravagant imagination in which the Irish are so fond of indulging."[8] Croker depicted, for a presumably unaware public, the *humus* of folklore from which the fairy tales he had collected grew and were transmitted, a context that, from his point of view, accounted for the sociopolitical delay afflicting the entire population, solidly anchored as it was in its traditions and resistant to any idea of progress.

Taking this viewpoint into account, it is not surprising to discover that Croker's work is far from being faithful to the letter of the tales heard and little respectful of the spirit of the storytellers. His transcriptions (in *Fairy Legends and Traditions of the South of Ireland*, as well as in his later collections) are authentic recreations, dictated by personal taste and by the expectations of Croker's target audience, and following established practice in the contemporary European milieu. The writer expresses his freedom in completing tales that, according to a canon of "Aristotelian 'wholeness'" are unfinished, fusing, for example, into a single whole tales that were originally separate[9] or emending details considered coarse or in any case aesthetically invalid, and finally inserting rational explanations by which to correct the fallacy of popular belief. In practice, Croker used a sort of personal filter to compile his collections, one that allowed him to construct *a posteriori* a fictional framework in which to unite the most widely varying tales or to develop a conventional image of the popular storyteller, thus depriving him of personality and rendering him functional to the tone of every tale narrated.[10] Bearing this in mind, one should by no means be astonished on hearing that Croker's closest collaborator, Thomas Keightley, author of *Tales and Popular Fictions* (1834), admitted that he was capable "of inventing an Irish legend and the character of some old narrator."[11] This statement illustrates the extreme instability of the concept of *authenticity* relative to the tales in the collections, but also provides us with an image of an oral tradition with the power to nourish a literary current which, in one way or another, draws its inspiration from it.

The attitude of Croker, and of so many of his contemporaries, including Keightley and Samuel Lover,[12] toward the tale originating from folklore is, practically speaking, the exact opposite of that of Yeats, above all because the former perceived folklore in a negative light, seeing it as a decadent source of knowledge and in need of purification on the part of the rational intellectual. This devaluation of folklore also justified its being read humorously. Croker also set himself the task of casting light on the close relationship between Irish fairy tales and English literature, on the one hand (one cannot otherwise explain his references to Spenser and Shakespeare, in whose work one encounters characters very close to the fairies of popular Irish tradition), and to international folklore on the other.[13] In substance, Croker is taking a stand and does not or cannot recognize the autonomy and intrinsic value of Irish storytelling and folklore. Despite these impediments, Croker's work was Yeats' main source, albeit read from the point of view of an absolutely antithetical poetic.

Croker's example conditioned the approach to the oral tradition until at least halfway through the nineteenth century. Periodicals such as the *Dublin University Magazine* and the *Dublin and London Magazine* satisfied the requests of an extremely wide public for traditional tales not published in their genuine form, but rewritten on the basis of the literary module provided by Croker and completed by the comments of an "enlightened narrator."[14] The interest in folklore and its narrative products spread as a fully fledged fashion that penetrated even more properly literary texts, as witnessed by the practice of many writers who, throughout the nineteenth century, inserted oral narrations into their novels or short stories to add truthfulness or a certain note of color to their work as a whole. The intention was also to provide comic counterpoint to a tragic contest or, again, to fill up the empty spaces in the main action with pleasant tales in which the creative inspiration of the author could vent itself more freely.[15] The literary use of the fairy tale, although on the one hand, it evinced its aesthetic function, on the other, distanced it from its specific oral and popular nature, the fruit of the convergence between individual creativity and ancestral legacy, between narrative pleasure and the needs of the community.

Patrick Kennedy

The fairy tale and the rest of the narrative production attributable to popular storytelling was given entirely different treatment in the work of Dublin librarian Patrick Kennedy. His two main collections were *Legendary Fictions of the Irish Celts* (1866) and *The Fireside Stories of Ireland* (1870). In both, we see the disappearance of the literary mannerism that distinguished Croker's work and that of many influenced by his teaching. This was easier for

Kennedy because he was not a writer but a simple scholar, who, moreover, had heard the oral narrations of the storytellers during his youth, an experience that provided him with a personal repertory from which to draw in the composition of his texts and instilled in him a fair dose of respect for folklore, to which he gave a certain credit, at least as far as Yeats affirms.[16] In Kennedy's transcriptions there is an unprecedented fidelity to the idiom and structure of the oral narrations. The text was intended to express the real characteristics of the rural life in which the tales were set, far from the sentimental or humorous excesses in which Croker and his followers had indulged themselves. Kennedy's contribution, on his own admission, limited itself to making each tale presentable "in a form suitable for the perusal of both sexes and all ages," including the choice to omit "scenes of blood and cruelty,"[17] a sort of preventive censure intended to make the tales accessible to the widest readership possible without offending the delicate sense of decency typical of the Victorian age.

This substantial respect for the specificity of the oral tradition was rooted nonetheless in a traditional devaluation of the literary dignity of the narrative products of Irish folklore. They were considered valuable only insofar as they were the expression of a certain popular culture that was not thought capable of offering a real alternative to classic literature, a point of view that, under a new guise, reintroduced a sort of prohibition regarding the phenomenon of folklore as an autonomous object of narrative creativity. Although Croker frequently used folktales as mere drafts to be completed according to his literary tastes, Kennedy was as faithful as possible to the originals, not considering them suitable to literary use.

Letitia McClintock, Lady Wilde, Douglas Hyde

Although not enjoying the renown of her literary predecessors mentioned above, Letitia McClintock deserves particular mention. Much of the evolution of the approach of the intellectual élite and writers to folklore must be ascribed to some articles published by McClintock in the *Dublin University Magazine* in the 1870s and 1880s, especially those published in 1876–1877 under the title "Folk-Lore of the County Donegal." The author presented a series of fairy tales transcribed directly from the living voices of the peasants of Donegal, one of the most traditional regions of Ireland. Her transcription was not only innocent of literary tampering, but also remained free of influences of a moral or political nature. Absolutely no attempt is made to rationalize the information contained in the tales, which are called instead to demonstrate "human interaction with the world of the spirits."[18] This is an aspect of McClintock's work that, in addition to the favor it might have found with Yeats, witnesses to the deeper value that was beginning to be attributed to a phenomenon until then deemed the fruit of a "subculture." McClintock may be considered the first real example, in the Irish context, of a folklorist, since in her texts we find "a living *Irish* tradition which she had observed all around her in County Donegal,"[19] a narrative tradition considered absolutely alive and properly speaking *Irish*—and hence capable of being assimilated into an indigenous ferment that had the requisites to make an original contribution to the birth of a real national literature.

The work of Jane Francesca Elgee, or rather Lady Wilde, mother of the famous Oscar, seems to move along the same lines. In her *Ancient Legends, Mystic Charms and Superstitions of Ireland*, which came out in 1887, just before Yeats' first publication, we find a faithful and accurate transcription of material gathered previously by her doctor husband, whose interests as an antiquarian and occultist led him to prefer being paid with fairy tales, rather than with geese and eggs.[20] What emerges above all is the loving care that a nationalist devotes to that patrimony of beliefs, usages, and tales that make her country unique and different from the rest of the world. Therefore, in her work, and even more strongly than in McClintock's works, there is an impulse to discover, first, what it is that renders the folklore tradition a "uniquely Irish phenomenon," and second, to explore the occult dimension of that tradition (in keeping with literary and intellectual fashions of the time) that made it even more worthy of being intensely studied. Here, however, one notes the influence of political propaganda and a marked "ethnological nationalism," rather than serious study of the narrative object. This is borne out further by a lack of noted sources and the effective absence of any correspondence between the ideas of the author and those contained in the material collected.[21]

In Yeats' opinion—and it is clear that this is what counts most in this context—the most remarkable work in the field of the transcription of traditional tales is Douglas Hyde's *Beside the Fire: A Collection of Irish Gaelic Folk Stories* (1890). From its title, one can note a detail of primary importance that distinguishes this work from almost all the collections previously published: for the first time, a collector, thanks to his bilingualism, could hear tales narrated directly in Gaelic, then translate them into English for his readership. Although, as shall be seen, written translations of texts from Gaelic to English had been flowering for some time, this was a novelty for the oral tradition, and it allowed an entire repertory of tales that had remained for the greater part unexplored to be uncovered. What is more, storytellers were offered the opportunity to express themselves in their usual idiom, and hence to tell their stories in the original form, thus guaranteeing a stricter adherence of the transcribed text to its source. Perhaps it was for this reason that the tales gathered by Hyde were marked by a singular "imaginative extravagance" that "needed no literary embellishments to make them interesting."[22] In practice, the compiler's faithful approach to the letter of the tales he heard was rewarded by their assuming an intrinsic value, since, from the source itself, they were invested with a by no means negligible aesthetic quality. Furthermore, what Yeats appreciated in Hyde was his ability to simultaneously exercise scientific rigor and poetic evocativeness: Hyde was capable of giving an absolutely faithful image of the reality of the oral tale, without renouncing his identity as a "man of letters."[23]

But as Hyde himself was to demonstrate later, maintaining an ideal equal distance between the scientific and literary approaches to folklore was an arduous task,[24] one that could not be completed, in that a real science of folklore had not yet emerged from the study of popular storytelling. This paralleled the situation that existed before Yeats, in which no organic literary movement had emerged that could really bring to fruition the wealth hidden in the oral tradition. The entire work of collection discussed above can be considered as a series of steps toward the discovery and appropriation of a patrimony that, until then, had remained hidden in shadows. The intrinsic value of these collections resides above all in their having laid the groundwork for the more mature and culturally aware treatment that the phenomenon of folklore would receive in the twentieth century. Within the ambit of our research here, one should again underline the multifaceted dialectic that had established itself in the field of the fairy tale between orality and writing, between tradition and innovation. This was to reach its climax in the Irish Revival, and especially in the early works of Yeats, in which the work of recovery lasting more than a century was to find expression.

The Literary Reception of the Written Gaelic Tradition

Throughout the course of the nineteenth century, Ireland was remarkable for the rediscovery of its traditional literature, which had been transcribed in the Middle Ages by Irish monks working to preserve the Celtic narrative heritage. I speak of "rediscovery" because it was in this century that Irish writers finally realized that they possessed "perfect material for a creative literature . . . the most plentiful treasure of legends in Europe."[25] This was possible because it was only in the nineteenth century that writers had at their disposal a conspicuous corpus of translations from the Gaelic, the language in which the greater part of the mythical and legendary tradition of the Celts had been transmitted. The availability of this material offered Irish literature a precious opportunity to escape from English and continental models and to renew itself through the reacquisition of an entirely indigenous treasure.

As one might imagine, the approach to the translation of texts dating so far back in time was by no means univocal. This was all the more so evident because these texts had been transmitted for centuries in manuscript form, which had necessarily compromised, on who knows how many points, the originality and correctness of the tradition. One must also take into account the personal taste and ethical and aesthetic exigencies of those authors who had chosen to draw from the texts in order to transform them into high literature. Thus, analogously the case of the fairy tale originating from folklore, different orientations developed in the literary recovery of the written tradition, which was a more or less legitimate heritage from the Celtic epoch. This written corpus had always been the main repertory of themes, motifs, and characters for oral narrative, and for the fairy tale in particular, especially in those zones where the substratum of the Gaelic language had proved most resistant. In virtue of this undoubted connection, it seems opportune to dwell briefly on the protagonists and modalities that gave birth to the wide variety of orientations that the reception of the early stories provoked. This is a subject that interests us closely, especially if the culmination of the literary events discussed below is believed to be reached in James Stephens' *Irish Fairy Tales.*

As a point of departure, it seems logical to me to choose Gerald Griffin and Denis F. MacCarthy, the two principal exponents of the most elementary approach to the text: that is, a faithful adherence to the form and content of the original, a fidelity maintained even when some characteristics of the transmitted texts seemed *dystonic*, so to speak, to the sensibility of the contemporary reader, and did not take into account the errors inevitably caused by the manuscript tradition. Using this approach, as passive as it was impersonal, one can perceive, on the one hand, an effectively exaggerated respect for the classical source, and on the other, the intention to place all the value—and hence merit—of their work exclusively in having brought to light and offered to the public something absolutely new and original, renouncing *a priori* any kind of re-editing and therefore managing a real appropriation of the text.

For the greater part of the "early myth-users,"[26] such a scrupulous approach to the sources proved impracticable. On the one hand, it was necessary to take into account the inevitable corruption lying hidden in a good part of the tradition, to the point of compromising its original aesthetic quality. On the other hand, these scholars faced the widespread presence of elements contrasting decisively with the idealized image of the Celtic age popular at the time, and also in opposition to the morality of an era in which certain kinds of expressive license were frowned upon.

The leading personality in a more active approach to the tradition was Patrick W. Joyce, who, despite considering himself a scholar, in the composition of *Old Celtic Romances* awarded himself the freedom of a writer, as he proposed restoring to the transmitted texts what, in his opinion, was their original spirit. Although on the structural level Joyce remained substantially faithful to the sources, on the level of form and language, his approach was far more incisive, to the point of emending whatever he considered the sloppy handiwork of clumsy or ignorant copyists. On some occasions, he opted for the omission of sections of the text that he considered to be subsequent additions; at other times, he was driven by a certain "prudishness":[27] his aim was to recover the original spirit, possibly in harmony with a sense of contemporary morality.

With the declared intention of turning "the old legends into 'good stories,'"[28] other authors were responsible for an even more active approach to the traditional material. This is the case of Henry de Vere, who approached the various versions of the same legend in such a way as to combine those elements that would make it more aesthetically valid. With the intention, once again, of restoring the original spirit of the tales, he added passages not present at the source, or expanded or condensed sections according to his own sensibility. Motivated by a personal ideal of native poeticalness, de Vere intervened so deeply in the texts as to frequently erase what might be considered the effective "spirit of the originals."[29]

Thomas W. Rolleston also aimed at getting good stories from traditional sources through a careful re-editing that would restore the original spirit—purified, however, of those trivial tracts that Joyce had attributed to subsequent interpolations. Rolleston instead acknowledged that "the early Gale *was* capable of grossness and other faults,"[30] so that his task as a man of letters was to select his material in such a way that his readership would discover only the "good side" of the Celtic spirit.[31]

In contrast to the reverence shown by his brother to the original sources, Robert D. Joyce composed two poems, *Deirdre* and *Blanid*, in which only the theme is derived from episodes narrated in the legendary tradition. The rest is almost complete re-elaboration, in which the original spirit is consciously betrayed in the name of a freedom of approach to the tradition, which was affirming itself more and more over the course of the nineteenth century (as proved by the great success, albeit brief, of the second Mr. Joyce). Yeats himself recognized Robert D. Joyce as a sort of precursor.[32]

Samuel Ferguson, on the other hand, offers us the most significant example of a re-elaboration of traditional material whose aim is moral and religious edification. His work does not limit itself to the simple exclusion of "'vulgarity' and 'turbid extravagances and exaggerations' in the old stories,"[33] but isolates in particular those aspects of the narrative patrimony more suitable to being interpreted in an ethical key, so that the text becomes a vehicle through which to further the Christian message so dear to its author. It is hardly coincidence that many of Ferguson's poems end with the prophetic announcement, on the part of a still pagan character, of the advent of the new faith.

In conclusion, we come to Standish J. O'Grady, whose work may legitimately be termed the definitive consecration, if not the most organic ordering, of the entire Celtic narrative tradition. It was appreciated and elected as a model by all the main exponents of what would shortly become the Irish Revival. O'Grady recognized the substantial superiority of the indigenous Irish tradition to any other, including the Greek, which, although it could boast of "polish and artistic form," was not capable of exhibiting "the sentiment deeper and more tender, the audacity and freedom more exhilarating, the reach of imagination more sublime, the depth and power of the human soul"[34] (all exclusive properties, in his opinion) of the Celtic narrative patrimony. O'Grady's aim, therefore, was to spread a highly idealized image of the myths, legends, and characters themselves, handed down from the noble Irish past, by virtue of which he was careful to purify the originals of all the immoral and grotesque elements that might have obscured this image. He described his heroes in such a way as to exalt their greatness while depriving them of superhuman qualities, as in the exemplary case of Cú Chulainn, who was meant to be "the noblest character"[35] of all literature. His *History of Ireland* offered, therefore, an artistic rather than strictly academic reading of Irish history, in which the past event was seen "through an imaginative medium."[36]

With O'Grady, the process of fusion between *fabula* and *historia* reached its pinnacle. In his wake, followed those who more knowingly appropriated the Irish narrative tradition as the privileged source of their artistic creativity.

Notes

1. Foster, *Fictions of the Irish Literary Revival*, 205.
2. Joan Fitzgerald, "Yeats's Irish Traditions," *Textus* II, 1–2 (1989): 27–28.
3. I am referring to the introduction by Séamus Ó Duilearga to the new edition of *Royal Hibernian Tales*, *Béaloideas* 10 (1940), 148–50.
4. Cf. ibid., 152: "I thought I could not benefit my readers more than by committing them [the stories in the collection] to print for their *instruction* and *amusement*" (my italics).
5. Cf. ibid.: "In fine, what will greatly enhance the value of this production is, that all the stories in it will be found to be genuine and never before offered to the public."
6. Cf. Zimmermann, *The Irish Story Teller*, 172: "Thackeray bought a copy [of the *Royal Hibernian Tales*] in 1842 and found in it 'the old tricks and some of the old plots that one has read in many popular legends of almost all countries, European and Eastern' (*Irish Sketch Book* 156, 189ff.)."
7. See ibid., 173.
8. Passages taken from Croker's introduction to *Fairy Legends and Traditions of the South of Ireland*, quoted in Zimmermann, *The Irish Story Teller*, 175.
9. Neil C. Hultin, "Anglo-Irish Folklore from Clonmel: T. C. Croker and British Library add. 20099," *Fabula* 27 (1986): 293.
10. Cf. Zimmermann, *The Irish Story Teller*, 176: "Croker contributed to the elaboration and diffusion of the image of the truculent Irish storyteller, well settled in a local community, which partly replaced the rather incredible solitary 'bard' and was definitely offered as contemporary." Croker places the figure of the storyteller in a realistic framework, far from the ideal image of the traditional bard. However, in this framework, the bard loses his individuality, becoming a representative figure from the point of view of the writer.
11. Ibid., 181.
12. Regarding the work of Samuel Lover, which in many respects can be traced back to that of Croker, see Zimmermann, *The Irish Story Teller*, 193–95.
13. See Mary H. Thuente, "W. B. Yeats and Nineteenth-Century Folklore," *The Journal of Irish Literature* 6 (1977): 65–66.
14. Ibid., 66.
15. To get an idea of the varied relationships that developed between Irish writers and the oral tradition in the first half of the nineteenth century, see Zimmermann, *The Irish Story Teller*, 225–62. In synthesis (260): "When novelists of the first half of the nineteenth century referred to or represented aspects of Irish rural storytelling, their purpose may have been just to add picturesque touches to their books, but they could also make it significant—to emphasize social polarities, or point to an ambiguous relationship between truth and lies (Edgeworth); or romanticize a more or less mythical past and a relatively elementary conception of national specificity (Lady Morgan); or exaggerate supposed national characteristics so as to meet demand for stage-Irish monologue and comic situations (Lover); or

preach education and reconciliation while providing an element of local colour (Hall); or expose a symptom of Irish Catholic Barbarity (O'Sullivan) . . . The Banim brothers and Griffin showed that storytelling and rumours were a normal social activity associated with both pleasant and horrible aspects of Irish life. Carleton offered a view of diversified kinds of oral arts and their essential roles in the life of a society which was vanishing like his own youth." In the last two positions, one can begin to make out what would prove to be the approach of Yeats and the Irish Revival to the traditional material.

16. See William B. Yeats, *The Four Winds of Desire*, in Id., *The Collected Works: Early Articles and Reviews* (New York: Scribner, 2004), vol. IX, 125: "Kennedy, an incomparably worse writer, had one great advantage: he believed in his goblins as sincerely as any peasant. He has explained in his *Legendary Fictions* that he could tell a number of spells for raising the fairies, but he will not—for fear of putting his readers up to mischief."

17. Thuente, *W. B. Yeats and Nineteenth-Century Folklore*, 66.

18. Ibid., 67.

19. Ibid.

20. See ibid.: "For when grateful patients would offer to send him [Lady Wilde's husband] geese or eggs or butter, he would bargain for a fragment of folklore instead."

21. Ibid., 68.

22. Ibid., 70.

23. Yeats, *The Four Winds of Desire*, 125.

24. Cf. Thuente, *W. B. Yeats and Nineteenth-Century Folklore*, 70–71: "This blend of the scholar and poet in Hyde is what always appealed to Yeats, but as Hyde directed his attention more and more to politics and the revival of the Irish language, Yeats complained that Hyde the nationalist and the scholar was completely eclipsing Hyde the poet and tale-teller."

25. Marcus, *Yeats and the Beginning of the Irish Renaissance*, 223.

26. Ibid., 226.

27. Ibid., 227.

28. Ibid., 228.

29. Ibid., 229.

30. Ibid., 231.

31. See ibid.: "We want the Irish spirit, certainly, in Irish literature; but we want its gold, not its dross; its spirituality, not its superstition; its daring fancy, not its too frequent recourse to mechanical exaggeration."

32. See ibid.: "They [Robert D. Joyce's works] were read by a number of other Irish writers who were working with similar materials, and Yeats wrote one of his earliest 'Irish' articles about them."

33. Ibid., 232 (the words of Ferguson himself in *Lays of the Western Gael* are quoted between inverted commas).

34. Standish J. O'Grady, *History of Ireland: Critical and Philosophical* (London-Dublin: Sampson, Low & Co.-E. Ponsonby & Co., 1881), 201.

35. Ibid., 235.

36. Standish J. O'Grady, *History of Ireland* (London-Dublin: Sampson, Low, Searle, Marston & Rivington-E. Ponsonby, 1878): vol. I, pp. IV–V.

A Rebirth in the Light of the Tradition **3**

The National Question and Literary Rebirth

THE PUBLICATION, BETWEEN 1878 AND 1880, of the *History of Ireland* by Standish J. O'Grady may undoubtedly be considered as a cardinal moment in the development of Irish literature. Purely aesthetic judgments aside, the *History of Ireland* can with good reason be numbered among those texts that gave birth to, or rather created the premises for the Irish Revival, also termed the Irish Renaissance or the Celtic Revival. In his *fabulosum* approach to national history, O'Grady created the premise for the refoundation of Irish literature, a definite parting from the knowing reappropriation of a far too long neglected indigenous patrimony that had been suffocated by a passive adherence, more or less imposed, to Anglo-Saxon models. This adherence had been favored by the adoption, centuries previously, of the English language, which had distanced the majority of the Irish not only from their native Gaelic idiom, but also from the tradition to which it was so closely linked. O'Grady's work brought the Irish back into contact with a past in which an Irish nation existed, and consequently a literature genuinely identifiable as Irish, too. The latter, it must be understood, had been preserved in the orality of the storytellers and in medieval manuscripts, and, in the course of the nineteenth century had undergone extended recovery, according to a more or less wide margin of elaboration. This native tradition, however, at least until the 1880s, had not succeeded in giving birth to an authentic, renewed national literature, one which stood out from all others by means of its well-defined identity, was capable of producing artists in the fullest sense of the word and, in the final analysis, could provide the imaginative energy necessary for the rebirth of an entire nation, by then intolerant of accepting passively the foreign yoke. This situation had been facilitated by what we could define as a prolonged cultural acquiescence on the part of the dominated country.

John O'Leary, one of the leaders of the nationalist movement and playing a very important role in the formation of the young Yeats' thought, was convinced that "the great misfortune of Ireland in the nineteenth century was that she had never produced a great poet" and that "a political revolution would not succeed without a cultural revival."[1] On the other hand, Yeats himself, who would fill the poetic vacuum denounced by O'Leary, stated that "There is no great literature without nationality, no great nationality without literature."[2] These two points of view demonstrate how intense, at the end of the nineteenth century, was the felt need for the redemption of a people. Yeats' view was strictly linked to the flowering of a new literary era, with the aim of restoring the lost glory of a by then mythical past and giving expression to the most original ferments maturing in a nation that desired to discover its real identity.

In this cultural, and more widely social, climate were born, in broad outline, two fundamental intellectual orientations.

The first was the more specifically nationalist approach, incarnated in Douglas Hyde's *Gaelic League*. He was engaged, in the first instance, in the complete recovery of the Gaelic language. Many saw Gaelic as a depository of the deepest national values; thus, its centuries-old decline had to be arrested absolutely. This decline in Gaelic among the Irish was caused by the prevailing of a foreign language (English), an occurrence that, in the course of time, had led to the modeling of a culture that had gradually emarginated the original. In this regard, the Gaelic Leaguers moved in a substantially antiquarian direction, in the sense that they strove to exhume all that was connected to the purest national tradition, not only the oral tales of the peasants, but also the music, Christian names, clothing, and anything else that could contribute to a radical de-Anglicization and impose an idea of "Irishness as exclusively Gaelic and Catholic."[3] Encouraging an original literary flowering was certainly not one of their main objectives, oriented as they were toward the mere preservation of a patrimony that already existed, and believing that, through this restored patrimony, they could save their fellow countrymen from the detrimental cultural influence, in the broadest sense of the term, of a foreign country. From this point of view, the figure of the Western peasant became a main point of reference, a myth of purity linked to a tenacious attempt to protect the most ancient traditions, attested to primarily by the correct use of the Gaelic language.

The other orientation to take form in this period was that devoted more specifically to the literary question, albeit with strict links to the nationalist movement just discussed, as the passage quoted from Yeats testifies. This approach developed within the Irish Revival (from now on, this term will be employed). The Revival, far from dedicating itself to a rigid conservation of the transmitted patrimony, promoted a highly fecund dialectical relationship with it, which led a series of writers to produce, finally, an original literature, which O'Leary maintained was the indispensable catalyst for a wider and deeper national revolution. The main aim of the Revivalists was to adopt "ancient mythology and the contemporary set of oral traditions *creatively*, looking for *universal* significance."[4] Everything making up the national tradition, both past inheritance and present reworking, had to pass through the channel of the creative genius of the single writer, who, as an artist in addition to an Irishman, had the duty of expressing in his work a message that would pass beyond the narrow confines of his own island. On the basis of the latter, the leading lights of Irish Revival—particularly Yeats, who had scarce knowledge of Gaelic, but who was also the most conscious proponent of the need to make his country's culture less provincial—reserved for itself the consolidated use of the English language: the movement aspired to be the representative of its national identity, but aimed consequently to be understood by the rest of the world. What lay hidden in the Irish tradition was a wealth of universal proportions, analogous to that of Greco-Roman civilization: "The discovery of Celtic literature, that 'untouched marble block,' had opened 'a new fountain of legends' for Europe."[5] This discovery placed at the disposition of writers—and not only Irish ones—a substantially new source of inspiration; it was the harbinger of unexpected horizons, a *malleable marble block* to which an aesthetically valid form had to be given: "To become superior art, oral tradition needed writers who could control the 'wild anarchy of legends' and give it 'deliberate form.'"[6] The exponents of the Irish Revival had thus found, within the indigenous tradition, the material most suited to their increasing need to reestablish Irish literature, a reestablishment occurring under the auspices of the always more mature criteria of poetics, in the light of which this material, rather than being conserved in museums, was revitalized. In this, the typical dialectical process that inserts itself between contemporary literature and illustrious tradition, it was possible to trace a continuity with a typical mechanism of the oral tradition, a mechanism according to which a text is never definitive. Furthermore, the great dream of Yeats and other exponents of the Irish Revival was that of restoring to the cultured and popular components, on the level of artistic elaboration, their original, mythical unity; to harmonize in their work the individual contribution and the collective tradition. This objective could be pursued, not through the passive celebration of the peasant as such, as the Gaelic Leaguers maintained, but in an active approach to the imagination conserved by the peasant himself—the only factor that could truly connect the present to the past and project the term "Irishness" beyond its merely parochial value.[7] The concept of Irishness was a wide one and, most importantly, revealed itself to be the most suitable means by which to create a fusion between the Anglo-Protestant and Celtic-Catholic factions that, in many respects, divided Irish society. The Irish Revival considered itself called to take the helm of the movement for national redemption, but also to prevent politics from making use of literature to its own ends.[8]

The greatest success of the Irish Revival was without doubt the foundation in 1899 of the Irish Literary Theatre. It represented an intensely pursued objective that had to overcome significant sociopolitical difficulties that were linked to the reluctance of the English to concede to the Irish the institution of a cultural pole around which could aggregate the ever more accentuated drive toward independence. The newborn theatre proposed to provide to those writers engaged in a decade-long literary rediscovery of the traditional patrimony the most efficient means to give expression to their innovative work. These writers had to deal with academic prejudice, represented primarily by the intellectuals of Trinity College, for whom the entire Gaelic tradition was not worthy of being considered in a literary key. This stance is by no means surprising if one considers that Trinity symbolized the cultural enslavement of the island to the English world.[9] The birth and affirmation of the Irish Literary Theatre was the most incisive response to anti-Celtic prejudice, because the public demonstrated a growing appreciation of the staging of subjects that had never been shown before—*indigenous* subjects, moreover. In theatre, the first real step toward independence was taken.

Yeats, the Inspiration of the Irish Revival

Let us now take a step backward, to a period before that in which the Irish Revival assumed the organic form it was to reach between the nineteenth and twentieth centuries. We have glimpsed the most important characteristics of the phenomenon of Celtic rebirth, giving space in particular to the national question by which it was in one way or another influenced, to the degree that the institution of the Irish Literary Theatre can be considered the first point of arrival of an intense literary season and of an ever more inflamed patriotic ferment. But now we must turn back to begin to circumscribe the specific ambit of our research, an ambit in which I think it is correct to identify one of the founding moments in the successive development of the Irish Revival. I am referring to the first work of W. B. Yeats, whom, one will have intuited, was undoubtedly the most eminent figure among the revivalists and the most tenacious upholder of the literary rebirth of his country. Before beginning his extraordinary career as a poet and dramatist, he dedicated himself to the compilation of a collection, *Fairy and Folk Tales of the Irish Peasantry*, published in 1888. This was followed, four years later, by *Irish Fairy Tales*, a far briefer collection, which from now on will be considered an integral part of the first, so that we can gain an overall vision of Yeats' relationship with the main area of our analysis, the fairy tale.

In fact, before compiling the anthology, he had composed, but not published, an autonomous work, the poetry collection *The Wanderings of Oisin* (1887), from which clearly emerged his interest in Celtic material, selected as his main source of inspiration. More precisely, he had quickly become aware of the inestimable value inheriting to a narrative and poetic tradition that was sedimented in time and that represented the purest spirit of the national community. His first poems reflected this conviction, but failed to satisfy the need to approach directly those considered the living sources of this tradition. Hence, Yeats preferred to make his public debut first as a compiler of fairy tales and only later as a poet of remarkable individuality. Yeats presented himself as a poet engaged in a preliminary activity of recovery—conducted following entirely personal canons—of a traditional corpus that would provide the material for his creative elaboration. My impression is that his choice of appearing in public for the first time with a collection of folk narratives was linked to the necessity, clearly felt by Yeats, of creating a significant hinterland from which to extract an interpretive key capable of clarifying the entire edifice of his successive art, an interpretive key undoubtedly revealed by the form that the collection takes in his hands. This finds confirmation in a statement of principle from some years later, according to which "no conscious invention can take the place of tradition."[10] Thus, Yeats seems to say that the poet in his individuality will never be able to invent anything that substitutes for that already elaborated in the interminable and collective creative chain of tradition.

Certainly, at little more than twenty years of age, Yeats did not yet avail himself of the expressive means that would distinguish his later poetic career, and hence he was presumably far more inclined to recognize his dependence on the authoritative patrimony of those themes and forms that he had chosen as his point of reference. It should be clarified, however, that this dependence, even in those early years, never resolved itself into passive reception. Yeats made a choice and ordered a variegated narrative material by, on the one hand, taking into account an original folkloric valency and, on the other, by reaching an exact estimate of the (pseudo)-intellectual encrustations caused by the work of previous collectors. His approach was one of active acquisition of sources, in that his objective went well beyond the simple compilation of an anthology, but also involved in the creation of a national literature, of which he would be the seer. And the first duty of a seer—of an illuminated guide—was that of breaking ground, of making a scrupulous choice of items from those that his predecessors had preserved of the tradition and then organizing this material according to the canons of a more sophisticated poetic design.

It seems to me fitting to see in Yeats a man who initiated the "history of the relationship between folk tale and fiction in Ireland,"[11] since it was only after his intervention that folklore ceased to be simply the expressive channel of popular fantasy and rose to the dignity of art. The fairy tale ceases to be ordinary fare when one sees in it the presence of an imagination, through which it is possible to link back, albeit through an indefinite number of intermediaries, to a primordial past. In this lies the pure source from which to draw an immense treasure of images that can function "as allegorical vehicles, sources of symbols, 'objective correlatives' for his own feelings and ideas."[12] This source is all the more effective in that it is invigorated by its native origin, a quality that guarantees it a more active and knowing reception than that reserved until then for the imported stock of images from a foreign culture. From this point of view, whereas the recovery of the bardic tale, which was linked to the classical tradition of medieval manuscripts, was more easily accepted in that it was already a part of literature, the status of the folk narrative was different, insofar as it was extraneous to a literary approach to narration, or at least far distant from it. The task of giving an artistic dimension to the folktale is given to the poet and prophet, who places himself at the head of a movement working to embrace the entire narrative corpus created and handed down within the nation. Whether one is dealing with the legendary song of an ancient bard as transcribed by a medieval cleric, or with the account of a meeting with the fairies given by a contemporary peasant and transcribed by a folklorist, the context is unchanging and is localized by narration. The folk narrative has the capacity to transcend the contingent reality of events and experiences deemed worthy of being remembered, an ambit in which the barriers between *historia* and *fabula* tend to dissolve, finding common ground in folklore.

In the end, our poet pursues a *perennially virtuous circle of narrativity*, causing a continuous exchange of contexts that, with the passing of time, have grown distant. Although he cannot approve of Croker's or Lover's approach to the traditional material, Yeats cannot remove himself from an implicit appreciation of those authors who have accepted a creative confrontation with the folkloric patrimony, inserting themselves fully into the circle upheld for centuries by oral storytelling. It is not surprising, therefore, that for his first anthology he does not conduct research directly in the field of his folk narratives. This is a type of research more adapted to the scholar, who needs direct contact with the oral source due to the urgency of reconstructing scientifically the nature of the phenomenon he is studying. From the viewpoint of Yeats' work, the individual voice that tells a given tale is just one of the innumerable links in a collective chain. The single storyteller is no more than a contingent instrument, the historical interpreter of a timeless phenomenon. This should not make one think that Yeats is indifferent to the specific characters of the men and women who had concretely preserved a precious tradition. Recognition and affection bind him to his fellow countrymen, although it is undeniable that his main point of view is that of the artist, one who holds most dear the imaginative potential that popular tales can lend to an inexhaustible literary elaboration, *original* and *aboriginal* at the same time. Yeats confronts himself with those who have preceded him because it is from this confrontation that tradition has always nourished itself; through the centuries, it has been fed by the most disparate contributions to the point of elaborating in itself an image so protean as to attract into its orbit writers of every kind. The fairy tale is at once the most genuine expression of the character of a people, even when they only pretend to believe in fairies to keep the collectors happy,[13] and the most direct expression of a typically human inclination to make a story out of events linked to a specific vision of the world, which in itself tends to dispute the canonical concepts of verisimilitude.

For the writer, the phenomenon is to be accepted in its totality, as it presents itself each time, and hence in its substantial elasticity, due to which it does not tolerate being reduced to rigid analytic schemes. Or rather, the phenomenon may tolerate it, but only at the cost of an alteration to, or even a debasing of, its intrinsic nature.

Yeats, in contrast to other collectors of the time (e.g., Hyde and Lady Gregory), clearly understood that any given storyteller, as a single representative of the peasant class and so much exalted as the depository of a primordial tradition, was an unpredictable variable, or rather *an il-legible* variable, unable to facilitate, within himself, an interpretation of the traditional tale. Direct contact with the informant can illuminate the current conditions in the narration of a given tale. It can provide all the external data needed to insert this single example into the framework of a specific cultural and socioeconomic climate, identified through a comparison with other examples collected elsewhere. But it does not provide that synthetic vision that is equipped to evince "the power of folklore to keep alive ideas and symbols that had not always been, and ought not to be, in the exclusive possession of the peasantry."[14] Here, it is necessary that the writer should not submit to the contingent conditions linked to individual storytelling, and he should attempt instead to appropriate the universal values lying beneath a tradition that called an entire nation—not simply a single class—to exploit it (albeit the latter had been determinant in preserving it). The writer can draw from the tradition, modeling it in his own way, and without any obligation to the occasional realization connected to the single peasant.

In this figure of the single peasant, Yeats discovers a visionary dimension, an intermediary between the sensible world and another, ordinarily inaccessible world. In light of this issue, the historical dimension—which drove Hyde to the relentless recovery of the Gaelic language and Lady Gregory to attempt to imitate the speech of the informant in her collections—can be devalued. In this instance, the historical dimension does not serve a project of a strictly spiritual nature, by which literature can raise itself onto an ideal level and hence translate itself (to adopt a title from the mature Yeats) into a Vision, the superb vision of a reality no longer subject to the bonds of History. Hence, the popular storyteller has also to be free of the dross that the prejudices and self-interests of previous authors has accumulated around his figure. In the same way, the tales must be cleared of everything not directly pertaining to their purely imaginary function, of all that circumscribes them in an extranarrative dimension and that may banalize or distort them. It is here that the intervention of the poet-editor displays itself in all its discretional power; he sets himself up as arbiter of the specific form that a tradition of collective matrix, situated at the meeting-point between popular, aboriginal elaboration and successive, intellectual reworking, must assume in the eyes of the entire nation. Yeats avails of this status to exclude from his exemplary collection all those tales that are irremediably corrupt due to their improper treatment at the hands of previous collectors, but also those tales dealing with themes that are, *ab origine*, extraneous to the horizons of the anthology, inadequate to the role assigned them of founding a new literary canon. Thus, one can see the exclusion of fairy tales with a moralistic orientation or of those finalized in political or religious propaganda, and of others distinguished by an unacceptable characterization of the Irish peasant or set in a foreign context. Sometimes, it is the presence of an overly "earthly" subject that leads to the tale's being rejected. Furthermore, those tales are left out that, despite their widespread diffusion in the ambit of folkloric narration, lend themselves too easily to an overtly historical interpretation, as in the case of themes dealing with the first colonizers of the island. If instead, within the tales selected there is, "authorial commentary and superfluous literary atmosphere which did not support Yeats' presentation of Irish folklore as a uniquely Irish subject matter free from stale English literary conventions,"[15] then the intervention of the editor becomes selective. He limits himself to omitting all those sections of the text that are dissonant or deviant with respect to the poetic ideal he is pursuing, by which the selected tale must appear in all its autonomy as a regenerating phenomenon, entirely free of interference on the part of a stale literary tradition.

The adoption of these discriminative criteria show us how our poet editor or national seer allows himself noteworthy freedom, and at the same time presents himself as the depositary of truth, able to restore to the traditional material its most authentic form and its deepest meaning. For Yeats, the truth resides in considering that "these folk-tales are full of simplicity and musical occurrences, for they are the *literature* of a class for whom every incident in the old rut of birth, love, pain, and death has cropped up *unchanged* for centuries: who have steeped everything in the heart: to whom *everything is a symbol.*"[16]

Yeats' words are very clear as to where the founding value of the tradition he has recovered lies, a tradition which in its capacity to read every real event symbolically takes the form once and for all of a literature, for which nothing changes because everything, or everything fundamental, has already been understood in its totalizing stare. To the collector remains only the task of presenting this literature in all its richness, allowing it to express fully that vast semantic range that resides nonetheless in a simple form, forged in the image of the popular class that has preserved it through time.

The Distinguishing Characteristics of Yeats' Collections

The fact that Yeats was not a simple collector is demonstrated by the way in which he introduces his fairy tales, in general and in particular, and also by the criteria he adopted in classifying them. Above, I quoted a passage from the introduction to *Fairy and Folk Tales of the Irish Peasantry*. Before Yeats, no one had prefaced a narrative collection of folkloric matrix with such a highly developed explanation. The introduction gives us a more precise idea of how he felt himself to be engaged in a national mission, one aimed not only at spreading among the Irish a knowledge of and love for their narrative patrimony, but also of placing the latter in the correct context, that discussed up to now. He is aware of having to educate his fellow countrymen in how to approach material that, until then, had been distorted and even degraded by those who had preceded him. Yeats, as seen, draws from this work, but places it in a context that the introduction is intended to illustrate in advance. However, prior to submitting the single collectors to judgment, Yeats' criticism is aimed at what he calls the *Spirit of the Age*, understood substantially as the depository of those principles of contemporary progress that would obstruct a serious understanding of the fairy tale. It is seen as an "old and much respected dogmatist" who soon, nevertheless, "will be covered over decently in his grave," and will be supplanted by "another and another and another."[17] It seems to me that Yeats wants to stress the substantial inconsistency, if not the instability, of all those prejudicial judgments that, in order to uphold a rigidly dogmatic idea of progress, are formulated in a way detrimental to the intrinsic value of everything pertaining to the concept of tradition.

The intention of the writer, therefore, is to give due attention to a world in which time seems to stand still, where everything left by the past maintains its perennial validity. The particular reference is to the set of beliefs that lies at the basis of the creation and fruition of the fairy tale: to fully appreciate the latter, a suspension of disbelief is required, which Yeats is the first to assume as his guiding principle in the compilation of his collection. At the end of his introduction, he even quotes a passage from Plato's *Phaedrus*, to justify his intention not to seek rational explanations for the figures and phenomena of the fairy, as they are encountered in the selected tales.[18] Yeats needs the reader's complicity to succeed in his "attempt to present fairy land as representative of a separate spiritual realm which was to be taken seriously even if it could not be understood."[19] He introduces his public to a world in which it is not important to *understand* what happens, but rather to *participate* in a realm that is probably not so far away, as demonstrated by the many references given in the course of the introduction to the typical figures of the popular storytellers, who are treated with unprecedented respect and consideration. This stance is reinforced by Yeats' negative judgments made regarding his predecessors, who had degraded the folk narratives, its creators, and its narrators into mere material for entertainment. It is by no means casual, therefore, that, having to adopt a criterion of choice between a number of fairy tales, he should lean invariably toward "the weirdest and most inexplicable materials available in them . . . the most unusual and mysterious versions he could find."[20]

Apart from the general introduction, Yeats includes specific introductions at the beginning of each section of *Fairy and Folk Tales of the Irish Peasantry*; these are lacking from the later *Irish Fairy Tales*. These introductions constitute a novelty in the field of folk narrative collections and are strictly connected to the innovative criteria adopted by the writer in classifying his narrative material. He rejects an ordering based on the origin of each text. This would have divided the tales according to the collectors from whom they had been received and put them into chronological order in such a way as to give an idea of the historical and literary evolution of almost a century of fairy tale collections. He also rejected an ordering into genre, which would have been plausible for a man of letters, and all the more so when one considers that Yeats himself had postulated a division of traditional storytelling into three parts: *fairy legends*, *folktales*, and *bardic tales*.[21] He opts instead for a more suitable classification based on the subject of each tale. Hence, *Fairy and Folk Tales of the Irish Peasantry* is divided according to the following scheme:

1. *The Trooping Fairies* (divided in turn into *The Fairies, Changelings, The Merrow*)
2. *The Solitary Fairies* (divided in turn into *Leprecaun, Cluricaun, Far Darrig, The Pooka, The Banshee*)
3. *Ghosts*
4. *Witches, Fairy Doctors*
5. *Tír-na-n-Og*
6. *Saints, Priests*
7. *The Devil*
8. *Giants*
9. *Kings, Queens, Princesses, Earls, Robbers*

Irish Fairy Tales, following the same criterion, is divided thus:

1. *Land and Water Fairies*
2. *Evil Spirits*
3. *Cats*
4. *Kings and Warriors*

Altogether, there are thirteen main categories in which are grouped the sixty-six tales in the collection (there are also thirteen ballads, which do not concern the present research). The adoption of these categories allowed Yeats to cast into relief the most specific aspects of Irish folklore. They offered him, in consequence, the chance to present his material as *autonomous*, in that it had been removed from canonical interpretive criteria. The classification appears to be extremely heterogeneous, based as it is on subjects pertaining to contexts at a great distance from each other, in space, time, and system of reference. However, this heterogeneity is purely superficial since it exists precisely to show just how wide is the thematic spectrum embraced by the oral and popular tradition—and in particular by the fairy tale—in which the most disparate subjects flow together into a common structure, as will be seen later.

Yeats' intention is apparently encyclopaedic: "I have tried," he says in the general introduction, "to make it [*Fairy and Folk Tales of the Irish Peasantry*] representative, as far as so few pages would allow, of every kind of Irish folk-faith."[22] In the brief space of a volume, the author leads his reader along a path winding through the history of an entire nation, guiding the reader in the discovery of its most important and most representative *loci*, which, from Yeats' point of view, tradition has protected from the passing of time and from the progress of civilization. From this viewpoint, one can understand better Yeats' decision to include an introduction intended to present and illustrate the subject or subjects on which each section of the work is focused. These introductions becomes all the more useful when one comes across typically Irish figures or phenomena unfamiliar to a foreign readership—and frequently unheard of even by an indigenous but mainly urban population completely ignorant of popular tradition.

Faithful to his commitment to avoid rationalism, even in the specific section introductions, Yeats gives no space to hypotheses that could unveil the mystery in which the existence and attributes of the various species of fairies or the singular power of witches and healers are wrapped. His introductions are intended to avoid disturbing in any way the delicate equilibrium between *historia* and *fabula* that oversees the development of each fairy tale and its characters. The introductions explain the phenomenon from within, as if Yeats were simply the voice through which this or that element of tradition express itself. One example is what he writes about *Tír-na-n-Og*:

> There is a country called Tír-na-n-Og, which means the Country of the Young, for age and death have not found it; neither tears nor loud laughter

have gone near it. . . . One man has gone there and returned. The bard, Oisen [sic], who wandered away on a white horse, moving on the surface of the foam with his fairy Niamh, lived there three hundred years, and then returned looking for his comrades . . . . Not three years ago a fisherman imagined that he saw it. It never appears unless to announce some national trouble.[23]

Yeats affirms, without the slightest hesitation, that *there is* a land of everlasting youth. He gives a summary description of it, attests that the legendary Oisin went there and returned after three hundred years, produces the testimony of one of his contemporaries, and interprets its appearance as an ill omen. In a certain sense, the introduction is a preliminary tale, through which the author prepares his reader spiritually, in such a way as to make him ready to cross the threshold, beyond which he will find himself in another dimension, that upheld by the laws of the fairy tale.

After all that has been said, it seems correct to me to consider Yeats' work not as a mere collection representative of folk narratives (as may be the case with all the other products of the Irish Revival and those produced earlier on the Continent), but as a composition in which the various tales are chosen to provide an organic whole, in which the author blends his voice—neither superimposing nor submitting it—with that of his people, so as to break down the canonical barriers between the two ambits and open the way to an innovative, expressive model for Irish literature.

The Fairy Tale according to Stephens

Whereas the collection edited by Yeats may reasonably be considered the point of departure for the movement toward the rebirth of Irish literature in light of national tradition, a work close to it in many ways—James Stephens' *Irish Fairy Tales*, published little more than thirty years later—may be considered the point of arrival of the Irish Revival itself. At least, it seems correct to me to see in the two narrative collections the beginning and end of a specific literary itinerary, the culminating, if not extreme, points of a process of innovative appropriation of the traditional patrimony, a process that involved (albeit not always to the same degree) all the exponents of the Irish literary scene in the thirty years separating the two works. The two collections, in their position at the boundaries of the movement, furnish a significant synthesis of what, in substance, was Celtic rebirth, all the more so if one recognizes the organic evolution that exists between the works of Yeats and Stephens, an evolution that, more than anything else, should be seen as the most mature, and hence, in this sense, the final expression of the literary reworking of the narrative genre of the fairy tale. The fairy tale, as discussed, rather than being a genre, may be considered a model with which to approach the reality implicit both in Irish folklore and in the literature regenerated from it. For this reason, it seems plausible to me to read Stephens' work as an exemplary synthesis of an entire cultural climate, rather than of a single literary current.

The narrative material from which James Stephens draws in the compilation of his *Irish Fairy Tales* pertained to a context—that of literature transcribed in Gaelic—that had already been widely explored by his precursors, as seen at the end of the last chapter. Moreover, it is through the work of these contemporary interpreters themselves that the writer appropriates a tradition that finds its roots in the Late Middle Ages, when Irish monks possessed themselves of the patrimony of Celtic myths and legends. In particular, he is indebted, as others before him, to the *Silva Gadelica* by Standish H. O'Grady, a collection of ancient tales, both in the original language and in translation.[24] As Yeats had approached the fairy tale of folkloric matrix through the filter of the nineteenth-century collectors, so Stephens approaches the tales from the Mythological and Fenian cycles—not directly, through the medieval manuscripts, but through modern transpositions. The fairy tale is hence introduced into a totally aesthetic dimension, one in which a comparison with the original source is not only unnecessary, but also impossible to find (the monastic manuscript itself being the reworking of an oral source). It is instead in the dialectic discourse with other writers that the authentic literary acquisition of a traditional context is found. Yeats had foretold this acquisition with his collection, but it had yet to be realized. Above all, the fairy tale, in Stephens' hand, ceases to be placed at the service of ideology and becomes the autonomous object of artistic elaboration, the expression of the personality of its author, who can define himself as such because he is aware of creating an original work. This originality not only permits the traditional texts to display characteristics inconceivable until that moment, but because their recreation is free of extranarrative ties, seems intended to bring to the surface the authentic spirit of the old tales.[25] In this respect, Stephens walks the narrow line of an almost imperceptible equilibrium, in which the desire to make the fairy tale a principal field of expression and that of incarnating the purest character of traditional storytelling seem to reach a balance.[26] The equilibrium pursued by Stephens is furthermore the fruit of an objective situation. The immense narrative patrimony that his age had received is full of gaps. Texts that had been transmitted as pure drafts needed to be completed because they had "lost the flow, the liveliness and the wealth of particulars pertaining to oral exposition"; Stephens believed that it was the writer's task to "restore them life."[27]

The choice of the Fenian Cycle (and the Mythological one in the case of his first tale) reflects a precise intention to institute a particular poetic. Stephens sees in the fairy tale above all the possibility of giving form to elements that can be included in a single category: the *indefinite*, which will be discussed shortly. In contrast to what takes place in the Ulster Cycle, in the Fenian Cycle much more space is given to the invisible, parallel world which, by means of Finn himself (Stephens employs the alternative name *Fionn*) and his companions, makes itself visible to the human eye. This aboriginal character permits the author to find a suitable terrain for the cultivation of his favorite themes, those which distinguish the rest of his work: "Reincarnation, metamorphosis and the different planes of being."[28] This group of themes can be ascribed to Stephens' mystical inclinations, which in many respects recalls Yeats and finds in the Celtic tradition the characters, settings, and situations most suited to inexhaustible spiritual research, which, as mentioned earlier, is also a distinctive inclination of the Irish mentality in general. However, the intention of the author is not so much that of casting light on a characteristic of his countrymen as of bringing to the fore the universal resonance of a narrative patrimony in which, from his point of view, unequivocal links can be unearthed with the mystical doctrines of Platonic thought and with the sacred texts.[29] The fairy tale in this way assumes a function going well beyond the simple, naïve folkloric document or the pure entertainment of the popular classes. It perhaps goes beyond the aboriginal value that its creators and beneficiaries attributed to it. But the uses that the author makes of it demonstrate the potential of the traditional tale, a potential that he—an integral part of the community that has preserved it and a worthy heir of Yeats—has the right to bring to fruit according to his own needs, both literary and cultural in a general sense.[30]

Fortunately, Stephens does not sacrifice his work exclusively on the altar of a mystical intellectualism or of the theories connected to it. The fairy tale is not reduced to being a cognitive tool, an intermediary between different realities. It is called upon chiefly to exhibit its primary narrative qualities, to manifest almost the very principles on which the construction of a tale—any tale—is founded. In this regard, it should be noted that Stephens searches for a "deliberate complexity of structure"[31] that, on the one hand, testifies to a decided progress with respect to all his predecessors, and on the other, evinces an absolutely specific attention to the mechanisms that preside over the passage from event to narration. One may certainly speak of *metanarrativity* as the specific characteristic of Stephens' text, a characteristic incarnated in the figure of St. Finnian, the metanarrative protagonist par excellence of the first and last tale, in that he is "listener, interlocutor and recorder"[32] of the facts narrated by the two exemplary characters from Celtic tradition. St. Finnian is basically Stephen's own image, the image of an intellectual attracted by the inheritance of an exemplary past, especially because it is the depository of an immeasurable narrative wealth. But he is also a filter that the author employs to bring the reader back to the climactic moment in which the tale passes from the oral memory of the bard—or of the protagonist himself, as happens in the opening passage—to the written page of the monk, placing him in direct contact with the more or less hypothetical background that he has before him. Stephens is furthermore paying homage to the precious act of storytelling, homage that leads writing to confound itself with orality, to exalt the improvisation of living dialogue with respect to the immobility of literary tradition, albeit of bardic matrix.[33] Hence, Stephens' tales are populated by almost as many interlocutors as there are characters, each called to make their personal contribution to a narration that seems contemporaneously to shape itself for reading. There is certainly no need to be surprised that an Irish author should apply himself with so much interest to the dynamics of narrative when, for an Irishman, this means basically to interest himself in his own personality, a trait absolutely typical of "Irishness." Stephens inserts himself into a wider context that, in substance, includes all the main exponents of the Irish Revival, a context that leads to the daring metanarrative experimentation of James Joyce and Flann O'Brien.[34]

One of the most interesting and attractive aspects of Stephen's text is undoubtedly the "calculated alternation of narrative registers,"[35] a constant variation of tone that produces the image of a world that, beyond its distance in time and space, reflects a spectrum so wide as to take in practically all the manifestations of human life. The choice of the tales itself seems to underline the author's intention to create a sort of global vision of his country's mythical and legendary past. We are, hence, far from the work of previous collectors, in which fairy tales were bent to this or that exigency, more often than not deviating from the real nature of the transcribed text. Now, the fairy tale assumes a fullness and universality of sense that incontrovertibly legitimates its entry into high literature. Stephens, following Yeats' teaching, raises a traditional genre to the same aesthetic level as the modern short story or novel. Basically, the ten texts chosen and placed sequentially by the author can be read as the chapters of a novel, each of which illuminates one or more aspects of a reality that assumes consistency only to the extent that it is upheld by a meditated narrative design.

This design manifests itself in the two tales that frame the entire collection and that seem intended to enclose the world evoked by the fairy tales in a purely narrative dimension, a dimension that the first and last texts connote thanks to the metanarrativity mentioned above. In particular, the first tale, by means of the testimony of an exemplary character, provides a species of account in which all the main events in the Irish mythical and legendary past find space, events that are followed through the successive metamorphoses undergone by the protagonist, Tuan Mac Cairill. Thus, a theme dear to the author weds itself, in a functional manner, to the content of the traditional tales. Within this frame, the eight texts develop to portray the events directly connected to Fionn, to his infancy and adolescence, to the birth of his faithful greyhound Bran, to the meeting with his wife Saeve (who comes, moreover, from the fairy world), to the birth of his son Oisin, and to the events related to a variegated array of characters orbiting around this central figure. Albeit not bearing the same weight in all of the tales, the attention drawn to the relationship between the human and supernatural dimensions is tangible throughout. In any case, the work is made up as follows:

1. *The Story of Tuan Mac Cairill*
2. *The Boyhood of Fionn*
3. *The Birth of Bran*
4. *Oisin's Mother*
5. *The Wooing of Becfola*
6. *The Little Brawl at Allen*
7. *The Carl of the Drab Coat*
8. *The Enchanted Cave of Cesh Corran*
9. *Becuma of the White Skin*
10. *Mongan's Frenzy*

All ten stories are far more highly developed than the tales in Yeats' anthology: whereas in the latter each section was composed of a certain number of tales intended to portray a particular aspect of Irish folklore, in Stephens' work, every text treats a multiplicity of themes, albeit well organized around a center of attraction, which can be equally a character, a setting, or a situation. From this viewpoint, one can understand better what has been discussed earlier about the alternation of narrative registers and also about the subdivision into chapters of each of the fairy tales. Moreover, the sheer size of the text is justified by the fact that the author does not stint in inserting "meticulous, redundant descriptions," and "wise, philosophical considerations,"[36] all aspects that bear witness to Stephens' full and personal acquisition of the traditional sources.

This acquisition manifests its originality more than ever in a clearly evident quality of the text, which Augustine Martin defines "the cultivation of comic grotesquerie."[37] This is perhaps the writer's most important innovation, at least insofar as it is the first real attempt to rework traditional tales in a humorous key; this created a trend exemplified by, among others, *Finnegans Wake* by Joyce, and *At Swim-Two-Birds* by Flann O'Brien, novels in which Stephens' intuition is brought to its extreme consequences.[38] In effect, grotesque or comic traits could already be seen in the texts transmitted from the Middle Ages, as in the oral narrations of the storytellers; traits which, as seen in the previous chapter, were frequently cancelled out or distorted by nineteenth-century collectors. Thanks only to the modern sensibility of a writer such as Stephens, these characteristics were given the space that they deserve.[39] On the one hand, Stephens works to elaborate the text in conformity with his poetic exigencies; on the other, he contributes to resuscitating an aspect that formed an integral part of the Irish narrative heredity, thus providing a clear example of how innovation and tradition can be welded together in protecting the originality of both. Eminently heroic characters transmitted by an honest translator such as O'Grady, by Stephens' pen are transformed into figures who are as heroic as they are comic or grotesque, while their feats are as adventurous as they are parodic.[40] The supreme art of the author resides in balancing attentively both components, so that his fairy tale does not transform itself into self-parody, but into an instrument distorting reality so as to reveal a deeper image of it—and, at the same time, providing the contemporary public with a pleasant read. Definitively, Stephens' objective is that of reestablishing the aboriginal value of the fairy tale as an exemplary tool of formation and delight. It seems to me that this objective is brilliantly realized.

Notes

1. Ulick O'Connor, *Celtic Dawn: A Portrait of Irish Renaissance* (Dublin: Town House and Country House, 1999), 105–6.

2. William B. Yeats, *Letters to the New Island*, quoted in Peter Ure, *Yeats and the Anglo-Irish Literature* (Liverpool: Liverpool University Press, 1974), 64.

3. Zimmermann, *The Irish Story Teller*, 324.

4. Ibid. (my italics).

5. Ure, *Yeats and the Anglo-Irish Literature*, 74 (an essay by Yeats is quoted, *The Celtic Element in Literature*, 1897).

6. Zimmermann, *The Irish Story Teller*, 328 (an article by Yeats is quoted, "Bardic Ireland," which appeared in *Scots Observer* on 4 January 1890).

7. Cf. Zimmermann, *The Irish Story Teller*, 325: "Country people would have kept something of the 'early phase of every civilization' where myth and dreams gave access to wisdom. According to him [Yeats], if Douglas Hyde and his League 'sought the peasant, . . . we sought the peasant's imagination'" (two passages from Yeats' *Explorations* are quoted). The peasant is therefore the depository of a function and a value that transcend absolutely mere individuality: he is the intermediary who allows the intellectual to renew his relationship with an aboriginal phase of civilization in which the imagination was at its maximum potential.

8. Yeats affirms quite clearly that literature must enjoy unquestionable autonomy, beyond any extrinsic exigencies. Consider, for example, the following passage from *Explorations*, 1903, quoted in Fitzgerald, *Yeats's Irish Traditions*, 23: "Literature must take the responsibility of its power, and keep all its freedom: it must be like the spirit and like the wind that blow when it listeth; it must claim its right to pierce through every crevice of human nature, and to describe the relation of the soul and the heart to the facts of life and of law, and to describe that relation as it is, not as we would have it be."

9. See O'Connor, *Celtic Dawn*, 101–2.

10. William B. Yeats, *The Message of the Folklorist*, 1893, quoted in Birgit Bramsbäck, "William Butler Yeats and Folklore Material," *Béaloideas* 39–41 (1973): 59.

11. Foster, *Fictions of the Irish Literary Revival*, 206.

12. Marcus, *Yeats and the Beginning of the Irish Renaissance*, 240.

13. Cf. Foster, *Fictions of the Irish Literary Revival*, 211: "The informant must surely have tailored what he said to such a collector [the reference is to the net sociocultural gap between the peasant telling the story and the intellectual transcribing it] *by playing the expected role* and telling the collector what he wanted to know (in this case that the peasant believed intensely in the supernatural), taking advantage of the collector's earnestness and credulity and embroidering along the way so that he too might enjoy this peculiar occasion" (my italics). The fact that the peasant might simulate his fairy lore is important only up to a certain point, because what matters is the outcome, especially from the viewpoint of the writer. And the outcome is the conservation of a fundamental source of narrativity, without taking into account that, even in fiction, the peasant expresses his link with beliefs coming from the past.

14. Ibid., 210.

15. Thuente, *W. B. Yeats and Nineteenth-Century Folklore*, 75.

16. William B. Yeats, *Irish Fairy Tales* (Thirsk: House of Stratus, 2002), III–IV (my italics). In this edition, contrary to what the title might lead one to believe, only the tales in *Fairy and Folk Tales of the Irish Peasantry* are included.

17. Ibid., I–II.

18. See ibid., VIII, where Socrates, in answering Phaedrus who asks him whether he believes in the myth of Boreas and Oritia, among the other things says: "And if he [who looks for rational answers to "traditional and inexplicable natures"] is sceptical about them, and would fain reduce them one after another to the rules of probability, this sort of crude philosophy will take up all his time. Now, I have certainly not time for such inquiries. Shall I tell you why? I must first know myself as the Delphian inscription says; to be curious about that which is not my business, while I am still in ignorance of my own self, would be ridiculous. And, therefore, I say farewell to all this; the common opinion is enough for me" (taken from Plato, *Phaedrus*, 238b–239a).

19. Thuente, *W. B. Yeats and Nineteenth-Century Folklore*, 76.

20. Ibid., 74.

21. See ibid., 73.

22. Yeats, *Irish Fairy Tales*, VII.

23. Ibid., 213.

24. Cf. Foster, *Fictions of the Irish Literary Revival*, 241.

25. Cf. ibid., 243.

26. Cf. ibid., 241: "Stephens imbibed stories by word of mouth or word of print and in retelling them was perhaps the nearest thing to a *shanachie* the Anglo-Irish Revival produced. . . . But in particular sequence of tales and in its elements of pure modern artistry, Stephens was justified in calling *Irish Fairy Tales* 'an original book.'"

27. Melita Cataldi, *Introduction* to *Fiabe irlandesi*, by James Stephens (Milano: RCS Collezionabili, 2001), 15.

28. Augustine Martin, *James Stephens: A Critical Study* (Dublin: Gill and Macmillan, 1977), 128.

29. Cf. ibid.: "That spiritual Overworld our Gaelic ancestors beheld was in essential the same as the Overworld revealed in the sacred books; and in the wonder tales the Gael we find a great secular corroboration of sacred literature and of half-sacred philosophy such as Plato utters through the lips of Socrates. Earth, Mid-world, Heaven-world and the great deep of deity they knew as they are expounded in the Upanishads" (passage taken from James Stephens, *Candle of Vision*, 1918).

30. On the literary exploitation of Irish folklore see, for example, the brilliant analysis of Marguerite Quintelli-Neary, *Folklore and the Fantastic in Twelve Modern Irish Novels* (Westport: Greenwood, 1997).

31. Martin, *James Stephens*, 128.

32. Ibid., 132.

33. Cf. Foster, *Fictions of the Irish Literary Revival*, 245: "It was folk speech rather than bardic or folktale conventionalism that Stephens wished to achieve."

34. Cf. ibid., 249, in particular where "Irish revivalists" are assimilated to "modernist artificers."

35. Cataldi, *Introduzione*, 77.

36. Ibid.

37. Martin, *James Stephens*, 128.

38. Cf. Quintelli-Neary, 1: "The serious treatment accorded to heroic figures of Irish folklore in the works of late nineteenth-century and early twentieth-century Irish Renaissance writers such as William Butler Yeats and Lady Augusta Gregory could not be sustained very far into the twentieth century. Near religious fervor vis à vis traditional Gaelic writings would be supplanted by satirical and parodic handling of Irish mythological source works."

39. Cf. Martin, *James Stephens*, 137: "There is a quality in traditional Irish story-telling that seems to perplex the translator while providing a comic opportunity for the *deliberate parodist*. This is the frequency of the conventional epithet, the epic simile and the accumulation of sonorous adjectives in the set pieces" (my italics). Obviously in the list of deliberate parodists we can include, apart from Stephens, also Joyce and O'Brien, without forgetting their numerous followers.

40. Cf. ibid., 137–41.

The Fairy Tale Between *Fabula* and *Historia*   4

THE PRECEDING CHAPTERS can be considered a long but synthetic voyage through the principal stages in the rise and forging of Irish narrativity, clearly from the point of view of what we have defined as the fairy tale. From this voyage, it seems to me that a definite link has emerged between the narrative elaboration pertaining to a *folk* in the broadest sense and the events, more or less historical, of the Irish land and nation. So consolidated was this link that it convinced the main advocates of national independence to see in this patrimony of oral tales the most efficient means to restoring a strong identity to a people who, if they were to give life to a coherent and incisive national rising, had necessarily to strengthen their roots in the purest native tradition. In this narrative patrimony lay hidden the most consistent and unique part of the immense heritage—cultural in the broadest sense—that the Irish had inherited from the past. This was a past, moreover, that could not be reconstructed according to objectively historical criteria,[1] but rather required the persistence of a quality radically innate to the Irish spirit: the absolutely fundamental value attributed to the narrative act, which was jealously conserved even at the cost of regressing to a prescientific dimension, to the *irrational*, in purely Celtic style.

The *congenital narrativity* of the Irish people has already been discussed. This concept must now be reviewed and analyzed more specifically as regards its sources before we can begin a deeper exploration of the particular, indicative context that, from the point of view of a discourse on narrativity, is the fairy tale. Although the fairy tale presents the most suitable form with which to represent the particular historical and cultural stratification of Ireland, one should not undervalue its eminently recreational function, in the double sense of the "re-creation" of the real and of entertainment. This function, in both cases, assumes even more value in the context of the Irish countryside, at least until the beginning of the twentieth century,[2] in which poverty and the monochord scansion of time could be opposed in a practically univocal manner by means of storytelling, an activity of the spirit (in the words of Jolles) characterized *by its seriousness*. This last concept is valuable, insofar as it leads us well beyond the distorted idea of the fairy tale, in the strictest sense, that was widespread in Europe following work of the Grimm brothers. This concept of associating the tale with an audience of children never took root in Ireland, even up to the present day. Those tales that various collectors before Yeats gathered from the voice of the Irish peasants in the course of the nineteenth century were an integral part of contexts made up primarily of extremely attentive *adult listeners*.[3] Far more so here than elsewhere, the universal, aboriginal value of storytelling had been preserved. An Irish proverb asserts that "it is a bad thing not to have some story on the tip of your tongue":[4] homespun wisdom that seems to convey in the most vivid terms possible the spirit of a people for whom there is no need for a real barrier between reality as it is lived and as it is transported into storytelling. In Ireland, the social integration of any individual depends on his being capable, at any occasion, of offering to the community his personal contribution to the construction of a collective patrimony of stories. Should a native capacity as a fabulist not come to one's aid (either by giving life to a new tale or recalling one from the depths of memory), it is always possible to resort to events from one's own biography, since, once lived, they are immediately classified as material that can potentially be narrated. This is by no means a singular observation, as can be seen from the remarkable number of examples drawn from Irish tradition. I am referring to the many tales focused on the subject of the man without a story, who, within the narration, becomes a real *character* only when he is made to live, in the first person, a fairy experience: experiences of another type could definitely be narrated, but were less effective in riveting the public's attention. Only the fairy tale is able to magnetize the interest of any listener. Into it flow all the data and values having the power to make recognizable and to strengthen links between individuals and, at the same time, provide escape into a parallel universe, another world—frequently very close by—in which are conserved the dreams and illusions of an entire community.

We have already seen how historical and pseudo-historical contexts and the narrative genres pertaining to them meet in the fairy tale. The theoretical possibility of the fairy tale is insolubly linked to the existence of multidimensional reality, on the basis of which the reality to which it refers is seen to consist of two qualitatively distinct levels—normally separate—that enter into contact when the fairy tale, as a sort of neutral ground and place of abnormal movement, offers its intermediation. It comes to the fore when the *unity of being* proper to Myth disappears, outdone by the advent first of a legendary and then of a historical context, contexts that assume given valency depending on the use made of them in the classification of Celtic literature. This is based on four main cycles, each of which gives witness to (in fabulous key, but frequently with a clear historical intent) the complex story of a nation that, only with the advent of Christianity, turned to writing.

If we take into consideration again the sections into which Yeats divides his collection, we will observe that each of them refers to the existence of a certain *category*: human, animal, and, above all, supernatural. They all have a specific identity, and sometimes are antithetical to each other. Each of them reflects a given aspect of folk-lore, which assumes consistency in that listeners to the tale are held at a certain distance from the figures evoked, who become representatives of a heterogeneous world into which, without the intermediation of the fairy tale, it would be impossible to enter. This may occur in a direct manner, or in an indirect one, as in those categories based on a human character who enters into contact with another world—for example, saints and priests, kings, queens, princesses, earls, robbers, and warriors (but not witches and fairy doctors, because these human figures themselves are repositories of supernatural powers).

If the meetings and visions that compose the tales put together by Yeats did not denote a more or less elevated degree of *extraordinariness*, they would not display all the weight attributed them. Converging in them are all the data and values that permit a genuine dialectic among the most distant planes, in time, space, and in system of reference, that have sedimented themselves in the Irish collective tradition. This mode of proceeding, bypassing the continuum proper to a history in the strictest chronological sense, allows the storyteller and his audience (as well as those writers who approach the stories) to appropriate and interpret with the widest margin of liberty the inherited past. To determine the structure and significance lying at the basis of the fairy tale, it is necessary to identify the theoretical premises on which it operates, the nature of the material that it elaborates.

The Space-Time Coordinates of the Fairy Tale

But the People of Dana do not withdraw. By their magic art they cast over themselves a veil of invisibility, which they can put on or off as they

choose. There are two Irelands henceforward, the spiritual and the earthly.
. . . Where the human eye can see but green mounds and ramparts, the
relics of ruined fortresses or sepulchres, there rise the fairy palaces of the
defeated divinities . . . . The ancient mythical literature conceives them as
heroic and splendid in strength and beauty. In later times, and as Christian
influences grew stronger, they dwindle into fairies, the People of the Side;
but they have never wholly perished; to this day the Land of Youth and
its inhabitants live in the imagination of the Irish peasant.[5]

This passage taken from a work—half tale and half essay—by Thomas W.
Rolleston, an exponent of the Irish Revival whom we have already met, is
definitely emblematic, since from it can be gained a sufficiently clear idea
of the foundation from which the edifice of the fairy tale takes origin and
on which it is built. This synthesis is a particularly fortunate one, because
it brings to our attention the sources from which are born not only a narrative genre, but also the cultural code of an entire people.

What is described is a kind of epochal alternation between a declining and a rising civilization. Rolleston (who, as we know, had a certain
knowledge of the medieval manuscripts, which he employs as the only
usable documentation on which to base his approximate historical construction) refers to the conflict between the primitive colonizers of Ireland,
the *Tuatha Dé Danann*, and a race of new invaders, the so-called *Milesians*.
The success of the latter, albeit fabulous to a degree, is of great importance
in the history of the island: tradition has it that the Milesians stood at the
origin of the Irish people. In parallel, we observe the definitive decline
of the mythical age (properly speaking) and the beginning of what was
gradually to become the *History* of the Irish nation, marked by a recognizable humanity that gradually imposed itself through the occupation of a
space in which a group of superhuman individuals previously lived and to
which they gave form. However, the alternation of epochs did not lead
to the cancellation of what, for a long period of time, had distinguished
Irish reality. The victor did not assimilate a number of characteristics of
the loser, nor did the loser adapt to living subordinate to the victor. Instead, the victor took possession of the *visible, earthly* space and the loser
abandoned the field—but did not abandon *Ireland*, since he retired into an
entirely new *invisible, unearthly dimension* or, let us say, a *subterranean* one.
In substance, the race of the Milesians superimposed itself on that of the
Tuatha Dé Danann not only in the temporal sense, but also physically: it is
by no means accidental that one speaks of *two Irelands*. A space subdivided
into two reciprocally opposed but coexisting worlds came into being.

This coexistence is not usually perceptible, in that, as Rolleston emphasizes, from the human point of view (which affirmed itself after the Milesian invasions), it cannot be located. All that appears are hills and architectonic ruins, the sites to which was transferred the reality of those who had been the uncontested masters of the entire country and its sole inhabitants. On the contrary, the latter, gifted with powers unknown to man, have the capacity to make their presence visible, or rather to become, exceptionally, perceptible to the natural senses. One is dealing with a clearly divine race, at least from the point of view of the literature preceding the advent of Christianity, as Rolleston specifies, or rather in view of the characters forming that part of the narrative tradition set in a pre-Christian epoch. In parallel to the affirmation of the faith imported by St. Patrick, in part of the literature but above all in popular tradition, on which the oral transmission of fairy tales depends, the Tuatha Dé Danann are reduced to the rank of *Fairy Beings*. Whether considered divine figures or fairies, their significance remains the same. In one or the other form, they are products of a *supernatural reality*, coexisting with humanity and acting as repositories of qualities and values that reflect the aspiration to transcend from within the narrow confines of a purely material world. It is in this respect that Rolleston speaks of a *Land of Youth*, the *Tír-na-n-Og*, under which Yeats lists a section of his collection—in other words, Fairyland. And we have already discussed how great, not just in the literature, but in the entire Celtic, and by consequence Irish spirit, is the anxiety for the *absolute*, the *infinite*.

I agree with Rolleston when he interprets the Milesian invasion as a sort of *caesura* imposed by a rereading of the narrative tradition in the Christian key, on the basis of which it was inadmissible to connect the origin of the Irish people with ancestors of an explicitly pagan nature.[6] I am also convinced that the Danann were overloaded with divine connotations, so that their defeat would become all the more disastrous, thus suggesting the idea of an omnipotence that becomes apparent only when compared to that of men who, later, would convert to the True Faith. However, they have remained, at all levels—from the collective imagination to literary elaboration—imperishable symbols of a dimension proper to humanity itself, one that is not only pre-Christian, but more generally primitive, preceding so-called civilization, with all the limits that civilization has imposed on existence and the barriers that it has raised to destroy an aboriginal unity. Where a relationship is established between this primigenial dimension and the representatives of what has superimposed it, we witness the intersection, not only of spatial ambits, but also of temporal contexts, between an *immanent* and *transient* element, subject to historical *becoming*, and a *transcendent* and *eternal* one, pertaining to the sphere of spiritual being: between a continually mutable *present* and a *past* that tends to return, perhaps in an altered guise, on the basis of a transformation of the system of reference. But the significance underlying this type of relationship remains substantially unchanged.[7]

If we keep scrupulously to what tradition narrates, the Tuatha Dé Danann are not the first colonizers of the island; they are not, that is to say, the genuinely aboriginal race, before which nothing existed. The first sections of the Mythological Cycle, which in truth are extremely lacking in consistency, describe the alternation of at least three peoples who sequentially settled in the island, the last of which is named the *Firbolg*.[8] However, none of them left tangible signs of their passage, thus extinguishing themselves when they were replaced by the next invader. The Firbolg have a certain importance in virtue of their unsuccessful war against the Danann. After this event, the latter assumed dominion of the island and the defeated race is lost from sight. However, they did not disappear as preceding invaders did, but, albeit in a condition of subjection, were assimilated (a concept that takes on a certain importance, as will be clarified further on). Thus, they did not install a parallel dimension, separate from, but coexisting with that of the newcomers. The Tuatha Dé Danann, therefore, found themselves in a reality organized on a single plane; theirs was a unitary Ireland, in which they were the only paradigm. Above and below them were no qualitatively different interlocutors with which to confront themselves, no past that had survived to offer an alternative to the order imposed by them. For as long as their dominion over Ireland lasted, they were the only conceivable plane of humanity. Their battles with the evil *Fomorian*, who frequently came from an indefinable *elsewhere* to contend their dominion, are not, in my opinion, the manifestation of a dialectic between two parallel dimensions of primitive humanity. They are instead the two sides—*obscure* and *infernal* (even *demoniac*, in the later Christian interpretation) and *luminous* and *divine*—of the same mythical dimension. Moreover, the Fomorian, having lost the decisive battle and being absolved of their function as a testing ground, were adopted by the narrative tradition to demonstrate the superiority of their adversaries and disappeared for good.[9]

The Tuatha Dé Danann, therefore, establish the mythical plane already mentioned as the indispensable point of departure for and foundation of the entire narrative tradition, in particular as regards the fairy tale. The latter can only originate after a mythical age, both in the temporal and causal sense. The fairy tale must draw from a mythical patrimony, but only after

this has become the heredity of an indefinite past. For as long as a mythical context lasts, or rather the one-dimensional reality of the Danann, the
tale can have only a single dimension in which everything is contained
and in which *everything is definite*. This is because the mythical tale—and
hence every narrative exemplar from the Mythological Cycle of the Irish
tradition—is constructed following a univocal logic, framed by a unilinear
conception of space and time organized along a single line, which can be
represented, according to an elementary graphic exemplification, as shown
in figure 4.1:

Figure 4.1.

The "O" (= Origin) indicates the moment at which the Tuatha Dé
Danann settled in Ireland and therefore that point in the past (obviously
not datable, at least according to rigid historical criteria) in which the
mythical age began, and consequently, also began the possibility of mythical storytelling itself. The half-line, which takes in an indefinite arc of time,
represents therefore a universe organized on the basis of a unitary scheme,
in which exists only the reality imposed by the Danann. This lasts until
an upheaval occurs drastic enough to definitively upset the status quo.
Hence, we must imagine the entire history of the mythical characters as
taking place along this line, characters for whom there is no other system
of reference than their own. Because of this, everything narrated in regards
to them takes place in an *internal* context that does not contemplate the
"shifting of a persona across the borders of a semantic field."[10] This semantic field is single one, an *open space* in which the concept of the boundary
is unknown insofar as its horizons are universal and totalizing, and there
is no reason for a distinction to be made between the ideal and the real.

But myth—or rather the world fashioned by it—as a configuration of
an aboriginal and ideal dimension has to reach a conclusion so that it can
give way to the properly human events of History. This takes place, as already mentioned, by means of an invasion of individuals from an external
world,[11] who come to permanently disturb the equilibrium preserved until
then by the Danann. The Milesians conserve almost every characteristic
of the latter, with the fundamental distinction that each of these characteristics is set in a context connoted according to canons of humanity.[12] It
is here that the mythical unity is disrupted and the evolution of the two-
dimensional space begins; from now on, the *historia* and *fabula* of the Irish
tradition will be framed. The withdrawal of the Tuatha Dé Danann into

a supernatural dimension (that we can call Fairyland and is to be found in subterranean realms beyond the sea, as well as in more accessible places, in strict contact with man, although going normally unnoticed) unveils for the first time the persistence, albeit in a new guise, of a past that no longer allows itself to be overcome and assimilated by the present, a heredity that does not live only in the memory of the mythical tale, but coexists with the new reality, thus offering the possibility of a direct confrontation between two semantic fields. The horizon against which the tales of the Ulster Cycle and the Fenian Cycle are framed can be represented as shown in figure 4.2:

Figure 4.2.

In this case, the "O" indicates the moment at which, having been definitively defeated, the Tuatha Dé Danann cede dominion over the visible Ireland to the Milesians and withdraw, as demonstrated by the perpendicular line linking the half-lines, into a parallel dimension This is *invisible*, both in virtue of its supernatural significance and the superimposition on it of what, from now on, will be configured as reality—or rather the *norm*, on the basis of which this reality is *definite* and *objective* and drives the preceding mythical norm into an *indefinite* and *subjective* field. From this point of view, the distance between the two half-lines is explained. They represent the separation between the planes, which continue separately, according to specific values and parameters, as indicated by the use of two different colors representing the qualitative difference between the two contexts.

This is the space–time system within which the fairy tale is conceived, or rather within which it is *conceivable*, since, although the environment suited to its birth has been installed, the borders have not yet been passed. The intersection of the two semantic fields has not taken place; or rather, the fairy movement has not occurred to interrupt the stasis in which the tale will otherwise find itself. For as long as the two half-lines remain parallel and distant from each other, the fairy tale will exist only in *potential*, whereas in reality, one-dimensional tales will continue to be handed down, whether mythical or legendary. Regarding the use of the latter adjective, it must be specified that I am referring to the tradition pertaining to the Ulster Cycle and the Fenian Cycle, included within this category to evince their nature as intermediaries between Myth and History, and also to emphasize the heroic character of their protagonists. This said, it is only when the plane of Myth and the plane of Legend, when mythical and legendary characters meet, or when the two half-lines cross, that one may speak effectively of the fairy tale. It will cover the vast part of legendary tradition in which are narrated the feats of human heroes who go out to meet those characters, raised to a divine or semi-divine level, who make up Fairyland, and also, in the opposite direction, when the Tuatha Dé Danann come out into the open to join up with man. In both cases, storytelling will become the locus in which two opposed semantic fields meet, and hence the means through which the storyteller—and with him an entire community—can reappropriate an ideal dimension that once was real. In the fairy tale, for a certain period of time, the aboriginal unity is recomposed.

However, the legendary age is also destined to end, giving way to a third phase of history and of Irish narrative tradition. The legendary age is supplanted when a more properly historical age comes into being, whose origins in my opinion are to be found when St. Patrick began his preaching.[13] With the advent of Christianity, one enters, gradually but inexorably, into a new context, in which the points of reference change radically as do, consequently, the nature of the figures involved, who assume entirely human connotations. With St. Patrick, in short, one has entered a historical dimension (and the relevant narrative cycle is defined precisely historical) that superimposes itself on the two dimensions inherited from the pagan past, which is framed within new schemes, but certainly not cancelled out. The representatives of Myth, demoted to fairies because their primitive divine character is obviously irreconcilable with the new faith, and the protagonists of Legend, only now retrospectively assimilable as the heroes of an ideal humanity, do not disappear from a horizon as spatial as it is conceptual. Instead, they withdraw into two parallel dimensions that act as two alternatives—coexisting, yet invisible—to the reality imposed by the advent of History. Space and time are hence organized on three planes, which may be represented as shown in figure 4.3:

Figure 4.3.

This time, the "O" indicates the moment at which, beginning with St. Patrick's first sermons, the Christian faith affirmed itself in Ireland, thus making the pagan dimension of legend sink to the same level as it had imposed on the mythical dimension. The latter, for its part, is consequently distanced even more from the light of day—or rather, its distance from objective and visible reality increases insofar as it becomes almost entirely *fabula* in comparison with something that is all *historia*. At the same time, its proximity to the legendary context, in which *fabula* and *historia* balanced each other, is greater. Naturally, these are absolutely relative concepts, expressed from a viewpoint internal to the narrative tradition, which, along its path, reflects in broad outline the process leading from a purely fabulous dimension to an ever more historical one, thus reflecting the gradual passage from orality to writing. But, and this is the important point, we are in the exceedingly mobile field of narrative and of culture, whose impatience regarding rigid schemes evinces itself in the *virtuous circle of narrativity*, which is capable at any moment of disrupting a presumed equilibrium.

This equilibrium based on three dimensions, in which, on each of the parallels, an independent tradition of one-dimensional tales can at any moment develop, is in fact entirely disrupted by the fairy tale, which now avails of a more complex, richer horizon within which to unfold its convergent dynamic. This new horizon, as suggested by some sections of Yeats' collection, makes it necessary to take into consideration the presence of a fourth dimension, one that is *transcendent* and *celestial*, linked to the Christian hereafter and hence to angelic or diabolical figures, or to specters that originate from a reality considered superior. From this viewpoint, the mythical Otherworld, albeit supernatural, must be interpreted in terms of *immanence*, situated at best halfway between heaven and earth, as evidenced by the popular identification of fairies with fallen angels.[14]

The Dynamic Established by the Fairy Tale

At this point, we can claim to have a complete picture of the space–time context within which the fairy tale operates, and this permits us to verify how this narrative genre, in its dynamic, is able to break down the semantic barriers imposed by a certain historical and narrative evolution. It can display, in its substantial unity, a tradition that, in effect and despite the fractures identified above, conserves an underlying continuity, which is frequently demonstrated in contexts other than the fairy tale.[15] Thus, figure 4.4 summarizes in overall terms what has been discussed until now and should be interpreted simply as an attempt to offer a general model

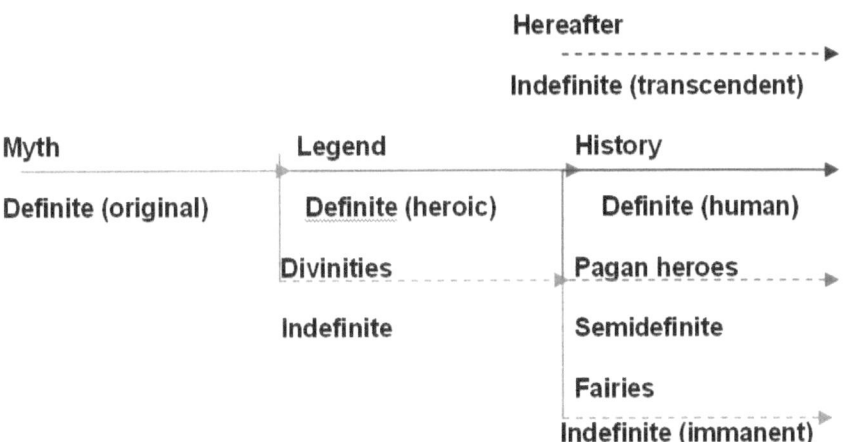

Figure 4.4.

in which the *theoretical presuppositions* of the creation and circulation of the fairy tale may find an organic and intelligible systematization. It should be emphasized again that the tradition of the fairy tale is intimately connected to the reconstruction, *sub specie narrativa*, of the phases that led to the formation of the Irish nation.

In contrast to the preceding examples, it is here possible to gain an overall vision, both in extension and depth, of the development of Ireland as described in the four principal cycles of which the narrative tradition is composed. This time, conceptual categories have also been employed, on the basis of which it is possible to interpret, depending on the angle of observation, each of the dimensions that gradually complete the horizon within which the fairy tale operates. The basic principle on which the model is founded is the opposition between the *definite* and the *indefinite* (the notion of the *semidefinite* indicates the intermediary nature of the legendary dimension in relation contemporaneously to the mythical and historical dimensions), an opposition that, as can be seen, alters its terms when the contingent situation alters. The *definite* is the level of the objective, the visible, the present, from the viewpoint of those who, in a certain space–time context, have imposed their vision of reality, thereby creating a norm that relegates the previous one to the level of the *indefinite*, to a subjective dimension, invisible and pertaining to the past, which may no longer be directly drawn on, unless by a movement that interrupts the established equilibrium. The *definite*, in its evolution from Myth to Legend to History, always remains at the top level of the diagram, indicating its imposition over those dimensions that, once supplanted by a new *definite*, sink lower into the field of the *indefinite*, where the broken line represents the relative consistency of a reality that can subsist only insofar as the higher level one admits of its existence. The issue is obviously different when one deals with the *transcendent indefinite*, since it is a category that has the same reason for existence as the historical dimension introduced by the advent of Christianity, and thus must be situated at the higher level, in a position appropriate to what should be understood as the indispensable otherworldly norm on which the vision of the world introduced by the historical definite is founded.

In the diagram, it is also possible to follow the evolution that the exponents of each level have undergone in accordance with the alteration of the norm of reference in which, in the course of time and of the tradition, they have gradually been framed. As long as one remains in the higher part of the model, each level represents a type of humanity, which passes from an aboriginal level in Myth (a sort of primigenial race from the *age of gold*) to a heroic level in Legend (distinguished in turn by the giant and monolithic heroes of the Ulster Cycle and the less magnificent and more fictional heroes of the Fenian Cycle), to arrive at humanity as it is conceived of today and that affirmed itself historically in the Christian age. This same humanity, as already mentioned, declasses the exponents of myth to the range of fairies, after they had been made divine in the legendary and pagan ages. The heroes of Legend, although not surviving properly speaking in a real parallel world, as do the fairies, remain nonetheless within the horizon of the narrative tradition of the fairy tale, both directly, when the return of one of them from Fairyland is narrated (as in the case of Oisin, who meets St. Patrick), and indirectly, when the tale is told of sublime characters who, by virtue of their characteristics, recall the legendary context, particularly if it is contrasted to a popular ambit. In any case, and above all as regards the heroes of the Fenian Cycle, one can easily observe this assimilation on the historical plane of characters pertaining to the legendary age by a tradition that reworks its subjects in a Christian key. The boundaries between one plane and another of the edifice of the fairy tale are not impermeable, because, inevitably, the final word awaits whosoever avails, on the concrete level of storytelling, of what these planes contain.

Using the theoretical premises thus laid out, or rather the *static* factors on which the fairy tale is founded, one may now approach the *dynamics* of its composition, enucleating its fundamental structure so that we may begin an analysis aimed at opening up a new perspective on the relationship between oral tradition and written elaboration, between the popular and the authorial tale. But before setting out on this examination, which will occupy the next chapter, I wish to clarify through a final graphic representation in what way, in my opinion, one should individuate the space that the fairy tale occupies in the categories analyzed up until now. My idea is that it stands as a species of *intermediate* space, not only with regard to its function, but in the literal sense. If we consider that Myth, Legend, and History individuate three spatially and temporally distinct contexts, separated by semantic barriers (I exclude, for expositive purposes, only the transcendent dimension of the Christian hereafter, which is implicitly included in a context that extends from History, due to its present and substantially objective connotation, to Myth, due to its indefinite and invisible nature), then the fairy tale occupies the open space between the closed systems just mentioned. This is a *communal* open space, in which exponents of any of the closed spaces may converge according to a modality that we shall call *escape*, a term whose exact meaning will be explained later. Escape concretizes itself in border zones, such as a wood, the banks of a lake, or ancient ruins, most probably in the liminal moments of night and twilight. Whosoever escapes from his plane does not enter immediately into another, but rather into this sort of *free zone* represented by the fairy tale, from which it is then possible to proceed by means of a genuine *invasion*, caused by a character passing the confines of a new dimension: this is the case when a character, rather than remaining on the banks of a lake, goes to the bottom, thus entering into an area pertaining properly to a fairy dimension, or when, vice versa, an *indefinite* character penetrates a house inhabited by human beings.

In the final scheme proposed here (see figure 4.5), the various combinations on the basis of which one can identify a fairy tale are contemplated. As can be seen, there are three. In order of their appearance they

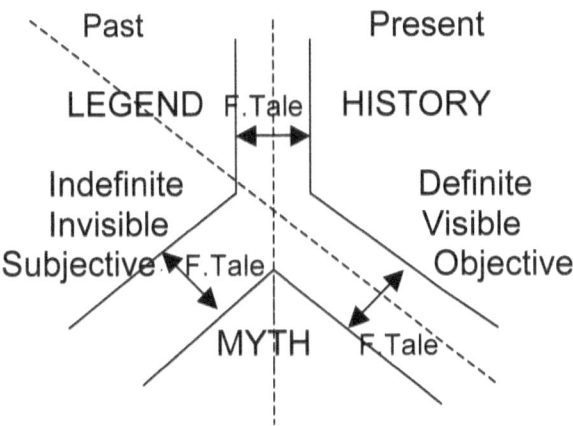

Figure 4.5.

are Myth-Legend, Legend-History, and History-Myth (in the last pair the relationship of History-Christian Hereafter is implicitly included), as if to trace a circle closing on itself. Moreover, the three space–time dimensions are set out in such a way as to connect them precisely to the concepts previously adopted to illustrate the fundamental nature of the oppositions that they represent, but also to evidence (through the broken line) how these concepts pass gradually and fluidly from one dimension to another.

Notes

1. In fact, in the tales that narrate mythical or legendary events, rather than historical reconstruction, one finds anthropological data pertaining to the society and culture in which the tales were elaborated. At the least, it is necessary to consider various aspects linked to the creation and fruition of the single tale. Cf. Kay Milton, "Irish Hero Tales as a Historical Source: An Anthropologist's View," *Occasional Papers in Linguistics and Language Learning (Approaches to Oral Tradition)* 4 (1978): 88: "Whether a particular narrative can be treated as an account of things happened in the past, as an entertaining story, or as a comment on what people hold to be ultimately true depend, not on the content of the narrative, but on what people do with it, the way in which it is brought to bear by them in social life. At the same time, what is said in a narrative will depend on the purposes for which it is used. The content of a narrative can only be understood, therefore, with reference to the social context in which it is told, learned, written down, or whatever."

2. That is until progress imposed new, more sophisticated forms of entertainment. Cf. Ó Danachair, *Stories and Storytelling in Ireland*, 111: "Before the penetration of modern media of entertainment into the countryside, the folktale took the place now filled by the glossy magazine, the novel, the radio and television, not forgetting, of course, the theatre and the cinema. With the coming into the countryside of all of these, the storyteller has lost most of his audience to the newer forms of entertainment. There still are storytellers, but now they must be sought out and coaxed to tell their tales, where formerly they held court night after night—especially in the long winter nights."

3. Cf. Gose, *The World of Irish Wonder Tale*, XIX: "In Germany the brothers Grimm came upon these tales through nurse-maids and old wives, who told them to children more than to adults. The situation was quite different in late nineteenth-century Ireland. There the men (and a few women) were the *proud bearers of an active oral tradition*. Since the tales were often told long into the night, young children were usually neither present nor welcome during these sessions" (my italics). Preserving a tradition of fairy tales is not simply an *adult* business, but a question of *pride*.

4. Zimmermann, *The Irish Story Teller*, 519.

5. Rolleston, *Myths and Legends of the Celtic Race*, 136–37.

6. See ibid., 120–21.

7. Cf. Carolyn White, *A History of Irish Fairies* (Dublin: Mercier Press, 1976), 17: "Mighty gods [the Tuatha Dé Danann] they were, of gigantic proportions, and humans honoured them as such. But when they went underground and became known as the fairies, human perception of them altered . . . . The size with which fairies appear to a mortal is proportionate to the belief that the mortal has in them."

8. In order to deepen a theme not strictly connected to our research here, see Rolleston, *Myths and Legends of the Celtic Race*, 96–107.

9. See ibid., 117.

10. Jurij Lotman, *The Structure of the Artistic Text* (Ann Arbor: University of Michigan Press, 1977), 233.

11. The journey that brought the Milesians from their native land to Ireland, in the tradition, takes the form of a passage from death to life. See Rolleston, *Myths and Legends of the Celtic Race*, 131–32: "They come from 'Spain'—the usual term employed by the later rationalising historians for the Land of the Dead. . . . Some mysterious law, indeed, brings together in the night the great spaces which divide the domain of the living from that of the dead in daytime. It was the same law which enabled Ith [Miled's grandfather, the Milesian's progenitor] one fine winter evening to perceive from the Tower of Bregon, in the Land of the Dead, the shores of Ireland, or the land of the living." The second passage, in which Ireland seems like a promised land in contrast to an external space inundated with the idea of death, is taken from D'Arbois de Jubanville, *Irish Mythological Cycle and Celtic Mythology*, 1903.

12. See Rolleston, *Myths and Legends of the Celtic Race*, 138–39.

13. Cf. Patrick K. Ford, "Aspects of Patrician Legend," in *Celtic Folklore and Christianity: Studies in Memory of William W. Heist*, ed. By Patrick K. Ford (Los Angeles: McNally and Loftin, 1983), 29: "The problem of Patrick is a very vexed one, as Celtic scholars know. Most studies have concentrated on historical issues, including the authenticity of the two works attributed to the saint and the sources available to his earliest biographers, Muirchú and Tírechán, both writing in the late seventh century—perhaps. But what interests the folklorist and the mythologist is not the historical problem but the persistence of a symbology in the developing legends concerning the saint, whom tradition has credited with the conversion of the Irish people." The question of the historical consistency of St. Patrick should in no way challenge his deep symbolical significance. In the ambit of an internal study of the Irish narrative tradition, the figure of the saint should be analyzed in terms of its functionality in an eminently narrative context, beyond any other implication. In substance, it is his character and not his actual person that acts in the present study. Or, at least, the first prevails over the second, considering moreover that it is far more verifiable than the other.

14. Yeats in the introduction to the section "The Trooping Fairies," questioning himself on the origin and nature of the fairies, furnishes three hypotheses, as

different as they are dependable (Yeats, *Irish Fairy Tales*, 1): "'Fallen angels who were not good enough to be saved, nor bad enough to be lost,' say the peasantry. 'The gods of the earth,' says the Book of Armagh. 'The gods of pagan Ireland,' say the Irish antiquarians, 'the *Tuatha de Danan* [sic], who, when no longer worshipped and fed with offerings, dwindled away in the popular imagination, and now are only a few spans high.'" Each of these hypotheses reflects not only a specific point of view, but also a whole group of meanings and values associated with the fairies.

15. See, for example, what is said regarding the hagiographic genre in Ford, *Aspects of Patrician Legend*, 30: "The Lives of the Irish saints not only continue the tradition of heroic literature, but have in some degree borrowed from the sagas even their motifs." Although it is true that St. Patrick inaugurated a new era for Ireland, it is also true that the preexisting tradition brought all the weight to bear of its traditional heritage.

The Process of Composition of the Fairy Tale

5

THE GRAPHIC MODEL APPEARING at the end of the previous chapter is probably the best point from which to begin an analysis aimed at identifying the dynamic factors underlying the composition of a fairy tale. This follows the conviction that we will be able to isolate a fundamental structure for all the single examples of fairy tales forming part of the Irish tradition, trusting in the representativeness of the texts in Yeats' and Stephens' collections. These texts, presenting an extremely wide typology, both thematic and formal, reveal themselves to be a field of research and comparison ideally suited to our objectives. Moreover, having at our disposal a number of texts in which, in one way or another, orality and writing, folklore and literature, fuse together, opens a wider view to our research, permitting us to trace a principle of composition, as functional in the oral/popular tradition as in the written/literary one. Thus, in practice, from an analysis of the fairy tale we can gain an integral understanding of the narrative phenomenon.

Our model is the most appropriate point of departure for the scope of this chapter because, on the one hand, and in virtue of the analysis made until now, it provides the most suitable image of the theoretical conformation that has been created in the course of a process of evolution that took place on both the levels of *historia* and *fabula*, a conformation that forms the static platform—or, let us say, the *constant background*—on which the fairy tale operates. On the other, the model already suggests an idea for identifying the more properly dynamic valency of the fairy tale, not so much in its faculty for connecting qualitatively different (if not opposed) levels of reality, but rather in its situation in a substantially indistinct ambit, an *intermediate* space in which the barriers between one context and another fall and the founding principles of the initial situation are cast into doubt or reworked. In the scheme under discussion, one notices three bi-univocal vectors connecting the three dimensions of the Irish tradition (keeping under consideration the implicit presence of the fourth dimension, the Christian Hereafter, not included for reasons previously explained). These represent, more than bridges linking in one direction or the other, spaces that otherwise would remain separate, the movements of these spaces, through their exponents, enter into contact, converge, and situate themselves on the same level. This is because the fairy tale is a phenomenon that disturbs an equilibrium imposed in a contingent space–time dimension. This phenomenon is capable of manifesting itself because it avails of a territory of its own in which to attract the elements—or rather the *characters*—that are the depositaries of the subsisting order on the near side of the semantic barriers erected over the course of time.

In the Introduction, I attempted to lay out—albeit upon an expansion of the traditional current of thought and study—a certain idea of the fairy tale, an idea that led me to recognize some fundamental characteristics of a genre that, as seen, left its decisive mark on the entire narrative tradition examined until now. This idea derives from the multidimensional context that has just been illustrated, but becomes operative by means of a certain structure that I have been able to distinguish from an analysis of the entire collections of Yeats and Stephens. Setting out on a path inaugurated by Propp, I have attempted to individuate a limited number of *fundamental functions* that might lie at the basis of the fairy tale's composition, a field in which—although larger than the nonetheless extended one of the *tale of magic* studied by Propp—it is even easier to be overpowered by the idea of an overwhelming variety and variability.[1] In effect, the proliferation of Irish tales endowed with their own specificity, but also the elevated quantity of variants of the same narrative type, pass a threshold beyond which it seems pure sacrilege to attempt a theorization of a Structuralist kind. We find ourselves facing a natural predisposition to a potentially unlimited extension of our area of examination, and a relative, constant enrichment of form and content on the part of the frequently mentioned phenomenon of narrativity. This phenomenon, nevertheless, is able to operate profitably since, from its origins, it has acquired a fundamental structure that offers, in the case of the fairy tale, a sort of internal stability, starting from which it has been possible to definitively perceive an entity that we now can undeniably assume is a narrative tradition. The fairy tale maintains its continuity despite the constant, natural evolution of themes, forms, and paradigms precisely due to the persistence of an underlying structure; it is able to preserve in time a characteristic mode of acquisition of reality connected to a determinate narrative genre. Once organized according to the scheme we are about to examine, the fairy tale has not only forged its own particular identity, but has also established a model of reference for other narrative genres.

The model we wish to propose here, precisely because of the theoretical premises that arose in the last chapter, is given much support by the spatial conception in Lotman's work. Particular importance is given to the idea that "the structure of the space of a text becomes the model of the structure of the space of the universe," while the internal syntagmatic structure of the elements within the text become the language of spatial simulation.[2] What does the fairy tale operate on if not on a spatial organization that has developed according to the dictates of a tradition born from the meeting between a historical discourse and a narrative one? When Lotman states that "the spatial order of the world [in a text] becomes an *organizing element* around which its non-spatial features are also constructed,"[3] does this not seem to suggest that we should see in the fairy tale a structure designed to furnish an *explicit* image of the concepts operating in the *implicit* underbelly of a tradition, one not disposed of other means to express its contents in perceptible form? Lotman himself refers to the work of art in general as a *translation*, by means of which, in a finite space, the image of an infinite world is given.[4] The fairy tale is likewise oriented toward the exploration of an infinite world, while remaining nonetheless radically rooted in the finite world in which it is elaborated. Through this typology of tale, the narrator detaches himself temporarily from the definite, from a space delimited by known confines, and transfers himself and his public, by means of exemplary characters, into the indefinite, a space in which lies all that, initially at least, it is impossible to define according to preestablished criteria. This space is unknown, or only partially known, and individuated by Myth, Legend, and the Christian Hereafter; these are loci modeled by tradition, as many dimensions with which the exponents of History come into contact and question themselves. This happens thanks to a movement in space (and, implicitly, in time) that is not figurative but real, clearly in terms of a logic internal to the tale, even though, given the ambiguous relationship that a narrative of folkloric origin has with historical truth, this logic might be subject to expansion. One should consider in particular the case in which the narrator and protagonist of a fairy experience are the same person, a case in which the narrative movement coincides with a historically probable, albeit debatable, event.

But, leaving aside these issues connected to the concrete and specific reception of a tale in a given context, what is of primary importance in general research is the identification of those functions—or rather the *constant quantities*—making up the fairy tale and adopted by it to appropriate the space–time context delineated until now. To reach this end, once again, a direct approach to the Irish narrative tradition is indispensable. A direct approach makes it possible to recognize an emblematic tale, one capable of establishing itself as a model for all others and of offering an outline on which it is possible to elaborate a hypothesis regarding underlying structure. As if to demonstrate a sort of conscious self-referentiality, it is the narrative tradition itself that undertakes it to clarify the foundation on which its multiform edifice is built. It explicitly leads us to the birth of the fairy tale, and this is made possible by a tale that, not by chance, is called the *priomscel*.[5]

The *Triangle* Composed of Étaín, Midir, and Eochaid, and the Origin of the Fairy Tale

Shortly after the arrival of the Milesians in Ireland, the tradition narrates an event that, for the first time, displays the *bidimensionality* that followed the withdrawal of the Danann to Fairyland, where the tale begins, as described by Rolleston.[6] It is told that Midir, a prince of the once dominant race, takes the extremely beautiful Étaín as his second wife, causing the terrible jealousy of his first wife to explode. She transforms her rival into a butterfly, leaving her to wander from one part of Ireland to another until chance has it that, in this form, she ends up in a cup from which the wife of a Milesian chief is about to drink. At this point, Étaín's fate changes radically and she is reborn from the womb of the woman as a mortal baby, forgetting completely her immortal past. Growing up, Étaín again becomes the symbol of beauty, so that she is given in marriage to the supreme king, Eochaid. Midir, therefore, first in the semblance of a brother of the king and then as himself, goes to Étaín to remind her of her past in Fairyland, describing it in all its properly mythical splendor. But the girl does not accept the invitation to go back to her first husband, since she is lacking the permission of her present husband, the king. Sometime later, the Danann prince presents himself at court to challenge Eochaid to a game of chess. After winning the last game, Midir asks as his prize to be able to embrace Étaín. The king, suspecting a trick, asks his guest to come back a month later. But when he returns, despite the ranks of soldiers drawn up in defense of the palace, he manages nonetheless to reach Étaín and to fly away with her, both in the form of swans. Hence, Étaín returns to her original dimension. Eochaid nevertheless does not resign himself to this state of affairs and, with the help of a druid, tries to discover where his rival is hiding with his bride. After nine years of battle, Eochaid finally forces Midir to surrender, but, in consigning him Étaín, the latter has her accompanied by fifty handmaidens, all identical to her, making it impossible for the king to recognize his bride. But Étaín, with a sign, succeeds in making her second husband recognize her, thus preferring to return to the human dimension, a choice in which we must probably read the definitive sanction of the passage from one epoch to another. Étaín undergoes this passage in the first person, and Midir and Eochaid are the first witnesses. In contending for the shared object of desire, they reveal the change that had recently taken place in the general plane of Irish reality.

In summarizing the adventures of this sort of love triangle, I have attempted to evince the fundamental passages, or rather those necessary for the identification of the functions suited to sustaining a discourse on the universal structure of the fairy tale. This structure is formed of series of *actions* performed by specific characters who become *archetypes* for all those who follow them in performing the same actions, leaving, despite the differences, a sort of trace that cannot be erased. Returning to an idea expressed by Frye,[7] it seems fair to me to affirm that the model delineated by the *priomscel*, as an act of creation, is ultimately the only fairy tale really necessary for an understanding of the entire successive tradition—one that, made up also of tales that are chronologically anterior to those in question, refers to a model in which it can find its original identity. If the *priomscel* was elaborated after other fairy tales, this does no more than further underline its founding value, for which the tradition feels the need and which it hence reflects in a single tale, thus making it an *exemplum* in the deepest sense of the term. In this tale a narrative potential, latent in the new situation that had established itself with the separation between the definite and the indefinite Ireland, was finally liberated in a narrative act. The contrast between the mythical and the legendary dimensions is a paradigm that, through the figure of Étaín and the conflict that breaks out in her name, is manifested on a syntagmatic plane.[8] This fundamental passage takes place according to the particular modality of the *priomscel*, a modality that, with the progress of the narrative tradition, assumes a universal connotation.

Let us go back, therefore, step by step, over the original fairy tale from a Structuralist point of view, such that this modality appear in its *functional* aspect, or rather as holding the constant quantities for the composition of each fairy tale. To make things clearer and to provide visual support for an analysis that follows the spatial approach adopted by Lotman, I will furnish an elementary graphic representation. Instead of a purely explanatory channel of the concepts theorized, this representation aspires to be an autonomous instrument for the structural analysis of the fairy tale.

An Analysis of the *Priomscel* and the Structure of the Fairy Tale

The situation presented at the beginning of the narrative lies within the mythical dimension arising from the defeat of the Tuatha Dé Danaan. In fact, the characters in the initial stages all pertain to Fairyland, and there is no connection between them and the *definite* plane of the Milesians, although it is implicitly present. The love between Midir and Étaín, and the jealousy of the first wife, are all set within the ambit of the mythical tale, and it remains such through all the vicissitudes faced by Étaín, before she falls into the noblewoman's cup from which she will be reborn. In order to represent this first part, we must resort therefore to two parallel lines (as we did in chapter 4), but with two important modifications. The lines will no longer have a universal value, but will refer specifically to characters who, in the given fairy tale, represent both dimensions of Irish reality. The distinction between the continuous and broken lines, which previously represented the difference between a *definite* plane, depository of present norms, and an *indefinite* one, hidden in an abnormal condition, assumes now a properly narrative connotation. The solid line indicates the plane on which, in a certain moment, the narration focuses; the broken line indicates the situation that will obviously be beyond the narration, albeit present in its paradigmatic horizon. On these premises, figure 5.1 shows the structure the *priomscel* assumes in its opening stages:

Figure 5.1.

In this first sequence, the tale takes place in one dimension, since the fairy tale has not yet concretized. However, knowing the successive development of events, we are able to discover in this initial situation the necessary *introductive* form of the tale, or rather a fundamental function for the composition of the fairy tale. This function is of a *static* nature, both in regard to the properly *dynamic* development of the fairy tale and due to its one dimensionality. Considering all this, I believe that the label INITIAL STASIS is appropriate.[9]

Étaín, who at the beginning belongs to the *indefinite* plane, after many vicissitudes ends up in the womb of a woman pertaining to the *definite* plane. Following this, she is reborn into new life, because she loses her previous divine nature and is transformed into a human being. As such, her adventures proceed, taking place now in the legendary dimension, with the mythical, in this phase, disappearing from the narrative. The scheme now assumes the form shown in figure 5.2:

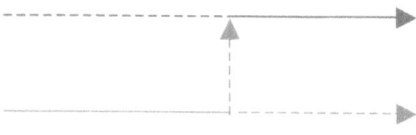

Figure 5.2.

The line rising up to join the higher one presents what we may define as Étaín's *assimilation* into the legendary dimension. This function is not fundamental to the fairy tale but has its importance insofar as it causes changes, also determinative, within the tale: it may even become indispensable in the institution of a dimension initially not contemplated in the narration. This does not happen here, but the way in which the main character alters her function diametrically in the tale should be emphasized. Her assimilation is permanent, in contrast to the temporary nature of the movement pertaining properly to the fairy tale. The fairy tale, at this stage of the adventure, has not yet materialized, since what was a mythical tale has become a legendary one. The two dimensions have not yet met: Étaín interacts with the Milesian characters as their fellow-creature and not in her original nature.

Midir, after a long search within his own plane, manages to find his love beyond it. Although presenting himself in a false appearance, in the instant that he appears before Étaín he makes the first *escape* of the tale insofar as he, a character pertaining to the *indefinite*, annuls the semantic as well as physical distance between his own dimension and that parallel to it. He finds himself in "a house outside of Tara,"[10] which is a space pertaining to the *definite* plane, in which Étaín is to be found. Thus, he must be considered precisely as an *invasion*, at the moment in which he breaks down the barriers that separate the definite from the intermediate area between the two dimensions. His invasion manifests itself as an apparition, in the sense that we do not follow the journey through which he makes his movement: indeed, it is fair to say that the invasion of the fairies and of all the other characters of the indefinite manifests itself constantly under the form of apparitions, in that the point of view of the tale is normally oriented toward those characters belonging to the definite. Leaving his own dimension and entering that of Étaín, Midir has finally given form to the fairy tale and, at the same time, established a second fundamental function, which I will call MOVENS, if I may be permitted the Latin license. The term is not intended so much as it is currently accepted as being linked to the concept of causality—which nevertheless is present, in a modality dealt with later—but rather in its reference to the idea of movement. This function, of putting a character from one plane into contact with that of another, whether through escape or invasion, is the first step toward what we may define as the *movement* of the fairy tale. In the case in hand, as will be seen in the following scheme, one is dealing with an *ascending movens*, in the sense that it passes from the lower level of the indefinite to the higher level of the definite, in which the higher and the lower levels are spatial simulations of concepts connected to the notions of the definite and the indefinite discussed in the previous chapter.

The *movens* is followed by the third fundamental function, which is central in every sense. During all the time that Midir and Étaín are in conversation, and hence in the course of the relationship that temporarily links the two figures from two different dimensions, there takes place what I will call INTERACTION. Here, the term refers to an action taking place between at least two characters who are naturally different and interacting. For as long as this function lasts, the fairy tale holds in check the normal order, preestablished and foreseen, of the *initial stasis*, in order to substitute an *abnormal* intersection between two logically separate dimensions. Moreover, in the course of the interaction, the plane of origin of the character who has made the escape and/or invasion disappears from the horizon of the narration. For those who listen to or read the *priomscel*, the mythical plane is represented by Midir and no one else. When he is with Étaín on the legendary plane, Myth no longer exists since it has flown into Legend, thus recreating a condition of primordial unity. In the reconstruction of this unity, which is at once spatial, temporal, and between narrative contexts, the fairy tale reveals its principal value.

This reconstruction is momentary, however, ending at the moment that Midir must leave Étaín to return to his own plane. His return manifests itself, in analogy with his coming, as a *disappearance*, to the extent that we are ignorant of the route he takes to return to his own world. Strictly speaking, indeed, it is not even possible to state with certainty that Midir has returned into his own world, since in his capacity to become invisible, a characteristic trait of the Tuatha Dé Danann withdrawn into Fairyland, he could remain among men without being perceived. Equally, when he appeared, it was impossible to discern whether he had reached the higher world or whether he had already for some time been in a state of invisibility. One can say that, as far as the tale is concerned, what counts is what appears in an *evident* manner, what may concretely be *narrated*, and that the invisible presence of figures from the Otherworld should be considered simply as a *potential* source of the fairy tale. In any case, the disappearance of Midir should be interpreted as a return into his dimension of origin, and the function connected to this return we will call REDIENS, a Latinate label that evidences the semantic contrast between this function and the *movens*. Whereas with one the idea of movement in *one direction* was expressed, the other indicates an idea of movement in *the opposite direction*, or rather a return that annuls the preceding movement, precisely *rediens*. Hence, whereas the *movens* was ascending, the *rediens* is descending.

At this point, the graphic design can be enriched by three fundamental functions representing the movement of the fairy tale, which inserts itself into the preceding *initial stasis* (figure 5.3):

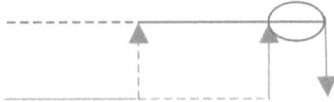

Figure 5.3.

The oval marking the interaction represents its nature as an invasion into a closed space, whereas an escape would have been portrayed by two separate curved lines to indicate the intermediate open space of the fairy tale. The rising and falling solid arrows represent, respectively, the *movens* and the *rediens*, which, lacking temporal consistency, insofar as they manifest themselves as an appearance or a disappearance, are perpendicular to the two dimensions of the tale. These do not develop horizontally, as does the interaction, which has temporal duration and a space in which to operate. In this regard, it should be underlined that the graphic makes it possible to follow the fairy tale in a *diachronic* sense, or rather in the succession of events that take place in the tale, and in a *synchronic* sense, in that it takes into account the contemporary coexistence of two separate contexts, which for the narration is impossible. The *movens* and *rediens* of Midir have only spatial consistency, deriving from the distance that separates the two planes of the tale. As soon as the distance is annulled, as can be seen in the figure, a void is created in correspondence to the mythical dimension, since for the entire duration of the interaction, it has flowed into the legendary dimension.

The *movement* ends after the *rediens*. Following it, a new static situation is installed that individuates the fifth fundamental function of the fairy tale or, in symmetrical opposition to the first, the FINAL STASIS, which recomposes the order preceding the movement but on different bases and according to the more or less clear changes caused by the interaction that has just taken place. With the final stasis ends the parabola of the fairy tale, and it is as if the datum of *historia*, suspended for the entire duration of the movement, prevails again over the *fabula*.

But the *priomscel* does not betray its importance as the complete model of the fairy tale and, as such, does not end after a single movement, but proposes another three, which are formed differently from the first. Hence, what takes place after the departure of Midir is not yet the final stasis, but simply the installment of a *provisional* order, in which one can recognize the existence of a sixth function, which we shall call the INTERMEDIATE STASIS, a function to be found naturally only in those tales composed of more than one movement. This provisional order instigates a situation of, so to speak, precarious equilibrium, since it is destined ultimately to be disturbed. Thus, this function, although static in *concept*, reveals itself to be in *fact* dynamic, manifesting through this the premise for a new movement. Hence, figure 5.4 has still only partial validity:

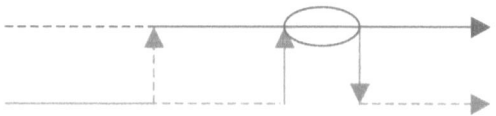

Figure 5.4.

We know that Midir makes another two invasions, the second of which interests us most from a structural point of view. Although the *movens* remains the same, the *rediens* differs in two aspects. On the one hand, one notices the temporal consistency which, this time, a *rediens* linked to a figure from the indefinite assumes, since the escape of Midir and Étaín under the form of a flight of swans is observed by Eochaid and his men. On the other hand, it is seen how what is a *rediens* for Midir corresponds to a *movens* for Étaín, or rather the escape of a human figure from its own world to another world to which it no longer pertains. In this case, the graphic first represents the *rediens* with an oblique vector that conveys its diachronic significance; second, it flanks it with a parallel to indicate Étaín's *movens*. This latter circumstance introduces a possibility that is to be found in other fairy tales—that is, the superimposition of *rediens* and *movens*, which in itself renders a further movement predictable, as long as the character connected to the *movens* is not assimilated.

The rest of the tale demonstrates just how Eochaid in turn escapes his own dimension to go and combat his enemy in his. Hence, we witness for the first time an invasion of the definite into the indefinite, ending only when the sovereign manages to recover his bride. This time, the graphic will display a descending *movens* and an ascending *rediens*, the second of which will be double insofar as it coincides with the *rediens* of Étaín. Moreover, both functions, as is normal in the case of actions performed by human figures, will have temporal consistency, so that they will be indicated by oblique vectors. Naturally, in the course of the prolonged interaction in Fairyland, a void will exist on the legendary plane, since it will have temporarily flown into the mythical one, indicating the recomposition of a unity, this time in the lower world.

With the return of Eochaid and Étaín into their dimension of origin after an assimilation and four movements, the tale ends with the definitive restoration—at least as regards the *priomscel*—of the initial equilibrium, albeit under a new light. Thus, the fifth fundamental function manifests itself, or rather the *final stasis*. At this point, it is possible to represent graphically in figure 5.5 the entire structure of the original fairy tale, through which we can discern the whole corpus of fundamental functions that create and compose all the traditional exemplars deriving from it:

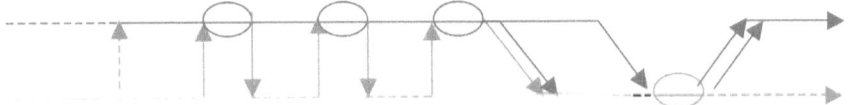

Figure 5.5.

The choice of representing the final stasis through two vectors indicating continuity rather than the closure of the single fairy tale is connected to the idea of preserving the open nature of a tale that is strictly linked to the whole successive tradition, which it resumes directly. There is also the need to demonstrate how the single fairy tale does not exhaust the dialectic between two or more dimensions—in this case Myth-Legend—which is instead always susceptible to being reproposed, perhaps through the uses of the same characters as in the tale. Only in the case of a tale that contains the definitive disappearance of a character who alone represents a dimension—perhaps because he has been assimilated—would the corresponding line be interrupted, indicating that, at least in that tale, it no longer has any reason to exist.

Through the recognition of the ordered succession of the five (or six) functions identified up to now, it is possible to recognize the fairy tale itself, which avails of this basic structure to appropriate and act upon a traditional context that in itself would remain inert. One is dealing with functions and not simply with phases into which the tale can be divided. This occurs because, if it is truly possible to split up the tale into *macro-sequences*,[11] it is even truer that their value descends primarily from the *functionality* inherent to the tale, so that it evolves according to the rules of the fairy tale and in no other way. Basically, it is the same situation that one encounters in Propp's apparatus of the *functions of the characters*.[12] Moreover, as the specific cases will display, the functions do not necessarily enter, all together, into the horizon of a concrete narration. A storyteller who omits the initial stasis to pass immediately to the fairy movement, or who skips from the interaction immediately to the final stasis, furnishes an incomplete tale, but the basis on which this is founded is not implicitly disputed: it represents the necessary postulate for the composition of any fairy tale, but also for the comprehension of its real range. In consideration of this, the fundamental structure shown in figure 5.6 emerges:

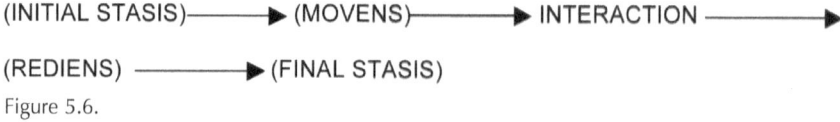

(INITIAL STASIS)————▶ (MOVENS)————▶ INTERACTION ————▶

(REDIENS) ————▶ (FINAL STASIS)

Figure 5.6.

From this scheme, on the one hand, is evinced the ordered sequence of functions through which each fairy tale is constructed, and on the other, the fact that the narration can allow the omission of each of the functions in parenthesis (the intermediate stasis can be considered in the same terms when the tale is composed of more than one movement). It is, however, absolutely incapable of tolerating the concealment of the interaction, insofar as this is the cardinal function around which the very sense of the fairy tale rotates. It can be considered as such because it contemplates the interaction between two dimensions of reality. Thus, the ideal, complete fairy tale—to which the *priomscel* comes close—presents all the functions *explicitly* although, following the tradition, multiple factors lead often to incomplete realizations of the model. The tale can be recomposed in its entirety during the writing phase, which in its nature is much more predisposed to completion and to the respect of an order than the oral tradition could ever be, since oral transmission often contains omissions connected to the mutability of the occasion and the inevitable blank spots deriving from the memory loss of the single narrator. Writing avails of an ease of composition not conceded to an oral narration that must take place within a limited arc of time. Of importance, the mnemonic process at the basis of orality can be facilitated by the adoption, perhaps unconscious, of a functional model such as that proposed here.[13] In any case, it is undeniable that the particular conformation through which the structure of the fairy tale manifests itself in the single narration is a significant test for determining the oral or written origin of text and in determining those traits of orality and those of written elaboration in texts presented in both modes. This takes on notable importance in the transcription of traditional tales. In this field, the outcome of the encounter or clash between the two fundamental modalities of narrative transmission is always unpredictable. A structure recognized as a common model of reference certainly favors a less traumatic convergence.

Classification of the Functions and Characterization of the Fairy Tale

Finding it necessary to frame in a more general scheme the problematic treated until now, it seems legitimate to me to sustain the dialectic identified regarding the functions of the fairy tale, founded on the interpenetration among three orders of fundamental factors. The first is a constant, represented by a space–time organization, in itself *immobile* (at least on the synchronic plane), modeled on the planes of reality imposed on the basis of a narrative-historical evolution. The second is variable, made up of characters intended to represent the relative plane of pertinence and to give body, through their mobility, to the narrative dynamic. The third factor, the *movement*, is a sort of *connective* between the former ones, which, through the three dynamic functions of *movens*, *interaction*, and *rediens*, permits the convergence, on a single plane, of contexts that would otherwise remain separate.[14] From a diachronic point of view, as has already been clarified, the multidimensionality of the real has not always had the same configuration. On the other hand, the characters, who theoretically are infinitely variable, reveal a functional constant that *depersonalizes* them and renders them merely *representative* of a certain time–space order. Constancy and variability are therefore concepts that can intersect, albeit within the limits of a well-determined narrative logic. Analogously, in the study of the notion of movement, or rather in the succession *movens-interaction-rediens* it is possible to find partial traits that permit a more complete approach to what still remains the constant factor through which the dynamic of the fairy tale unfolds. With this, I wish to underline that by conducting a deeper examination of the three aforementioned functions as they manifest themselves in the narrative tradition, it is possible to group them into an elementary classification, one which, on the one hand, would allow for a more specific characterization of the fairy tale in general, and on the other, would allow a more effective qualitative distinction between single examples of the fairy tale.

If we take into consideration the system of the thirty-one *functions of the characters* developed by Propp, we cannot fail to notice the evident qualitative characterization of large numbers of them.[15] For example, the cardinal function, A, or rather the damage caused to a member of the family, implies a conflictual relationship between two or more characters, an opposition. The same could be said of the pair of functions, Q–M, or the struggle of the hero with his antagonist and his eventual victory. Moreover, the function of the donor, D, implies a wide range of solutions, from which in substance one can identify a friendly or hostile attitude of the donor toward the hero. On the one hand, therefore, Propp defines the functions not only on a strictly structural plane but also on a more widely qualitative one; on the other, he recognizes how the same function can manifest itself according to contrasting modalities.

In the same manner, one can proceed with the three functions of *movement* identified up to now. (I exclude the functions of stasis both because they already belong to a specific dimension and because, since a logical continuity exists between the *initial stasis* and the *movens* and between the *rediens* and the *final stasis*, the categories adopted for the two dynamic functions would necessarily reflect on the other two, offering a sufficiently clear picture of the fairy tale in its entirety.) Thus, to obtain an exhaustive understanding of the fairy tale, it is vital to apply logical categories that are able to cast light on the *distinctive* characters through which the *dynamic* functions make themselves explicit. These categories, on the basis of an attentive analysis of the material at our disposal, can easily be reduced to nine, three for each function.

For the *movens*, the function which sets off the movement and which, therefore, must in some way furnish an explanation of it that is linked naturally to the background provided by the initial stasis, a classification on the basis of a principle of causality seems to me correct. The three fundamental causals can be individuated in the following categories:

VOLUNTARY (symbol v), which implies a *clear* and *free* intention of the character to escape from his own dimension and/or to invade another;

IMPERATIVE (symbol i), which implies the *imposition* of the escape and/or invasion on the character by another character or a given circumstance;

ACCIDENTAL (symbol a), which implies the *unawareness* and/or *involuntariness* of a character in escaping from his own dimension and/or invading another.

The interaction, being the function through which a temporary fusion between two or more dimensions is established should, in my opinion, be classified according to a *relational* principle. Three fundamental relations can be identified as:

FRIENDLY (symbol F), in which *definite* and *indefinite* meet on a plane of *concordance* and/or *complicity*, so that a *synthesis between opposites* is realized;

CONFLICTUAL (symbol K), in which *definite* and *indefinite* meet on a plane of *discordance* and/or *diffidence*, so that an *antithesis between opposites* confirms itself;

EXTERNAL (symbol E), in which the relationship between *definite* and *indefinite* limits itself to a simple *coming to awareness* (reciprocal or not) of the other's existence, so that there exists a certain *distance between opposites*.

Finally, the *rediens*, being the function which brings the movement to an end, and that hence bears its consequences, which reverberate in the *final stasis*, should be classified according to a principle of *consequentiality*. In this case, three fundamental resultants can be identified:

BENEFICIAL (symbol β), in which *definite* and/or *indefinite* show an *improvement* of the initial condition from the *interaction* or avoid a *deterioration*;

DAMAGING (symbol δ), in which *definite* and/or *indefinite* show a *deterioration* of the initial condition from the *interaction* or lack an *improvement*;

NONE (symbol ω), in which *definite* and/or *indefinite* emerge from the *interaction* with no change in their initial condition, either better or worse.

Regarding the *rediens*, it should be noted that, since it follows an interaction, it implies in turn a double interpretation and hence a double resultant, one for the *definite* and one for the *indefinite*, particularly when it follows a conflictual interaction in which one character draws an advantage and one is damaged. However, to preserve a correspondence with the *movens*, it is the resultant pertinent to the character and to the dimension responsible for the movement that counts the most; thus, if it is not strictly necessary, the indication of the other can be avoided.

Applying the above categories (with the help of their corresponding symbols) to the model already delineated and graphically illustrated, one can complete the determination of the purely dynamic development of the fairy tale. This is now identifiable as the *deep level* of its structure, while we also recognize a *modal* or *descriptive* development,[16] assimilable to a sort of *surface level*, which is the practical manifestation of the structure. This implies above all the characterization of the approach that the specific characters in the tale have with the context of the fairy tale. Thus, the nature of the *movens* can reveal the level of *consciousness* that the definite has of the existence of the indefinite or vice versa; the modality of the interaction can tell us what is the effective *gap*, in the widest sense of the term, between one dimension and another; and the genre of the *rediens*, finally, can display what palpable value is attributed to an experience undergone beyond the canons of daily life. The status of the character alters then with the alteration of the categories that define both his or her being and actions within the tale. Hence, if the nine categories are inserted into a table, it will be possible each time to identify the path taken by a character in the realization of his movement and, consequently, his *typology*. One could also individuate the subgenres incorporated within the wide range of the fairy tale (see figure 5.7).

Mov.	Int.	Red.
v	F	β
i	K	δ
a	E	ω

Figure 5.7.

If, for example, we were to isolate the sequence v–K–β, referring to *a definite* character, we would have identified, on the one hand, the classical typology of the hero and, on the other, would have evinced the development most typical of the *tale of magic* studied by Propp, which would demonstrate only one of the possible narrative developments of the fairy tale. In fact, by simply substituting β with δ, we would have a sort of *antihero* and hence the form of the *antifable*, in which the canonical victory of the protagonist is supplanted by his defeat. Or, by isolating the sequence $a–E–\omega$, we would have individuated a sort of *hero by chance*, who undergoes the experience of the legend as traditionally understood—the supernatural vision—from which he draws nothing other than the discovery of another dimension. The fairy tale envisions potentially all the sequences in the table and in this demonstrates its value as a transversal category.

But to observe concretely how this system of categories is applied to the fairy tale, one must return to the *priomscel*, or rather to the graphic scheme illustrating its structure (figure 5.8):

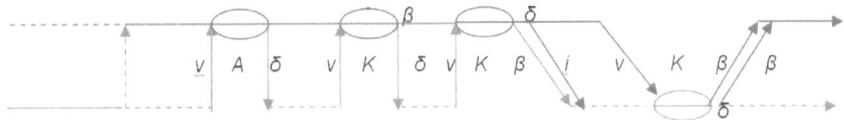

Figure 5.8.

This can be considered the complete representation of the structure of the fairy tale, which takes the form primarily of a multiple succession of stases and movements. As well, it correspondingly individuates specific triadic sequences that mark each of the key moments of the tale. The sequences expand when they imply a double resultant, fruit of a conflictual interaction that has provoked consequences in both of the dimensions involved, or when two functions manifest themselves contemporaneously, a *rediens* and a *movens*, as when Midir escapes with Étaín, or two *rediens*, as when Eochaid brings Étaín back to his world.

But these, like the other innumerable, unobservable forms in the *priomscel*, denote the natural variations on theme of a genre that, in the great liberty allowed to individual elaboration, remains nonetheless firmly anchored in its fundamental structure. This structure can be found in the entire narrative tradition that Yeats gathered in an exemplary collection and that Stephens reworked according to personal canons of poetics.

Notes

1. Cf. Propp, *Morphology of the Folktale*, 20–21: "Running ahead, one may say that the number of functions is extremely small, whereas the number of personages is extremely large. This explains the two-fold quality of a tale: its amazing multiformity, picturesqueness, and color, and on the other hand, its no less striking uniformity, its repetition."

2. Lotman, *The Structure of the Artistic Text*, 217.

3. Ibid., 220 (my italics).

4. See ibid., 209.

5. See Rolleston, *Myths and Legends of the Celtic Race*, 164: "To this great story the tale of Etain and Midir may be regarded as what the Irish called a *Priomscel*, 'introductory tale', showing the more remote origin of the events related."

6. See ibid., 155–63.

7. Cf. Northrop Frye, "The Mythical Approach to Creation," in *Myth and Metaphor: Selected Essays 1974–1988*, by Northrop Frye (Charlottesville: University of Virginia Press, 1991), 241: "Creation myth is in a sense the only myth we need, all the other myths being implied in it."

8. Cf. Algirdas J. Greimas, *On Meaning* (Minneapolis: University of Minnesota Press, 1987), when he occupies himself with identifying the *Elements of a Narrative Grammar*; in particular, he states that narrative grammar is made up of an *elementary morphology*, which is furnished by the taxonomical model, and by a *fundamental syntax*, which operates on the previously inter-definite taxonomical terms.

9. The implicit meaning of the expression *initial stasis* can be compared to the notion of *introduction* adopted by Labov and Waletsky and to that of *setting* used by van Dijk and Kintsch. In both cases, one is dealing with the reconstruction of the tale into five *micro-categories*, similar to the theoretical proposal put forward in the present chapter. But, apart from the *introductive* categories, the system is oriented in a totally different way. As seen further on, the *final stasis*, for example, which closes the narration, has little in common with Labov and Waletsky's *coda* and with the *moral* of van Dijk and Kintsch: see Mihály Hoppál, "Narration and Memory," *Fabula* 22 (1981): 286–89.

10. Rolleston, *Myths and Legends of the Celtic Race*, 159.

11. Cf. Hoppál, *Narration and Memory*, in particular 284–86.

12. Indeed, he declares that the functions "constitute the fundamental components of a tale" (Propp, *Morphology of the Folktale*, 21).

13. Cf. Hoppál, *Narration and Memory*, 281: "From the recalled propositions, and *by the help of the narrative and of linguistic formation rules*, a given narrative text could be retold by the narrator again and again with relatively slight or minor modifications" (my italics).

14. Lotman is moving in the same direction when, by plot "means an eventful action sequence with three components:

1. some semantic field divided into two mutually complementary subsets;
2. the border between these subsets, which under normal circumstances is impenetrable, though in a given instance (a text with a plot always deals with a *given* instance) it proves to be penetrable for the hero-agent;
3. the hero-agent" (Lotman, *The Structure of the Artistic Text*, 240).

15. See Propp, *Morphology of the Folktale*, 25–65.

16. Cf. Greimas, *On Meaning*, in which the French scholar distinguishes a *simple narrative utterance* from *modal* and *descriptive utterances*.

Plurality and Metanarrativity in the Fairy Tale

6

Is THE STRUCTURAL MODEL PROPOSED as the foundation for each exemplar of the Irish fairy tale tradition something to which each narrator *unconsciously* returns in creating and recreating his tale? Or, is it *a priori* consciously present in the minds of those who wish to venture into the ambit of the fairy tale? (These questions stay within the limits of our research here, but the validity of the model in question can be extended well beyond the confines of Ireland, to the extent that similar material conforms naturally to the canons developed in the course of the preceding chapter, no matter what its country of origin.)

The first hypothesis would assume a sort of *ineluctability*, on the part of the fairy tale, to develop according to a certain consolidated scheme. The second would instead see in this scheme the recognized premise from which every storyteller would take the cue for his performance, a sort of elementary draft on which to model the individual's contribution to the narrative tradition. The answers to these questions lay on the subtle margin between mere structural necessity and autonomous creative intent. The individuation of a fundamental structure lying at the basis of the narrative genre that we have identified in the fairy tale lends itself to varied interpretations according to the approach that, over the course of time, the individual establishes to the model of referral. This model is exemplified in the so-called *priomscel*, which may be read as the logical expression of the state of affairs that, at a certain moment, came into being in Ireland, and conversely, as the possibility of appropriating this state of affairs *narratively*. Put differently, this structure that, with its fundamental functions, permits the interaction of characters and dimensions pertaining to a certain conception of the real, can be read both as the heritage of a past in which these functions had extranarrative significance[1] and as the appropriation by a certain part of humanity of its own context in an eminently creative, and hence narrative, function. The fairy tale, located on the boundaries between *fabula* and *historia*,[2] is the terrain most suited to giving a univocal answer to the questions posed at the start of this chapter—questions, moreover, that form part of a dialectic between liberty and necessity that has a by no means negligible influence on the creation and circulation of the most typical Irish narrative product. This dialectic can be understood correctly only after a careful examination of the relationship, in time and space, established between a tradition that continuously brings its weight to bear on a collective scale and the innovation introduced by the individual in a field that has already repeatedly taken form.

Substructure and Metastructure

The identification of the relationship between collective heritage and individual intervention should be conducted through the introduction of conceptual categories that can isolate the principles from which the variable characters intrinsic to each of the tales making up the tradition ensue. The structure is the constant, immutable aspect of the construction of the fairy tale, thanks to which continuity is preserved and the identity of a specific narrative mode is set up. However, this mode would remain pure theoretical potentiality if it were not realized through the act of a narrator and the reception of a public. Two factors, the individual (re)creator and the group of individuals who receive the message, must give consistency to a peculiarity that otherwise could easily be reduced to a cold and elementary sequence of fundamental predicates. This operation is even easier when one is dealing with the written version of a fairy tale that, due to its static nature, allows the reader to rationally possess himself, so to speak, of the text. However, the reading of the text also clarifies how the structural factor is just *one* component of the narrative. To put it more clearly, the structural factor is the *implicit* component of an *explicit* whole represented by the text in its formal and thematic evidence.

Since each narrator who adopts a traditional plot elaborates it according to his own needs and his own tastes, and to the specific requests of the public that he is addressing, it is clear that although the structure of the plot will remain unchanged—in that it maintains the continuity and identity of a tradition—the same will not occur in the case of those aspects in which a natural process of variation takes place. As an example, we can take the case of the narrator *b*, who will employ twice the number of words to illustrate the tale's initial stasis than will a previous narrator *a*. Narrator *b* may describe the hero's *movens* according to motivations that are quite different from those given by narrator *a*; or, narrator *b* may move directly from the interaction to the final stasis, on which he will perhaps dwell longer than his predecessor. Whether these changes depend on the taste of the narrator or on the demands of the public or both is of no importance. What it is important to notice is how, using a preestablished structure, individual innovation has a wide margin of liberty. The deep nature and sense of the tale do not change; rather, its *exterior* characteristics, those within the power of the single recreator/beneficiary, change. If we assign the five structural functions of the fairy tale to fill as many empty compartments—the whole of nouns, adjectives, verbs, and so forth with which, in each narration, these spaces are concretely filled—it takes on *intelligible* form, and this can be defined as the *substructure* of the tale itself. This term implies a certain idea of subordination with regard to the structure, in the sense that a species of invisible but indivisible link is established between the practical narrative act and the abstract theoretical model in which the steps to be taken in the telling of the tale are laid out.

The substructure, therefore, in the widest sense, is the properly aesthetic component of the fairy tale. It marks the passage from structural necessity to liberty of expression, from the generic to the specific; it is the aspect that, in the oral context, makes it possible to distinguish one variant of the same traditional exemplar from another. Migrating then into the written context, this can become constant and also establish a model on the substructural level. However, writing, when its scope is artistic, tends to correct the substructure of the oral text, in order to give it a form and a content in line with determinate literary canons. When the end in view is instead the documentation of an oral tradition, then the transcription will attempt to follow the original substructure as faithfully as possible. The variation of names, attributes, circumstances, landscapes, thoughts, gestures, actions, and so forth that makes up the narrative material allows the structure of the fairy tale to manifest all its intrinsic expressive potentiality and its capacity to adapt to the most disparate contexts through the two fundamental channels of orality and writing. These channels, whether converging on the same objectives or following separate paths, and despite the change in time and space, repropose each time a universally valid model.

A second variable quantity can be identified in the composition of the fairy tale. Along the lines adopted until now, a *metastructure* can be defined as a sort of metanarrative frame in which the voice of the narrator himself

is foregrounded, sounding explicitly above his more or less fictional characters to the point of involving his audience (which, in the oral tradition,
frequently interrupts the storyteller's performance). This component lies
beyond the tale itself, linking it to the real context in which the act of narration takes place.[3] The metastructure is therefore the *present* in its relationship
with the heredity of the *past*, the space that the storyteller occupies to give a
current identity to his narration, an opportunity for him to observe the fairy
tale from without. It is the chief space of orality, directly connected to the
circumstances of the tale. Writing tends to neglect this space, to the extent
that it is not functional to the economy of the text.

In Yeats' collection, there are many tales in which the metastructure
is preserved, since it certainly gives a more accurate idea of the specific
reality of oral narration. But there are also examples in which the collector has cut it out, symptom of the desire to render the tale a literary object, freed from a context that, on the written page, no longer makes any
sense.[4] However, one should also mention the case in which the writer
himself has added a metastructure to the text to provide his own personal
comment on the events narrated, perhaps to impose an illuminated vision
of a phenomenon popularly understood in supernatural terms, or simply
to give an account of the occasion on which he heard the tale; or again,
as seen in Croker's work, to create, more often than not *a posteriori*, a
frame in which to link up the most disparate texts. Regardless of the
motivation, one is dealing in any case with interventions that alter the
perception of the text and, in substance, place the writer on the same active level as the storyteller from whom he has heard the tale. Moreover,
when the collector's metastructure contaminates the purity of the tale,
Yeats himself eliminates it to restore the more authentic value of the text,
most suited to his idea of popular tradition.[5]

Substructure and metastructure should therefore be understood as
dynamic factors on the basis of which the fairy tale—otherwise *static*, as
the depository of a model imposed once and for all—is able continually
to renew itself. Each exemplar of the fairy tale, in the course of oral
transmission, is subject to the variations dictated by the substructural and
metastructural elaboration of each storyteller and the circumstances of
the narration. This continues until one arrives at the written version of
the tale, in which substructure and metastructure are permanently fixed
by the writer. The same structure, therefore, can develop an infinite
number of variants.[6] By this, I do not intend only to consider the various
versions of a specific fairy tale that it is possible to collect in the field as,
for example, Yeats' *Master and Man*. I intend also to demonstrate how

the structure of this particular tale can be found identically in numerous other fairy tales, in no way connected to it—or rather, only connected to it by sharing, at root level, an authentic model of composition that reveals itself to be indispensable to a certain number of narrative types.

Deep Structure and Surface Structure

The structure is the constant system overseeing the composition of fairy tale. But one may also identify in it a variable component. In effect, what remains constant is the immutable succession of functions that make up, invariably, each fairy tale.[7] There also exist, however, numerous modalities through which these functions can organize themselves within the tale. One can affirm that although, at a deeper level, the structure remains identical to what we saw in the case of the *priomscel*, at the surface level, it is characterized by criteria of mutability, which respond to narrative exigencies that obviously differentiate it from the original fairy tale. The scheme of the *priomscel* demonstrates how, in the phase of realization, the model can assume various other forms. It is enough to analyze other fairy tales to see how the same basic structure can manifest itself according to different organizational strategies and, consequently, how it is possible to identify, within the general whole delimited by the narrative category of the fairy tale, a finite series of subsets from which to obtain an overall idea of the formally adoptable outlines of the tale.

As verified in chapter 5, the particular structural identity of each tale can be identified through graphic symbolism, from which, at the same time, one can trace the equivalence, always at a structural level, between single tales.[8] But how can one designate the criteria by which the deep structure of the fairy tale operates on the surface level? According to what circumstances is it possible to explain the structural variability that distinguishes exemplars of the same tradition? We were furnished a first example by the notion of *completeness* and *incompleteness*, with regard to the explicit presence of all the functions within the tale or not; a second example was found in the nine categories used to identify a corpus with the fundamental attributes necessary to define the dynamic functions. All the others, albeit indirectly, have been enunciated, or at least given graphic representation, in the progressive construction of the scheme of the *priomscel*. These criteria regulate the specific plot through which the universal *fabula* of the fairy tale expresses itself.

Dimensionality can be taken as the first category: once established that the fairy tale operates in a multidimensional context, one can have a tale that connects two dimensions—one *definite* and one *indefinite*; one that connects three, with the inclusion of the *semidefinite* dimension; and finally, one that gives an account of all four dimensions present in the Irish context in the historical age. In the first case, one would be dealing with *binary* dimensionality, which distinguishes all the stories in Stephens' collection, centered on the relationship of Myth to Legend (apart from two texts that focus on the relationship of Legend to History, which nonetheless remain secondary with respects to the main body of the text, which they frame). Binary dimensionality also marks the greater part of Yeats' collection where, instead, the meeting of Myth-History prevails, exemplified particularly in the first three sections, in which encounters between men and fairies are narrated; in the section *Ghosts*, it connects men and exponents of the Christian Otherworld, whereas in the two tales making up the section *Saints, Priests*, we see the interaction of Legend and History.

Ternary dimensionality is far less frequent, found, for example, in Yeats' tale *The Little Weaver of Duleek Gate*,[9] in which a historical character first arrives in a legendary context and then enters into a relationship with a creature of mythical stamp. *Quaternary* dimensionality, at least as regards the material under examination, remains pure potentiality.

A fairy tale may also distinguish itself according to the number of movements that it contemplates. In this regard, it seems opportune to create a fundamental distinction between tales with a single movement and tales with more than one movement. Fairy tales focused on the simple discovery of a given aspect of the Otherworld tend toward the first solution. This is seen, for example, in *How Thomas Connolly Met the Banshee*[10] by Yeats, whose title announces its bare plot, based solely on the meeting between the main character and a specific figure pertaining to the indefinite, the *Banshee*. Fairy tales in which the attention is focused on the feats of the character tend toward the second solution, as in the case of *The Fairy Greyhound*,[11] in which the unfortunate hero goes three times to an enchanted tumulus in search of treasure and three times is undone by a diabolical greyhound. This latter example has a precise number of movements, but there are also tales, as for instance the above-mentioned *Master and Man*,[12] in which the exact number of movements cannot be estimated and in which, indeed, the interaction between the definite and the indefinite assumes an iterative aspect, as if to give an impression of normality to an event that is entirely abnormal.

Moving now from quantitative to qualitative variability connected to the aspect assumed by functions within the tale, one notices above all that the two static functions—leaving aside the intermediate stasis, which is superfluous in this context—adopt two fundamental modalities, one *definite* and one *indefinite*. By this I intend that the *initial stasis*, in its func- tion of introducing the event on a one-dimensional level, usually in the definite dimension. This is by far most frequently the case, as evinced by the two collections that I have examined. However, *The Priest's Supper*,[13] which opens directly on a scene involving a group of fairies whose initial equilibrium is disturbed by the arrival of a priest, opens in the indefinite dimension. The same is true of the *final stasis*, which normally and logi- cally corresponds to the *initial stasis*. This apart from the case in which the tale, as in *The Priest's Supper*, begins in the indefinite and ends in the defi- nite, or in which, in ternary dimensionality, the protagonist moves from the definite to end his adventure in the semidefinite, passing obviously through a decisive interaction with the indefinite. In *The Lazy Beauty and Her Aunts*,[14] the main character, belonging to a humble historical context, is raised by the classical Prince Charming to a higher plane, thus recalling Legend, but only through the intercession of three witches, who evoke the mythical dimension.

Besides the nine categories in which, in the qualitative sense, the dy- namic functions have been framed, there are other criteria on the basis of which these functions influence the plot of the fairy tale. Hence, we need to identify the direction that the *movens* takes in the tale: as mentioned in the previous chapter, this can be descending or ascending. In the first case, a definite character descends into an indefinite dimension, as for example does Jamie Freel in the tale of the same name by Yeats,[15] when he decides to go to the place where he thinks that the fairies dwell. The second case regards instead the representatives of the indefinite who ascend to the definite plane, as the fairy who presents himself in the house of the wife of Paddy Corcoran to explain her ills.[16] A particular case is given by those tales, as found in the section *Ghosts*, in which the indefinite, represented by the superior level of the transcendent, undertakes a descending motion toward the definite. What has been said concerning *movens* is also valid for *rediens*, taking into account that, since the movement is the contrary, ascent and descent are also in the opposite direction to that indicated for *movens*.

The interaction also assumes two fundamental forms, based on the al- ready mentioned concepts of escape and invasion, depending on whether one or the other (or both) are present. When the definite moves toward the indefinite, both modalities are possible, perhaps paired. This happens in *The Soul Cages*,[17] in which the main character meets a merrow, first on the neutral territory of the beach,[18] and then under the sea, where he discovers the normally inaccessible place where the merrow dwells. If one considers that the apparition in a neutral field of the indefinite would not take place without the escape of a figure from the definite, as long as the indefinite stays *out there* and nobody goes out to meet it, the fairy tale remains pure potentiality. This is so because it lacks the figure who might make its presence evident to the rest of the historical community; one can understand why the interaction provoked by the indefinite always takes the form, logically, of an invasion: even when, as for example in *The Legend of Knock-grafton*,[19] the human character is immobile in a wood and the fairies come toward him. Here, it is supposed that the meeting would not have taken place if the man had not ventured into the wood, and, moreover, at night.

The interaction can also be classified according to a quantitative criterion; that is, it can be single or multiple. In the first case, between a *movens* and a *rediens*, there is only one interaction, recognizable by the fact that (its length aside) it involves the same interlocutors from the beginning to the end. In the second, there is more than one interaction within the time–space dimension enclosed between a *movens* and a *rediens*: obvious examples are the meetings or battles between the hero Conn-eda and the indefinite sustained during the mission given him by his stepmother.[20] One should be careful not to confuse the number of interactions with that of the movements: the latter begin with a *movens* and end with the corresponding *rediens*. Hence, one should not be surprised at the existence of a fairy tale, such as *The Story of Conn-eda*, in which a single movement, being divided into numerous interactions, gives birth to a very long tale; conversely, a far shorter tale, such as the above-mentioned *The Fairy Greyhound*, is organized into three movements, all based on a single interaction.

We are already aware of the concept of *assimilation* within the fairy tale, one that, although not representing a fundamental quantity, can influence structure. In fact, this process, which implies a permanent passage from one dimension to another, is frequently crucial in creating within the tale the specific plane of the indefinite with which the representative of the definite will interact. In Yeats' collection, we find the example of a "beautiful lady . . . that the fairies took away"[21] to turn her into white trout; in a lake, she awaits the return of her prince, but during the tale she enters into contact with the definite in the person of an arrogant English soldier. On other occasions, assimilation involves the disappearance from the narrative context of the plane on which the tale began, as when the main character of *The Lazy Beauty and Her Aunts*, abandoning her mother's home and not coming back (a *movens* not followed by a *rediens*), not only assimilates herself to the semidefinite plane of her prince, but also cancels the definite plane from the context of the narration.

The combination of all the elements taken into examination until now provides, I believe, an extremely exhaustive reply to the heterogeneity of plot characterizing the tradition of the fairy tale. This tradition has left room for numerous attempts at classification that have proved mostly unnecessary in face of the uniformity that lies at the basis of so much variety. This structural uniformity is so significant as to make converge, in the same field, not only a folklore collection and another of consciously literary tales (albeit strongly linked to an oral and popular tradition), but also a collection of *absolutely* literary tales, in no way oriented toward the revival of a traditional patrimony. Although the first two references are obviously to Yeats and Stephens, the third is to Joyce's *Dubliners*, a work that apparently shares nothing with the fairy tale but, as shall be seen later, is not so far removed from it. Evidently, in this recurring structure lies hidden a preeminent quality of narrativity, which can adapt itself to more than one narrative context, both because of its archetypal form and its capacity to carry a universal *significance* (an aspect dealt with in the next chapter).

The Narrativity Produced by the Fairy Tale

In Ireland, speaking about narrativity means above all repeating how the narrative phenomenon here receives unparalleled attention, as underlined by the abundance of stories about storytelling,[22] tales in which the protagonist is the act of narration itself and the sources from which it can draw. One is struck in particular by those stories in which the characters have no story to tell, a lack that exposes them to danger until they are able to remediate it. This implies that, in the absence of previous knowledge and in an urgent situation, it is necessary to draw from personal experience, thanks to which "everybody should be able to narrate."[23] In this way, a symptomatic fusion is set up between the hero of the tale and the narrator, a coincidence that places the listener or reader face to face with the birth of the tale itself and of the relative tradition. When a character lives out a story, to be able to narrate it later in first-person, the audience witnesses the fateful passage that takes place from event to narration, where the former is organized according to the particular rules of the second.

As the examples in Yeats' collection demonstrate, finding a story to tell means living out in the first person a supernatural experience, entering into contact with any aspect of the indefinite, so that this can then be testified to before a larger public. Pat Diver, the main character of *Far Darrig in Donegal*,[24] is a tinker who is denied hospitality because he cannot satisfy the desire of his hosts to hear a story; in fact, he holds the custom of storytelling in contempt.[25] Later, however, he is involved personally in a triple interaction with four *far darrig*, a species of solitary fairy, due to which, despite himself, he acquires a story to tell—as one of the *far darrig* brings to his attention in the meeting that ends the tale. The impression one receives on reading this tale is that both the inhospitable house owners and the fairies conspire to create a fairy tale,[26] which acquires even more value in that its protagonist and witness is a character who opposes the narration and does not accept its foundational function for the community.

In *A Fairy Enchantment*,[27] we meet a certain Michael Hart who narrates in the first person how, finding himself alone in a strange house, he receives the sudden visit of two fairies who give him the duty of turning a corpse on a spit. Returning to him, the fairies ask whether he knows a story and, on receiving a negative reply, throw him out in the middle of the night. Later, one of the fairies goes back to him and repeats the question. This time, the reply is in the affirmative, since the protagonist now knows a story—none other than what has just happened to him with his two interlocutors from the indefinite. Thanks to this, he gets back indoors and goes to bed, until, waking up, he finds himself in the middle of a lawn. In practice, Michael Hart is involved in a spell, from which he nevertheless emerges enriched by something he previously did not possess—a story to tell, a fairy tale procured for him directly by a pair of fairies. Although the main theme should be the deceitful art of the fairies, one can understand how, in reality, the entire illusion undergone by the main character was designed to turn an ordinary figure into a storyteller able to witness to a supernatural event, so as to lend to the illusion a tangible dimension, albeit purely verbal.

In these two examples, as in all the vast corresponding tradition,[28] an equivalence can be seen between the lack of and the desire for a narration and the need to have a meeting with the fairies to narrate; it is as if one can improvise oneself a storyteller if one possesses at least one fairy tale to tell. What emerges from these two tales is a sort of *narrative triangle*, made up of the narrator/hero, antagonists who provide the narration, and an audience. This triangle is organized according to a scheme, which, in practice, reworks the structural scheme of the fairy tale. If, as the initial stasis, we identify the audience who want to hear a story and a hero who is devoid of one; if we identify as the *movens* the hero who, consciously or unconsciously, escapes from the reality that has rejected him; as the interaction the space and time in which he obtains story at his own expense; as *rediens* his return to the reality temporarily abandoned; and as the final stasis the moment in which the hero, possessing a story, is able to satisfy the preceding requests of his audience, then there is a correspondence between the fairy tale itself and the dynamic underlying the process that generates it. Behind a movement that is only figurative, in the course of the narration there lies a *real* movement, responsible for the birth of this particular fairy tale. And in this real movement we discover that at the roots of the fairy tale hero is a character with the need to become a narrator, and hence that his adventures do not have autonomous value but are finalized in the acquisition of a plot to be made available to traditional narrativity, a discourse that gains even more credit in the Irish context, where one is denied social integration if one is incapable of participating *actively* in the communal activity of storytelling.[29]

From this viewpoint it seems to me possible to interpret Fairyland, and therefore all the indefinite reality that one imagines lying beyond the definite world, as a formidable *locus narrativus*, which invests so much importance in the popular mentality precisely on the basis of its capacity to furnish the raw material for the narrative tradition. On the value intrinsic in a phenomenon as variegated as fairy lore, the most differing theories can be built, all in their way open to discussion; what is definite, however, is that on it is founded the most conspicuous and significant part of a narrative patrimony that, evidently, cannot do without it. Representing the movement that leads to the acquisition of a tale on the basis of the structural scheme of the fairy tale implies recognizing a modality that forms part of the popular spirit, for which there exists a sort of perpetual repertory from which to draw in order to enrich a tradition that is never saturated. Narrator, audience, and indefinite figures are the three angles of a dialectic that extends inevitably toward that synthesis *par excellence*—the fairy tale.

This synthesis is divided into two fundamental parts. The first can be individuated in the *narrative triad* of *lack–acquisition–transmission*, which reflects the adventures of an individual who, to satisfy the request of a certain public (although one might also be dealing with an individual desire), becomes first the character in an exceptional event and then its narrator; hence, he is responsible for the first transmission of a fairy tale. From this, we can move to the second part, the *traditional triad* of *memory–reworking–narration*, which reflects a later stage, when the tale has entered to form part of a tradition, of a collective memory from which all can draw in order to satisfy a communal or individual desire, thus setting off a movement that only metaphorically reproduces the real movement lying at the origin of the tale itself, a movement that ends with a new narration.[30]

On the basis of these fundamental processes, it is possible to identify the principles on which an entire narrative tradition is built, that avails of the immediate relationship set up between the individual as a character and as a narrator. Almost all the tales in Yeats' and Stephens' collections include a reference, more or less direct, to the narrative dimension. One receives the distinct impression that the events themselves, despite being undeniably extraordinary, are undergone by the characters principally so that these characters can narrate them as soon as possible, to share them with other human beings; thus, the moment of narration is, so to speak, anticipated in the tale that the storyteller is telling. One can perceive that an internal *metanarrative* dimension (not to be confused with the external metastructure) is always present in the fairy tale. In practice, we are put in touch not only with the events themselves, but also with the very process that made them tellable. When this takes place through a narrator who, in the first person, exposes an experience of his own, one can speak of *immediate narrativity*, in which a minimum distance is created between the event and the tale. As an example, in *A Fairy Enchantment*, Michael Hart himself recounts his nocturnal adventure. When, instead, the person who is narrating is someone who has heard the tale from the direct protagonist, or when the narrator describes the manner in which the latter transmitted his experience for the first time, then one has *explicit narrativity*. An example of the first modality is the extremely short *A Donegal Fairy*,[31] in which the narrator relates a story directly confided to him by his aunt. An exemplar of the second modality is *Teig O'Kane and the Corpse*,[32] in which the narrator recounts the moment at which the protagonist relates his story to his father, the only person to whom he entrusts it: hence, Teig O'Kane's parent is to be considered as the filter through which the directly lived event becomes a tale. Here, the distance between event and narration has grown, but a recognizable link exists between the source and the successive tradition. One encounters *implicit narrativity* when, instead, the effective moment in the tale in which the story is transmitted by the protagonist to the tradition dispersing it in time and space is no longer identifiable. In this case, a link with the original source is not excluded, but upon it has sedimented an entire series of intermediate narrations, which have considerably increased the distance between event and narration. But it is also possible that the current narrator, especially if he is a writer intending to free the tale from its oral origins or instead wishing to subtract it from any link with contingent reality, decides consciously to conceal the circumstances that led to the event's becoming a tale. The *Far Darrig in Donegal* is indicative of this third genre of narrativity, in that the narrator does not communicate if and how Pat Diver has handed down to posterity his adventures with the fairies. Clearly, from the point of view of the purely fictional tale,[33] the question of narrativity poses itself in an ambit of *free invention* on the part of the author, from whom is demanded complete responsibility for the text. Moreover, the progression individuated in the three grades of narrativity just illustrated implies a parallel ascent or descent, according to the viewpoint, from a purely oral context to a more plausible written one. One observes the progressive decay of the metastructural component and a corresponding distancing of the factual aspect of the tale.

In any case, the fairy tale is always connected to a certain event, either one deriving from fact as something that really took place or one that can be totally invented. We already know that, in this field, it is impossible to trace a clear line of demarcation; the traditional concepts of truth and falsity have to confront themselves with a properly narrative logic.[34] This logic comes into play every time a given event is entrusted to a purely *fabulosa* transmission, a context in which the oral word dictates the conditions according to which the event should be transmitted. The value to be attributed to it will be determined by the particular treatment it receives each time from the single narration. In this way, the fairy tale becomes a specific channel of knowledge of a past that cannot be reconstructed according to the canons of veracity. Apart from its purely aesthetic or hedonistic value, it is reinforced by the absence of records of *historia*, sanctioned by written documents and possibly contemporary to the fact, that can provide the one definitive word on the events in question—even if this proves to be partial, tendentious, or entirely fictitious. In fact, an event could be immediately written down by a poet, who would certainly have less at heart the historical truth of the fact than its aesthetic value. Thus, from a *historicum* approach, too, it is possible to give birth to a fairy tale, and from a written text to begin a new oral tradition—hence, sanctioning the circularity of the relationship between *fabula* and *historia*. On the other hand, there also exists the possibility of *aphasia*, or rather that an actual event is not in fact transmitted, so that there is no trace of it, *fabulosum* or *historicum*. In this case, one is dealing with a genuine invention, which simulates, through the narration, the existence of an event that is consciously devoid of any reference to reality, an occurrence that subtracts the fairy tale from the folkloric and traditional context and transposes it to an exclusively literary one. There, it can follow an entirely autonomous evolution, leading it to encourage the most innovative ferments intrinsic to its narrativity.

In this final concept lies the crucial point on which we can seek an answer to the questions posed at the beginning of the chapter. The structure that from the *priomscel* onward has created and transmitted all the fairy tales in the Irish tradition is at once cause and consequence of narrativity. This is in the sense that it has revealed itself to be the ideal model on which to construct an eminently dynamic process, but that, in the moment that its archetypal value has been constructed, has been adopted as an instrument with which to test reality and appropriate oneself of the occasions that will expand the narrative patrimony.

Notes

1. Cf. Susan Reid quoted in Gose, *The World of Irish Wonder Tale,* 53: "The fairytale retains with precision a structure which is necessary to the ritual but has, in the main, forgotten the reason for this structure. From half memories and the rationalizations which make up for this loss spring many of the motifs of the tale." On my part, I by no means criticize those who seek a mythical or ritual origin for the fairy tale, but am also of the opinion that there has been some exaggeration in this respect, without considering that the preexisting value of the fairy tale as a narrative object has too frequently been undervalued.

2. In the fairy tale, the two fundamental modalities of the acquisition of reality combine to give birth to a third that substantially distinguishes itself from the other two. Cf. Zimmermann, *The Irish Story Teller,* 588: "With *truth* and *lies,* we may consider *fiction* as the third angle of a triangle, linked with the other two and often closer to one of them, but relatively independent."

3. Cf. Stephen Belcher, "Framed Tales in the Oral Tradition: An Exploration," *Fabula* 35 (1994): 1, in which the evolution of the concept of the metanarrative frame in the context of folklore is considered, at least as far as American studies are concerned: "Indeed, the concept of the frame, in current American folklorist usage, has shifted and no longer suggests primarily a narrative mechanism for the linkage of possibly unrelated tales, but rather the series of devices by which a narrator signals, and exploits, the disjunction between the fictive world evoked in the story being performed and the immediate human context of narration." Beneath the concept that I have adopted of *metastructure* fall both of the meanings given by Belcher.

4. *The Lazy Beauty and Her Aunts* is, for example, symptomatic of a rich metastructural apparatus, and it is no coincidence that Yeats should take it from Kennedy. At the end of the tale, we read (Yeats, *Irish Fairy Tales,* 307): "And in troth, girls and boys, though it's a diverting story, I don't think the moral is good; and if any of you *thuckeens* [a popular term which can be translated as *little sillies*] go about imitating Aunty in her laziness, you'll find it won't thrive with you as it did with her. . . . Thus was the tale ended by poor old *Shebale* (Sybilla). Father Murphy's house keeper, in Coolbawn, Barony of Bantry, about half a century since." As one can see, in the metastructure, pride of place is found in the moral that the old narrator gives to her young listeners, then in the intervention of the collector, who inserts the transcribed text into a precise space–time context. *Rent-Day,* once again significantly drawn from Croker, is an example of a text devoid

of metastructure; the narration opens with an exclamation of the main character in the first person (ibid., 216): "'Oh, ullagone! ullagone! This is a wide world, but what will we do in it or where will we go?' muttered Bill Doody, as he sat on a rock by the lake of Killarney." The conclusion is completely inherent to the event narrated, without any external reference (ibid., 219): "From that hour Bill Doody grew rich; all his undertakings prospered; and he often blesses the day that he met with O'Donoghue, the great prince that lives down under the Lake of Killarney."

5. Whosoever has had the chance to read the text from Lover from which Yeats drew *The White Trout: A Legend of Cong* (ibid., 36–39) would discover that originally the text was far longer, since in the source a series of introductive pages preceded the narration itself. Questions of textual economy apart, one should note, in Yeats' substantial editing, his intolerance for the excessive presence of a collector, albeit in dialogue (who knows how real . . .?) with his female informer, which seems to diminish the authentic center of attraction.

6. I would emphasize that this affirmation is theoretical, since in the reality of the narrative tradition one observes very frequently the reintroduction of events that are not necessarily structural. Cf. Éilis Ní Dhuibhne, "'The Old Woman as Hare': Structure and Meaning in an Irish Legend," *Folklore* 104 (1993): 80: "The concrete details which are in theory infinitely variable but which in practice vary only slightly."

7. As Propp teaches, moreover, about the functions of his *tale of magic*: "The number of functions known to the fairy tale is quite limited. . . . The sequence of functions is always identical" (Propp, *Morphology of the Folktale*, 21–22).

8. Cf. the scheme proposed by Propp in "Appendix" (ibid., 119–27), where the structural analysis assumes a graphic guise.

9. See William B. Yeats, *Fairy and Folk Tales of Ireland* (Gerrard Cross: Colin Smythe, 1973), 372–80.

10. See Yeats, *Irish Fairy Tales*, 118–21.

11. See Yeats, *Fairy and Folk Tales of Ireland*, 325–28.

12. See Yeats, *Irish Fairy Tales*, 89–96.

13. See ibid., 10–14.

14. See ibid., 303–7.

15. See ibid., 54–61.

16. See ibid., 32–34.

17. See ibid., 66–79.

18. Regarding the beach as the place joining the two dimensions of the real, both temporal and spatial, cf. Wilhelm F. H. Nicolaisen, "Concepts of Time and Space in Irish Folktales," in *Celtic Folklore and Christianity*, ed. Patrick K. Ford, 157–58: "The beach becomes the *seam* between land and sea and a metaphor for the *border* between the known and *familiar*, the firm land, on the one hand, and the *threatening* or at least *unpredictable* other, the infirm sea, on the other. It is a *place of ambiguities*. . . . It [the beach] is also the *limit of temporal existence*, for there beyond the horizon, at the faraway edge of that expanse of water lies *Tír na nÓg*,

the island of eternal youth from which there is no return for ordinary mortals" (my italics, apart from *Tír na nÓg*).

19. See Yeats, *Irish Fairy Tales*, 42–47.

20. See ibid., 323–36.

21. Ibid., 36.

22. For an ample and complete vision of the question, see Zimmermann, *The Irish Story Teller*, 517–49.

23. Ibid., 548.

24. See Yeats, *Irish Fairy Tales*, 96–99.

25. So much so that, in contrast to what has been said up to now regarding the seriousness of the relationship between the Irish and storytelling, Pat Diver states: "A story, indeed . . . Auld wives' fables to please the weans!" (ibid., 97).

26. It is not surprising that in this conspiracy, the figure of *far darrig* should appear, whose exclusive activity is soon described by Yeats: "The *Far Darrig* . . . busies himself with practical joking, especially with gruesome joking. This he does, and nothing else" (ibid., 86).

27. See Yeats, *Fairy and Folk Tales of Ireland*, 319–20.

28. Cf. Zimmermann, *The Irish Story Teller*, 539–40.

29. So precious is this activity as to make pass into the background the personal qualities of the given narrator. Cf. ibid., 549: "A fictional storyteller could be cunning or silly, brave or cowardly, lucky or victimized; but his function was essential."

30. A general synthesis of the two phases identified in the birth and evolution of the fairy tale can be discerned in the triad individuated by Carlo Tullio-Altan regarding the mythopoetic process: *dehistorification–transfiguration–identification* (see Tullio-Altan, *Ethnos e civiltà*, 14).

31. See Yeats, *Irish Fairy Tales*, 47–48.

32. See ibid., 17–32.

33. Cf. the definition given for this term in Northrop Frye, *The Anatomy of Criticism: Four Essays* (Princeton: Princeton University Press, 1957), 366: "Relating to literature in which there are internal characters, apart from author and his audience; opposed to thematic."

34. Cf. Zimmermann, *The Irish Story Teller*, 588: "[In the fiction] the referents may be an illusion accepted by the recipient of the story, or 'reality' itself— often a mixture of both. What matters is inner cohesion, clarity, opportuneness and interest."

The Significance of the Fairy Tale in Historical and Cultural Contexts

An Indicative Metaphor

THE CELTIC TWILIGHT CAN BE CONSIDERED the work with which Yeats ends his exploration of the world of the folkloric fairy tale. In this work, according to an entirely interior logic, more or less brief essays alternate. This presentation should be understood as reflecting themes held dear by the author (more often than not inspired by first-person experience) and tales drawn directly from the popular voice, at least as declared by the writer. The text in question is, in fact, an autobiographical account of a series of journeys made by the author to the west of Ireland, in particular to the area of Sligo, where he found his family roots. It is a sort of *catabasis* into a reality that preserved its links with the world depicted by the fairy tales previously collected in written sources. We face an attempt to acquire in a deeper, more personal way the values on which a new poetic was being built, to approach directly the context from which the *primigenial* energy needed to renew literature came and also to widen the common rational perception of reality that was being unleashed.[1] In substance, this return to the places of the author's childhood translates itself into an analogous regress into an aboriginal dimension, the *unitary* dimension of the universe in the mythical phase. According to the orientation of Yeats, this dimension can be both recreated and relived by means of the patrimony of fairy tales offered to the poet by the voice of those peasants who, thanks to the uninterrupted activity of storytelling over centuries, preserved their links with a past otherwise destined to oblivion. The loss of these tales would have deprived the contemporary age of a traditional heredity made all the more precious by the awareness of its function as an irreplaceable instrument with which mankind in general, and the poet in particular, can go beyond mere "knowledge" and reach authentic "wisdom."[2]

This last observation opens the way to the type of analysis to be conducted here, whose objective is to identify those characteristics of the fairy tale that can be conveyed by the term *significance*, or rather its capacity to carry one or more fundamental meanings. As mentioned in the previous chapter, this is essential to verifying the universal importance of a narrative genre which, from the point of view of our research here, takes in an extremely wide semantic spectrum. An article that appeared in the *Irish University Review* is very interesting in this respect.[3] It puts forward a convincing hypothesis, aimed at unveiling the underlying unity of *The Celtic Twilight* that given its (permit me the license) *Menippean* nature seems rather to subtract itself from any coherent identification. This hypothesis is based on a careful analysis of the text, from which emerge a body of recurring elements that, whereas on the one hand, they recompose in an organic whole an extremely heterogeneous text, on the other, reveal a significant expression of the message conveyed by the fairy tale, particularly from the point of view of an artist who approaches it with the greatest of expectations. Whereas the three key elements identified by Kinahan are intended to connect the apparently disconnected threads of *The Celtic Twilight*, they can also be read as the fundamental supports on which to model the principal dialectic of the fairy tale, that which opposes and composes the already examined concepts of *stasis* and *movement*.

According to Kinahan, *The Celtic Twilight* is founded on the assumption that the sensible world is manifestation of "a fall from grace," after which man has been trapped "in the *web* of mortal limitations."[4] The term *web* (as *net* and the more complex *cobweb veil*[5]), which Yeats uses in the work, is the preliminary element for an interpretation of the sense of the fairy tale, the metaphor through which to interpret the state that the tale, and hence mankind, have to face. This, as we know, follows a primitive situation of grace, in which the concept of a limit has no reason to exist. However, man and his world are not wrapped in a continuous cobweb, because here and there are gaps through which it is possible to open up to a wider dimension. In the moment that the "myths of fall are also as a rule myths of regeneration," then the "images of entrapment give way to images of openness, and most specifically to images of *doors, thresholds, gates* and *gateways, ways out*."[6] By adopting these terms, Yeats draws the reader's attention to the existence of a *threshold*, an opening that can put man in contact with a world lying beyond the confines of daily life, an element that, from the point of view of the fairy tale, implies the potentiality of a passage from one dimension to another, but which also implies the ability to recognize, albeit under a false appearance, one of the openings to the Otherworld. In the text, one reads of the authentic supernatural experiences undergone by Yeats and by people whom he has met, but these are absolutely rare and destined to the privileged few. Moreover, they are concentrated in that corner of Ireland in which modern civilization has only partly corrupted the ancestral Celtic heredity. The element that permits a much wider public to pass the threshold—albeit not in the first person—is identified in the third cardinal figure of *The Celtic Twilight*, the storyteller, who, in Homer and in more or less historical Irish narrators, is celebrated by Yeats as the one who through the force of words can stem the flow of time. In *The Celtic Twilight*, and in the fairy tale in general, there is a rejection of the chronological conception of time, to the extent that in both the narrator lends his voice to something immortal.[7]

A similar reading of Yeats' work offers a vision of the world in which a given situation that presents an absolutely partial image of reality is set in opposition to the ability to transcend this situation, both on the real level (perhaps through a journey to those places in which this is most probable) and on the imaginary level, using the means provided by the storyteller. The storyteller reveals himself to be a sort of *privileged interpreter* who, with his gifts as an *affabulator*, is able to put into contact two coexisting but distant planes of reality. He puts into action what, from the viewpoint of the *Weltanschauung* of the fairy tale, is a constant potentiality. We can recognize the intersection between the definite and the indefinite dimensions only when this is made explicit by the tale, which has a reason to exist only in virtue of the fact that an opening has been made in the web that, due to a historically imposed norm, limits human perception. It is not enough that a human being should meet a fairy to have a fairy tale. It is necessary that the former is in a condition to be aware of his interaction with a figure from the indefinite, or that the latter should be willing to show himself. In Yeats' *A Donegal Fairy*,[8] we find ourselves in an ordinary house, in which an ordinary woman is cooking. The story could continue on this everyday level, if it were not that an unexpected event takes place: a fairy falls accidentally into a boiling pot. If this incident had not taken place (a rare example of an *accidental movens* connected to an indefinite character), the woman would never have noticed all the fairies who immediately rush to the assistance of their companion (in this case, the *movens* is *voluntary*). Without an unexpected event, the woman would have remained completely ignorant of the fact that she cohabits with representatives of the indefinite, and consequently, despite having the potentiality, could never have narrated the fairy tale which finds itself among the pages of Yeats' collection.

In light of this example from the text, one can understand better the antithetical pair of attributes with which the planes of the definite and the indefinite have previously been identified. The human character, as part of an objective daily reality, has no more than limited awareness of what surrounds him. He is not able to grasp the reality of something discussed simply on the level of the subjective experience of someone else. The existence of an invisible microcosm within the visible world escapes his purely terrestrial sight. Figures from the fairy world form part of a past that, until they manifest both their presence and prerogatives, cannot disturb the present equilibrium. In short, there is an entire group of elements and phenomena that lie hidden beneath a veil, at least until this veil is removed. The fairy tale, through one or more heroes, raises this veil and, by means of its diffusion among an ever-widening public, renders always less subjective the knowledge of the existence of a world that may have been considered well canceled by the inexorability of progress. The woman who had the chance to observe the fairies in her own home had probably already heard tell of these beings, so that her adventure provides further testimony of the consistency of what collective tradition had already handed down. As soon as his adventure is turned into a tale, the latter becomes an *involucre*, through which deeper awareness of reality manifests itself and is offered to a more or less extended community. No less than a rite, the fairy tale permits the shift of a *latent* mythical aspect into a *conscious* historical context.[9]

The *Epihanic* and *Pragmatic* Components of the Fairy Tale

What arises at this point is the *epiphanic* aspect of the fairy tale, its capacity to reveal reality under a particular light, to display its darker side, placing man face to face with all that is *other* than himself. Dealing with the epiphanic significance of the tale implies also paying attention to the other fundamental aspect, the *pragmatic*, which corresponds in practice to the spatial and temporal sequence identified in the structure of the fairy tale. The characters move against a determinate paradigmatic horizon with the double objective of performing an action that alters, in a more or less obvious way, an initial situation, and coming to consciousness of something that, before the action began, was either partially or completely unknown.

On an elementary level, the two components are strictly linked in that there can be no epiphany without at least the pragmatic action of a character. Likewise, it is impossible to conceive of any action without a conceptual horizon within which to identify the context and the characters who must act. It should be noted, however, that it is unlikely that, in every tale, both sides of the coin will have the same importance. From time to time, one will be predominant over the other, to the extent that, in some cases, one will almost seem to disappear because of the exuberance of the other.

Returning for a moment to what was said in chapter 5 regarding the triadic sequences identifiable through the application of the nine qualifying categories adopted for the classification of the dynamic functions: in the presence of a tale characterized by the scheme ν–K–β, one can intuit the preponderance of the pragmatic category, since the attention of the narrator is naturally directed toward the actions of the hero, and we are little interested in ascertaining, for example, the nature of the supernatural being in the role of antagonist. On the other hand, a narration that develops on the scheme a–E–ω is decidedly oriented toward the discovery of a given indefinite phenomenon and takes little interest in how the hero has arrived at the place of the meeting.

Let us return, finally, to the classical opposition between *Märchen* and *Sage*, between the tale of magic identified by Propp and the legend as it was conceived by Lüthi, an opposition that finds its *raison d'etre* in a large part of the European tradition. In this tradition, the fairy tale tends easily to divide, creating almost a rift between tales oriented toward the pragmatic datum and others oriented toward the epiphanic datum. In the Irish context, the situation assumes far more subtle contours. In Yeats' collection, we practically never encounter the narration of the feats of heroes entirely detached from a living context,[10] just as one always notices an unparalleled interest in providing a clear and serious identity for figures and phenomena pertaining to an indefinite plane. If anything, one can see in the Irish tradition a greater predisposition toward the epiphanic aspect, a tendency in which, as can easily be intuited from what has been said up to now, an innate component of the Irish spirit is reflected, a never-satisfied attraction to everything belonging to an otherworldly dimension.[11]

If one compares Yeats' text *The Man Who Never Knew Fear*[12] with variants of the same fairy tale collected by the Grimm brothers[13] and Afanas'ev,[14] one notes how, despite the fact that they all develop on the same structure, which varies substantially only in the number of escapes that the hero makes in search of fear (it should also be underlined that the Irish version contains the greatest number of movements, in confirmation of the fact that the importance of the epiphanic datum in no way overshadows the pragmatic potentiality intrinsic to the fairy tale), the approach toward the figures from the indefinite is decidedly different. On the part of heroes from German and Russian variants, figures of the indefinite are considered no more than bench tests on which to exercise one's courage, without the slightest attention paid to their identity by the hero. Thus, the effort of the struggle is not indeed noticed.[15] In the Irish variant, the hero performs his feats with a fair dose of respect for something that goes beyond his understanding. Whereas the German and Russian heroes act pragmatically, in their own interest, the Irish hero not only acts for the common good, but also takes on the responsibility of revealing to the community the nature of events that, prior to his arrival, were wrapped in the deepest mystery. Finally, the German and Russian heroes learn the meaning of fear, but this takes place in a humorous key, linked to events that are obviously natural (it is enough to surprise them in their sleep with a chest full of darting fish). The Irish figure, however, remains a spotless and fearless hero, because, I would suggest, of the correct relationship he has established with the indefinite dimension, which had been a source of fear for the rest of the community. Whereas the tales of the Grimm brothers and Afanas'ev concentrate exclusively on the more or less heroic feats that lead the characters to easy rewards, Yeats' tale seems to want to exalt the feats of the hero (who still is given the reward that he deserves), but with the objective of instituting a new universal order, in which *the definite and the indefinite*, reciprocally revealed, can coexist peacefully.[16]

If, on the one hand, the movement of the fairy tale is finalized in a transition from a phase of mystery to one of consciousness through the cardinal passage of epiphany, on the other, it is the factor of *disturbance* that conducts an initial situation of equilibrium to a final situation in which this equilibrium has been modified. Both aspects shape themselves perfectly on the structural model of the fairy tale, so that the epiphanic process can be depicted in the following graphic guise (see figure 7.1):

Figure 7.1.

Simply changing the terms, the pragmatic process can be illustrated as in figure 7.2:

CONFRONTATION

UNSTABLE EQUILIBRIUM   STABLE EQUILIBRIUM

Figure 7.2.

In both illustrations, I have attempted to employ terms that give the clearest idea possible of the fundamental processes that the fairy tale brings into being. However, if instead of the two triads adopted I had limited myself to reproposing the structural triad *initial stasis–interaction–final stasis* (the arrows conserving the functions of the *movens* and *rediens*, respectively), I think the nature of the two processes identifying the conceptual dynamic of the fairy tale would have been equally clear. In both cases, of decisive importance is the movement that leads one or more characters from one dimension to another, following which the event takes place that, in one way or another, modifies the initial situation imposed by the contest. What varies is the function of the hero who, on the epiphanic plane, is first simple *representative* of his dimension, then the *witness* of another dimension, finally assuming the function of *divulger* of what he has discovered. On the pragmatic plane, whereas at the beginning the hero was *quiescent*, in syntony with the calm of the contest to which he pertains, in the course of the interaction he is transformed into an *active* hero, to return, after his escape and/or invasion, to *quiescent* again; but this only occurs after having changed, for good or evil, his and/or others initial state.

Allowing that no strict correlation exists, it is fair to state that when the interaction is *external*, one presumes that the story is oriented toward the epiphanic aspect (for example, Connor Crowe in *Flory Cantillon's Funeral*[17] remains hidden and at a distance on purpose, in order to discover the secret of the burial that the *merrows* offer to members of the Cantillon family). Here, a *conflictual interaction* (one should consider that the term *confrontation* is used to indicate the central phase of the pragmatic process; the more explicit *contest* could have been used) individuates logically a story oriented toward the pragmatic aspect (for example, the vicissitudes undergone by Daniel O'Rourke in the story of the same name,[18] on account of the hostility of a *pooka*). The *friendly interaction* seems to be the most neutral, at one moment limiting itself to a simple dialogue between characters pertaining to different dimensions (as happens in *Rent-Day*,[19] where the interest of the story is focused on the meeting between the poor Bill Doody and the legendary figure of O'Donoghue, who permits his interlocutor to attend to his own state of poverty); whereas at the next, this involves far more lively action (as demonstrated by *The Piper and the Púca*,[20] in which, after a ride on a *pooka*'s back, a human musician must play his bagpipes at the feast of the *banshees*, to then return home having been gifted with exceptional mastery of his instrument).

From all the examples given, one can see that, in each case, it is impossible to individuate an exclusive predilection of any fairy tale for one aspect or another. The tale is firmly rooted in a dialectic between the epiphanic and pragmatic lines that reflect the necessary interaction between the heredity of folklore and narrative structure, between traditional paradigm and syntagmatic elaboration, and between the *functionality* and *availability* of the story.[21] It is significant that Yeats, having discovered in folklore an indispensable source of literary inspiration, aspired to creating himself, in the figure of *Red Hanrahan*,[22] a character capable of passing from literature to folklore, according to the logic of the *virtuous circle*, for which literary writing and popular orality could set up a profitable relationship and create an ever more solid bond. Stephens himself, when he made his first literary approach to the stories in the Fenian Cycle, imposed limits on himself that kept him firmly within a traditional context.[23]

To the traditional context belongs the concept of *deep structure*, in which the formal identity of all fairy tales has been recognized. This also forms the matrix that can liberate the compositional freedom of the individual, which manifests itself instead in the *surface structure*. But to this context also pertain a certain *imaginative store*, the whole of figures and phenomena that a millennial tradition has sedimented in the popular mentality. Now, although the storyteller has an almost inexhaustible faculty for varying the plot of any fairy tale (and hence of intervening personally on the pragmatic aspect of the text), he is conceded far less liberty in approaching the imaginative store, on which the epiphanic character of the text is plainly based. In the preceding chapter, we saw how a narrative tradition can be born, or at least how this event is represented within the narration itself. We were faced with characters who, presumably for the first time, were put into contact with an indefinite dimension, from which they drew the fairy tale, which was handed down from then on. But did the trials they underwent (or simply narrated) have no link with similar or identical events registered previously? Yes and no. From a strictly narrative point of view, the experiences of Pat Diver and Michael Hart, insofar as they were individually conceived of and disclosed, are a point of departure, a *unicum* that opens up a new front within the tradition. But if one's glance widens, it becomes clear that one is dealing once again with the theme of the meeting with a particular type of well-recognizable figure belonging to the indefinite. In this case, the figures are *far darrig*, who significantly occupy a section of Yeats' collection. The two characters may be ignorant of these creatures belonging to the popular imagination, supposing their extremely hypothetical isolation from the community, but when their disclosures become traditional, they are absorbed into the wider horizon of folklore, in which they are reregistered simply as two new *interpretations* of a known phenomenon.

In practice, every new fairy tale is based on a *preexisting* imaginative store, which, consciously or unconsciously, has a determining influence on the characteristics attributed by the given storyteller to the figures, phenomena, or circumstances that distinguish his story. The preexisting character of what is narrated can be implicitly perceived from the exterior, as in the case of the stories of Pat Diver and Michael Hart, or be explicitly declared by the narrator himself. Consider, for example, how the storyteller of *A Donegal Fairy* begins his story: "Ay, it's a bad thing to displeasure the gentry, sure enough—they can be unfriendly if they're angered, an' they can be the very best o'gude neighbours if they're treated kindly."[24] Before narrating the supernatural encounter, the storyteller introduces the theme of the tale on the basis of the traditional image of the gentry—or rather, the fairies—as if in this image he seeks complicity with the interlocutor so as to justify his testimony. In *The Soul Cages*, it is instead the main character, Jack Dogherty, who complains of the fact that "though living in a place where the Merrows were as plenty as lobsters, he never could get a right view of one."[25] In this case, the character is aware *a priori*—an awareness deriving from the previous disclosures of his grandfather and father—of the existence of the merrows before actually meeting one of them.

However, one must also contemplate the possibility of encountering a fairy tale focused on the *native* imagination store, in no way linked to a preexisting tradition, but rather the first testimony in absolute of the existence of a determinate aspect of the indefinite. This is extremely improbable in the case of more recent stories, but going back in time becomes all the more plausible. One must return to the more or less historical moment in which a certain folklore tradition began. But, as can easily be intuited, it is very unlikely that the fairy tale has been conserved that, for example, speaks for the first time of the leprechaun or explains perhaps his link with the art of the cobbler. Faced by a tradition that, for centuries, has entrusted itself exclusively to orality, it is obvious that a continuous exchange occurs by which, as one proceeds, the most ancient examples of a certain type of fairy tale disappear to leave space for more recent interpretations. Only writing would be capable of putting us into contact with the native phase of a figure or phenomenon from the indefinite.

In any case, an example of this native imagination is to be found in Yeats' collection, where the account is given of a twelfth-century writer, Giraldus Cambrensis, regarding the first appearance of a *ghostly island*, able to rise or sink at will, until the inhabitants of the region, by means of a flaming dart, manage to stabilize and colonize it.[26] The storyteller in this case states clearly that he is able to explain the origin of the phenomenon, so that all the stories focused on ghostly islands (which from the twelfth century onward enrich the tradition) will have to be considered in one way or another indebted to the native testimony of Giraldus Cambrensis. The same could be said of any storyteller who, perhaps in far more recent times, was capable of creating a figure entirely independent of the tradition and to impose it in the popular imagination. Although this is plausible in the literary context, where the writer has a far wider margin of liberty, it is much more difficult in the field of folklore, where the traditional imagination exercises a force of attraction as efficacious as it is rooted in a past that—ultimately—always originates from a mythical dimension.

The Dialectic Between *Signifier* and *Signified*

As previously mentioned, each fairy tale, operating on a preexisting imaginative store, forms a sort of ulterior interpretation of a consolidated tradition. In substance, what presents itself to the popular memory is a more or less wide repertory of elements, each of which has given origin to determinate traditional thread. Each storyteller can choose into which thread to insert himself, with the intention of offering his personal contribution to the *a posteriori* transmission of a theme from folklore, reworked in determinate narrative structure. Thus, he will have once again erased the distance that separates a nonetheless indefinite phenomenon from definite context in continual change. He will have brought past and present onto the same plane, with the past becoming ever more distant with the passing of time. This necessitates a continual reinterpretation, to prevent the past from becoming simply a memory that ultimately disappears, thus leading to the vanishing of an entire traditional thread—an irretrievable loss both on the level of folklore and of narrative. The task taken by the fairy tale is, therefore, that of guaranteeing a certain consistency to events that, given their nature, tend to escape any attempt at coherent systematization. This occurs unless a writer such as Yeats intervenes, ordering the traditional patrimony according to a personal, but rational classification, or, on a higher level of elaboration, Stephens, who makes of the Fenian material a poetically ordered whole and further frames it between two metanarrative texts. But the main task of the fairy tale is, at the same time, that of keeping alive a narrative tradition in which Irish folklore has its principal resource.

Obviously, the tale cannot give any *real* consistency to material that, until proved to the contrary, is purely verbal. But, from the point of view of the characters who act in the story, this consistency is possible. Between the figures from the definite and those from the indefinite, a dialectic is set up that, in a certain way, reflects de Saussure's distinction between *signifier* and *signified*, or the relationship between *name* and *object*. Thus, the fairy tale opens, more often than not, with an explicit awareness of elements that only later will be put to the test, but which at the level of the initial stasis can only be *named* or, at least, implied.

In the town where Jamie Freel lives "it was well known that fairy revels took place; but nobody had the courage to intrude on them":[27] everyone knows about the fairies, and everyone talks about them, but no one is willing to take the step that would annul the distance between the named and the object. If it were not for the hero, who eventually decides to go to the place where the fairies are said to live, the real meaning of the concept would remain unknown; it would be a void signifier. Only when Jamie Freel escapes from his dimension and invades the castle inhabited by the fairies is a conjunction made between the mere mental image evoked by a name and the effective consistency of the object so denominated, since, on his return home, the hero will be fully aware of the meaning intrinsic to the verbal involucre—fairies—and, albeit indirectly, he can involve other human beings. The clearest image of the direct experience of Jamie Freel will remain incontestable until an epigone emerges willing to follow in his steps and, in altered conditions, to join the name again to the object, to complete the signifier with its exact signified. As the tradition linked to that specific category of fairy goes on, each main character of the fairy tales will furnish to the community, depending on the case in hand, a reconfirmation or a redefinition of the images and conceptions inherited from the past, or perhaps a rediscovery of something that had been removed from popular memory.

From the viewpoint of the conscious appropriation of the meaning intrinsic in the indefinite, the figure of Tuan Mac Cairill, the main character of the story that opens Stephens' collection,[28] seems exemplary to me. In the adventures of this character, practically all the mythical, legendary, and historical events of Ireland are reproduced, up to the meeting with St. Finnian, who gathers his testimony. Tuan assists in the first person at all the successive invasions of the island and thus, in his eyes, all the figures and events that are to become part of the narrative tradition and enter into the popular imagination gain consistency. What permits him to live more than a thousand years is a progressive metamorphosis by which he first becomes a deer, then a boar, a hawk, and a salmon. He becomes a man again in the end, so that he can communicate his extraordinary experience to a representative of the definite. It does not seem casual to me that Stephens should begin his collection with such a story, since it is the most appropriate introduction to the themes that fill his pages. We could define it a sort of *guiding* fairy tale, in that any narrator can start from it in developing any fairy tale, or especially those focused on the relationship between Myth and Legend. But, above all, in this metamorphosing hero we discover the illustrious predecessor of all the heroes who will break down the barriers between those worlds which Tuan has seen born: his testimony is the unshakable guarantee for the entire edifice that supports the fairy tale. And Stephens is definitely conscious of this function.[29]

Characters such as Jamie Freel and Jack Dogherty represent better than any others the typically human desire *to know* and the necessity of knowing the reality that surrounds one.[30] Undoubtedly, in such figures one cannot but notice the notable drive provided by the desire for adventure, as there is likewise a definite intention to procure a pleasant story to share with other people. But, in the depths of the fairy tale lies a fundamental tension aimed at unveiling the meaning of what exists beyond the veil of appearance and at shaking up the dust that time naturally accumulates on the data and values preserved by a relatively stable memory. In such an opening, in full relief, in my opinion, should be understood the peculiar, universal value that led writers such as Yeats and Stephens—so attentive to the epiphanic function of the literary text—to become involved actively in the virtuous circle of the fairy tale, a circle in which space exists for many other Irish writers, including the most illustrious of all—James Joyce. Besides, how could one discuss epiphany without invoking the name of Joyce? I hope to respond to this question in the next chapter, through the specific reading which I propose of *Dubliners* and, more generally, of the relationship between the fairy tale and the tale properly speaking, or again between the fairy tale and the pseudo-fairy tale. These are conceptually relevant pairs, capable of instituting a stimulating dialectic of narratological interest.

Notes

1. Cf. Rosita Copioli, introductory note to *Il crepuscolo celtico*, by William B. Yeats (Milano: Bompiani, 2001), 7–18. See in particular 15: "Yeats had turned

to popular poetry as the first of the paths to consciousness. From the images and myths in which it abounds and which were so familiar to him, he must have understood that consciousness always proceeds through models and symbolic forms, not only in poetry, but also in science, philosophy and all disciplines."

2. See Frank Kinahan, "Hour of Dawn: The Unity of Yeats's 'The Celtic Twilight' (1893, 1902)," *Irish University Review* XIII, 2 (1982): 197.

3. See ibid., 189–205.

4. Ibid., 191 (my italics).

5. See ibid., 192.

6. Ibid., 193 (my italics).

7. See ibid.; cf. also Thuente, "Traditional Innovations," 96–102, in which a spatial and temporal conception is given which Yeats drew directly from the oral and popular tradition.

8. See Yeats, *Irish Fairy Tales*, 47–48.

9. Cf. Dario Sabbatucci, *Il mito, il rito e la storia* (Roma: Bulzoni, 1978), in particular 340–44.

10. Cf. Nicolaisen, *Concepts of Time and Space in Irish Folktales*, 156: "The landscape of Irish folktales, whether in this world or the other, is—and this has to be said, although it may sound trivial—the landscape of Ireland. In particular, since protagonists have to leave home in order to complete their assigned tasks and ultimately to find themselves, it is the landscape of the roads of Ireland."

11. Besides the attraction that the Irish feel for what lies *beyond*, one must also take into account the *harmony* that this people has reached in its relationship with supernatural beings. In this regard, Yeats draws attention to the fact that there is a notable difference of approach between the Irish and their Scottish cousins, dedicating to the theme a chapter in *The Celtic Twilight* (London: A. H. Bullen, 1902). See in particular 178–79: "You have burnt all the witches. In Ireland we have left them alone. . . . You have discovered the faeries to be pagan and wicked. You would like to have them all up before the magistrate. In Ireland warlike mortals have gone amongst them, and helped them in their battles, and they in turn have taught men great skill with herbs, and permitted some few to hear their tunes. . . . In Scotland you have denounced them from the pulpit. In Ireland they have been permitted by the priests to consult them on the state of their souls." This last remark sanctions once again the peaceful interpenetration that, in Ireland more so than elsewhere, took place between the pagan heritage and the Christian faith.

12. See Yeats, *Fairy and Folk Tales of Ireland*, 344–51.

13. See Jacob and Wilhelm Grimm, *Grimm's Fairy Tales* (Teddington: Echo Library, 2006), 318–29: *The Story of the Youth Who Went Forth to Learn What Fear Was*.

14. See Aleksandr N. Afanas'ev, *Russian Fairy Tales* (New York: Pantheon, 1945), 325–27: *The Man Who Did Not Know Fear*.

15. One of the distinctive characteristics that, for Lüthi, distinguishes the *Märchen* from the *Sage* is precisely the effortless way in which the hero of the fairy tale performs his feats, where the main character of the *Sage* allows all the tension

he undergoes in facing his adversary to be felt. Since in the story from Yeats in question the hero performs his feats in the style of a *Märchen*, but behaves like a character from a *Sage*, one is led to think that the distinction proposed by Lüthi is not so binding, or that the Irish story, taken altogether, is more easily inserted into the category of the fairy tale examined until now.

16. Obviously, it must be mentioned that, in the inclusion of one variant rather than another of the same narrative type, the criterion of selection employed by the editor is definitive. Hence, while it is plausible that Yeats would have consciously chosen the more serious variant because it was closer to his own poetic of the fairy tale, it is also fair to think that the Grimm brothers and Afanas'ev, according to a different criterion, preferred to leave space for the humorous side of their narrative tradition.

17. See Yeats, *Irish Fairy Tales*, 80–83.

18. See ibid., 105–12.

19. See ibid., 216–19.

20. See ibid., 102–5.

21. Cf. Northrop Frye, "The Archetypes of Literature," in *Fables of Identity*, (New York-London: Harcourt, Brace and World, 1963), in which the Canadian scholar sets up an interesting dialectic between *narration* and *meaning* on the basis of the literary phenomenon. Of particular interest is the idea according to which "just as pure narrative would be *unconscious act*, so pure significance would be an *incommunicable state of consciousness*, for communication begins by constructing narrative" (15, my italics). The epiphanic and pragmatic planes are hence reciprocally dependent.

22. Cf. Foster, *Fictions of the Irish Literary Revival*, 236–40, in particular 239: "Yeats hoped that Hanrahan might be accepted as a once-historical figure and then, by way of Yeats's stories, pass into Irish legend and thence into folklore." In creating a character who follows the opposite path to many characters drawn from the tradition, it is correct to recognize Yeats' desire not only to *emulate* the tradition, but also to *repay* in person its great generosity in terms of material offered to his poetry.

23. Cf. ibid., 243: "Stephens was in fact happiest when observing *unconsciously* the laws of folk narrative" (my italics).

24. Yeats, *Irish Fairy Tales*, 47.

25. Ibid., 67.

26. See ibid., 227.

27. Ibid., 54.

28. See James Stephens, *Irish Fairy Tales* (Dublin: Gill and Macmillan, 1979), 3–31.

29. The first story in *Irish Fairy Tales* is not only a refined example of the *tale within the tale*, but its function extends to the very value that Stephens asks his reader to understand. Cf. Martin, *James Stephens*, 133: "It is not only an infinitely reflexive narrational method, it is also a method by which the reader is never per-

mitted for long to suspend his disbelief that what he is reading is fiction: continually he is startled by a casual shift from one world to the next, from one narrator
to the next, one story to the next."

30. A necessity felt all the more in a context in which "Fairyland actually
exists as an invisible world within which the visible world is immersed like an
island in an unexplored ocean, and it is peopled by more species of living beings
than this world, because incomparably more vast and varied in its possibilities"
(Walter Y. Evans-Wentz quoted in the "Introduction" to Yeats, *Fairy and Folk
Tales of Ireland*, XI).

Between the Fairy Tale and the Tale 8

The Five Phases of the Fairy Tale

TO RETURN TO AN ISSUE only touched on at the end of the Introduction, I think the moment has come to examine a question that is central to our research. We must identify the fundamental levels through which to observe the birth and development of a traditional story. The objective is now focused specifically on the forms assumed by the fairy tale on the basis of the various levels of elaboration that, in the course of time, mold it and guarantee it a certain configuration. We are entering an area very different from that put forward by Foster.[1] As the classical conception of the genre imposes, he adopts the notion of the fairy tale (or the folktale) exclusively in terms of the extreme outcome of the narrative itinerary set off by an event or an experience, the final stage in a precise evolutionary process. Now, instead, the opportunity is offered to our analysis to recognize and study the principal *phases* on which the evolution of the fairy tale is modeled, which from a partial level of the narrative progression extends to take in all these levels. It will no longer represent a point of arrival but a structural constant. In view of this constant, a rigid codification of the narrative material into genres and subgenres will demonstrate all its relativity, since each of the phases identified will not only outline a partial aspect of the elaboration of the fairy tale, but also a form subject to *transitoriness*. Hence, a purely dynamic scenario emerges, in which each step should indeed be analyzed and appreciated in its particular nature, but always relocated in the wider context of the general principles on which the transversal validity intrinsic to the fairy tale rests. Whereas Foster limited his range of action exclusively to the context of folklore, in our case, the horizon must be widened to embrace the literariness true and proper of the story. In the phases that distinguish the evolution of the forms, contents, and functions of the narrator in the fairy tale, it is correct to perceive an exemplary itinerary that leads progressively from orality to writing, from folklore to literature, from the unknowing character to the skillful author. Moreover—and this aspect deserves all our attention—in the course of its trajectory, the fairy tale is able to lead us back to the original phase, in which it is possible to hypothesize the congruency of the conflictual visions of *fabula* and *historia*. This congruency declines precisely at the moment that the fairy tale begins its voyage, accentuating constantly its *fabulousness* at the expense of *historicity*, which is obliged to follow an independent path.

From my point of view, we can divide the parabola of the fairy tale into five fundamental phases, according to a scheme that tends to claim wider validity, to the point of including the entire sphere of narrative expression. The scheme is a general one, within which it is possible to observe the specific path taken by each fairy tale. Thus, as it is possible to individuate what develops along the entire spectrum of the five phases, it is also possible to verify what restricts it to a more limited arc, arresting its course in an intermediate phase or skipping one or more phases and moving directly from the first to the last. This variety of outcomes is explained by the fact that each of the phases following the first always represents a narrative form that, although susceptible to transformation (with the passing of time, the spreading into space, and the change of the narrating subjects), also possesses the capacity/opportunity to arrest the chain of mutation and to crystallize it.

At the basis of any disquisition concerning narrativity, and all the more so regarding the fairy tale, it is necessary to theorize the existence of a *preliminary* phase, corresponding to the moment at which what will later be absorbed and expressed by the narrative act itself is *enacted* or only *imagined*. In substance, this is the phase, constantly evoked in the preceding pages, which up to now has been indicated by the neutral and all-inclusive term *event*, which is moreover the term adopted by Foster. Foster also speaks about *experience*, a notion that better reflects the *lived* nature of so much of the material connected to the folk narrative. But neither term weds itself now to the needs of a discourse that is becoming deeper and more specific.

It seems to me indispensable, therefore, to adopt a less neutral term, more suited to reflect the characters and values intrinsic as much to the fairy tale as to the narrative tradition as a whole. Both ambits cannot, in fact, be restricted or extended, according to point of view, within a perspective in which any event has the faculty to propose itself as a source of inspiration. Potentially, nothing is irreducible to a narrative rendering. But this capacity must measure itself with a set of parameters that regulate its approach to the context, whether real or imaginary. I refer back to what was said in the previous chapter about the fairy tale as a vehicle of meaning. An effective meaningfulness can only be obtained if the discourse starts from a background that forms a repository of what is recognized as really meaningful. One presumes, therefore, that all that passes from pure *eventuality* to the narrative act is held to pertain to this exemplary background, a background in which lie the indispensable foundations for a discourse that aspires to acquiring universal validity. Here, inevitably, the term *myth* returns to our attention, to the extent that it seems to me the best adapted to expressing the sense of the concepts to be included in the first phase of the fairy tale. The word *myth*, in the lowercase, having been already adopted in a somewhat different perspective, is now taken up again.

We have already seen the significance which Myth (with a capital letter) had for the narrative tradition. In the wake of this, one now comes to deal with *myth*. It returns to the idea of the primordial, from which every story flows and gains substance. In this term, it is possible both to distinguish a system of data, parameters, and factors of *archetypal* scope[2] and to recognize the presence of figures and events in a context in which the common notions of reality and fiction[3] intersect so closely as to render a repertory of themes and motifs that give origin to the most varied of narrative modalities. Interpreting as myth every event, or part of it, that lies at the origin of a narrative tradition implies recognizing its independence from questions linked, for example, to the common notions of veracity or credibility. Any event able to distinguish itself from limited context of time and space and to be absorbed even within the simplest narrative elaboration ceases to be an event and becomes myth. Beginning as the patrimony of a single individual, this situation extends to take in an ever wider community, given that the circumstances favor its diffusion. In any case, that particular myth will enrich a patrimony in which all the exigencies of narrative will be satisfied. Myth is to be considered as the first indispensable phase with which the evolutionary parabola of the fairy tale must measure itself. Myth can be considered as such insofar as it provides the evolutionary parabola that the fairy tale must embrace. It can be conceived as the ground zero of narration, in that it furnishes the material that can potentially be narrated. At least one successive phase is required, however, that is capable of fashioning, according to the given narrative canon, this material itself, so that it is effectively available to an audience that can enter into the *virtuous circle* of narrativity.

Myth is followed by the phase of the *anecdote*, which should be interpreted as the simplest phase of narration since it refers to the first testimony available for a particular event. Anecdote is the passage leading to a personal experience, undergone in the first person, indirectly or in pure imagination. It opens itself to an initial relationship with the exterior. It is fair to say that this second phase functions as a channel through which the myth in question embeds itself in a narrative context. And it is in this eminently *pragmatic* context that resides its main function and its extreme instability on the temporal plane, in the sense that it maintains its validity only insofar as the account of its narrator lasts. Nor is it without significance that one speaks here of an *account* and not of a story, to the extent that there is still no authentic narrative *project*. This is true in the sense that the properly narrative function is superimposed by the *informative* function, which renders the *anecdotalist* no more than a source—the only one—that can furnish visibility to an event perhaps far distant from the listening community.

One may speak of a project only when the anecdote is taken up by a member of the audience, one who is capable of grasping a narrative quality in what he has heard from the source and of exerting himself, so that the anecdote may take the next step and become *legend* (note the use of the lowercase to avoid confusion with the use made previously of the same word). This marks the third phase of the narrative elaboration of the fairy tale. At this level, myth depends above all on the logic of the *community*, in the sense that, spreading within a given community, it undergoes a process of appropriation on the basis of which its meaning depends strictly on the conditions and the needs of those who are at the same time beneficiary and recreator of the narration. Legend involves *participation* in what is narrated, since it remains thus only as far as the link is preserved between the event and the context in which it was received for the first time (which, moreover, is presumably where it was set). Hence, preserving this link implies preserving, in theory at least, the *truth* of what is narrated because in this way one preserves a founding tradition for the community.

The fairy tale can arrest its development in the legendary phase, and there are outstanding examples of this in Yeats' collection. This is all the more plausible when narrative tradition remains confined within the limits of a small community in which oral transmission, albeit altering in form and content, maintains its original value as a legend connected to local myth. It is also the case that legend can be acquired as such thanks to the advent of writing, which imposes an artificial limit on the evolution of the fairy tale. But writing can also move in the opposite direction,

permitting a legendary plot to pass into the fourth phase, perhaps by intervening directly on the anecdote or even on myth itself and immediately giving it a *folktale rendering*. The *folktale* (*fiaba* in the original Italian
of this text) is in fact the fourth phase of the evolution of the fairy tale, a
phase, that can be reached also on the basis of the natural oral progression
of the legend. It is certain that, with the process being illustrated here,
folklore allows always more space to literature, orality to writing. The
phase of the folktale comes into play when community logic is replaced
by a wider one in which narration, rather than limiting myth to a more
or less particular context, displays its general value, so that more than one
community is capable of recognizing itself. This explains how, in this
phase, the concept of a more or less historical truth is replaced by a wider
human truth,[4] without taking into account that the purely aesthetic value
of the story gains greater relevance. These changes of perspective are reflected in the form and content of the folktale, which tends to obliterate
any precise reference to time and place and to stylize its characters, thus
giving an increasingly accentuated impression of *artificialness*,[5] or at least
of an elaboration on the part of a narrator for whom the consistency of
the myth narrated has decidedly passed into the background. Moreover,
it is the inexorable passing of time itself that tends to distance to an ever
greater degree the traditional memory of the original source[6] and subject
it to the "jurisdiction of narrative laws of type and genre."[7]

In any case, the fairy tale, even in the phase of the folktale, continues
to be the product of an oral tradition, regardless of the extent to which
the latter has widened its perspective with respect to the restricted original
context. The phase of the legend and of the folktale are the two fundamental levels, coexisting and evolving into each other,[8] through which
the patrimony of myths pertaining to a particular tradition gains narrative
expression. The fairy tales in Yeats' collection conform to this. Despite
how they have been modified more or less in the transition from orality
to writing, they are the popular elaboration, in the broadest sense of the
term, of all that enters into the category, adopted in the last chapter, of the
imaginative store. This store is made up of myths that are identifiable as such,
in that they have been elaborated through the process, complete or partial,
of anecdote–legend–folktale. Without this store, Yeats' and Stephens' collections would have been inconceivable, as would scientific works, such as
the *Handbook of Irish Folklore* by Ó Suillebhain, which attempts to gather
the entire corpus of themes and motifs in the Irish tradition. If we isolate,
within this repertory, the chapter entitled *Mythological Tradition*, we find
ourselves in practice dealing with all the myths from which the greater part

of our fairy tales originate and gain substance, since this section contains the most relevant number of figures and events connected to the category of the indefinite.[9] This repertory can never be considered definitive, both because it is always possible that a new myth will emerge on which to build a tradition and because it is fair to think that others have been canceled out by an insufficient narrative tradition, either through conscious choice or unfavorable conditions.

The evolutionary parabola of the fairy tale does not exhaust its potential here, however. There is in fact a fifth phase, which leads to a definitive detachment, on the one hand, from the oral context and, on the other, from the folkloric. This narrative form that, in the absence of a valid alternative, I shall call the *novella*, avoiding thus both the insufficiently precise term *tale* and the adoption of the word *fiction*, which would probably provide the most exact sense of what one is attempting to theorize.[10] (The original value of the "novella" will be set aside, despite the fact that no great difference exists between it and the topic under consideration here.) By *novella* is intended the literary story, hence it refers to the phase in which the fairy tale has been completely absorbed into a literary logic, in which the original myth has been completely uprooted from its live context and is transferred to an absolutely aesthetic context, subject to the poetic of a single author, who is always a writer. In this way, the fairy tale ceases to be common property and ceases to undergo the continual alteration of oral reworking. In this phase, an artistic object is produced and deposited once and for all in the literary tradition. Whereas in the preceding phase writing was an external factor that arrested an evolution in action, the novella is immediately identified with the form that written elaboration imposes at the origin. Thus, if a writer is the first to approach a myth handed down in no other form, an immediately definitive version of this myth will be transmitted. In the case in which this writer is a historian, the myth will be subjected to the more rigid laws of historiography and transmitted as a historically real event, attested to by a written document. The consequence is, if testimony such as that, for example, cited in the last chapter of Giraldus Cambrensis regarding the ghostly island is considered reliable, then it will take on the value of *historia* and can aspire to being studied from a scientific viewpoint; if, on the other hand, it is not considered reliable and is the pure fruit of invention, then we are dealing with an approach of *fabula* within the creative logic of the author in question. Writing, therefore, in parting from the one source, can impose both a historical and a literary tradition.

The texts collected by Stephens are certainly fairy tales and derive certainly from elaboration in legend or folktale of a tradition with its roots in mythical patrimony. However, these texts have been absorbed into a fully formed poetic, for which the figures and events inherited from tradition assume an entirely innovative value, comprehensible exclusively for their author, who is the most advanced exponent of a formal and thematic evolution which, as has been seen, is divided into five phases. While the logic of Yeats' collection is that of faithful conservation—beyond the more or less wide margins of literary elaboration introduced by the collectors—of a narrative patrimony that maintains, even in a written context, its relationship with the oral and popular background, in Stephens we observe a decisive leap toward the independence of the text, in which the fairy tale becomes to all effects a literary genre, that we have defined as the novella.

What has been preserved, from the first to the fifth phase, is the dialectic definite–indefinite, without which one could not speak of the fairy tale. *The Twelve Wild Geese*[11] is one of the purest examples of the folktale, but no one can prevent us from thinking that if Yeats had been capable of approaching the same fairy tale one or two centuries previously, he would have found it in the legendary phase, with whole series of precise references to the original context. Likewise, what seems actually to be a fairy tale still in the anecdotal phase—*How Thomas Connolly Met the Banshee*[12]—if it had been collected a few years later, could already have been a folktale, with Thomas Connolly transformed into an anonymous hero in search of adventure. In each case, one is dealing with forms that can decline from one moment to the next, in which the movement manifests itself and, albeit in an altering context, breaks down each time the barriers separating one or two dimensions of the real. This movement should be read as the unchanging peculiarity of the fairy tale, and it is only on the basis of it that one can set up a profound comparison with other narrative ambits. The five-phased model of evolution just outlined is only the exterior manifestation that can plausibly be discovered in contexts that lie outside the fairy tale, since the model not only traces back narrative processes, but also traces more widely historical and cultural ones.

The Fairy Tale and the Pseudo-Fairy Tale

It has already been said that Stephens' collection should justly be considered a collection of fairy tales, at least according to the canons developed in the course of this research. Each of the ten tales is effectively founded

on the dialectic of definite–indefinite, two notions that gain specific meaning on the basis of a precise theoretical framework. However, one should
note that when reading the text of *The Little Brawl at Allen*[13] not even the
shadow of this dialectic appears almost until the end. It is, in fact, the narration of a contest, as cruel as it is comic, between the ranks of two Fenian
heroes, Fionn and Goll mac Morna, characters belonging to the same
dimension, and the tale lacks even minimum intervention from indefinite
figures. The events take place on the plane of Legend (note the capital letter), until in the last paragraph it is narrated how Goll mac Morna liberates
Fionn and his knights from the Christian hell: there is, therefore, an opening toward the transcendent indefinite, the Otherworld imported by St.
Patrick's preaching.[14] Without this, it would have been impossible, strictly
speaking, to rank it as a fairy tale.

On the other hand, the following story, *The Carl of the Drab Coat*,[15] is
based on events set almost entirely in the indefinite dimension, in which
Fionn again interacts with his army: here, one is dealing with a fairy tale
in the fullest sense of the term.[16] What distinguishes one from the other,
given that both belong to the same category, is the *fairy density*, if one can
use such an expression, in the sense that one tale allows much more space
than the other to interaction with the indefinite. The second story furnishes a much more detailed image of an otherworldly dimension, whereas
in the first, this seems to be a simple corollary to a story focused on a far
different theme. Thus, one is faced with quantitative differences, just as in
both cases the context remains, so to speak, that of the *pure* fairy tale.

The issue becomes more delicate when one comes to examine the
stories in Yeats' collection. Can one consider as a fairy tale a story that
narrates the conflict (or better, the lack of conflict) between Finn and
Cú Chulainn, or between two heroes both belonging to the plane of
Legend?[17] And how is one supposed to assess the events narrated in *The
Haughty Princess*,[18] in which a prince and princess pertaining absolutely to
the same dimension first confront each other and then get married? Finally,
what should one say about the tricks with which Donald O'Nery repays
the misdeeds of his two jealous neighbors?[19] From a theoretical point of
view, all three stories are absolutely extraneous to the logic recognized up
to now in the fairy tale. In none of them does a dialectic occur between
totally different dimensions—everything takes place on a one-dimensional
plane. In these stories, one is dealing with three exceptions from a whole
made up of pure fairy tales. Into what category should these three exceptions be placed? There seem to be two possible paths to a solution. On the
one hand, one could eliminate the adjective "fairy" and define the three

stories in question as simply unspecified "tales." In this case, the fairy tale would become a more complex expression of a zero degree represented by the one-dimensional tale. On the other, one could examine the texts more deeply, to discover whether sufficient elements exist to make them candidates, albeit by a shortcut, for the class of fairy tale. This second path would profile instead the existence (or at least the identification) of spurious forms gravitating around the fundamental category of the fairy tale, a sort of constellation of *pseudo-fairy tales.*

Adopting the first strategy would mean recognizing the importance of the theoretical framework through which the notions of the definite and the indefinite were individuated, notions based on a conceptually complex systematization of the world, so that a story becomes a fairy tale only if it can make this complexity perceptible. From this point of view, it is permissible to infer that the simple tale, whatever its exterior characteristics might be, represents a *limitation* to the more authentic potential of narration. What may be simply evoked or imagined by a tale becomes *real* in the fairy tale. Confrontations that remain imaginary in the tale, in the fairy tale gain *pragmatic* consistency. The three stories in question, therefore, are located beyond the threshold discussed in a previous chapter and develop a dialectic between characters in a system that remains closed to the exterior. Hence, their epiphanic value is limited to a context that is presumably known from the beginning.

If, instead, one examines the texts under discussion according to a less rigid conception of the dialectic of definite–indefinite (and is thus less obsequious to the multidimensional conception proper to the Irish fairy tale), it is possible to recognize elements that, organized from the correct point of view, can identify alternative or weak variants of the fundamental, strong model of the fairy tale—almost as if the latter were the first source of storytelling, from which forms gradually less marked by the original dialectic descend. Hence, the contest between Finn and Cú Chulainn would be confrontation between a *more definite* character (Finn) and a *less definite* one (Cúu Chulainn), according to a model that has been reorganized with respect to one of real opposition between the pure definite and the pure indefinite.[20] Nor should one undervalue the fact that two concepts, such as those just evoked, can be interpreted in a different manner depending on the space–time context in which they are elaborated. Thus, one may also hypothesize a context, human or purely narrative, in which Finn and Cú Chulainn represent the maximum tension between definite and indefinite. Just as, vice versa, a context can be hypothesized in which such a tension cannot be established insofar as everything is perceived in a definite key and no element is able to institute an indefinite dimension: this holds true when considering the situation presented in the age of Myth. In practice, the value assigned to the notions of the definite and the indefinite is connected to a sort of *preestablished pact* between the storyteller and his audience, between the text and its context, which, in its totality, accounts for the plausibility of the fairy tale. From this point of view, it is with some surprise that one notes the presence of the three pseudo-fairy tales found between the pages of a collection oriented programmatically toward demonstrating the dialectic between parallel planes of reality. However, one would be no less surprised to come across a drift into the fairy tale within a collection of realistic tales. In both cases, an ineluctable fact remains: narrative—and above all apparently irreconcilable cultural typologies—can, according to the context in which they operate or on the basis of specific choices of the storyteller, cross paths and give birth to narrative products that cannot be better specified, or that can be most correctly characterized precisely by virtue of their *mixed* nature.

The fact remains, however, that one may conceive of a sort of antithesis between the neutral notion of the tale and the qualitatively determined notion of the fairy tale through a confrontation in terms of the approach to the reality narrated. If one is justified in maintaining that every story requires a dialectic to be set up between *one's own* and *the others'*—hence to a relationship between at least two poles at a more or less greater distance from each other—it is equally correct to recognize the substantial nature of this relationship. When literature sends its characters off on otherworldly journeys or faces them with supernatural apparitions, events that, in general, overflow any threshold of verisimilitude more or less imposed or more or less accepted, it constructs an *effective* relationship between one's own and the others'. It operates analogously to the situation of the storyteller, who acts in such a way as to lift the veil that normally hinders human perception. It is as if, in syntony with what happens in the field of the oral tradition, an *open system* existed, in which the story unveils a universe whose confines separating space–time dimensions reveal themselves to be porous and open to an exchange between planes of reality that otherwise would be hidden from each other. When at least one character is allowed not only to depart and move in a horizontal direction, but also to escape (moving, therefore, in a vertical direction), it seems fair to me to recognize in the story a fairy tale. The latter denomination models itself clearly on an Irish context, influenced decisively by the interaction between folklore and literature, and hence set against a determinate background of myths (in the sense given in this chapter) in which *fabula* and *historia* interpenetrate, but which could equally permit the identification of a given whole transcending the narrow limits of a single narrative tradition.

However, just as limiting ourselves to the Irish context has made it possible to elaborate a certain idea of the fairy tale, in the same way one must limit the field of research when one moves to examining that area pertaining to the *closed system*. This area is delineated by an unspecified conception of the tale, in which there exists the expression of a universe containing an impermeable barrier between a preexisting reality and another potentially extending above or below it. The character of this sort of tale is able to depart, to make a movement, but, in effect, he remains anchored to his plane of origin—that of History—even when he simulates, perhaps through an act of imagination connected to the fairy tale itself, an escape to a territory lying beyond an insurmountable border. It is necessary, then, to recognize James Joyce as an author who best presents, in a work that re-evokes the narrative collections examined up to now, a tale built in this way. This author is as close as possible, in time and space, to those who have been chosen as representatives of the fairy tale, one who has perhaps taken a critical stance with respect to the literary renewal of the traditional patrimony adopted as a source for the specific definition of the fairy tale.

The Joycian Tale in the Light of the Fairy Tale

Joyce was a writer who, from the outset, maintained an openly dissonant attitude to the Irish Revival and substantially rejected a certain "imaginative incompleteness and senility of mind,"[21] expressed by the folk narratives that so many of his colleagues strove to recover from the living voice of the peasants. Joyce chose voluntary exile to limit the influence, which he maintained detrimental, of his homeland on his creativity. He could express, therefore, in the most effective manner, the capacity of literature to free itself of the conditioning of the oral and popular tradition. To test the solidness of this hypothesis, it would be opportune to examine Joyce's short story collection, *Dubliners*, as a text that can most easily be compared to the collections of Yeats and Stephens. Examining this on the basis of the criteria established in the analysis of the fairy tale, we seek to locate a less neutral and more specific sense and link it to the notion of the tale and everything connected with it. The objective I have set myself, conscious of the limits of such partial research, is that of discovering what type of relationship exists between two ambits that could create a fundamental bipartition in the field of narrative, just as they could institute a sort of convergence on shared ground, where eventual relationships of dependency between one and the other might perhaps be perceived.

It seems to me that *Dubliners* can be considered the ideal and most coherent conclusion of the process that began with the works of Yeats and Stephens. Whereas Yeats' text represents the complete acquisition of a national tradition in which folklore makes its entrance into a renewed literary context, and whereas in Stephens there is a partial readoption of this, in keeping with a more autonomous literary poetics, Joyce's text displays instead a definitive detachment of literature from tradition, or rather—in keeping with our aim—of the tale from the fairy tale. Through *Dubliners*, it is in fact possible to take a step backward and reconnect to the ambit from which Yeats made his start. The stories set in Joyce's Dublin seem to provide the most representative image of the antithesis between closed and open systems, but in this same context, the idea of a synthesis between the two forms of the same universe seems perceptible or conceivable.

Although admitting that this is not the most suitable context in which to attempt an intensive analysis of a work as complex as *Dubliners*, which would also require a parallel treatment of the rest of Joyce's work, I shall approach a reading of the text in question by isolating a few significant passages, best adapted to the scope in hand and examined naturally through the more or less deforming interpretative lens consolidated in the preceding pages. These brief passages are nonetheless capable, in my opinion, of revealing a deep structure that sustains the work as a whole. This structure manifests itself with certain immediacy in *An Encounter*, which, as Harry Levin correctly deduces, is a crucial crossroads, with its emblematic title, for a large part of the other stories in the collection.[22] This observation evinces a theme (which is also a narrative instrument) central to *Dubliners*—that of the *encounter*, in which two or more characters, antithetical in some way and repositories of more or less divergent worldviews, cross paths on their journey through Dublin and set up a more or less close confrontation.

The main character of *An Encounter* is a boy who, like his playmates, is enthralled by the marvels evoked "in the literature of the Wild West,"[23] hence by a reality that is entirely *another* with regard to the limited space of the city. An authentic attraction leads the narrating voice toward the limitless horizons of the American plains. His desire for adventure is expressed eloquently: "I wanted real adventures to happen to myself. But real adventures, I reflected, do not happen to people who remain at home: they must be sought abroad."[24]

On the one hand, there is the need to escape, and on the other, the awareness that a movement is required to reach the desired dimension. For as long as the boy continues to simulate the adventure while staying at home with his friends—and thus on the definite plane—the situation is still that of initial stasis. More particularly, it seems to me that one can introduce a specific concept, that of ELUSIO, in the Latin etymological sense of being *ex-* (out of) *lusio* (play, entertainment), intending the second term as much in an immediate meaning of hedonistic pleasure as in a profounder sense of spiritual wholeness.

Just as the hero of a fairy tale, the character in Joyce's story decides to escape from his context, to enter into material contact with a superior dimension known only through stories told by others. His journey to the Pigeon House—in reality simply a power-station—is to be understood as if it were a *movens*, a long voyage toward something never seen before from close quarters. However, the journey is too long and costly to be brought to an end and must finish in a field that is simply far from home. In this field, the interaction of the main character and his companion with the indefinite takes place. The indefinite takes on the appearance of an old man, the encounter with whom provides the title of the story and is therefore the most important section. This phase of interaction can be read, in this context, as a sort of ILLUSIO, also here adopting the etymological sense of *in-lusio*, hence of being within the game that previously was only imagined.

It is nonetheless clear that this equivocal character, albeit other than the main character, is far distant from the mysterious and coveted Pigeon House. From this viewpoint, therefore, the term *illusion* should also be read in the immediate sense of a *deception* undergone by the hero who has searched for the indefinite in the wrong place—rather, a real escape has been denied him.

Faced by this discovery, there is no alternative but for the hero to retrace his steps (*rediens*), with the added fear of having met a character who is perceived as being dangerous. The boy returns to the everyday reality from which he had attempted to escape for a day, but which in the end imposed itself to reestablish the situation of initial immobility without anything new having been brought into play by the movement. This is the final stasis, which should be interpreted in the canons of a DELUSIO, in which to the etymological sense of *provenance* and *exit* from (*de*) the game (*lusio*) should be added the specific sense of the Italian term *delusione* (disappointment), or rather that of an experience that has betrayed one's expectations.

Proceeding in such a way as to re-evoke the form of the fairy tale, Joyce's story has demonstrated the previously mentioned impermeability that encloses the definite plane identified by the tale. Whereas in the fairy tale, the hero witnessed an epiphany of another world, the hero of this tale observes an auto-epiphany of his own world which, deceptively, does nothing else than continually reassert itself. It is not by chance that Joyce himself spoke of *Dubliners* as the expression of *paralysis*, on both the dynamic and the mental levels. The same can be said regarding the use of the term *epiphany*, from which transpires as much the *meaningfulness* of the story as the degraded revisitation of a concept originally of far deeper significance.[25]

In the attempt to clarify further the structure of *An Encounter*—in which it is possible to recognize a form that practically distinguishes almost all other texts in the collection—it would be opportune to provide an illustration (see figure 8.1):

Figure 8.1.

Here, the arrows represent, respectively, *movens* and *rediens*, and one can see how the movement of the tale is enclosed within a polygon. Thus, the duration of the movement is limited by the restricting net of a context from which it is impossible to escape, one that allows only the *appearance* of motion.

But if the hero had succeeded in reaching the Pigeon House, could one have spoken then of a real escape, and hence of a fairy tale? This same question was posed regarding those three stories of Yeats that deviate from the norm, where we posited that it might be better to introduce the category of the pseudo-fairy tale. Also in *An Encounter*, it is correct to recognize that the Dublin power-station (The Pigeon House) cannot, strictly speaking, incarnate the category of the indefinite, but it is equally permissible to perceive in the main character's sublimated vision of this place the visible *materialization* of his dreams of escape, the only concrete possibility of reaching a reality that is *other* than everyday monotony. Under this light, the Pigeon House could be interpreted as a *pseudo-indefinite* and the tale would enter into the category of the pseudo-fairy tale.

We know, however, that the destination is not reached and that *An Encounter* therefore moves in an absolutely horizontal space. This space is also totally closed in on itself, as exemplified in the graphic illustrating the dynamic and conceptual progression underlying the story. This is demonstrated by the rest of Joyce's collection, in which one discovers an irreconcilable opposition between a vague desire to escape and the constant frustration of this posed by a static and hermetically sealed environment. No less significant in this regard are other passages from the text, in which one can see with further clarity this approach to Joyce's narration.

In *The Boarding House*, regarding the male character who has been trapped in a net laid by a mother in search of a husband for her daughter, one reads: "He longed to ascend through the roof and fly away to another country where he would never hear again of his trouble, and yet a force pushed him downstairs step by step."[26]

The man, finding himself with no way out, desires to *fly* from the roof and to land *in another country*, serving himself therefore of an authentic fairy tale image. His flight is purely imaginary, however, since he remains confined to the ground by an unknown *force*. He would like to move *skyward*, symbol at once of salvation and liberty, but the context obliges him to go downstairs, to remain at a *lower level* and to accept the consequences of the trap laid for him by the mistress of the boarding house and her daughter. If any character manages to escape from the initial stasis, it is the daughter who, with her mother's help, succeeds in making the man marry her. She abandons the family boarding house and moves to a less definite context.

In *A Little Cloud*, Little Chandler, enchanted by the exotic fascination emanating from an old friend from his student days coming to visit from London, reaches out toward a new life in an *elsewhere* that is even specified: "Every step brought nearer to London, *further from his own sober inartistic life*."[27] A few pages further on, the main character finds himself again faced by the opening dilemma: "Could he go to London? There was *the furniture* still to be paid for."[28] Following a revelatory encounter, the hero becomes aware of the prosaicness of his life, compared to the poetic life that his friend leads in faraway London. Hence, the desire matures to reach that indefinite place in which he hopes to make a decisive change in his life. However, returning home, the prosaic consideration that there is furniture to pay off is enough to dissuade him from any real movement and to fix him once and for all in the definitive stasis of Dublin.

In *Counterparts*, the main character, Farrington, lives a gray existence confined to an anonymous office. This is the ideal situation in which to instill a strong desire to escape to an elsewhere that would give sense to an absolutely static life: "His *imagination* had so *abstracted* him that his name was called twice before he answered."[29] Once again, it is the imagination

CHAPTER 8

that leads the hero far away from reality, if only for an instant, to a much more satisfying dimension than that in which he really lives. However, at the second call, he is obliged to return, also in the mind, to the close confines of his workplace. Farrington's frustrating condition becomes even clearer in the compensation he seeks by getting drunk in the pub, then returning home and mistreating his son, on whom the rage of a man continually constrained to coexist with an unsatisfying definite vents itself.

We have seen three examples demonstrating unequivocally the closure imposed by the city, but also the inability of the characters of the tales to pass the threshold of the imagination, to acknowledge and give substance to their desires. A claustrophobic environment has unfolded before our eyes, closed in on itself. Here, too, are an array of authentic *antiheroes*, who never manage to undertake the journey leading finally to the discovery of the indefinite lying beyond the limited, but comforting, reality of Dublin. The escape takes place on an exclusively mental level, where there is no risk of being overcome by the unpredictable experience of the other, or rather of what escapes consciousness, because no one has taken the responsibility of leaving and returning with testimony of the epiphany of another world to share with their community.

However, an examination of *Dubliners* cannot exhaust itself with the awareness of the stories being incapable of transforming themselves into fairy tales or even pseudo-fairy tales. To glimpse more enticing horizons, it is necessary to approach the most complex story, which significantly closes the collection. I refer to *The Dead*, a text in which the dialectic of the tale–fairy tale opens on a far wider perspective and permits therefore a far deeper understanding of the phenomenon under examination. In effect, for almost all the long story, we seem to find ourselves immobilized in the classical Dublin situation, between the four walls of a house in which is celebrated the traditional rite of Christmas dinner, during which range of definite humanity does no more than reflect itself. Only the last pages open up an unexpected horizon, when the young couple Gabriel and Gretta Conroy, return to their hotel. There, the woman is surprised by the memory of a youth, Michael Furey, so in love with her as to have unhesitatingly put his delicate health at risk, up to the point of encountering an early death. This traumatic event emerging from the past disturbs not only Gretta but also Gabriel. Two passages are particularly significant regarding what happens to the main character:

> A vague terror seized Gabriel at his answer ["I think he died for me," as Gretta says regarding the death of Michael Furey], as if, at that hour when

he had hoped to triumph, some *impalpable* and vindictive *being* was coming against him, gathering forces against him in *its vague world*.[30]

His soul had approached that region where dwell the *vast hosts of the dead*. He was conscious of, but could not apprehend, *their wayward and flickering existence*. His own identity was fading out *into a grey impalpable world: the solid world* itself, which these dead had one time reared and lived in, *was dissolving and dwindling*.[31]

The first quotation reports Gabriel's reaction to a critical moment of his wife's story, when she reveals that a boy died out of love for her. He becomes aware of the presence of an *impalpable being*, coming from an indefinite (*vague*) world, which seems ready to revenge itself, at his cost, for its bad luck. The main character, although remaining in a hotel room, perceives the presence of a figure pertaining to the indefinite true and proper; he becomes the witness of an invasion by a figure pertaining to the transcendent. His experience is a purely interior one, to the extent that Gretta is not even slightly aware of it (at least as far as the narrator lets us know), but it is nonetheless indicative to note that, after so many vague attempts at escape, in the last tale Joyce, putting a close to the context of Dublin, should include mention of an interaction with an indefinite dimension.

The second paragraph portrays Gabriel's situation after his wife has finished her story and fallen asleep. He is alone now and is aware of an episode from Gretta's past of which he had been completely ignorant. This awareness is an epiphany in the fullest sense of the term, because through it the main character enters into contact with a dimension to which he had paid no attention until now. His wife's story leads his soul almost to detach itself from his body and escape into a region inhabited by the "vast hosts of the dead," no longer just Michael but all those who pertain to the otherworldly dimension that now presents itself to Gabriel's perception. He is not simply imagining an escape into another world, but is conscious of the existence of a world parallel to that in which he is living, of its different nature and of the elusiveness of a world that removes itself from the definite laws of the solid world. Through the altered consciousness of the hero (no longer an antihero), two dimensions coincide in the same space; it does not seem that one is dealing with a purely interior interaction, since Gabriel feels his identity disappear and sees his definite reality dissolve, both absorbed into a "grey world" that seems to want to envelope the entire universe. It is as if a primigenial unity of being were being reestablished, as if one were returning, albeit in a decidedly faded light, to the one-dimensionality of Myth. In the last tale, one observes therefore a sort of drift into the fairy tale, or that the narration, which until this moment had remained within an absolutely definite context, has now found the way to break down the barriers of an exceedingly oppressive realism. If we consider *Dubliners* as one long story, we can note how, after numerous failed attempts to reach an epiphany from a world that is other than the static point of departure, one arrives in the finale itself at reestablishing the link with a dimension that was believed buried for good. Hence, *Dubliners* is a fairy tale, although of extremely low *fairy density*. In any case, *The Dead* seems to demonstrate that the conceivableness of the fairy tale has not entirely disappeared. It remains a narrative potentiality that simply needs the correct conditions in which to manifest itself. And the correct conditions are provided not by any real movements of the characters, but by the narrativity of the text itself, as demonstrated by Gretta's *tale within the tale*, through which the gates of the fairy tale open for Gabriel.

More generally, in Yeats' work as in Stephens' and Joyce's, one observes the efforts made by the story and its narrator to upset the stasis of the real through more or less *extraordinary* encounters. Nothing of any importance would happen if it were not for the epiphany provided by the narrative movement. The profoundest potentiality of this movement expresses itself in the fairy tale, but this requires the active participation of its characters and for the suitable conditions to manifest itself. Hence, when this cannot occur, the tale, despite availing itself of a more limited and limiting point of view, operates in such a way as to invest reality with the *magic* of the other, an operation that acquires all the more value in a context—such as Joyce's Dublin—that would seem to offer only the barest resources for the development of a narrative discourse. The analysis of *Dubliners* demonstrates how, between the *realist* tale, in the broad sense of the term, and the fairy tale no effective antithesis exists, but rather a convergence in the common intention to displace the "nightmare of history," to quote Joyce. On the one hand, the realist tale depends on the fairy tale as far as the means—structural and conceptual—adopted to appropriate the tellable material are concerned. On the other hand, the fairy tale depends on the realist tale for the formation of a static context in which to begin the exploration of the (probably boundless) universe that is intrinsic to the idea of the fairy tale.

Notes

1. See *supra*, "Introduction," 22.

2. Cf. Frye, *The Archetypes of Literature*, 16: "The myth is the central informing power that gives archetypal *significance* to the ritual and archetypal *narrative* to the oracle" (my italics).

3. There can be no distinction in a field in which there tends to prevail a substantial unity of concepts which only later, in parallel to a certain evolution of humanity, could be theorized separately. This discourse is very close to that concerning Myth as the first stage of the Irish narrative tradition. One can say that myth, in its independence from a precise space–time context, renders something feasible each time that, in the Myth in question, was confined to a rationally inaccessible past. Cf. David Bidney, *Myth, Symbolism, and Truth*, in *Myth: A Symposium*, ed. Thomas A. Sebeok (Bloomington: Indiana University Press, 1965), 8: "According to Cassirer's Neo-Kantian approach, we must understand the mythical symbol, not as a representation concealing some mystery or hidden truth, but as a self-contained form of interpretation of reality. In myth there is no distinction between the real and the ideal; the image is the thing and hence mythical thinking lacks the category of the ideal."

4. Cf. Foster, *Fictions of the Irish Literary Revival*, 216: "The transformation of personal experience into story does not mean that the original conviction or belief is rendered unfounded, insincere, or duplicitous: but it does mean that validity or sincerity or verifiability becomes irrelevant."

5. Here, the utility of the previously quoted contribution of Lüthi to the definition of the formal differences between *Sage* and *Märchen* becomes clear, once their pertaining to a common *platform* is recognized.

6. Cf. Zimmermann, *The Irish Story Teller*, 583: "After a certain time the eyewitness's account is replaced by a *stylized* and *stereotyped* version" (my italics).

7. Foster, *Fictions of the Irish Literary Revival*, 216.

8. Not only the natural progression anecdote–legend–folktale, since the opposite must be taken into consideration, a sort of *devolution*. Cf. ibid.: "I suspect, too, there might be some devolution: a *Märchen* . . . is localized, a local legend is passed off to the outsider as personal experience."

9. See Seán Ó Suillebhain, *A Handbook of Irish Folklore* (Dublin: Educational Co. of Ireland for Folklore of Ireland Society, 1942), 440–519.

10. Cf. Frye, *The Anatomy of Criticism*, 366: "FICTION: Literature in which the radical of presentation is the printed or written word, such as novels and essays."

11. See Yeats, *Irish Fairy Tales*, 297–303.

12. See ibid., 118–21.

13. See Stephens, *Irish Fairy Tales*, 157–72.

14. In Stephens' text, there is an authentic rebellion on the part of Goll mac Morna, who is not willing to allow his world be eaten up by the infernal *perdition* imposed by Christian law. His rebellion is successful, as if to confirm the capacity of Legend to survive the advent of a new Otherworld and its coexistence with the plane of History. In the following passage, one can see his attraction and nostalgia for a period more suited to the spirit of the last true exponent of the Irish Revival. See ibid., 172: "And, later on, when time did his worst on them all and the Fianna were sent to hell as unbelievers, it was Goll mac Morna who assaulted hell, with a chain in his great fist and three iron balls swinging from it, and it was

he who attacked the hosts of great devils and brought Fionn and the Fianna-Finn out with him."

15. See ibid., 173–200.

16. Stephens' first lines, moreover, leave little room for misunderstanding (ibid., 175): "One day something happened to Fionn, the son of Uail; that is, he departed from the world of men, and was set wandering in great distress of mind through Faery. He had days and nights there and adventures there, and was able to bring back the memory of these."

17. *A Legend of Knockmany*, in Yeats, *Irish Fairy Tales*, 283–96.

18. See ibid., 311–13.

19. *Donald and His Neighbours*, ibid., 317–20.

20. Albeit through the deforming lens of humor, which probably owes much to Carleton's transcription. In Cú Chulainn's return to Ireland to establish his superiority over Finn, who is guilty of having obscured his fame (but avoids the meeting in every way possible), one can glimpse a sort of confrontation between the epic idea of heroism, incarnated in the protagonist of the Ulster Cycle, and a more modern conception of it, reflected in the far from heroic behavior of Finn. Where the latter avoids direct conflict with Cú Chulainn, knowing he cannot compete on the level of brute force with an individual closer to Myth than himself and therefore more superhuman, and in the bloodless defeat that Cú Chulainn undergoes due to the tricks hatched by Finn's wife, one can read the incompatibility of the Celtic Heracles with a time in which Legend had assumed more fictional tones and required more human characters.

21. Foster, *Fictions of the Irish Literary Revival*, 203.

22. Cf. Harry Levin, introduction to *Dubliners*, by James Joyce, in *The Essential James Joyce* (London: Jonathan Cape, 1948), 21: "Not one but many of these sketches might be titled 'An Encounter.'"

23. Joyce, *Dubliners*, 29.

24. Ibid., 30.

25. Cf. Levin, introduction, 21: "In calling his original jottings 'epiphanies,' Joyce underscored the ironic contrast between the manifestation that dazzled the Magi and the apparitions that manifest themselves on the streets of Dublin; he also suggested that those pathetic and sordid glimpses, to the sentient observer, offer a kind of revelation."

26. Joyce, *Dubliners*, 62 (my italics).

27. Ibid., 66 (my italics).

28. Ibid., 73 (my italics).

29. Ibid., 78 (my italics).

30. Ibid., 172 (my italics).

31. Ibid., 174 (my italics).

Narrative Construction and Reconstruction of the World

9

Paradigm and Syntagma, *Fabula* and Plot

IS IT CORRECT TO SAY that a marked distinction is to be found between the *realistic* tale (pertaining in the broadest sense to the weak and limited conception of the tale developed in the last chapter) and what is defined as the *fairy* tale in the paradigmatic significance of the latter with respect to the more markedly syntagmatic approach of the former? Paradigm and syntagma are the two fundamental axes on which fairy tales, as well as any other narrative texts are constructed. They represent the vertical and horizontal dimensions within which the narration is modeled. Borrowing from linguistic theory, let us say that on the paradigmatic axis a *selection* is made, based on the choice of one element above others, all belonging to the same category or function, but each with its own semantic value. On the syntagmatic axis, there is instead a *combination* of the self-same elements that, each time, are extracted from the paradigmatic axis until, one after the other, they go to form a chain of varying length providing a determinate *sense* both to the simplest phrase and to the more complex tale. Whereas combination presupposes a more or less extended temporal development—and hence a *diachronic* dimension—selection is marked by the contemporary coexistence of elements lying on an indefinite number of planes, forming, as it were, an ideal edifice: the operation is effected therefore in a *synchronic* dimension. This consideration allows us to perceive in the syntagma the *univocal* realization of a narrative project which, remaining on the level of the paradigm, would contemplate an almost infinite number of realizations, always relegated nonetheless to the field of *potentiality*. History, understood as the irreversible succession of events that man has undergone in the temporal arc of his evolution, is the most explicit manifestation of the *unilinear* development following which the syntgmatic level of the narration unfolds. From the point of view of *historia*, it is only possible to follow and record the effective, and hence the only, concatenation of elements and actions on the basis of which a given event has developed diachronically. Each of the elements present, along with what has become *real*, is destined to oblivion or in any case to remain hidden, at least until history has taken an innovative path.

To ask to what extent the nature of the fairy tale can be considered paradigmatic in comparison to a certain syntagmaticity in the realistic tale, broadly speaking, implies research aimed at clarifying to what degree the first can bring to light all the signifying potential that the merely historical approach is incapable of unveiling and that the tale, circumscribed in the world of History, limits itself to evoking. The fairy tale, being the result of an interaction between folklore and literature, between collective tradition and individual innovation—and hence an accumulation, more or less amalgamated, of *historia* and *fabula*—is the ideal location for the meeting between a vertical dimension (depositary of potential planes of reality) and a horizontal dimension in continual and inexorable progress. From this point of view, the fairy tale is a means to preserve and indeed render explicit all those elements that, on the basis of a certain historical evolution, are to be found above and below the level of referral on which the *official* events of human history take place (up to now identified as the plane of History). As seen in the previous chapter, none of the myths pertaining to the Irish area would have come down to us if a narrative tradition had not been constituted in the course of time and capable of giving them a form. From this perspective, the fairy tale becomes above all the depository of precious semantic wealth, a perspective that gains ever greater weight when seen from the viewpoint of a literature oriented to reinforcing the link with an exemplary past. What becomes inevitable is an immediate paradigmatic reading of the fairy tale, as if it were the tool most suited to piercing the veil that time has progressively laid over the eyes of those who observe the world from a *partial* point of view.

Whatever its nature and ends may be, the tale necessarily develops in a horizontal dimension, is built up through the juxtaposition of logically linked elements, and takes on consistency thanks to the actions of a hero who consumes time and space in the name of those who either hear or read about his feats. However, these feats acquire an even deeper significance when the existence of a space–time dimension is perceived in them that is not perceptible to common sense. And the more importance that is given to the exploration of levels parallel to and simultaneously present with that of the one being used as a reference, the less predictable will it be to find in the tale—and hence on the part of the storyteller—a significant elaboration on the syntagmatic level, or rather within the *plot*.

Mentioning the plot leads us to consider the other fundamental pole individuated in the narratological debate, that of the *fabula*. *Fabula*, leaving aside the meaning that we have given it up to now, is "the content, or better its [the text's] cardinal elements, reorganized in logical and chrono-logical order," where by plot is understood in "the content of the text in the order in which it is presented."[1] In this definition can be found both the components on which to reconstruct the *content* of a narrative text, and also two specific orientations of view through which it is possible to direct the progress of a tale. Whereas on the axis of the *fabula* the interest is in the *substance* of the tale, on the axis of the plot increasing value is given to the *form* assumed by the elements going to make up the text. Whereas the *fabula* can be considered the simplest and most explicit stage of the expres-sion taken by a given myth (to remain faithful to our terminology), the plot is the progressive complication of the myth provided by the *fabula*, a complication through which—the more it moves ahead—the storyteller's formal elaboration increasingly operates.[2] Hence, although every tale is necessarily based on a *fabula* that, in its orderly *a posteriori* reconstruction, clearly evinces its paradigmatic value, it is the specific plot that makes it possible to perceive the content implicit on the syntagmatic level. Indeed, one *fabula* can give birth to a potentially infinite number of plots, since each storyteller, especially in an oral context, can organize the content of a given myth according to an order responding more or less to logical and chronological criteria and on the basis of collective necessity or personal taste. The many variants of a traditional tale are basically the outcome of the continual alteration and interweaving of a shared patrimony.

It should nevertheless be emphasized that, in the case of the popular storyteller—and even more so when his narration is a personal experience—what must above all be communicated is the specific nature of the element or elements with which he or his hero has come into contact. Hence, it is vital to follow as faithfully as possible a logically and chronologically ordered sequence, in such a way as not to distract the listener from the main theme but also to preserve the storyteller's memory;[3] form becomes strictly func-tional to the explication of a paradigmatic message, or of material dealing with the founding values of a community. Thus, its indispensable *recreational* function apart, the folk narrative, and therefore the fairy tale in particular, bases its general validity on the capacity to maintain constantly alive the relationship of the individual with a series of elements that constitute his most deeply rooted identity, focusing in particular on the individuation of an *otherness* that is fundamental in the fairy tale to a greater degree than elsewhere.

Tales oriented toward the explication of the universal dialectic between identity and otherness are characterized by a *perspective* view, one which, organized according to simple plot, goes well beyond merely chronological datum, being attracted instead to an atemporal sphere, as if every event did not *take place* but rather *existed*.[4] In this sense, the syntagmatic dimension becomes a sort of essential link between material that is perennially present and in potential and its recreation within the canons of rigid space–time schemes. What else is the structure identified as constitutive in the composition of the fairy tale if not this, a sort of *filter* through which myth becomes the tale, the tool by which what is beyond time and space acquires humanly valuable consistency? Lévi-Strauss was not entirely in the wrong, therefore, when in the famous debate with Propp, author of the *Morphology of the Folktale*, he proposed, for the analysis of the folktale, rather than Propp's chronological scheme with 31 Functions, one according to a *matrix* composed of a limited number of elements susceptible to transformation.[5] The latter system brought out the multidimensionality of the fairy tale and was capable of demonstrating how the narration, apart from being "in time (consisting of succession of events)" is also "beyond time (its signifying value is always in the present)."[6]

As seen in the examination of Joyce's *Dubliners* in the light of the fairy tale, the progression of the Joycian tale remains imprisoned in a dimension from which there is no effective escape. Hence, an in-depth selection of elements with which to compare characters pertaining to the historical level is not admitted. Leaving aside *The Dead*, what is developed in *Dubliners* is a dialectic between elements that can be traced back to a preexisting identity. One can see, therefore, how the author, operating on a limited paradigmatic axis, has concentrated his efforts on the plane of syntagmatic elaboration, lending complexity to the plot and making up for the lack of real depth by means of symbolism; he invests objects and actions pertaining to an absolutely historical plane with meanings not visible at first sight. From this viewpoint, too, one can explain the far greater attention to the description of setting and the marked individualization of the character, two characteristics that create a net distinction between the tale and the fairy tale precisely because the first requires greater *construction*—a further deepening of what lies, so to speak, at hand and not having the conceptual width of the second, which instead draws from surface elements not considered absolutely necessary.[7] Metaphor, in its function of linking far distant levels of meaning, makes sense in a context in which the character is allowed only to move horizontally; it becomes superfluous when the narration effectively contemplates *transference* beyond a purely historical dimension. Basically, the metaphorical process is located in a dialectic between *historia* and *fabula*, hence between reality as given and as imagined, a dialectic that emerges in differing quality and quantity according to the context under investigation. Proof of this is clearly given by the three narrative collections examined up to now, which, in the final analysis, identify three points of view from which to judge the capacity of the tale to relate the *stasis* of the real to the *movement* of the imagination (the latter term should be understood in an extremely *active* sense, in its capacity to recreate the datum of *historia*).[8]

In short, it is precisely through the comparison of points of view that it is possible to clarify how, from one tale to another, from one narrative context to another, the relationship varies between paradigmatic depth and syntagmatic extension, between *fabula* and plot, between the categories of identity and otherness. When Yeats decides to collect a certain number of fairy tales (or pseudo-fairy tales), his aim is mainly to save from disappearance not only the authentic production of his people, but also to find a way of narrating and, at the same time, of conceiving of reality. His objective, therefore, is to form a repertory *par excellence* on which to develop a literary movement. On the one hand, the fairy tale in itself is the purest expression of the *fabula*, in contrast to the complexity of the literary plot, to the extent that it is the main expression of a universe that represents paradigmatically the reality of an entire people whose identity, as previously mentioned, is built precisely on an incisive relationship with otherness. On the other, however, the fairy tale must be inserted into a wider dialectic, that in which a new idea of literature is opposed to a traditional one (where by traditional is intended to represent the literary canon imposed by the writers preceding the advent of the Irish Revival). An exclusively *contextual* object—such as the oral tale of the Irish peasantry—by means of an acquisition *from above*, is detached from a specific space–time context and is absorbed into the universal logic of the literary text. Already in this first passage, in substance from orality to writing, the original characteristics of the fairy tale inevitably undergo an evolution. This evolution leads the fairy tale to complicate, to a greater or lesser degree, according to the collector or the writer involved, its elementary plot, since, in consequence, the folkloric paradigm is distributed *with greater care* in the literary syntagma. A powerful opposition between identity and otherness as it is felt at the source is *diminished* on the literary page. Thus, although not reworked, the elements of folklore are acquired in a necessarily *fictional* key, functional to the needs of the author, who in this case is more precisely a "re-creator."

In Yeats' collection, despite the presence of a marked poetic project, one can identify, precisely due to the *purifying* care of the editor, a fairy tale produced in conformity to the original point of view, using a lens that is substantially faithful to the nature and functions of the original context. In Stephens' collection, however, we observe the authentic literary (and therefore *personal*) acquisition of traditional material that has already passed through medieval transcription. Stephens operates according to the point of view preached by Yeats, and hence appropriates not only the substance, but also the form of the fairy tales provided by the tradition. He does this not to become a passive imitator, but rather to weave into a tale that maintains its fundamental identity a plot that casts his own poetics into necessary relief. The imaginative approach to reality furnished by the fairy tale, albeit a reality pertaining to Myth and Legend, is the ideal key for an author such as Stephens, who is decidedly impatient of the limits imposed by his own milieu.[9] On the other hand, the escape allowed to the writer by the multidimensional paradigm of the fairy tale is a fundamental necessity in any narrative context and should indeed be considered the indispensable cipher through which the fairy tale can lead its recipient beyond the purely *historicum* datum. Whereas at the source the fairy tale is unaffected by the detachment between *fabula* and *historia*, given that the two aspects tend (potentially at least) to coincide, on a literary level, this detachment becomes clearer, leading authors such as Yeats and Stephens to seek nowhere else than in the fairy tale *fabulosum* refuge from the nightmare of History, which one must ultimately re-enter.

From the point of view of Folklore (i.e., Yeats' peasants) and Legend (i.e., Stephens' heroes) indefinite planes of reality are always close at hand, frequently a few steps away; from a modern or literary point of view, these planes can be reached only through the fabulist magic of the tale, and in particular of the fairy tale, which is moreover the most complete manifestation of the first point of view. Joyce's intense efforts to find escape from the suffocating reality of Dublin do not lead to the rediscovery of Myth and Legend. These remain nevertheless indispensable points of reference for an Irish writer, but in a dimension that, *other* as it may be to the tale's point of departure—and hence identifiable as fairy—was imposed by a properly literary dialectic (specifically that established by Joyce using Ibsen's plays, one of the favorite models in his artistic formation). This dialectic demonstrated itself to have absorbed definitively the function originally performed by the fairy world.

An *Essential* Dialectic

When reference was made to the dialectic between identity and otherness, an allusion was also made to the dialectic set up between the absence and the presence of a tale. As one has seen, in a text such as *Far Darrig in Donegal*, the rejection of the tale implies the rejection of contact not only with *the other*, represented by a certain category of fairies, but also with the *identical*, or rather with the two people who do not welcome the main character into their home since he is incapable of bringing a tale with himself. The identity between the person who requests hospitality and those who have the faculty to concede it or not is recognized thanks to the ability of the tale to put the *similar* into direct contact with the *dissimilar*. The main character, who explicitly declares his desire not to enter into the *lusus* of the narration, finds himself excluded from the community in which he should be peacefully accepted. Only after having had a direct experience of the fairy world do the doors of the community open to Pat Diver,[10] insofar as he has finally been inserted into a paradigmatic dimension on the bases of which he is capable of giving a more profound consistency to a vision that previously was exclusively syntagmatic. Perhaps this will be his only direct experience of the indefinite; yet, this does not exclude the possibility of his being elected as a figure in the collective imagination, a figure able to generate a tale that, in turn, will generate a potentially infinite number of similar figures, rendered meaningful thanks to the dialectical depth intrinsic to the narrative movement itself. The area of the tale represents the zone of human existence in which it is possible to enter into the game mentioned with regard to *Dubliners*, one that lasts as long as there is a willingness to halt the course of nature in human affairs. Hence, the fairy tale can be taken as an authentic paradigm of narrative creation, in that it is the fundamental expression of a dialectic in which the twin poles mark an eternal conflict between the immanent and the transcendent, the mutable and the unchanging—in short, it marks the point where what is already definite and what is still indefinite confront each other. The indefinite remains as such, at least until it enters into the possession of History, which puts on the same level all that it manages to encompass and assimilate of what it receives from a more or less traditional *fabula*. The more the tale aims at the recognition of (or indeed has already recognized) a substantial distinction between definite and indefinite, the more there is mirrored in it man's ability to create and see beyond the visible, perhaps by scrutinizing himself.[11]

How is the paradigmatic depth of a tale such as *The Dead* born? It is, broadly speaking, realist, despite a temporary detachment from the logical sequence of the events and the consequent summoning up—through a tale within the tale—of a past that conceals a whole range of values that transcend the common datum provided by the preceding, merely syntagmatic account. What else was the detailed description of the Christmas dinner if not the most eloquent manifestation of the absence of *lusus* conceded to the imagination, and in turn connected to the tale's property of creating a *lusus*? *The Dead* becomes almost the illusion of an *eternal illusion*, thanks to its closing evocation of correspondence between the living and the dead, or rather between what exists and can be seen and what (may) exist but cannot be seen: it is a fairy tale devoid of a final stasis, and hence is a story that remains permanently as such. Although admitting that Joyce is employing a grandiose metaphor, one cannot but recognize that it creates a link with a primigenial dimension of narration, a dimension in which nothing is really comprehensible and everything is imaginable. Gabriel Conroy rejects the prosaic datum and listens to the poetic one connected to his wife's tale; this tale is innocuous at first sight but, having found an appropriate recipient, it triggers off the spark that ignites the paradigmatic deepening with which *The Dead* surprisingly ends. The parabola of the story outlines a decidedly fundamental dialectic, such as that between the opposed poles of life and death, which can be extended to take in the entire collection which, as such, becomes two-dimensional. This recalls the fairy tale (in particular when one thinks of the section entitled *Ghosts* in Yeats' collection, in which living human beings face their fellow men returning as ghosts), but, differently from it, *The Dead* is not based on a net opposition between divergent planes, but rather on a gradual transition from one plane to another, as if to evince the impossibility of perceiving any real distinction between what is living but seems dead and vice versa.

Although in the Joycean tale, therefore, it is impossible to individuate an authentic dialectic between opposites, since the traditional opposites flow together in a single, not exactly identifiable dimension, in the fairy tale, the sense of the tale is built instead on the clear opposition between poles. As we know, one can be dealing with a conflictual or friendly relationship or a purely external one, in a context in which the boundaries between one plane and another are not always recognizable:[12] in any case, mankind must unequivocally face something that is different from it. In the opposite case, moreover, there would be no sense in a structure based on the concepts of *movens* and *rediens*, of escape and invasion, which refer undoubtedly to the infraction of barriers which, impalpable as they may be, have precise semantic validity. From this point of view also, one can easily individuate a paradigmatic dimension in the fairy tale with respect to what occurs in a narrative modality in which the syntagmatic plane tends to level out parameters and values that were opposed at the source. Hence, the fairy tale reveals itself to be the key, and Yeats is the first to be aware of this. He realized that literature can serve to restore an absolute value, connected *ab origine*, to the fundamental categories of human experience. Life and death are two exemplary categories that conserve their original sense only if they are adopted as the poles of a well-defined paradigmatic dialectic, where they are represented, that is, by clearly distinct elements that can always be traced back to the antithesis definite–indefinite. On the contrary, where this antithesis has been supplanted by a sort of spurious synthesis, the original categories tend to become confused and to be perceived in an ever more relative way.

Faced by the opposition between an absolute and a relative conception of the paradigmatic apparatus underlying narrative elaboration, there emerges, on the one hand, a necessary relationship of dependence between the relative and the absolute approach, in that it seems undeniable to me that modern narrative—operating according to a scheme that complicates and renders problematic the elementary outline given originally by an exemplary narrativity (represented by the fairy tale)—is a continual reworking of what can be identified in the broadest sense as tradition. On the other hand, a process of an evolutionary nature comes into being in the passage from a tradition that can be ascribed to the fairy tale, and hence to the collective elaboration, and one which can be traced back to the *modernity* forged by the individuality of authors whose intention is to construct and impose new models of narrativity, if not of *Weltanschauung* itself. The sense of Yeats' work, and I am referring to the entire corpus, resides basically in the attempt to mediate between the absolute of the fairy tale and the relativity of modernity, between the indispensable patrimony inherited from a tradition that is a depository of universal values and the no less indispensable novelty of modern individuality, including that of the author himself. The idea is that the fundamental *fabula* has been composed once and for all, but that there is also plot that can be woven and rewoven each time. The paradigm of referral remains the same, albeit observed every time from a differing angle. Whereas to the legendary bard death appeared under a well-recognizable, or at least unmistakable, guise, to the writer, immersed in History, it displays itself in a far more problematic manner, thus admitting that one can attempt to identify it in the first place.

Assuming, or rather reassuming, the patrimony of concepts and values deposited in a *national* tradition means once more weaving together the loose ends of a web in continual becoming, since it contains the main traits of an ancestral identity that is never complete as long as those who survive can alter it with their personal contribution. A given approach to reality on the part of a Yeats or a Stephens is not merely a personal choice or a question of poetics,[13] because the fairy tale becomes the expressive means through which to let re-emerge from the darkness an identity that would otherwise be buried by the evolution of modernity. This identity can be further enriched by the active intervention of the writer on the same narrative form, based on his capacity to introduce themes and modalities received from other ambits, either literary or pertaining to foreign traditions.[14] The function of the writer is decisive in this regard because he keeps the national literature alive and capable of confronting itself with others, rather than sterilizing itself within the narrow confines of tradition.[15] Furthermore, it is the task of the true writer, from the Yeatsian point of view, to direct literature toward occupying itself with themes that can justly be considered profound.[16] Reviving the identity linked to the fairy tale implies a parallel revival of an *essential* modality of observing the world, a capacity to identify the elements that constitute *the immortal substance of literature*.[17] This means redefining what can be defined as the *paradigmatic map*, on which the plot introduced by each writer who intends to make of his text a deep exploration of the reality that he is setting out to represent, organizes itself. Joyce's epiphany, moving, as seen, from a supposition of the fairy tale evoked and left punctually unrealized, finds its force in the deepening of aspects of a reality that, at first sight, seemed devoid of meaning. Hence, he created a sort of degraded, but absolutely revealing, alternative to the eagerness for the absolute visible in the fairy tale itself.

But this eagerness should be individuated primarily in the natural inclination of the entire Irish people to pay attention principally to what lies beyond the veil of *appearance*, a tendency that concedes the widest powers to the *fabula* intrinsic to the narration. This power is, in effect, conceded because, in the context of folklore, it is by no means easy to locate the precise confines between *fabula* and *historia*, to the degree that both concepts are entirely entrusted to orality. And orality is incapable—by its very nature, but often by choice—of establishing criteria by which to judge the events conserved in and handed down by popular tradition. When writing eventually imposes criteria that can provide a definitive interpretation of a given event, this enters into a sphere of relativity, or rather is absorbed into a purely *historicum* context and is hence removed from the dominion of the fairy tale, which acquires force precisely on a terrain in which definitive confines cannot be fixed.[18] If one is to speak of confines, one must do so with regard to the aforementioned absolute polarity around which is built a narrative discourse intending to give an extremely *essential* image of the world, in the sense, that is, of revealing the essence of a universe that, time and space apart, remains constantly faithful to itself.[19]

Discovering, or at least imagining, the essence of an immutable universe means, at the same time, isolating the essence of narrativity itself, at least in its function of organizing on an ordered syntgmatic plane the fundamental acquisitions of which the paradigm of humanity consists. Therefore the writer, such as Yeats, who dedicates himself to the recovery of tests of oral and popular origin, displays not so much the intention of guaranteeing to writing a patrimony that it would otherwise be denied as the desire to make writing itself pass through the essentiality proper to the fairy tale. This essentiality implies returning narrativity to its origins, to the, so to speak, real consistency of the movement through which the tale sets in motion a dialectic that, as already seen, takes in the planes both of time and space, to the point of involving the very suppositions underlying our conception of the world. In the same way, a writer such as Stephens, who organizes his collection around the main developments in the life of a legendary character such as Finn and readopts a modality typical of the Irish narrative tradition,[20] commits himself to evincing precisely those essential elements and values that render narrativity an instrument for the appropriation of a paradigm that is both heroic (pertaining to a well-defined literary and cultural climate) and more widely human (given that, in Finn's adventures can be recognized the existential parabola of each of Stephens' readers). Obviously, the fairy tale cannot be denied its faculty of widening and complicating its syntagmatic extension, which was also suggested by the identification of a five-phased evolution. This is the inevitable price to be paid for a progressive absorption into a literary context. But it is precisely in this that the opportunity of recognizing in the fairy tale its value as a narrative paradigm resides, in the sense that, in the very passage from an oral/popular ambit to a written/literary one, it displays its capacity to be taken as the fundamental point of reference in the construction of narrative discourse. Whereas between the mythical (potential) phase and the anecdotal one (the first, essential actuation) the fairy tale identifies itself organically with its paradigmatic plane, in the three following phases it matures an increasingly complex interaction with the syntagmatic plane, thus evolving effectively into the modern story, realist or not, as it may be. In any case, between *fabula* and plot, one observes through the fairy tale a process by which the universe reveals its secrets. This is because a narrative intention is operative on it, a capacity, connected to a sort of *creative imagination*, to restore through verbal material the essence of a reality preceding the word itself.[21] The word separates man from being, but reveals itself to be the indispensable means by which, each time, he can make a new voyage back to the roots of his existence. One is dealing with an illusion, a constant pitting of the self against *nothingness*, but it is precisely in this inexhaustible attempt that human nature resides. The fairy tale, in the ultimate analysis, tries to second and facilitate this attempt.

Notes

1. Cesare Segre, *Le strutture e il tempo* (Torino: Einaudi, 1974), 4.

2. It seems appropriate to me to note that the *fabula*, in its primitive simplicity, is the ideal test for measuring and appreciating the compositional effort of the writer. Cf. ibid., 8–9: "Šklovskij and Tomaševskij have brilliantly identified two co-existing syntagmatic lines, one of which, the *fabula*, acts as a neutral foil ingeniously employed to unveil, by contrast, the process of composition activated by the writers."

3. When the oral storyteller draws on literary tradition, his choice is carefully meditated on the basis of specific requirements that make the tale suitable to oral and popular reception. Cf. Gose, *The World of Irish Wonder Tale*, 5–6: "Alan Bruford, in his study *Gaelic Folk Tales and Medieval Romances*, presents evidence about the way the written romances entered the oral tradition. One of his preliminary conclusions is that 'only what *is easy to remember* and *interesting enough to be worth remembering*, has a good chance of being passed on' (167). This puts a premium on *brevity* and 'a *strong coherent plot line*' (168)" (my italics, except for the title of Bruford's text).

4. Cf. Thuente, "'Traditional Innovations'," 96: "Legend transcends history and time by depicting past events as *simultaneous* rather than *chronological*" (my italics). Needless to say, here, *legend* takes on the meaning of *fairy tale*.

5. See Claude Lévi-Strauss, "La structure et la forme. Réflexions sur un ouvrage de Vladimir Propp," *Cahiers de l'Institut de Sciences Économique Appliquée* 7 (1960): 3–36.

6. Ibid.

7. The strictly *functional* choice of narrative material, on the one hand, is part of the nature of the fairy tale, but on the other, leads to its being enjoyed by the public. Cf. Gose, *The World of Irish Wonder Tale*, p. 118: "Much of our enjoyment of a wonder tale [read fairy tale] is knowing that each character, event, and object that is described will play a part in its plot and theme."

8. Cf. Thuente, "'Traditional Innovations,'" 97; "According to Yeats, a country does not begin to produce great literature until it ceases to consider history 'merely as a chronicle of facts' and begins to consider history 'imaginatively'" (two passages taken from Yeats' *Explorations* are quoted).

9. Cf. James Stephens quoted in Foster, *Fictions of the Irish Literary Revival*, 250: "The constant engagement of every artist is to dodge his own atmosphere: environment, which is everything to the historian and the biographer, is poisoned air for an imaginative writer: imagination is in effect the escape from environment."

10. At the beginning of the tale, the main character is surprised by the lack of hospitality in a town renowned to the contrary: "Where was the boasted hospitality of Innishowen, which he had never before known to fail?" At the end of the tale, it is the *far darrig* himself who reveals, implicitly, the town's rejection of Pat Diver: "'Do you not know me, Pat?' Whisper—'When you go back to Innishowen, you'll have a story to tell'" (Yeats, *Irish Fairy Tales*, 96–99).

11. Cf. William B. Yeats, "First Principles," in *The Collected Works: The Irish Dramatic Movement* by William B. Yeats (New York: Scribner, 2003), vol. VIII, 58–59: "and in the end the creative energy of men depends upon their believing that they have, within themselves, something immortal and imperishable."

12. It is not by chance that the boundary dividing one world from the other is to be found in an unstable element such as water. Cf. Gose, *The World of Irish Wonder Tale*, 99: "Water was an important boundary in both the ancient Celtic tales and in the medieval romances. As John Reinhard concludes, entry to the other world was 'made by one of the three ways: *over water, through water*, or through the *sidh* or earth mound'" (my italics, except for *sidh*).

13. Cf. Marcus, *Yeats and the Beginning of the Irish Renaissance*, 24–25: "The spiritual, the visionary, and the occult are fit subjects of concern for Irish writers because they are essentially related to the true Celtic nature."

14. Cf. ibid., 16: "He [Yeats] would therefore have to create a new *Prometheus Unbound* in which Patrick or Columbkil, Oisin or Fionn would be substituted for Prometheus, Cro Patrick or Ben Bulben for Caucasus." Given the universal significance of a figure such as Prometheus, Yeats' ambition is to readopt him using Irish heroes and places, considering, on the one hand, the native figures worthy of incarnating such an illustrious myth, on the other, taking into account the need for the tradition of his country to enrich its mythical store.

15. Cf. Yeats, "First Principles," 63: "A writer is not less National because he shows the influence of other countries and of the great writers of the world. No nation, since the beginning of the history, has ever drawn all its life out of itself."

16. Cf. ibid.: "I mean by deep life that men must put into their writing the emotions and experiences that have been most important to themselves."

17. Cf. ibid., 57, where Yeats takes into consideration the *vivid imagination* of classical authors such as Boccaccio and Cervantes, whose fecundity of inspiration is, in his opinion, due to the fact that "they lived in times when the imagination turned to life itself for excitement. The world was not changing quickly about

them. There was nothing to draw their imagination from the ripening of the fields, from the birth and death of their children, from the destiny of their souls, from all that is the unchanging substance of literature."

18. Cf. André Jolles, *Einfache Formen: Legende, Sage, Mythe, Rätsel, Spruch, Kasus, Memorabile, Märchen, Witz* (Halle: Niemayer, 1930): "As soon as the fairy tale takes on historical characteristics, which happens sometimes when it meets the novella, it always loses part of its force."

19. In the essentiality of the content is reflected the simplicity of the form that the fairy tale assumes, particularly in confrontation with the literary sources. Cf. Gose, *The World of Irish Wonder Tale*, 6: "The folktale version usually drops 'irrelevant motifs' to dramatize scenes merely narrated in the romance, to reduce the number of characters, to preserve 'precise chronological order' (no flashbacks), and 'to knit the story together with small details.'" According to Bruford, who is the author of the quoted passages, the simplification introduced by the folktale (to use his expression) is "aesthetically far more satisfying than the original form."

20. Cf. Cataldi, introduction to *Fiabe irlandesi*, by James Stephens, 16.

21. Cf. Gose, *The World of Irish Wonder Tale*, 107: "Literature is 'constituted of words' but signifies 'more than words,' is 'at once verbal and transverbal' (156). But fantasy goes further; it uses words to recreate a vision of the world before it was divided up by words" (Todorov's *The Fantastic* is quoted).

Beyond Ireland: A General Perspective **10**

Narrativity as a Quest for Meaning

STORYTELLING IMPLIES, on the part of the storyteller, a more or less autonomous *interpretation* of a certain event that it was thought worthwhile to remove from the immanence and transitoriness of human history. It also implies a precise *choice*, when one decides to turn a certain event rather than another into a tale and hence to preserve it from oblivion; this is a criterion as valid for events that have really taken place as it is for those born from the imagination. Although, logically, the choice precedes the interpretation, one must recognize how a conscious choice cannot be taken without a previous interpretation that frames the object of the narration within a *meaningful* perspective. This last consideration allows us to underline how, by turning into a tale and therefore isolating a given segment of that otherwise continuous line that is human history implies, necessarily, investing with meaning the more or less complex series of events that make up the tale itself.[1] This meaning ultimately justifies the choice of isolating from the flow of time a certain happening rather than another, and furthermore can impose one particular form rather than another. This form must also have *substance*, or rather acquire a humanly perceptible consistency. Hence, in the tale, one encounters figures, more or less anthropomorphic, who, on the one hand, allow the action to take place, and on the other, become *vehicles* of a given part of the overall meaning of which the tale is the expression.[2] In practice, the characters involved in a particular narration lend themselves to performing a specific function and, to this end, undergo, on the part of the storyteller but also on that of the public, an interpretation functional to the internal coherence of the narration itself. The nature and action of the characters in a tale are therefore oriented in a *univocal* direction: that required for the tale to respond to the canons for which it was produced and handed down. Due to this, one must take into account the adoption, by the storyteller and by the writer, of a criterion of choice regarding the characters. This criterion exploits, entirely or in part, the semantic potential that has accumulated over time in figures authoritatively sanctioned by a narrative tradition.

It would not be pertinent to speak of a tradition if the storyteller could not avail himself of a more or less wide repertory of characters and situations connected to them. From this repertory the storyteller may draw every time that the present—whether linked to real historical events or to the imagination of the author—is insufficient for, or inefficient in, the creation of a tale or, more specifically, the production of a certain meaning. The force of a tradition moreover manifests itself in the ability to impose its interpretations on those events that then become narrative, according to a process that also works in the opposite direction. Thus, those very events that lend themselves to interpretation in conformity with a tradition enter more easily into the narrative sphere. This is sort of *vicious* or *virtuous circle*, depending on the point of view, thanks to which every narration is at the same time the gathering point of other narrations (or fragments of all previous narrations) and the point of irradiation for successive narrations, able to affirm itself both in the oral and written contexts. On the one hand, therefore, a tale can be defined on the basis of previous (traditional) interpretations. On the other, it can give rise to different, even antithetical interpretations, taking into account that, when dealing with a conservative reading (as might pertain to a community that is the depository of an oral tradition), the innovative readings of a writer, historian, or critic must be taken into consideration.[3] These readings rework the tale according to parameters diverging more or less from tradition. If, on the one hand, the tale, especially in the oral culture, lends organic form to a series of scattered and inhomogeneous *proto-narrations* that render traditional figures functional within an organized and meaningful space, on the other, it lies at the basis of successive elaborations that, where they alter the original meaning, make it functional each time to a specific interpretation.

To gain a clearer idea of these concepts, it would be worthwhile to deal with the fairy tale, a context in which these concepts have particular value. This context is already contained, as we know, in the adjective *fairy*—which immediately provides advance interpretation of what will be told in the tale and how it will be done. The tale is organized against a rich background, populated by figures, places, and situations that refer directly to the concept expressed by the word "fairy" and in the wake of which a whole series of events and phenomena can be catalogued, organized according to a criterion that is, in its way, *rational*. The various entries that make up the section of the *Handbook of Folklore* dedicated to the Mythological Tradition not only represent figures always functional to the dynamic of the fairy tale,[4] but also provide keys through which it is possible to approach human adventures and turn them into narration, according to a logic that lies above historical rationality.[5] The storyteller who refers to one or more of these elements, coming from a past inaccessible except through other tales, rises above his historical context to enter an ambit in which reality is confronted by a *virtual* image of the storyteller's creation. This image derives from the biblical and hagiographic tradition, from the heredity of Celtic literature or folklore, contexts far distant from each other, but ones that tend to meet when it comes to providing elements functional to the production of that specific meaning that we have defined as the prerogative of narrative elaboration.[6]

On the other hand, one should emphasize that the tale is not necessarily built upon figures *officially* included in consecrated tradition, insofar as individuals, situations, and events can always potentially be absorbed beyond the confines of the fairy tale. This possibility obviously displays itself *a posteriori*, after an interpretation has been made (one favored by a specific context) that assigns a determinate value to elements that otherwise would remain neutral, a value that renders them functional to the latest reproposal of a model that tends to include in itself all that the other models are incapable of making explicit. This last reference is addressed to those contexts in which, lacking a rational awareness—or let us say a *historiographic* consciousness—every explanation is derived from a corpus of traditional knowledge. It also refers to those *empty* spaces that inevitably characterize the historical reconstruction of the past and that originate from the absence of historical documents, thus offering the ideal opportunity for a narrative tradition to affirm itself unopposed by discordant interpretations.[7] Fragments regarding, for example, an anonymous Mrs. O'Brien are assembled and elaborated using the lens of the fairy tale in such a way as to obtain an organic and meaningful whole, even at the cost of distorting the real nature of the person in question: her image, only put together on the basis of more or less reliable information and testimony, assumes full characterization, functional to the rendering of the meaning intrinsic to the fairy tale, which, as said previously, in certain contexts can play the role of *historia*.[8]

Whether one is dealing with tales pertaining to an illustrious tradition or pieces of narration of popular hearsay, it is correct to say that those characters who reach down to the fairy tale are in a special way the depositaries of a more or less accentuated functional tendency on which the tale itself thrives, organizing its still coarse material according to the canons of its own interpretation. Rather than of *motifs*, therefore, one must speak of authentic *narrative units*, in the sense that the elements that come down to concrete narration already contain a narrative value, either partial or not organically expressed. The choice of the storyteller becomes fundamental when he glimpses in a given event—ordinary or even insignificant—the suitable conditions on which to build an exemplary narration. It is possible to obtain these conditions due to the fact that the vast category that I have defined as the *imaginative store* already exists. Therein not only do the aforementioned figures from Ó Suillebhain's repertory find place, but also a particular way of perceiving events, a specific point of view, which characterizes an entire human community; this permits a specific narrative form not only to be produced, but also to be perceived and enjoyed in an involved manner.

The fairy tale, therefore, becomes the meeting point of many related points of view, in which characters and situations take it upon themselves to provide *visibility* to that profound meaning that is recognized to be concealed in reality, fruit of an interpretation that finds consistency only in the intrinsic power of fabulation. This power must necessarily pass above the autonomy of those figures carrying the narration and meaning, in that, once *transfigured* in the narrative act, they lose or see weakened the attributes that render them organic to the plane of reality from which they derive. The fairy tale places the representatives of the definite on the same alternative plane as the beings of the indefinite. The former are chosen from all the components of a community, real or imaginary, present or past, on the basis of the fact that, apart from sharing characteristics with the human beings surrounding them, they reveal themselves, always from a point of view inherited from ancestral imagination, to be depositaries of one or more qualities raising them above an exemplary dimension.

If we examine Yeats' text *Bewitched Butter* (*Donegal*), we can see concretely how the fairy tale is built on the identification and connection of characters appropriate to staging the dialectic between definite and indefinite, even in the absence of properly supernatural figures. This process of identification, realized in how the characters are presented, demonstrates itself to be linked to the patrimony of proto-narrations that, as previously mentioned, lie at the origin of the fairy tale's creation. The fact that the four main figures in the narration have *really* come into contact, besides *how*, and that they have been associated only through the tale is irrelevant to our analysis here. Or, at least, it would only become useful in the case in which one desired to establish the boundaries between what can effectively be traced back to the biography of the individuals mentioned and what can instead be attributed to the autonomous reconstruction of the tale, albeit without any record of births and deaths. Indeed, it would be fair to doubt even the historical existence of the characters in question: one could, in fact, be dealing with characters with conventional names, who have been for some time part of the tradition and employed precisely by virtue of a nature suited to the specific narrative project. What one must instead individuate is the preexistence of *clues*, to adopt a term dear to Roland Barthes,[9] capable of setting under way a process of narrative elaboration that can be interpreted from the viewpoint of the fairy tale, leaving aside the consistency of characters who take on value only insofar as they are functional to the explication of a theme typical of folklore, such as "bewitched butter."

Let us observe therefore that the tale opens with the presentation of two families, the Hanlons and the Doghertys, with reference to whom the storyteller affirms that: "Both families had good cows, but the Hanlons were fortunate in possessing a Kerry cow that gave more milk and yellower butter than the others."[10] The possession of a renowned exemplar of the cow allows the tale to set up an initial distinction, based on the Hanlons' greater fortune with respect to the Doghertys. The cow is bereft of anything that can be assimilated, not only to a character, but also to a Greimasian *object of value*, to which, on the basis of popular anecdote (if not thanks to direct testimony), almost magical qualities are ascribed. Hence, its belonging to only one of the families establishes a situation of disparity that is a potential source of *conflictual interaction*, if only on the level of the definite.

Given this premise, a character from the disadvantaged family is introduced, who moves toward the home of the fortunate Hanlons. Her entrance is as follows: "Grace Dogherty, a young girl, *who was more admired than loved in the neighbourhood*, took much interest in the Kerry cow, and appeared one night at Mrs. Hanlon's door with the modest request: 'Will you let me milk your Moiley cow?'"[11] Her presentation is decidedly low key. Through it, we discover only that, apart from her young age, she is *more admired than loved* by those who make up her own community. Although no further elucidation is provided, the storyteller clearly implies that she has been involved in some not entirely praiseworthy adventures of which news has spread. One could even hypothesize a preexisting fairy tale directly linked to the girl. This hypothesis is reinforced by the insistency with which she asks Mrs. Hanlon to allow her to milk her munificent cow: it is, in fact, well known that this is how a witch casts her spell. It is easy to understand that Grace Dogherty represents, albeit in a vicarious form, the indefinite erupting into the tale, whose interaction with the definite is favored by the good faith of Mrs. Hanlon, who clearly neither knows nor gives weight to what is said about her neighbor. The prosperity of the Hanlons—connected to the value of the Kerry cow—and the fairy tale characterization given to Grace Dogherty are the clues necessary to set up the tale. More specifically, the preexisting narrations circulating in the community regarding these themes flow together into an organic and compact narrative construction, such as this fairy tale, which Yeats has included in his collection.

This fairy tale manifests itself as such when it is discovered that, after the intervention of Grace, the cow is no longer able to produce milk. In a context dominated by the folkloric imagination, it is almost natural that such an incident should be given a supernatural explanation, all the more so when a character with the reputation of the young Dogherty girl is involved. In the lack of a solid alternative, a fairy tale interpretation is required, according to which, at this point, it is necessary to introduce the right character, one who has the power to cancel out the consequences of witchcraft. The community knows that *black magic* must be contrasted by *white magic*, that belonging to the so-called "fairy doctors." It is predictable, therefore, that the Hanlons will invoke the help of a representative of this category, who is introduced as follows: "When this melancholy state of things lasted for three days, the Hanlons applied to a certain Mark McCarrion, who lived near Binion."[12] A more synthetic presentation could not have been offered (one should remember the *essentiality* of fairy tale characters, as mentioned in the previous chapter), but their immediately turning for help to a *certain* Mark McCarrion contains an implicit recognition of the function incarnated by this character. There is no need to mention that he is a healer, considering that he is already responsible for numerous other feats in similar situations, of which the Hanlons are definitely not ignorant. And their trust in him is soon repaid, if it is true that the spell he casts against hers obliges Grace Dogherty to put an end to her magic. The outcome of events, on the one hand, confirms that the fairy tale interpretation is correct and, on the other, sanctions once again the validity of the tradition circulating with regard to the main characters.

In substance, the tale ends with the reestablishment of the initial situation—or rather, the fairy tale concludes its parabola with the returning of the characters employed to the context from which they had been taken. They are returned nonetheless with a wider narrative dimension and a richer semantic value. Altogether, the new tale, built up on clues taken from tradition, is a more or less innovative reading of the world from the viewpoint of the fairy tale. But this reading is above all a momentary *escape* from the univocity of History, an active interpretation of the laws of nature, in which nature itself must bend to the power of and need for fabulation intrinsic to man.

Whereas the characters from this tale, like many other characters in Yeats' collection, can be considered the unconscious bearers of a preexisting narrative store—and hence ignorant of their ability to set up a new narration each time—in Stephens' collection we find instead conscious bearers of narrativity, characters who come to our attention insofar as they are depositaries and vehicles of a certain narrative patrimony. Stephens is extremely sensitive to the process that establishes itself between the transmitter and the recipient of a tale; as already noted, his texts are marked by meta-narrative awareness. Eloquent demonstration is provided by the two fairy tales that frame his collection. Both in *The Story of Tuan Mac Cairill*—whose particular function has already been discussed—and in *Mongan's Frenzy*, characters are presented who go in search of the narration, as well others who, in return, demonstrate their willingness to involve in an organic tale their conscious narrative store. What takes place is the voluntary sharing by a meaningful character—up to the point of the transcription by the Abbot of Moville of the tale of Mongan's frenzy, heard from the bard Cairidè—of a personal tradition which, perceived in all its exemplariness, naturally from the viewpoint of the fairy tale, enters to form part of someone else's tradition. Tuan and Mongan should be considered as if they were two walking narrative units, from whom the recipient can catch the deepest meaning of the fairy tale.

Tuan Mac Cairill reveals his extraordinary past to St. Finnian after the latter has managed to convert him to Christianity. It is as if to say that a tradition in eclipse, such as the Celtic-pagan one, in order to save itself from disappearance consigns itself to the newly emerging tradition. The long narration of the protean Celtic character becomes the means by which two worlds, two contrasting visions of the world, flow together to form what will become a single, syncretic tradition. The fairy tale thus officially takes its place in Christian faith, as is furthermore testified to by the following passage regarding St. Finnian: "He was one who loved God and Ireland, and to the person who could instruct him in these great themes he gave all the interest of his mind and sympathy of his heart."[13]

The interest of the Saint is equally divided between his faith (*God*) and *Ireland*, a term which recalls all the native characters of the land in which he preaches. And to deepen his knowledge of pre-Christian Ireland, St. Finnian has no alternative but to turn to its narrative patrimony, best incarnated by the adventures of his noble interlocutor. The tale parts from the origins, in response to the Saint's precise question: "Tell me of the beginning of time in Ireland, and of the bearing of Partholon, the son of *Noah's* son":[14] the reference to Noah, its connecting him to the first, mythical colonizer of Ireland, demonstrates unequivocally that the pagan and Christian traditions have quickly fused. The Christian filter has already begun to appropriate the Celtic narrative corpus, to make it an integral part of its interpretative system.

As the Abbot of Moville, in *Mongan's Frenzy*, St. Finnian returns as the representative of Christianity who, attracted by the Celtic narrative tradition, calls to his monastery all those who know one or more tale, so that they can be transcribed for his own enjoyment and that of those following him. However, Cairidè, differently from Tuan, is not the main character of the tale he tells. He is a storyteller who has inherited, from generation to generation, the tale of Mongan, in the sense that a homonymous ancestor of his has heard the tale from the lips of its hero. Cairidè's tale is a tale within the tale, in which Mongan's continuous refusal to tell his wife of a past experience of his frames the tale providing the title of the text, a tale that the main character finally concedes to his wife and to a chosen circle, of which the bard (who is an ancestor of Cairidè's) forms part. What is told is a fairy tale, but what is really specific is the context in which the storytelling takes place: we are, in fact, in the fairy world and the listeners include figures pertaining to that world, since, before the narration unveils Mongan's memories, those who are listening are put into direct contact with the foundation that holds up the entire edifice of the fairy tale. This so much so that Cairidè, before letting Mongan begin, gives a rapid and incisive description of it: "There is a difference between this world and the world of Faery, but it is not immediately perceptible. Everything that is here is there, but the things that are there are better than those that are here."[15]

In delineating the imperceptible difference that separates one world from the other, the storyteller reveals to his Christian interlocutor an interpretative factor fundamental to revealing the nature and function of his narrative tradition. Ultimately, Cairidè preserves the aboriginal idea in which the world of Faery is *better* than that of daily life, an idea that should go into direct conflict with the new awareness of reality imported by Christianity. However, the Saint, recipient of the melancholy song of the heir of a declining civilization, sets up no resistance and is in fact glad to widen the horizons of his knowledge to take in something of which, in the absence of this tale, he would have remained ignorant. But his attitude should not be read as passivity in face of the blinding beauty of a product of the popular imagination: in the bard's poetical and naïve (from the Saint's point of view) interpretation of the other world, St. Finnian glimpses the prefiguration of the Otherworld introduced by his faith, which from this viewpoint, *sublimates* an idea already well-rooted in the Celtic mentality. Thus, in the idea of the fairy connected to Cairidè's fairy tale, two interpretative threads of transcendence converge in an almost inextricable manner, producing an innovative vision of the world that extracts purity from the narrative category identified in the fairy tale, but further deepens the conceptual complexity of which it is depositary.

Cairidè's tale is one of the first manifestations of the reorganization of the interpretive apparatus, but this is realized only insofar as it explicates the narrativity intrinsic to Mongan's adventures, a narrativity that not by chance is diverted into the manuscript drawn up by the abbot, an exemplary figure in the change that has tacitly taken place in the semantic horizon of the fairy tale. This narrativity is preserved until it adheres profitably to the new tradition by which it has been received, perhaps to attain an ever more organic fusion with Christian dogma. However, this hypothesis is far from finding the activation it will be given when the tale in question falls into the hands of a writer such as Stephens, in whose literary approach an image of the text is consolidated in which none of the deeper ideas disseminated by a long tradition can be neglected. If anything, the writer does no less than to pursue the illusion of appropriating the original sense of the narration of Mongan's adventures (as those of Tuan) since his main prerogative in approaching the traditional text is that of locating material that will lead to a radical detachment from a present contaminated by an excessive number of spurious interpretations.

A Model of Universal Significance

The textual examples adopted allow us to intuit that it is possible to identify a sort of tacit pact between the (possible) witnesses of the narrated events, the storyteller or storytellers, and the recipient or recipients of the tale. This pact preserves not so much memory as the very motives leading to the birth of the fairy tale. This pact can be maintained until it comes down to the collector and the writer, should they decide to keep to the spirit that has created and preserved this particular narrative product, or at least to remain neutral in the face of something that goes beyond their historical and/or cultural context. The fairy tale displays mainly a human inclination toward the indefinite, a desire to accede to the many aspects of existence that evade objective categorization, a curiosity to explore dimensions of reality lurking in obscurity. Consequently, the fairy tale is equipped, at the source, with a particular interpretative system, which, as I hope has been understood, is not only a passive response to the mysteries of the universe but, above all, insofar as it is a tale, an active appropriation of the universe. This act of appropriation is made as much according to inherited schemes and images as to a marked tendency toward reworking, which involves above all those writers who, although remaining faithful to the aforementioned pact, approach the fairy tale with the manifest intention of making it suitable to the creation of new meanings, linked both to their own personality and to the need for universality. Respect for the tacit pact made by all those who have perpetuated the memory of the single fairy tale, both in the oral and written contexts, allows for the preservation of a piece, small or large, of that often extremely fragile mosaic that is the identity of a human community. Indeed, it permits this piece to conserve its function, in its capacity to express an absolutely specific meaning.

A clear example of how this pact is respected—and indeed, sublimated—is provided by Yeats' collection. Yeats purposefully adopts a stance in decided antithesis to those collectors—from whom it should be noted he draws many texts—who diminish the original value of the fairy tale, interpreting it in the light of a rationality that is entirely out of place, to the extent that an interpretative criterion is adopted that is completely extraneous to the reality of the tale and fails to recognize the legitimacy of the conceptual horizon against which it has been elaborated. A rational criterion would be fruitful if one desired to compare all the exemplars of fairy tales focused on the same theme, so as to obtain a sufficiently well-developed idea of the traditional interpretation of a given phenomenon.[16] In this way, not only would one deepen one's knowledge of a context extraneous to those who approach it, but above all, one would enter into syntony with the interpretative system responsible for the production of a particular object, such as the fairy tale.

But, due to its very nature as delineated up to now, the fairy tale is an object that lends itself to the widest possible interpretations, as many as the keys that can be adopted in referring to it. It is possible, and I would say more than legitimate, to analyze the tale in its narrative immediacy, and hence to individuate in it simply the explication of the *imaginative play* invoked by Boas; conversely, it is no less legitimate to deepen one's research to the point of localizing, beyond appearances, its most recondite signifi-

cance. A fairy tale may be striking as much due to its unfolding of a porten-
tous creative imagination as due to its ability to give symbolic expression
to the fundamental themes of existence. Even when it is deeply rooted in a
precise context, in an ambit, that is, which does not go beyond Ireland or
simply a small local community, one can still glimpse in it a dimension that
tends to embrace the entire sphere of humanity. Almost all the tales chosen
by Yeats fall within clearly delineated confines: time, place, and character
are set within an absolutely circumscribed reality. Yet it is clear nonetheless
that each of the elements making up the narration is capable of inducing
both in the listener forming an integral part of the community of origin
and in the reader, far distant in time and space, a reflection of a general
type, if not an encounter with his own interiority. The fact is that in the
fairy tale, more remarkably than in other narrative contexts, there appear
figures who, starting from their primary function of expressing a particular
corpus of more or less imaginary beliefs, almost imperceptibly transcend
mere appearance, which proves itself to be no more than the incarnation
of one or more universally recognizable concepts. When the tale has these
figures interact, not only is a narrative movement revealed to the recipient,
but the concepts that are the vehicles of these figures are also related and
hence cast into discussion. Properly human dilemmas are transferred from
the individual dimension to the collective space delineated by the fairy
tale,[17] a space in which reality gradually dissolves into a dream, in which
every question, whatever its weight, is filtered through the lightness that
characterizes the plane on which the tale operates, a plane for which one
cannot establish precise outlines.[18]

It should now be underlined how all the values, more or less universal,
that can be discerned in the fairy tale, in the final analysis, are to be ascribed
to the single interpretation of the individual who concretely hears or reads
the particular tale. The attempt to formalize an interpretative model that
could contain all the variety, and variability, intrinsic to this fact seems clearly
hazardous to me.[19] The text of Bewitched Butter (Donegal), as it was received
on the basis of Yeats' acquisition of it, has certainly little to do with its reception in the original popular context, regardless of how one must recognize
Yeats' tenacious pursuit of a literary (re)unification of the entire Irish nation.
And, in Stephens' texts, one can definitely not maintain that for the pagan
storyteller, albeit converted, and for the Christian receiver, the tale would
have had the same value, despite the syncretic efforts made by both parts.
It is undeniable, nonetheless, that both Yeats and the Donegal community,
saints and abbots and heroes and bards, derived from the fairy tale a perennial validity, although none of them, presumably, were aware of the original

sense that in its time had given birth to this expressive form. What counts in the eyes of the interpreter is that the tradition inherited from the past should conserve its functionality, whether one is dealing with a pleasant entertainment for a peasant community or with a corrective for a literature in crisis.[20] Moreover, one should not forget that the fairy tale is the ideal location for the encounter or clash between differing interpretations, both because of the fact that it is inevitably elaborated collectively, at least in the oral phase,[21] and because, as I have attempted to demonstrate, in it there meet traits of more or less historical epochs (each with their own cultural background) and narrative genres that lie far distant from each other. It seems to me that this consideration alone is enough to place the object of our study in the correct perspective, and also to ascribe it the value it warrants.

If one avoids the pretension of imposing a univocal interpretation at the level of meaning on the fairy tale as a whole and on its individual elements, the way is open to an analysis directing its efforts at the identification of a particular narrative strategy able to offer more objective answers to its own polysemy. If one can discern in the contrast between the Hanlons and the Doghertys the eternal conflict between abundance and destitution, if between Mrs. Hanlon and Grace Dogherty there is a conflict between the ingenuous and the cunning, if definitively in the struggle between *witches* and *fairy doctors* the clash between good and evil, life and death, is manifested, all this depends on an interpretative act on the part of whosoever listens or reads, if not on the part of whosoever has told or originally created the tale. But none of this would be perceptible if the interpreted elements were not presented, collocated, and connected according to the dictates of a specific narrative strategy that allows us to read in Stephens' characters, Tuan and Mongan, an entire set of values from which the recipient can choose what is most meaningful to him. Furthermore, if it is possible also to discover in *Dubliners* (and in who knows how many other literary texts) the functioning of a narrative strategy that can be modeled on the deep structure of the fairy tale, then it may be here that we should concentrate our research. And one must also accept that, among the nerve centers of this structure, it is possible to insert or derive a potentially infinite range of meanings, which in my opinion should be considered as a consequence rather than a cause of narrativity. The model proposed here finds its validity precisely in this, the identification of specific form assumed by narrativity. And this form, recognized in what has been baptized the fairy tale, aspires to impose itself as an overall model for narrative construction. The Irish tradition is where it has been discovered, and is its first test: all other narrative contexts can verify its universal significance.

Notes

1. Cf. Hayden White, "The Value of Narrativity in the Representation of Reality," in *On Narrative*, edited by William J. T. Mitchell (Chicago-London: University of Chicago Press 1981), 2: "Arising, as Barthes says, between our experience of the world and our efforts to describe that experience in language, narrative 'ceaselessly substitutes meaning for the straightforward copy of the events recounted.' And it would follow, on this view, that the absence of narrative capacity or a refusal of narrative indicates an absence or refusal of meaning itself."

2. Cf. Tzvetan Todorov, "Les catégories du récit littéraire," in *L'analyse structurale du récit* (Paris, Seuil 1969), 125–51: "The meaning (or function) of the work is its possibility of entering into correlation with other elements of the work or with the work as a whole. . . . Each element of the work has one or more meanings (if it is not deficient at least) in a finite number which can be established once and for all."

3. From the dialectic between the narrative and critical work is born the image of an interpretation that is never the same. The tale, in its totality or in the partiality of its single elements, must each time face a change in the context in which the critical reading takes place. Cf. ibid.: "The interpretation of an element of the work changes according to the personality of the critic, his ideological positions and the period. In order to be interpreted, the element is inserted into a system which is not that of the work but of the critic." This discourse may easily be extended to the heterogeneous relationship that is established between a specific folk context, oral or transcribed, and the literary work that desires to draw inspiration from it.

4. Apart from the numerous figures falling under the category of *supernatural beings*, Ó Suillebhain also inserts into his catalog specific references to places and phenomena connected to the following figures: *fairy places, abductions by fairies, ghosts and apparitions, supernatural places, hidden treasure, supernatural phenomena, the afterworld* (see Ó Suillebhain, *A Handbook of Irish Folklore*, XXVIII–XXIX).

5. A logic that could be defined *mythical*, following the specific use of the term *myth* adopted in chapter 8, but also with regard to what is stated in Zimmermann, *The Irish Story Teller*, 581: "One of the various senses of the word 'myth' may be relevant here: an imaginative construction of peculiar seriousness and emotional power, held to be true but without factual basis, and serving as explanation or justification of the present state of affairs."

6. In this regard, consider the marked tendency in the Irish narrative tradition toward syncretism between pagan and Christian elements, between the literary and the folk heredities. Cf. Ó Giolláin, *The Fairy Belief and Official Religion*, and Ford, *Aspects of Patrician Legend*.

7. Cf. Zimmermann, *The Irish Story Teller*, 581–83, where he proposes a fundamental quadripartition of the knowledge and interpretation of the past. In particular, 583: "But 'oral history' may preserve information concerning events that are not documented in other ways, or offer a corrective to other sources."

8. Cf. Henry Glassie, *Passing the Time in Ballymenone*, quoted in ibid., 584: "*Information* about past people and events floats free, *unorganized* in vast quantity, waiting to be *selected and attached* to something about which people do 'have the history'" (my italics).

9. See Marchese, *L'officina del racconto*, 54: "If the functions are narrative units distributed on the level of history, the clues can instead be saturated on the level of the characters. They are divided between *clues*, in the strictest sense, 'which refer to a characteristic, a sentiment, an atmosphere or a philosophy,' and *informants*, 'pure immediately meaningful data,' such as the age of the character, the descriptions etc." (Roland Barthes, *Critical Essays*, quoted).

10. Yeats, *Irish Fairy Tales*, 160.

11. Ibid. (my italics).

12. Ibid., 161.

13. Stephens, *Irish Fairy Tales*, 11.

14. Ibid.

15. Ibid., 266.

16. Cf. what Yeats adds at the end of the tale *Bewitched Butter (Donegal)*: "There is hardly a village in Ireland where the milk is not thus believed to have been stolen times upon times. There are many counter-charms" (Yeats, *Irish Fairy Tales*, 162). Rather than casting into discussion the plausibility of what has just been narrated, the poet takes note and makes his readers aware of the fact that the theme of the *bewitched butter* is widespread throughout the island and therefore is a privileged *narrative unit* for the fairy tale.

17. Cf. Gose, *The World of Irish Wonder Tale*, 7: "In the process of creating their simple and intense coherence, these tales also develop important psychic and spiritual concerns."

18. Cf. Bengt Holbek, "Interpretation of Fairy Tales," *FF Communications* 239 (1986): 406: "In traditional communities, fairy tales provided a means of collective daydreaming . . . . They depicted a true world, i.e., the world as it should be."

19. Cf. Segre, *Le strutture e il tempo*, 70–72.

20. Cf. Holbek, "Interpretation of Fairy Tales," 406: "The 'marvellous' [which should be considered as a synonym of fairy] elements are traditional expressions, i.e., they have been in use for centuries, perhaps millennia, but they are only retained because *they are still meaningful to their users*" (my italics).

21. Cf. Linda Dégh, "The 'Belief Legend' in Modern Society," quoted in Zimmermann, *The Irish Story Teller*, 577, note 103: "Current legends seem to be generated by certain groups at specific occasions through communal cooperation. The participants of legend-sessions put together their pieces of knowledge."

Selected Bibliography

Aarne, Antti, and Thompson, Stith. "The Types of Folktale." *FF Communications* 184 (1961).

Afanas'ev, Aleksandr N. *Russian Fairy Tales* (1863). New York: Pantheon Books, 1945.

Almqvist, Bo. "Irish Migratory Legends on the Supernatural. Sources, Studies and Problems." *Béaloideas* 59 (1991): 1–43.

Apo, Satu. "A Singing Scribe or a Nationalist Author." *FF Network* 25 (2003): 3–12.

Bachtin, Michail. *Rabelais and His World* (1965). Bloomington: Indiana University Press, 1984.

Belcher, Stephen. "Framed Tales in the Oral Tradition: An Exploration." *Fabula* 35 (1994): 1–19.

Benjamin, Walter. *Il narratore. Considerazioni sull'opera di Nikolaj Leskov* (1936). Torino: Einaudi, 2011.

Bettelheim, Bruno. *The Uses of the Enchantment: The Meaning and Importance of Fairy Tales*. New York: Knopf, 1976.

Bidney, David. "Myth, Symbolism and Truth." In *Myth: A Symposium*, edited by Thomas A. Sebeok, 3–24. Bloomington: Indiana University Press, 1965.

Bogatyrëv, Petr, and Jakobson, Roman. "Folklore as a Special Form of Creation." *Folklore Forum* 13, 1 (1980): 1–21.

Booth, Wayne. *The Rhetoric of Fiction*. Chicago: University of Chicago Press, 1974.

Bramsbäck, Birgit. *James Stephens: A Literary and Bibliographical Study*. Uppsala: Lundequist, 1959.

Bramsbäck, Birgit. "William Butler Yeats and Folklore Material." *Béaloideas* 39–41 (1971–1973): 56–68.

Breatnach, Deasún. "The Púca: A Multi-Functional Irish Supernatural Entity." *Folklore* 104 (1993): 105–10.

Bremond, Claude. *Logique du récit*. Paris: Seuil, 1973.

Breteau, Claude H., and Zagnoli, Nello. "Recherche sur les variables structurantes du récit." *Fabula* 22 (1981): 214–27.

Briggs, Katharine M. *The Fairies in Tradition and Literature* (1967). London: Routledge, 2002.

Briggs, Katharine M. *A Dictionary of British Folk Tales*. London: Routledge and Kegan Paul, 1970.

Bronzini, Giovanni B. *Il mito della poesia popolare*. Roma: Edizioni dell'Ateneo, 1966.

Bronzini, Giovanni B. *Elementi istituzionali di storia delle tradizioni popolari*. Roma: Edizioni dell'Ateneo, 1973.

Bronzini, Giovanni B. *Cultura popolare. Dialettica e contestualità*. Bari: Dedalo, 1980.

Bronzini, Giovanni B. *La letteratura popolare italiana dell'Otto-Novecento*. Firenze: Le Monnier, 1994.

Brooks, Peter. *Reading for the Plot: Design and Intention in Narrative*. New York: Knopf, 1984.

Burke, Peter. *Popular Culture in Early Modern Europe*. Aldershot: Scolar Press, 1994.

Calabrese, Stefano. *Fiaba*. Scandicci: La Nuova Italia, 1997.

Calvino, Italo. *Lezioni americane: Sei proposte per il prossimo millennio*. Milano: Garzanti, 1988.

Carrara, Lorenzo, ed. *Favole celtiche*. Milano: RCS Collezionabili, 2001.

Carrara, Lorenzo, and De Marco, Katia, eds. *Saghe e leggende irlandesi*. Milano: RCS Collezonabili, 2001.

Cataldi, Melita, ed. *Antiche storie e fiabe irlandesi*. Torino: Einaudi, 1985.

Ceserani, Remo, ed. *La narrazione fantastica*. Pisa: Nistri-Lischi, 1983.

Christiansen, Reidar T. *Studies in Irish and Scandinavian Folktales*. Copenhagen: Rosenkilde and Bagger, 1959.

Christiansen, Reidar T. "Some Notes on the Fairies and the Fairy Faith." *Béaloideas* 39–41 (1971–1973): 95–111.

Cocchiara, Giuseppe. *Storia del folklore in Europa*. Torino: Einaudi, 1952.

Cohan, Steven, and Shires, Linda M. *Telling Stories. A Theoretical Analysis of Narrative Fiction*. London: Routledge, 1988.

Colum, Padraic. "Story-Telling in Ireland." In *Folk Literature of the British Isles*, edited by Eloise Speed Norton, 115–18. London-Folkestone: Scarecrow Press, 1978.

Connolly, Sean J., ed. *The Oxford Companion to Irish History*. Oxford: Oxford University Press, 2002.

Courtés, Joseph. "Motif et type dans la tradition folklorique." *Littérature* 45 (1982): 114–27.

Dégh, Linda. "What Is a Belief Legend?" *Folklore* 107 (1996): 33–44.

De Giorgi, Fulvio. "Teoria, narrativa e storia." *Annali della Scuola Normale Superiore di Pisa. Classe di Lettere e Filosofia* XIV, 4 (1984, III series): 1465–1514.

Delargy, James H. *The Gaelic Story-Teller. With Some Notes on Gaelic Folk-Tales*. London: Cumberlege, 1945.

de Martino, Ernesto. *Il mondo magico*. Torino: Einaudi, 1958.

Eason, Cassandra. *A Complete Guide to Fairies and Magical Beings*. London: Piatkus, 2001.

Eco, Umberto. *Le poetiche di Joyce*. Milano: Bompiani, 1982.

Eco, Umberto. *I limiti dell'interpretazione*. Milano: Bompiani, 1990.

Fitzgerald, Joan. "Yeats's Irish Traditions." *Textus* II, 1–2 (1989): 17–39.

Ford, Patrick K. "Aspects of Patrician Legend." In *Celtic Folklore and Christianity. Studies in Memory of William W. Heist*, edited by Patrick K. Ford, 29–49. Los Angeles: McNally and Loftin, 1983.

Foster, John W. *Fictions of the Irish Literary Revival*. Dublin: Gill and Macmillan, 1987.

Frazer, James G. *The Golden Bough: A Study in Magic and Religion*. New York: Macmillan, 1923.

Frye, Northrop. *The Anatomy of Criticism: Four Essays*. Princeton: Princeton University Press, 1957.

Frye, Northrop. *Fables of Identity*. New York-London: Harcourt, Brace and World, 1963.

Frye, Northrop. *Myth and Metaphor: Selected Essays 1974–1988*. Charlottesville: University of Virginia Press, 1991.

Genette, Gérard. "Frontières du récit." In *L'analyse structurale du récit*, 158–69. Paris: Seuil, 1966.

Genette, Gérard. *Narrative Discours Revisited*. Ithaca, NY: Cornell University Press, 1983.

Gibbons, Luke, "'Some Hysterical Hatred': History, Hysteria, and the Literary Revival." *Irish University Review* XXVII, 1 (1997): 7–23.

Gnerre, Maurizio. "Lo spazio del mito." *La ricerca folklorica* 11 (1985): 29–33.

Gose, Elliott B. *The World of Irish Wonder Tale*. Toronto-Dingle: University of Toronto Press, 1985.

Gramsci, Antonio. *Letteratura e vita nazionale* (1950). Roma: Editori Riuniti, 1991.

Greimas, Algirdas J. *On Meaning* (1970). Minneapolis: University of Minnesota Press, 1987.

Greimas, Algirdas J., and Courtés, Joseph. "The Cognitive Dimension of Narrative Discourse." *New Literary History* XX, 3 (1989): 563–79.

Greimas, Algirdas J., and Ricoeur, Paul. "On Narrativity." Ibid.: 551–62.

Gregory, Lady Augusta. *Poets and Dreamers: Studies and Translations from the Irish* (1903). Gerrards Cross: Colin Smythe, 1974.

Grimm, Jacob and Wilhelm. *Grimm's Fairy Tales* (1812–1815). Teddington: Echo Library, 2006.

Hamon, Philippe. *Semiologia lessico leggibilità del testo narrativo*. Parma-Lucca: Pratiche, 1977.

Hartland, Edwin S. *Popular Studies in Mythology, Romance, and Folklore*. London: Nutt, 1914.

Hillis Miller, Joseph. *Reading Narrative*. Norman: University of Oklahoma Press, 1998.

Holbek, Bengt. "Interpretation of Fairy Tales." *FF Communications* 239 (1986).

Hoppál, Mihály. "Narration and Memory." *Fabula* 22 (1981): 281–89.

Hultin, Neil C. "Anglo-Irish Folklore from Clonmel: T. C. Croker and British Library add. 20099." *Fabula* 27 (1986): 288–307.

Hultin, Neil C. "Belief and Interpretation in T. Crofton Croker's Legends of the Lakes." *Folklore* 98i (1987): 65–79.

Hyde, Douglas. *Beside the Fire: A Collection of Irish Gaelic Folk Stories* (1890). New York: Lemma, 1973.

Hynes, John L. *Propp and His Progeny: An Evaluation of Story Grammars and a Reappraisal of the Value of Propp's Theories for Literary Analysis and Reading Research*. Ann Arbor: University Microfilms International, 1982.

Jolles, André. *Einfache Formen: Legende, Sage, Mythe, Rätsel, Spruch, Kasus, Memorabile, Märchen, Witz*. Halle: Niemayer, 1930.

Joyce, James. *Dubliners* (1914). In *The Essential James Joyce*, by James Joyce, 9–174. London: Jonathan Cape, 1948.

Joyce, Patrick W. *Wonders of Ireland and Other Papers on Irish Subjects*. London: Longmans-Green, 1911.

Kaivola-Bregenhøj, Annikki. "Homo Narrans. People Making Narratives." *FF Network* 29 (2005): 3–11.

Kinahan, Frank. "Hour of Dawn: The Unity of Yeats's 'The Celtic Twilight' (1893, 1902)." *Irish University Review* XIII, 2 (1983): 189–205.

Labrie-Bouthillier, Vivian. "Les expériences sur la transmission orale: d'un modèle individuel à un modèle collectif." *Fabula* 18 (1977): 1–17.

Lavinio, Cristina. "Potenza e magia della fiaba. La fiaba tra i generi della prosa narrativa orale tradizionale." *La ricerca folklorica* 12 (1985): 37–48.

Lavinio, Cristina. "Modello narrativo e intreccio nella fiaba: i condizionamenti della memoria." *La ricerca folklorica* 15 (1987): 41–48.

Lévi-Strauss, Claude. "La structure et la forme. Réflexions sur un ouvrage de Vladimir Propp." *Cahiers de l'Institut de Science Économique Appliquée* 7 (1960): 3–36.

Lévi-Strauss, Claude. *Myth and Meaning*. New York: Routledge, 2001.

Lo Nigro, Sebastiano. "La fiaba tra scrittura e oralità." *La ricerca folklorica* 12 (1985): 7–9.

Lotman, Jurij. *The Structure of the Artistic Text* (1970). Ann Arbor: University of Michigan Press, 1977.

Lotman, Jurij. *Universe of the Mind: A Semiotic Theory of Culture* (1974). Bloomington: Indiana University Press, 1990.

Lüthi, Max. *The European Folktale: Form and Nature* (1947). Bloomington: Indiana University Press, 1986.

Lysaght, Patricia. "The Banshee's Comb (MLSIT 4026). The Role of Tellers and Audiences in the Shaping of Redactions and Variations." *Béaloideas* 59 (1991): 67–82.

Marchese, Angelo. *L'officina del racconto. Semiotica della narratività*. Milano: Mondadori, 1983.

Marcus, Phillip Le Duc. *Yeats and the Beginning of the Irish Renaissance*. Ithaca (NY)-London: Cornell University Press, 1970.

Mariani Ciampicacigli, Franca. *La struttura narrativa: come funziona la macchina del racconto*. Ravenna: Longo, 1980.

Martin, Augustine. *James Stephens: A Critical Study*. Dublin: Gill and Macmillan, 1977.

Meletinskij, Eleazar M. *Introduzione alla poetica storica dell'epos e del romanzo* (1986). Bologna: Il Mulino, 1993.

Meletinskij, E. M., Nekljudov, S. J., Novik, E. S., and Segal, D. M. *La struttura della fiaba*. Palermo: Sellerio, 1977.

Mercier, Vivian. *The Irish Comic Tradition*. Oxford: Clarendon Press, 1962.

Milton, Kay. "Irish Hero Tales as a Historical Source: An Anthropologist's View." *Occasional Papers in Linguistics and Language Learning* (*Approaches to Oral Tradition*) 4 (1978): 88–97.

Mincu, Marin. *Mito-Fiaba-Canto narrativo. La trasformazione dei generi letterari*. Roma: Bulzoni, 1986.

Nagy, Joseph F. "Orality in Medieval Irish Narrative: An Overview." *Oral Tradition* 1–2 (1986): 272–301.

Naughton, Nora. "God and the Good People: Folk Belief in a Traditional Community." *Béaloideas* 71 (2003): 13–53.

Neeman, Harold. "Le conte et la théorie." *Fabula* 42 (2001): 297–303.

Nicolaisen, Wilhelm F.H. "Concepts of Time and Space in Irish Folktales." In *Celtic Folklore and Christianity*, op. cit., 150–58.

Nicolaisen, Wilhelm F.H. "Why Tell Stories?," *Fabula* 31 (1990): 5–10.

Ní Dhuibhne, Éilís. "'The Old Woman as Hare': Structure and Meaning in an Irish Legend." *Folklore* 104 (1993): 77–85.

Ó Catháin, Seamas. "Folklore, Preserving the People's Past." In *Folk Literature of the British Isles*, op. cit., 98–106.

Ó Coileáin, Seán. "Oral or Literary? Some Strands of the Argument." *Studia Hibernica* 17–18 (1977): 7–35.

O'Connor, Ulick. *Celtic Dawn: A Portrait of Irish Renaissance* (1984). Dublin: Town House and Country House, 1999.

Ó Danachair, Caoimnin. "Stories and Storytelling in Ireland." In *Folk Literature of the British Isles*, op. cit., 107–114.

Ó Danachair, Caoimnin. "Oral Tradition and the Printed Word." *Irish University Review* IX, 1 (1979): 31–41.

Ó Giolláin, Diarmuid. "The Fairy Belief and Official Religion." In *The Good People: New Fairylore Essays*, edited by Peter Narvaez, 199–214. New York-London: Garland Publishing, 1991.

Ó Giolláin, Diarmuid. *Locating Irish Folklore: Tradition, Modernity, Identity*. Cork: Cork University Press, 2000.

Ó hÓgáin, Dáithí. *Myth, Legend, and Romance: An Encyclopedia of the Irish Folk Tradition*. London: Ryan, 1990.

Ong, Walter J. *Orality and Literacy: The Technologizing of the Word*. Abingdon-New York: Routledge, 1988.

Ó Suillebhain, Seán. *A Handbook of Irish Folklore*. Dublin: Educational Co. of Ireland for Folklore of Ireland Society, 1942.

Ó Suillebhain, Seán, and Christiansen, Reidar T. "The Types of the Irish Folktale." *FF Communications* 188 (1963).

Prince, Gerald. *Narratology: The Form and Functioning of Narrative*. Berlin: Mouton, 1982.

Propp, Vladimir J. *Morphology of the Folktale* (1928). Austin: University of Texas Press, 2003.

Propp, Vladimir J. "La trasformazione nelle favole di magia" (1928). In *I formalisti russi*, edited by Tzvetan Todorov, 277–304. Torino: Einaudi, 1968.

Propp, Vladimir J. *Le radici storiche dei racconti di magia* (1946). Roma: Newton Compton, 1992.

Purkiss, Diane. *Troublesome Things: A History of Fairies and Fairy Stories*. London: Penguin, 2001.

Quintelli-Neary, Marguerite. *Folklore and the Fantastic in Twelve Modern Irish Novels*. Westport: Greenwood, 1997.

Ricoeur, Paul. *Time and Narrative*. Chicago: University of Chicago Press, 1984–1988.

Rolleston, Thomas W. *Myths and Legends of the Celtic Race*. New York: Crowell, 1911.

Ross, Miceal. "The Knife Against the Wave: A Uniquely Irish Legend of the Supernatural?" *Folklore* 105 (1994): 83–88.

"The Royal Hibernian Tales: Being a Collection of the Most Entertaining Stories Now Extant." *Béaloideas* 10 (1940): 148–203.

Ryan, Marie-Laure. *Possible Worlds, Artificial Intelligence, and Narrative Theory*. Bloomington-Indianapolis: Indiana University Press, 1991.

Sabbatucci, Dario. *Il mito, il rito e la storia*. Roma: Bulzoni, 1978.

Schenda, Rudolf. "Raccontare fiabe, diffondere fiabe. Trasformazione delle forme di comunicazione di un genere popolare." *La ricerca folklorica* 12 (1985): 77–83.

Scholes, Robert. "Language, Narrative, and Anti-Narrative." In *On Narrative*, edited by William J. T. Mitchell, 200–8. Chicago-London: University of Chicago Press, 1981.

Scholes, Robert, and Kellogg, Robert. *The Nature of Narrative*. New York: Oxford University Press, 1966.

Segre, Cesare. *Le strutture e il tempo*. Torino: Einaudi, 1974.

Segre, Cesare. "Narrazione/narratività." In *Enciclopedia*, vol. IX, 690–701. Torino: Einaudi, 1979.

Segre, Cesare. "Tema/Motivo." Ibid., vol. XIV, 3–23.

Sheeran, Patrick. "Genius Fabulae: The Irish Sense of Place." *Irish University Review* XVIII, 2 (1988): 191–206.

Shenhar, Aliza. "Metafolkloristic Additions to Stories by the Artistic Narrator." *Folklore* 98i (1987): 53–6.

Stephens, James. *Irish Fairy Tales* (1920). Dublin: Gill and Macmillan, 1979.

Stephens, James. *Fiabe irlandesi*. Milano: RCS Collezionabili, 2001.

Sturgess, Philip J. M. *Narrative: Theory and Practice*. Oxford: Clarendon Press, 1992.

Thompson, Stith. *The Folktale* (1946). Berkeley-Los Angeles: University of California Press, 1977.

Thompson, Stith. *Motif-Index of Folk Literature*. Copenhagen: Rosenkilde and Bagger, 1955–1958.

Thompson, Stith. "Myth and Folktales." In *Myth: A Symposium*, op. cit., 169–80.

Thuente, Mary H. "W. B. Yeats and Nineteenth-Century Folklore." *The Journal of Irish Literature* 6 (1977): 64–80.

Thuente, Mary H. "'Traditional Innovations': Yeats and Joyce and Irish Oral Tradition." *Mosaic: A Journal for the Comparative Study of Literature and Ideas* XII, 3 (1979): 91–104.

Tillhagen, Carl-Herman. "Reality and Folklore Research." *Béaloideas* 39–41 (1971–1973): 329–43.

Todorov, Tzvetan. "Les catégories du récit littéraire." In *L'analyse structurale du récit*, op. cit., 125–151.

Todorov, Tzvetan. *The Fantastic: A Structural Approach to a Literary Genre* (1970). Ithaca, NY: Cornell University Press, 1973.

Todorov, Tzvetan. *The Poetics of Prose* (1971). Ithaca, NY: Cornell University Press, 1977.

Tullio-Altan, Carlo. *Ethnos e civiltà*. Milano: Feltrinelli, 1995.

Ure, Peter. *Yeats and Anglo-Irish Literature*. Liverpool: Liverpool University Press, 1974.

Vittorini, Fabio. *Fabula e intreccio*. Scandicci: La Nuova Italia, 1998.

Wall, Richard. *A Dictionary and Glossary for the Irish Literary Revival*. Gerrards Cross: Colin Smythe, 1995.

Waugh, Patricia. *Metafiction: The Theory and Practice of Self-Conscious Fiction*. London: Methuen and Co., 1984.

White, Carolyn. *A History of Irish Fairies*. Dublin: Mercier Press, 1976.

White, Hayden. "The Value of Narrativity in the Representation of Reality." In *On Narrative*, op. cit., 1–23.

Williams, Noel. "The Semantics of the Word 'Fairy': Making Meaning Out of Thin Air." In *The Good People*, op. cit., 457–75.

Yeats, William B. *Irish Fairy Tales* (1888). Thirsk: House of Stratus, 2002.

Yeats, William B. *Fairy and Folk Tales of Ireland* (1892). Gerrards Cross: Colin Smythe, 1973.

Yeats, William B. "The Four Winds of Desire" (1893). In *The Collected Works: Early Articles and Reviews* by William B. Yeats, vol. IX. New York: Scribner, 2004.

Yeats, William B. *The Celtic Twilight*. London: A. H. Bullen, 1902.

Yeats, William B. "First Principles" (1904). In *The Collected Works: The Irish Dramatic Movement* by William B. Yeats, vol. VIII. New York: Scribner, 2003.

Yeats, William B. *Il crepuscolo celtico*. Milano: Bompiani, 2001.

Yeats, William B. *Fiabe irlandesi*. Milano: RCS Collezionabili, 2001.

Zimmermann, Georges D. *The Irish Story Teller*. Dublin: Four Courts, 2001.

Zipes, Jack D. *Breaking the Magic Spell: Radical Theories of Folk and Fairy Tales*. London: Heinemann, 1979.

Index

About the Author

Vito Carrassi is a writer and translator who teaches folklore at the University of Bari. His main fields of research are literary anthropology, narratology, and Irish and Italian folklore.